MW00769821

A CURSE

for the

HOMESICK

A CURSE

for the

HOMESICK

LAURA BROOKE ROBSON

MIRA

MIRA™

ISBN-13: 978-0-7783-6847-2

A Curse for the Homesick

Recycling programs for this product may not exist in your area.

Copyright © 2025 by Laura Robson

All rights reserved. No part of this book may be used or reproduced in any manner whatsoever without written permission.

Without limiting the author's and publisher's exclusive rights, any unauthorized use of this publication to train generative artificial intelligence (AI) technologies is expressly prohibited.

This is a work of fiction. Names, characters, places and incidents are either the product of the author's imagination or are used fictitiously. Any resemblance to actual persons, living or dead, businesses, companies, events or locales is entirely coincidental.

For questions and comments about the quality of this book, please contact us at CustomerService@Harlequin.com.

TM is a trademark of Harlequin Enterprises ULC.

Mira
22 Adelaide St. West, 41st Floor
Toronto, Ontario M5H 4E3, Canada
MIRABooks.com

Printed in U.S.A.

For Ariana,

text me when you get home

Prelude

Where the earth gives way, there is a man made of stone. The snow catches on his eyelashes and in the fine grooves of his lips, which are parted slightly—like he was about to say something. Behind him, frozen fog rolls relentlessly off the ocean.

Three women stand facing the edge of the cliffs with their shoulders touching.

The first says: "I don't understand."

The second says: "Fucking hell."

The third doesn't say anything at all.

The Return

2022

I returned to Stenland the day I turned twenty-six. I didn't mean to get in on my birthday. Originally I'd planned to get in the day before, but there was too much wind to land at the airport, so I ended up taking the overnight ferry from Aberdeen. I woke alone in the small, rocking bedroom and could not move the air from my throat into my lungs.

I got dressed and went outside. From a mile out, I saw the hazy shape of the island. The black sand; the turf-roofed houses; the craggy mountains. The only other passenger on the ferry was a twenty-something backpacker who was throwing up over the railing. The captain watched me, like he wanted me to be ill too, like this would be proof I'd been made soft in my absence. He didn't greet me by name, but I knew he knew me. Everyone knew everyone in Stenland.

I wasn't going to come, but it was all Linnea asked for. I tried to buy her things instead: a vacation, a dress, a collection of ceramic dishes. No, she said, no to all of it. The only thing she'd asked was that Kitty and I come home to be her bridesmaids.

When I climbed down the ramp to the concrete dock, I could see a banner hanging from Hedda's. *Congratulations, Henrik and Linnea!* Behind it, in the basin of fog, the old brutalist church was a solemn slab of gray. Red woolen clothes flapped on the bodies of stone statues.

I could not bring myself to look directly at them.

I opened the door to Hedda's with my boot, and a bell jingled. From behind the register, the painting of the Virgin Mary looked scandalized. As always, it smelled like fermented fish.

Had I missed it?

No.

I had not let myself.

I could hear Hedda rummaging around in the back room, and no one else seemed to be there, so I shoved my hands into my pockets and examined the counter. Hedda had finally bought a credit-card reader. So that was nice. According to the menu, this was the island's best *capachino.* I imagined tourists seeing that and tittering—those poor stupid Stenns who couldn't even spell the food they served. I felt embarrassed, then resentful.

Hedda emerged from the back room with her hands on her aproned hips. She looked older.

I lifted my shoulder to keep the strap of my duffel bag in place.

"You may as well sit down," Hedda said and set to work crabbily pouring me a cup of coffee.

I sat. The chair squeaked.

Hedda added a liberal amount of cream and sugar to my mug before handing it over. "You look like a corpse microwaved back to life," she said.

I took a sip of the coffee. Hedda nodded, satisfied, then went back behind the counter to retrieve a small pie, which she dropped unceremoniously onto the table next to the coffee. The pie smelled like mutton and kohlrabi. I didn't pick up the fork.

"Glad to see you're still the conversational equivalent of a dead seagull," Hedda said.

"Thanks for the coffee," I said.

She exhaled, exasperated.

The door opened, and in like a gust of wind burst Kitty. She was wearing over-the-knee suede boots and a long woolen coat. Her lipstick was bright purple. When she saw me, she barreled through the café, knocked aside a chair, and bodily forced me onto my feet so we could hug.

Hedda grumbled something about the two of us acting like we never saw each other. Stenns had no sense of scale. There was only the island and everywhere else. Since Kitty and I both lived "everywhere else," of course Hedda would assume we spent all our time together, though I hadn't seen Kitty since Christmas. Whenever we met, it felt like the world's smallest survivor's group.

"You're early!" Kitty said. "We agreed on nine, right? Okay, whatever. I've been at Linnea's just now, and she was trying on her dress again, and, I don't know, her mum thought it looked too tight on her, so *that* was a whole thing, and then Henrik showed up to do whatever it is Henrik does, so Linnie had to change out of her dress so she could—"

Over Kitty's shoulder, Hedda pinched her middle and ring fingers together with her thumb, making a *yap yap yap* sign.

"—which made me think, sure, if I'm going into town to meet Tess anyway, I might as well offer to drop the dress at the tailor's, so." Kitty flourished a hand. "Here I am."

"Hey," I said.

She took a sip of my coffee, made a face, and hugged me again.

Hedda wouldn't let me escape the shop without the pie and a loaf of hard, dark bread in my hands. Once the door jingled shut behind us, I said, "I have a bad feeling."

"Well, obviously. You let Hedda put what I can only assume was six tablespoons of sugar in your coffee."

"A bad skeld feeling," I said.

"We're only here for three days," Kitty said. "Don't be paranoid. I'm manifesting a very short and easy trip for us. Don't out-manifest me with something awful."

She looped her arm through mine as we walked. The September weather was colder than a California January. We zigzagged down the street between the stone fences, and I remembered how I used to love the way the air tasted on days like this—earthy and salty and sweet.

We reached the little red house by the cemetery. Linnea had added beds of wispy white flowers and a porch swing out front. In the windows, I saw lacy curtains like the ones Linnea used to have in her bedroom growing up. Back in California, I had a Polaroid of Linnea climbing out her window through those curtains; on the bottom, Kitty had Sharpied *Faerie Queen emerging from flower.*

We stared at the door. Eventually I said, "How's Georgia?"

"We're off again," Kitty said.

"I'm sorry."

She lifted a shoulder. "How's Noah?"

"He's good."

"He didn't want to come?"

"I didn't think he should."

From inside, I could hear a familiar fluty voice. Linnea was singing. Her voice was a time capsule, airy as the wind and pretty as anything. For a minute, I felt like we were all eighteen, my hair smelling of chlorine and Kitty with her books in a too small but very fashionable handbag and Linnea carrying a bottle of elderflower liqueur that we were going to drink down by the beach.

"How has it been?" I asked.

"Being here? Not, you know, super fun. On the list of things I would like to be doing with my time, this ranks somewhere near drinking rat poison."

"But you're not still in love with her," I said.

"If only we could all forget how it felt to be in love the first time," Kitty said.

"I never think about him."

Kitty said, "Sure," and opened the door.

I stepped inside after her and saw Linnea in profile. She was standing in front of the sink, looking at her reflection in the mirror as she applied mascara. Oh—no. Not Linnea. Saffi, her sister. Her blond hair was in two long braids on either side of her round face and elegant neck. When she heard the door, she turned and gave us a smile with a tiny gap between the front teeth. She looked like one of the dolls they sold in the gift shops in town—the perfect Stennish woman.

Saffi broke the spell by setting down her mascara and hugging Kitty and me in turn. I got the feeling she was only hugging Kitty—whom she'd surely already seen—because it was awkward to hug me. I stared at Saffi's neck. She smelled like Linnea, like jasmine.

"You look gorgeous," Saffi said generously. I knew what I looked like. Hedda had told me: a microwaved corpse. "I love your hair."

I looked down at my hair. The ends were blunt and frazzled from chlorine. Kitty laughed.

"Yours too," I said.

Apropos of nothing, Kitty said, "Tess, where did you get your boots and why don't I have a pair? Is this how you spend your ridiculous engineer money?"

She was trying to make Saffi feel bad. It was a very Kitty thing to do—to make someone else feel worse in the hopes of making me feel better. I wished she wouldn't.

"Noah got them for me, actually," I said.

"Oh!" Kitty said. "So that's how he spends his ridiculous programmer money?"

An awkward silence.

"Linnie's so excited to have you here," Saffi said finally. "She's out back."

We followed her through the house, and Kitty poked my spine. She mouthed something incomprehensible, and when I shook my head, she rolled her eyes and texted me.

Kitty: I'm being helpful!!!

Me: Please don't be that helpful

Linnea, in a fluttery dress, crouched over a collection of potted plants. When she saw me, she hesitated. It had been years since we'd seen each other in person. She seemed unsure of herself, like I was an unknown variable, possibly dangerous, and it made me wish I wasn't wearing the expensive rain boots.

I set down my duffel bag and the food from Hedda's. Linnea opened her mouth, and I was afraid she was going to say something terrible and banal: *How were your flights?* or *It's so nice to see you.* Instead, she said: "I had a dream last night that you turned into a Pembroke Welsh corgi, which is strange because I've always thought you'd be a greyhound."

Then we were normal again and hugging—Linnea and Kitty and Tess, thank god, thank god.

"Happy birthday, Tessie," Linnea said, which made Kitty shriek with rage.

"It's your *birthday*?" she said. "You were supposed to get in the day *before* your birthday!"

"But then she got in a day late, remember?" Linnea said.

Kitty made her rage noise again. "Well, then I have a fucking cake to order, don't I?"

"It's okay," I said.

"No, it's not," Kitty and Linnea both said. They looked at each other, then away again just as quickly.

The four of us got ready together, Linnea and her three bridesmaids. Linnea's parents kept rushing in and out of the house, as did Kitty's mum, who kissed me on the cheek without setting down the massive flower arrangement she was carting. I texted my dad asking if he wanted to drop by Linnea's, but he said he didn't want to interrupt and that he'd see me at the rehearsal dinner. I couldn't figure out how to tell him how badly I wanted to see him. We were both afraid my absence had made us strangers.

At one point, I was sitting on the edge of Linnea's old bed while Kitty did Saffi's hair, and my stomach growled. Linnea tossed me a sleeve of chocolate biscuits, a brand not available in the States, without needing to ask. As the biscuits arced through the air, time dilated; I had lived this moment a hundred times before. Kitty, who had exactly no coordination, would try to intercept the biscuits and end up dropping them. Then she'd insist it was on purpose—*Sugar is bad for one's dental hygiene, actually*, she'd say—and then I would shrug and scoop them off the floor; and Kitty would protest about germs and cavities; and I would hold the biscuits up high, out of her reach; and she would relent and ask for a biscuit; and Linnea would start laughing her irrepressible, gravitational laugh—the kind that made others laugh, the kind that went and on and on. I saw it all happening in my mind, in my memory, and then in front of me—that was how it all went. Exactly as I imagined. In this room, the particular rhoticity and lilt of the voices were precisely like my own. The pressure against the inside of my heart was a kind of longing, but I did not know how it was possible to keep missing them when they were right here.

They had the rehearsal dinner at this restaurant, Sjö, where I had never been but according to *Travel + Leisure* was The Place to eat if you visited Stenland. It was set tastefully back from Lundwall, outside of the town proper, with a view of the sea from the cliffs. The whole west side of the restaurant was made of windows, and the terrace had fire pits and heat lamps and globe lights. Apparently they were getting a staggering discount because Saffi was the owner's favorite waitress.

On our way to the cars, Kitty grabbed my arm. "We look like we're dressed for a sexy gallery opening, and they look like they're going to Mother's Day tea."

"What's a sexy gallery?" I said.

Kitty gestured at our dresses. She was wearing tight nude lace. I was wearing a black sheath with a slit up the side. Ahead of us, climbing into Linnea's parents' car, the Sundstrom sisters were both wearing loose, flowy pastels. When I'd packed, I'd run this dress by Noah's older sister, who was twenty-nine and had been to approximately a hundred weddings in the past six months. She'd said it was hot yet family appropriate.

"On the bright side," Kitty said, "I'm planning to record the moment Soren sees you for posterity. I bet he'll make that little choking noise—you know that one when he's surprised? And then I'll send it to you, and you can play it back whenever you forget what a catch you are."

"I am begging you," I said as we reached the car, "to shut up."

We piled in. I ended up squeezed into the way-back between Saffi and the window. She hummed softly and did not look at me. The whole drive, her spidery, pale fingers plucked at the thin cotton fabric of her dress.

Sjö was everything *Travel + Leisure* promised. The windows.

The ambience. The paralyzing panic when I saw a man in a suit with hair the color of sand adjusting a flower arrangement.

But it was just Magnus Invers, one of Henrik's ushers. When he saw us, he grinned and waved. It hadn't occured to me how obvious my panic had been until Saffi cleared her throat and stepped around me. I wiped my hands on my dress.

More people arrived. Kitty and I bobbed around, trying to keep busy. Soren was nowhere.

"Tess!" Henrik said.

I turned to see him weaving between tables, his arm linked with Linnea's. Oh, god, they were just *so Stennish*, so red cheeked and blue eyed. He was handsome in his suit. Handsome and square. Kitty had once called him an aesthetic quadrilateral, and the laugh jumped out of me before I could stop it. He hugged me. Still very square.

"I wasn't sure you'd come!" he said. "I'm so glad you're here."

Because he was Henrik, I believed him.

"Congratulations," I said. "You're marrying one of the two best people in the world."

Linnea made a pleased little noise, almost a hiccup.

Henrik grinned and started to say something, but before he could, his father was touching his elbow and asking about forks. Henrik nodded. God, he looked grown-up. Did I look that grown-up? He had an honest-to-god wrinkle on the outside of his eye.

"Let's catch up at dinner," Henrik said, squeezing my shoulder. It struck me as a very fatherly gesture, like what his own dad had just done. "I want to hear all about work and Noah and San Fran." And again, I believed him.

Once he and Linnea had gone to deal with whatever fork catastrophe was unfurling, Kitty passed me a glass of champagne. *"San Fran,"* she said.

"It's not as bad as Frisco."

"Frisco!" she said. "The old Silicone Valley."

I snorted, but I felt mean about it. It was too warm in the restaurant, and I stretched the fabric of my dress away from my sweaty ribs as I searched the growing crowd. I'd imagined the rehearsal dinner would be smaller; I'd imagined spending most of my time trying not to make eye contact with the best man, but I still hadn't spotted him.

I went off in search of my dad, but no one had seen him. Eventually, in the kitchen, I found Kitty's mum, Michelle, who was gesturing animatedly at a chef.

She acknowledged me with a squeeze of my hand while she said to the chef, "Well, I assumed you'd be making it if you're doing the catering for tomorrow."

"Not enough ovens," the chef said. "And buttercream nauseates me."

I hadn't realized Kitty followed me until I heard her ask, "What's all this about?"

"Margit just called from the bakery and said she can't deliver the cake, and that someone needs to pick it up as soon as possible," Michelle said.

"Oh!" Kitty said. "Tess's birthday cake. I called earlier today."

"I really don't need a cake," I said, and everyone ignored me.

"I'd go get it," Michelle said, "but I told Linnea I'd figure out where the rest of the flowers went."

"I can't go," Kitty said. "I'm getting along too well with the champagne."

"I can do it," I said.

"You can't pick up your own birthday cake."

"No, really." I set down my glass of champagne, which was only a few sips shy of full. "Can I borrow your keys?"

Michelle handed them over and called after me that I had to be back by seven thirty for the rehearsal. I probably could've found someone else to go to the bakery, or at least to drive with me, but I was starting to feel like the ceiling was descending and if I didn't get out soon, it might flatten me.

I unlocked the car and threw myself into the driver's seat before anyone could catch up. My shoes, strappy black heels, were not conducive to driving, but I didn't want to sit around taking them off. The tires squealed as I pulled out of the lot. Michelle had had the radio going, but I punched the power button so I could listen to the wind instead.

The world got sexier when you were driving. Low to the ground, hugging curves of black asphalt. The condensation on the windows and the growl of a motor. Michelle's car was powerful and twitchy, sleek and mean. I eased around an S-bend, taking the racing line from apex to apex. In front of me, a wall of fog marched off the ocean like an approaching army.

I missed the turn for town, which was embarrassing because there was pretty much only the one turn. I had to pull into the dirt driveway of a croft, which was covered in tire tracks from tourists who'd made the same mistake. It stung to realize I was no longer a local, even though that was all I had ever wanted.

I parked by the pub. I probably could've found a closer spot, but I had no desire to hurry back. As I walked along the harbor, I shivered. A weathered statue, one of the oldest on the island, stood guard by the pier—a remnant of a time when Stenland had wanted to tell outsiders to keep out. I avoided her gaze. Wind whipped at my hair and my dress. My shoes rubbed at the backs of my heels. When I passed a pair of men, vaguely familiar but at least a decade older than me, they stopped on the footpath to stare at me. It felt like rubbernecking—like they were trying to make sense of a disaster.

The bakery smelled like vanilla. According to the sign, it closed at four, but the lights were on and when I pushed the door, it opened. A man in a black suit was facing the abandoned counter, his hands in his pockets and his posture so still he could've been made of stone. The door started to close on me; it hit my shoulder. I just stood there. Soren turned.

He hadn't shaved that day. Not enough to look scruffy. Just—just this faint bronze shadow along the slant of his jaw, around the fine lines of his lips. His hair was short, neat, pushed away from his forehead enough that you could see the mole three finger-widths above his left eyebrow. If Kitty had been there to record his expression for posterity, I could have watched it again and again, the way his mouth flattened and his brows creased, and maybe after watching it a hundred times, I could've said what that expression meant. When you stop seeing someone you were in love with, you start to pretend they weren't as attractive as you thought or that you didn't love them as much as you thought you did. But sometimes when you see them again, you realize you were wrong. Sometimes you realize you actually did love them. Your body and your brain are on opposing teams; they don't understand that this person is not yours anymore. It's agony; it's euphoria.

As it turned out, Kitty was wrong. Soren didn't make a surprised, choking noise. He didn't make any sound at all.

Margit, the baker, emerged from the back room, saying, "I really am sorry about this. It should have…"

Neither Soren nor I looked at her. I didn't care that I was staring. I didn't care that I looked so out of place here, on this island, in this dress.

Margit cleared her throat. Soren turned back to her, and I became aware of the frigid wind. I stepped inside and the door banged shut.

"My niece has been helping me," Margit said to Soren. "She was meant to drive the cake to the restaurant, but her car broke down."

Soren shifted his weight. He touched the back of his neck, like he could feel my eyes there.

Margit, sounding increasingly uncomfortable, said, "And you're with the Holm-Sundstrom wedding too, I imagine?"

I nodded.

"Oh, right, of course," she said. "Tess. You were the swimmer." I felt like I was being discussed postmortem. "You must be the birthday girl in question."

She held up a hand and disappeared into the back again, leaving Soren and me alone. He kept facing the empty register. I stayed by the door. Our eyes met in the reflection of the pastry case, then broke apart.

Margit returned a minute later with a white box, lid open. She held it out for us to see. It was a chocolate cake, glossy as satin, with *Happy Birthday Tess* written across it. I wondered if it bothered Soren that *birthday* was capitalized or that they hadn't put a comma before my name.

"They must've gotten their wires crossed somewhere, sending two of you to come pick this up," Margit said. "I promise, I'll make sure the wedding cake gets there in time tomorrow. This doesn't usually happen." A pause. "I can give you a discount."

"It's fine," I said. My heels were too loud on the tile floor. I didn't look over at Soren as I raised my credit card.

"You can't buy your own birthday cake," Soren said. He wasn't looking at me either. Just the cake.

I tapped my card against the reader.

"No American Express," Margit said. "I really am sorry about all of this."

As I flipped through the cards in my clutch—California license, Stennish license, library card, BART pass—in search of a Visa, Soren reached in front of me and held his phone to the reader. It beeped.

"Soren," I said.

"Tess."

Margit held out the box, first to Soren, then to me. I took it and balanced my clutch and phone on top of the box. Soren smelled like soap. Like always.

I had never been so glad to hear my phone ring. When it lit up with Noah's name, I saw Soren notice and turn away.

"Thanks," I said to Margit. I held the box with one hand and tucked my phone under my ear. "Hey."

"Happy birthday, you withered crone," Noah said.

"You're two months younger than me," I said, opening the door with my foot. I felt Soren's gaze on my back. Or maybe I just wanted to. The door swung shut behind me, and I shivered.

"Stop being such a Gemini," Noah said.

"I'm pretty sure I'm a Virgo."

"Yeah, but you're a Gemini Waxing Gibbous."

"Is that a real thing?" I asked.

Noah conceded that it was not. In the background, I could hear the clacking of keys. He was working, I assumed. Once I got back into the car, cake nestled in the passenger-side foot well, I put Noah on speaker.

"How's the wedding?" he asked.

"The expected chaos."

"Run into any exes that might harm my delicate masculinity?"

"Ha ha."

More typing. The familiar metallic *ting* of a can getting set down—either LaCroix or an IPA.

"How's work?" I said.

"Eh. Hey, did the fancy HR person ever get back to you?"

"She wasn't fancy," I said. "She was just English."

"Fancy accent. Same thing."

"Do you think my accent is fancy?"

"No," he said, "your accent is Tess-y. I have heard your accent cry over *Moana*. I can't think that's fancy anymore. My question remains."

The fancy HR person—who was, as I said, really only English—had called last week to interview me for a job that would require me to move north of London. I had not told

Noah I was applying. I had not told anyone I was applying. Noah had only found out because he'd unexpectedly come home while I'd been on the video call. I'd told him I'd just applied on a whim, to practice my negotiation skills.

Noah had taken this news like he took everything else: calmly, with an easy shrug and a *Right on—that's cool.*

"They hired someone else," I said.

"Their loss," Noah said. "Ah, shit, I just deleted, like, twelve lines of critical code. Talk later?"

I kept my eyes fixed on the dark road. "Sure."

"Love you," he said. "Bye."

The call ended. I always thought that was interesting—that Noah never waited for me to say it back. Like he just assumed I would. Or wouldn't mind if I didn't.

Soren

2008

I don't remember when I first met Soren Fell. I don't remember when I first met anyone, actually, because I grew up on a small rock between Scotland and the Arctic where everyone is someone's cousin and the woman who owns the café also controls the nation's politics. You don't meet people. You just know them.

When I was twelve, my mum was arrested for accidentally killing Soren's parents. You can see why it is unfortunate, then, that he was the first person I fell in love with.

The day his parents died, I had to get to school early for a field trip. My mum was still asleep in her bedroom, and my dad was making me pancakes. He was so tall, he had to hunch over the stove. When he and my mum had started dating, he'd looked like a teenage film star: straight teeth, broad shoulders, fair hair that would turn dusty but never gray. His eyelashes were so pale, you'd think he didn't have them at all, but then you'd stand close and realize he actually has the longest eyelashes in the world. His name is Erik. Erik Eriksson; same as his dad. People from outside Stenland think it's a stupid name. My mum even made a joke about it in her memoir, about the famine of creativity ravaging Stenland, about how she had to fight to keep him from naming me Erika. My dad isn't the sort of person who would bother defending himself, but one time, I found an old photo of a woman in a drawer and asked him who it was. He said, *Oh, that was my grandma Tess. You were named after her.*

Before he gave me a plate, he got out the white plastic tub of Swedish lingonberries and spooned them onto the top pancake in the shape of a smile.

"See, look," my dad said. "He's happy."

I rearranged the face so it was frowning.

"He's about to be eaten," I said. "He's a realist."

He went to the garage to start working on a car that had to be done by nine. I washed my plate and zipped my parka and turned on my flashlight, since the sun wouldn't rise for two hours yet. I began the eight-minute walk to school just as I heard the first stirrings of movement from my mum's bedroom. I did not bother waiting for her to get up. If I had, I would have died instead of Soren's parents.

It was the last Friday before Christmas. That was why we were going on a field trip. Our teacher, Ms. Winwick, decided she could not possibly bear another day of students chattering about what presents they wanted and throwing peppernut biscuits at each other, so we were going to visit Fairhowe Cairn instead.

We waited in the playground while the bus lumbered toward the gates. It was a degree north of freezing, and puddles filled uneven gullies on the asphalt. Whenever I let the basketball hit the ground, it made a flat *thump* in the water. My hands were gray with wet dirt, and beneath, they were violent pink from the cold. I was shooting the ball at the hoop but only making it one try in four. I couldn't unbend my fingers.

Kitty stood just out of splash range. She had a hat pulled far over her forehead and her hands tucked under her armpits. Every few moments, she'd stomp her boots like she was making sure her feet were still attached to her ankles. Linnea was drifting around us, occasionally interjecting nonsense comments like: "Does the headmistress think you're ready for this mission, Sapphire?" I believed free time was for sporting pursuits; Kitty believed it was for talking; Linnea, for playing make-believe. We had given up trying to convince the others of our way and had instead settled on doing what we wanted in close proximity.

I'm not sure how people come up with an identity if they don't have two best friends. From the time I was born, Kitty Sjöberg and Linnea Sundstrom had been my best friends, so whenever I wondered what my personality was, I just looked at the gaps they didn't fill. Consciously or subconsciously, we didn't encroach on one another's interests. We didn't even look particularly alike. Linnea was, in every way, the prototypical Stenn, tall and thin lipped, her cheeks round and her hair blond and wispy. Kitty, who was Chinese Stennish, had the same dark hair as her mother but a spatter of freckles from her father. I didn't look as Stennish as either of my parents; apparently I took after Great-Grandma Tess, with light eyes and brown hair and solid little shoulders.

"I've decided we should start fancying boys," Kitty said.

I looked over at her. Linnea was hesitating, one foot up, her skirt flapping against her leggings.

"I don't think the headmistress would like that," Linnea said.

Kitty rolled her eyes, which she'd been doing frequently

and to great effect over the past few weeks because she'd read a book where the main character did it every other page.

"That sounds," I said, "tiring." I took another shot, and it bounced back off the rim. It landed near Kitty, and she didn't kick it back to me, but that was fine, just part of the compromise. I stooped to grab it, and when I stood, Kitty had a business-y expression on her face.

"I was reading this magazine my mum had by the toilet, and it said it can happen to your children when they're nine or ten, but it hasn't happened to any of us yet, so I think we better figure it out before we get left behind. Don't worry. I've already thought it all through." Kitty pointed at me. "You can like Thomas because he swims and you swim and you can have swimmy babies together." I made a face, and Kitty turned to Linnea. "And you can take Soren, because Delia likes Soren, and I don't want her to have him."

When Kitty said Soren's name, my stomach plunged with something like panic. I had not yet put a name to it—the fact that I knew exactly where Soren was in the geometry of the schoolyard, over playing soccer on the frosted grass, the same way I always seemed to know when he'd entered the classroom or what book he was reading for English.

"What if I already like someone?" Linnea said, and I felt my body slacken with relief.

"Is this Linnea speaking," Kitty said, "or are you playing a character right now?"

"This is Linnea. What if I already like someone?"

"You can't possibly," Kitty said. "You would've told us. And besides, it's so tidy if you like Soren because if you got married, we'd be cousins."

Soren's mother and Kitty's father were siblings. I forgot that sometimes because I saw so little of Kitty's father, who always acted like he was in a Very Big Hurry to see someone Much More Important than You.

"Okay," Linnea said, looking troubled.

Kitty rolled her eyes again. "Don't just say okay. You can't just say okay. If you have a crush on someone, you can't just… move it to the left."

I dribbled my ball once, twice. Jumped for another shot. It went in this time, not so much with a swish as with a slap against the sodden net. It fell with a thump, solid and dead against the ground, and in the same moment, wind came roaring off the sea. I shivered as the fence around the school clinked. Everything smelled abruptly like low tide.

Ms. Winwick called us to the bus, and we all piled on. Soren ended up in the line just behind us, and I was convinced he'd overheard our conversation. When I glanced back at him, trying to be surreptitious, his cheeks were pink and his sweaty hair was tangled. He was wearing a long-sleeved gray shirt and had a jacket slung over his shoulder. When our eyes met, he looked away quickly and his ears turned red.

On the bus, I slid into a row toward the middle and Kitty and Linnea pressed in after, squeezing me against the window. Soren and Henrik Holm took the row behind us, but I pretended not to notice.

The bus rumbled away from the school. I rubbed the squeaky fog from the glass. Outside, the potholed road curved to the right and slumped down the island. The sun was just starting to warm the air, turning the frozen fog the color of shortbread. We crested a hill, and for a moment, I could see all of Lundwall: down the hillside, past the turf-roofed buildings and stone fences, over the cement church with the clanging bells, all the way to the black-sand beach and out to the sea.

Fairhowe sat on the eastern edge of the island. It was past Lundwall, past the airport, past where all the stone walls ended and the hills rolled together unbroken. Without the big parking lot and the visitors' center, which sold excellent ice cream, you'd never know there was anything worth seeing out there.

Fairhowe was a burial site, one of many across the island—thousands of years old and surviving because it was made entirely of stone. I had already visited the cairn twice on various field trips.

When we got off the bus, there were no other cars in the lot. Three purple-black ravens took noisy flight from where they'd been perched on a plaque.

We followed Ms. Winwick in a scraggly line past the visitors' center and toward the mouth of the cairn. From the outside, it just looked like a little hill: a mound of frost-deadened grass surrounded on three sides by a plastic fence. The doorway was an open slot in the sod, and beneath it you could see the piles of stone that held the structure upright.

It was then, as we were waiting our turn to go in, that I overheard Delia Haugen say that a skeld season had just begun.

Delia was the only one in our class who had a phone. She had it peeping out of her jacket pocket as she read off text messages from her mum. One of the skelds, apparently, was my swim coach's girlfriend. No one knew about the other two yet. Kitty and Linnea and I glanced at each other, but none of us said anything, like speaking any fears aloud would call the curse closer to us.

Inside, the cairn was cramped as a coffin. Once you were through the hallway, it opened up slightly—just enough that Linnea and Kitty could fall into step next to me.

"Can you imagine living here?" Linnea said.

"Nobody lived here," Kitty told her. "It's a grave."

"How do you know no one ever lived here? They might've."

"Well, they didn't."

"There could be ghosts," Linnea said. "Ghosts are people."

"Right," Kitty said, and she shot me a look.

People said Linnea was scattered, which I'd always thought was unfair. Earlier that week, Ms. Winwick had told us the old riddle—the farmer with the fox, the chicken, and the sack of grain trying to get across a river—and Linnea had said, *Well, the river can't be more than a mile wide, can it?* Everyone had groaned and laughed—oh, that Linnie, at it again, entirely missing the point—and Linnea had looked confused and flushed. Afterward, I'd asked her about it, and she'd said, *Foxes can swim a mile at a time. They're very good at it. Why wouldn't you just make the fox swim?*

The inside of the cairn was lit by bare, buzzing bulbs that looked like something out of the last century. The walls were made of carefully stacked stone, and at eye level running around the perimeter there was a shelf that had once (if Ms. Winwick was to be believed) held human skulls. At each end of the space, facing each other, there was a stone figure: one a man, one a woman. They were naked, presumably because they'd been dead so long no one felt embarrassed for them anymore. Except me; I felt embarrassed, so I tried to distract myself with the jagged lines cut into the wall. All the walls were covered in carved inscriptions: modern graffiti, Norse runes, Pictish lines, maybe things even older than that.

"Can you read this?" I asked, pointing to the largest inscription.

"I think I can," Linnea said.

"No, you can't," Kitty told her. "It's in Stennish. The plaque outside said so."

We all went quiet and looked at the words. We did not speak Stennish. No one in Stenland did. It had died two hundred years prior.

"Has anybody translated it?" Linnea asked.

"Yes. Why does no one else read the plaques?"

"Because they're covered in raven poop," I said. "Tell us already."

But I did not get to hear what the inscription said. Ms. Winwick had appeared behind Linnea and was clearing her throat. The unsteady fluorescent light made her look solemn and sharp.

"Tess?" she said. "I'd like you to step outside with me, please."

I tried to remember if I'd done anything wrong. Ms. Winwick usually liked me because I was the only student who'd done the factorization chapter in our pre-algebra book and because I had never once spoken during silent reading. I followed her out of the cairn and blinked against the delicate morning sun.

Soren was already standing there, staring straight ahead. Delia was saying something and touching his elbow with one hand while she held her phone aloft with the other. When Ms. Winwick said her name warningly, she darted past us and back into the cairn. Soren did not move.

"Soren, sweetheart?" Ms. Winwick said. "I've called your grandmother. She'll be here any minute, and then she can take you home, all right?"

No reaction.

I looked up at Ms. Winwick, waiting for an explanation that did not come. To me, she said, "Your father is on his way." She did not call me sweetheart.

My dad arrived first. We lived closer. He got out of the car and had a hushed conversation with Ms. Winwick. I gathered he was offering to drive Soren home. Ms. Winwick raised her voice when she said, "That hardly seems like a good idea, Erik."

I climbed into my dad's car and looked out the window. Soren was still standing at the edge of the parking lot with his shoulders hunched to his ears and his face to the wind. When my dad started the car, Soren's eyes found mine through the window, and the moment they did, he flinched.

Once we cleared the parking lot, my dad said, "How much have you already figured out?"

All of it.

"Nothing," I said.

His hands were too tight on the wheel; his knuckles looked

like they might pop right through his skin. "A skeld season just started," he said. "Your mum was marked."

He kept glancing over at me, but I felt too ashamed to look at his eyes. I didn't want him to flinch, like Soren had.

"She—didn't check herself in the mirror, I guess," my dad said. "She came to say good morning, but I was under a car, so I didn't see her."

I picked at the stitching on the seat with the corner of my thumbnail. I got a whole tangle of it loose, long enough to wrap twice around my index finger.

"She said she was going to Hedda's for coffee. She was walking on the waterfront when Mattias and Sara Fell stepped onto the footpath. It sounds like they were just dropping off their younger son at school."

The thread was cutting off the circulation in my finger. I had pulled it so tight my nail was going purple.

"Tess?" my dad said.

"She turned them to stone."

Hoarsely, my dad told me she did not mean to. It was probably the first time he'd ever said it, but he already sounded tired of the excuse. I asked him if that made them any less dead. He turned on his blinker.

"No," he said. "I guess it doesn't."

A long time ago, people had thought the skelds were touched by the old gods. Later, people had thought they were touched by the devil. The word *skeld* meant *shield* in Stennish, which made sense because they were our protection from the outside world, from people who came to Stenland and tried to take it.

You couldn't tell when a skeld season was going to begin. Sometimes they came in rapid succession. Sometimes the island went years without. On the first day of a skeld season, three women woke up with marks on their foreheads: three black slashes like the wound from a raven's talon.

If a skeld's eyes met yours, you would turn to stone.

So the skelds went to Ramna Skaill, a stone tower at the northeastern reaches of the island, where they only interacted with each other and three keepers, selected to keep them safe or, depending on your perspective, keep everyone else safe.

After three months, the skelds would become human again. Their marks would disappear and their curse would go away. But the people they turned would never come back. You could not unmake stone.

In school, after Christmas, Delia came up to me at recess and said she couldn't believe I'd show my face here right now because didn't I know it was hurting people to be reminded of what my mother had done?

Soren was walking by when she said it. Maybe that was by design. He was surrounded by a tight knot of people, some his friends and others who had recently decided they were his friends. He looked up at me, and I wished I had said something to him when we'd been standing in that parking lot. This was the moment I took the thing I felt for Soren, the thing I had not yet named, and packed it away. There would be no more catching his eye when he walked into the room, no more subtly comparing the books on our desks, no more placing ourselves in adjacent bus seats.

My mother would be in prison for two years.

I would hate her the whole time.

Midsummer

2013

Around the time we started high school, people had begun telling Kitty, Linnea, and me that we would be skelds. Today, tomorrow—someday. They'd seen too many trios like ours, friends so close they might as well have been sisters, and they knew, by now, what it meant.

Unless we left.

By the summer before my final year of high school, I knew, down to the day, how long it would be until I could leave Stenland. We had not had a skeld season in thirty months. I felt the overdue pressure of it hanging above me like an overripe fruit on a bowing branch.

While in prison, my mum had written a memoir about her time as a skeld. After her release, she'd gone straight from the courthouse to the paisley-patterned couch of a women's morning talk show. She'd become medium famous among memoirists, which made her low-level famous among the general population. After reading her book, in which she'd categorized my dad as slightly sinister and deeply stupid, I'd developed a resentment toward her that lingered in my mouth like sticky candy. If she had not married my dad, she'd said, she would have left Stenland after high school. She'd wanted to flee the curse, but she'd made the mistake of falling in love, and wasn't it just like men to trap you? I agreed with some of her points but begrudged her for making them at my dad's expense.

Last I'd heard, she was living in Edinburgh. I could've gone with her, and there were times I wished I had, but the only thing I wanted less than to be a skeld was to spend all my time staring at her, at the serene and inspirational self-help feminist guru she had become. So I stayed in Stenland and plotted my way out. I swam every day. Talked to coaches at US universities. Took the classes and sat the tests and wrote the essays. With whatever time I had left, I helped my dad fix cars so we could have a little more money so I could buy a plane ticket away from this place forever.

There was, in fact, little I allowed myself to do that didn't relate to escape. Which was why Kitty and Linnea had spent so very many hours convincing me to join them on the beach on Midsummer.

It was nearly midnight, and though the sun had set, it wasn't dark; you could still see the fuzzy glow just below the horizon. We called it *simmer dim*, that kind of light. The sky and ocean were matching periwinkle, and for once the wind was calm.

I sat propped on one of the big flat rocks at the bottom of the cliffs with my knees bent and my elbows resting on top of them. An old skeld cave loomed behind me. A thousand years ago, the skelds had lived in these caves to protect the island from outsiders. The walls were etched with carvings of raven women and smeared with dark red paint. Down the black beach, some of the boys from my class were throwing peat bricks onto a bonfire that already loomed above their heads. Most of the girls wore white, but the boys were more mixed—a blue sweater here, a red T-shirt there. We had been a Viking island and a Norwegian territory, then we'd been part of Scotland and then part of the United Kingdom, and now we were part of nothing, just our own little speck out in the Atlantic. A few decades ago, someone had gotten the bright idea to start celebrating Midsummer in a big way to honor our Scandinavian roots. So now we had a parade and a maypole and girls in white dresses. It was unclear how much of this had been devised by the tourism board.

I was wearing black shorts and a large red flannel, thin from age. When Kitty had seen me that morning, she'd said, *Oh, so you're too good for tradition? You think you're better than everyone?*

Kitty was wearing a black jumpsuit.

That hardly seems fair, I'd said.

I mean, Kitty had said, *I think you're better than everyone. It's just a bad energy, you know? Very prickly.*

Linnea, who had chosen a pretty white dress for the day, had said, *You are both radiant like the sun and effervescent in spirit. Can we go now?*

I'd lost them a few minutes before because Linnea had said she had to pee and Kitty had decided to get us more drinks from the hole someone had dug in the sand. I was still sipping one, a cider in an amber bottle, and picking at the corner of the label. If I concentrated, I could make out conversations happening along the beach: one boy yelling at another about the best way to architect the fire, a flirtation in the shadows of the cliffs, someone saying something funny by the water's edge.

I'd never liked this beach because the caves down here were purported to have once been part of some sort of skeld ritual, so you were as likely as not to stumble on a carving of raven women and stone giants. In the '80s, a nineteen-year-old named Matilda had escaped the keep while she'd been a skeld, and she'd come to this beach while all her classmates had been having a party. She'd set out turning them to stone, one by one, and a handful had run into the ocean to try to escape, but she'd followed them out there. At low tide, when the surf was calm, you could see their stone heads and hands just breaking the surface. In the end, somebody had shot Matilda from the shore.

She was Hedda's daughter. In spite of Matilda, or maybe because of her, Hedda remained a fixture of the community. Plenty of Stenns were just one degree of separation from a skeld tragedy. Part of the reason Hedda was so beloved, I thought, was because she handled her proximity to Matilda's crimes in the way Stenns were meant to handle things: without asking for pity and with eyes set forward. Hedda did not behave as though Matilda's crime condemned her, so the rest of the island followed suit.

But Hedda was Hedda, and I was not. I felt that what my family did, what my friends did, most especially what my mother did bled into me. I wanted to move so far away that my mother's crime stopped feeling like my own.

Out of the corner of my eye, I noticed Kitty walking back down the beach toward me.

"I feel like I'm a hundred years old," she said, sitting on my rock.

Her hands were empty.

"No drinks?"

"I got distracted," she said.

I looked at her, waiting for the follow-up. Her hair, that morning, had been in a braided crown. The crown part had come loose, and now it hung in two long braids on either side of her face. Her lipstick remained immaculate and served to emphasize the sour knot of her mouth.

"The Faerie Queen," Kitty finally said, "continues to charm the masses with her ephemeral grace."

I followed Kitty's gaze to the bonfire. Linnea was standing in a group of three boys a year older than us, recent graduates. She looked, in the firelight, very slender, almost stretched. Her arms and legs were as pale as her dress: moon planes of skin in the dim. The boys were laughing as she gestured, and one of them was gathering the wild wisps of her long hair so they stopped flying into her face.

In every friend group, there are three types of people: one who likes everyone, one who everyone likes, and one who would like everyone to go away.

Linnea liked everyone. I had never seen her not forgive someone, no matter what they said or did. She wore floaty clothes and spent a lot of time staring at the horizon. Men tended to like her and women usually didn't. With some regularity, Linnea was accused of playing a character because no one could be so high and airy and innocent.

Kitty, everyone liked. As often as not, she didn't reciprocate, but that was part of her charm. She was sharp, untouchable, incisive, which meant that winning her approval felt like the sun. She wore shades of lipstick with names like Ferrari Bombshell and Incorrigible Harlot. She would tell you the truth, but she would probably couch that truth in seven metaphors and five paragraphs.

Which left me as the third type of person.

I had a habit toward silence that had been compounded by my mum's memoir. It struck me as so presumptuous to imagine that anyone would want to hear her innermost thoughts that I felt the need to even the scales; she had already said so much on behalf of the Eriksson women that I figured I may as well shut up. Once, Kitty had told me that if I swam less and talked more, I could be the smart one. I'd said I thought I *was* the smart one. She'd said, *Please.*

"Why are you angry at Linnea?" I asked.

Kitty gestured toward the fire. "She's being… Delia would say she's scrounging for attention."

"Delia would say."

"Yes. Delia would say she's being a—flirt."

"You can't pretend you aren't slut-shaming Linnea by blaming Delia for saying things she's not even here to say."

Kitty crossed her arms. "I'm not slut-shaming Linnea. She can do whatever she wants. Hashtag feminism. It's just that you and I both know Linnea doesn't have the best track record of taking care of herself, and I don't want to be the one holding her hair out of the toilet bowl when she starts puking."

"Don't you?" I asked.

"Piss right off," Kitty said. Then: "Of course I do." She leaned against me and scowled. "Say something distracting."

"Pulchritudinous."

"What? No, like, a distracting topic of conversation."

"Hedda just bought a '78 Mustang, and she's having it shipped here next Tuesday."

Kitty made a noise of disgust. "You're no help at all."

I shrugged.

"Wait," she said, "where's Linnea?"

I looked back to the bonfire, and sure enough, no Linnea—gone like mist in the wind.

The three older boys were still in a huddle, but they were turned the other direction now, backs to the fire and faces to the ocean.

My heart did a slow one-two beat as I looked out at the waves: ink dark where they weren't tinged with the simmering midnight sun.

That was when I heard Linnea scream my name.

I was already standing.

I was already halfway down the beach.

My flannel was coming off as I ran—the thread-ripping noise

of a button flying—and my shoes were somewhere behind me. I saw Linnea, a flash of pale, and I was running into the surf.

The water was pins-and-needles cold. So cold it was hot. When it got as far as my stomach, I couldn't breathe from the shock of it. I dove, and my skin sang in pain.

It had been calm just a moment ago, and now it wasn't. The waves were coming at me diagonally, splashing at my mouth when I tried to breathe under my elbow. I opened my eyes. Too dark, too cold.

My hip collided with something—hard.

I gasped. Water filled my mouth, and I had to stop, breaststroke paddling with my arms as the pain radiated out from my hip bone, down my leg, and up my torso.

I'd hit one of the petrified figures. The statues, reaching their hands toward the surface with their immovable stone fingers.

Linnea called my name again, and on the crest of the next wave, I saw her: her dress spinning out wildly around her, her hair in a tangled noose around her neck.

She kept surging away from me. The current was pulling both of us, so the longer it took to close the gap between me and her, the farther we got from shore. But then, finally, we were in the trough of the same wave. Her face was doll pale, bloodless. She kept reaching wildly like the water would solidify in her grasp, become something to hold on to. I was shouting at her—I didn't even know what I was shouting; I couldn't hear my own voice—and her eyes were wide and white. Her mouth and nose kept going under. She angled her face to the sky, and the waves knocked at her, and she just kept grabbing, grabbing at the water.

I wrapped my arms around her from behind. She seized my hands, trying to keep them in place or claw them off.

I frog-kicked on my back. It was something between treading water and survival backstroke. Linnea kept choking on the waves. I glanced over my shoulder, trying to make out the silhouettes around the bonfire. My heart was starting to beat faster—the first push of adrenaline giving way to a different kind of fear. I told myself we didn't need to get there quickly; we just needed to keep moving faster than the current could drag us out again.

Linnea was going boneless in my arms. She was still breathing. Almost there. Almost there.

I saw a wave coming for us. Not yet breaking but moving like a predator. I was only thinking of Linnea—angling her so she didn't swallow half the ocean. The wave lifted us, and I kicked. Then it dropped out from underneath us, so much water rushing away, and pain pierced my body like I'd been stabbed.

I let go of Linnea.

Everything was dark.

I couldn't breathe.

My legs and arms and face had all disappeared, turned to nothing with numbness; the entirety of my being was concentrated in a palm-sized point on my left shoulder. The pain blossomed and crescendoed: I moved out of myself, transcending, and I had a moment of sudden clarity. There I was, sinking through the water, Linnea grabbing for me. In the water nearby, a man made of stone was raising a hand toward the surface.

I fell back into my body with a crash of pain.

I gasped at the water. Found my way to the surface. Coughed lungfuls of ocean as Linnea's hands closed around my arms. That place in my shoulder shrieked, or maybe I was shrieking, or maybe I was silent, too out of breath to make any noise at all.

Everything was pulsing black as I paddled to shore. Linnea was kicking now, just a little, and I noticed it and forgot again just as quickly. It began to feel like this would be my whole life: fighting the waves to shore as my shoulder seared like it wanted to come detached from the rest of my body.

And then there was sand beneath me. I tried to put a foot

down but found I couldn't stand. I shoved Linnea farther ahead of me, and she stumbled out of the surf while I crawled on my hands and knees. The sand under my fingers was a depthless dark. When I inhaled, I felt like I was being set on fire.

Everyone on the beach had collected in front of us. I would learn, later, that one of the boys had dared Linnea to go touch one of the stone figures. Linnea had been too drunk or happy to remember that she could hardly swim at the best of times, in a pool with a shallow bottom and a lifeguard on duty. The waves had swept her out, and all the boys promised they'd been about to go in after her, but I had dived past them before they'd gotten the chance.

At the time, I was only vaguely aware of the conversation going on. Kitty was shouting. Linnea was crying softly. Everyone else was whispering.

I was too numb to feel the cold when the water frothed against my hands and knees. *Stand up*, I told myself. *You have to stand up.*

I did, slowly, and there was one angle that made my body spasm so violently I almost went crashing down again. But then, all the way upright, it was slightly better, hardly bad at all, as long as I didn't inhale or exhale or move.

Most of the group's attention was fixed on Kitty, who had one arm tight around Linnea's waist and was continuing to tell the group of boys that she would personally carve their eyes out with spoons. The boys were starting to get defensive, crossing their arms and looking taller than they had a moment ago, and I found my heavy legs moving—dragging me across the sand, taking me to the place I belonged beside Kitty and Linnea. It was probably only a few feet, but it felt like the whole length of the beach. By the end of it, my eyes were watering. I leaned against Linnea's side, and she shot me a concerned glance.

"How was I supposed to know she couldn't swim?" one of

the boys demanded of Kitty. "Who the fuck jumps in the ocean when they can't swim?"

"It was just a dare," one of his friends said. "She didn't have to do it."

Linnea hid her face against me as color bloomed across her cheeks.

"And I don't have to fill your car with bees," Kitty said. "But let's see if I do it anyway."

"You need to calm down," the first boy said. He was flexing and unflexing his hands in fists at his sides, the universal sign of hoping to punch someone. I wanted to go stand between him and Kitty. I wanted to flex and unflex my hands into fists. When I let out a breath, black fringed my vision from the outside in.

"Hey," someone was saying, "hey, hey, hey." It was Henrik Holm, who had been in our class since we'd been born, who had hands the size of steering wheels and big, broad shoulders and a pink-tinged face framed by shaggy blond hair. He played rugby and didn't do well in school and never watched where he was going, but when he inevitably crashed into you in the hallway and sent your things flying, he would kneel on the tile next to you collecting books and say, *Ah, shit, I'm sorry—here, let me buy you a coffee or something.*

Henrik's cheeks were red from wind or beer or frustration. He was bigger than the other boys, and they glanced at each other like they were trying to make up their collective mind about something.

"There's no need for this," Henrik said. His hands were raised in a placating way. More quietly, he added, "She's already rattled."

Linnea pressed her face harder into my shoulder. I tried not to gasp from the pain.

Gesturing past Henrik to Kitty, one of the boys said, "She's fucking threatening us, yeah?"

Kitty gathered her breath to spit something back, but Henrik quickly said, “Please, can you just leave it?”

The boys were still tensed, but then through them slipped someone else, and there was Soren Fell standing at Henrik’s side. I hadn’t noticed him on the beach earlier; maybe he’d showed up when Henrik had. Between the two of them, lean, soccer-playing Soren and solid, rugby-playing Henrik, they looked better equipped for a fight than the three older boys.

Soren didn’t say anything. He just stood there and looked at them. Since the deaths of his parents, Soren had taken over much of the responsibility of running the Fells’ croft with his grandmother. Each year that went by, he did a little more and seemed a little older, like he was aging twice as quickly as the rest of us. By the time we’d turned seventeen, the men of the island were treating him as one of their own, calling him *Fell* and asking him about bank loans and crop yields.

The longer Soren stood there silently, the more the pressure built, like everyone was waiting for a mic drop, something clever and scathing to make the boys look like children. In the end, Soren’s eyes just swept them up and down, and he turned away from them and faced the three of us.

“Thank you, O knight, for your heroic protection,” Kitty said.

Soren inclined his head toward her. To Linnea, he asked, “You okay?”

“I’m fine,” Linnea said.

His eyes found mine, but he didn’t speak. Behind him, Henrik was successfully coaxing the boys back to the bonfire, and the crowd was dispersing. The numbness from the water was starting to fade, and without it came a sharp awareness of the cold air and an incongruous heat across my back. Was I bleeding? I hadn’t thought to check.

Soren extended something to me. It took me moment to realize it was my flannel. I accepted it—and for the first time noted that I was wearing nothing but my shorts and a black bra. I put on the flannel slowly and tried to keep my face emotionless. When I lifted my arm to get my hand through the sleeve, my vision went temporarily black.

"You must be freezing," Henrik said. I thought he was talking to me at first, but no, his gaze was fixed on Linnea as he peeled off his fleece jacket and draped it over her shoulders. "Want to sit down? Make sure you're okay?"

Linnea was nodding, and I felt a weight come off me. I trusted big, gentle Henrik, and besides, Kitty was stomping after them, and I just wanted them gone for a minute so I could figure out what was wrong with me.

Soren was still standing there.

"What?" I said.

He shook his head, but didn't go.

"Can you look at my shoulder?"

If he thought this was a strange request, he didn't show it. He just tilted his head to the side, and I turned away from him.

I felt his fingers on the collar of my flannel as he eased it off my shoulders. His index finger skimmed the back of my neck, my spine, and then his thumb slid across the skin to the left of my shoulder blade. The breathlessness now was deeper than before, and I felt stupid about it because this was Soren.

Our school was too small for everyone to not consider everyone else carefully when it came to romantic potential, so it would've been pointless to pretend that I did not like the way Soren looked or that I had not noticed. His hair was still fair, but not yellowish white like when he was a kid. It was closer to gold now—and cut terribly, with lumpy edges around his ears. Haircut aside, general consensus was that he had become attractive rather spontaneously last year. Linnea said it was because of his face, which was sort of squarish when you looked at it straight on but angular from the side. Kitty speculated it was because he kept his mouth shut most of the time, so he seemed less stupid than everyone else. I refused to comment on the matter because I refused to concede that I found him attractive. Nothing could happen between us because of my mother. We'd had classes together over the years, but this was the first time we'd been alone since we were twelve.

"What happened?" Soren said. His fingers ran carefully down my shoulder blade, and I arched my back away from him. "Sorry."

"The statues," I said. "I think I hit one."

His hand rested around my bare arm, thumb angled toward the locus of the pain. I wanted to be less aware of his touch than I was. "You're bleeding," he said.

In a way, I was glad for this. If it was bleeding, it would scab and it would heal. The idea of an invisible injury was more terrifying.

He dropped his hand suddenly. The warmth evaporated as I felt him step backward. I turned slowly, feeling embarrassed and vaguely rejected. He was tugging off his sweater, briefly exposing a band of stomach and faint golden hair.

I accepted the sweater, which was dark red and smelled overwhelmingly like soap, and pulled it over my head. It swallowed my hands and stretched lower than the bottom of my shorts.

"Thanks," I said.

"Yeah," he said. "I should go."

Go where? "Okay. Hey—don't tell Linnea."

"About your shoulder?"

I nodded. He frowned slightly, but in a way that felt like an assent.

Then he was gone, and I was alone on the beach, wrapping his overlong sleeves around myself and trying to fend off the feeling that my life had lurched imperceptibly in a direction I could no longer control.

Hedda's

2013

I woke up the day after Midsummer and found I couldn't move.

I stared up at the ceiling of my narrow room and briefly wondered if I was dead. Sun lit the pale space, undeterred by my gauzy curtains. My bed was exactly the length of the room. In the remaining space, there was a chest of drawers with a mirror on top, and at the uppermost point of the mirror, a relief carving of Haakon the Old, king of Norway in god knew when. The only thing I had on my wall was a Renaissance-era portrait of a noblewoman who looked prepared to murder her painter if he made her sit there a moment longer. Across it, Kitty had painted the words: *I don't have anything nice to say.* She'd given it to me for my fifteenth birthday.

Again, I tried to move. This time, I managed to shift my foot under the covers, and I exhaled slowly. I wriggled my toes and fingers, creating an inventory of my body. When I finally forced myself onto an elbow, a stabbing pain radiated through my shoulder, and I had to pause to catch my breath.

I got to my feet inelegantly. Before I'd gone to bed, I'd cleaned the blood off my shoulder and dabbed antiseptic on the worst of it. I smeared on another layer of antiseptic now, wincing.

Over my footboard, I had draped a towel, still damp, and Soren's red sweater. I had the uncomfortable urge to wear it. I tugged on one of my own instead, plus leggings. When I passed the mirror, I looked at my reflection carefully, as I did every morning, looking for three long claw marks across my skin. There was nothing. Just my normal face and my salt-crusted hair and a spot on the side of my nose.

My phone said it was eight. Practice started at nine, once the wave of very young and very old swimmers had cleared out of the pool. I told myself my shoulder would loosen as I swam, and I stuffed my damp towel and a swimsuit into my bag.

In the kitchen, my dad was making French toast. His phone, which sat on the counter, was playing Lady Gaga. My dad listened almost exclusively to female pop stars; for Christmas, Linnea had bought him a Taylor Swift keychain.

"How was Midsummer?" he asked, nudging a plate in my direction.

I took it. The butter was melting into the syrup; everything smelled sweet and cinnamony. "Youthful."

"You got back late. Did you walk?"

"Kitty drove me."

We ate in peaceable silence. My dad's knife clicked against his plate as he divided his toast into a tiny grid of equilateral pieces. I considered telling him about my shoulder, but decided not to; if I didn't say it out loud, then it couldn't be that bad.

"Do you need the car this morning?" I asked.

"Not until tonight."

"Tonight?"

"I have something vaguely reminiscent of a date."

I raised my eyebrows and speared the last of my toast. "With?"

"Anna? From the hospital?" My dad kept his head ducked to his plate. Beneath his scruff—three days of pale stubble—his cheeks were going pink. "Figured. You know. Get back out there."

My dad had really only dated one person since my mother, and that was my kindergarten teacher. They'd been together for two years, and I had wanted to be supportive because it had meant a lot to my dad, but I knew I hadn't been. I resolved myself to regard Anna, from the hospital, with less suspicion.

"That's great," I said.

My dad nodded once and fished the car keys out of his pocket. I caught them by the keychain.

"Oh," he said with the air of someone saying something offhand that they had been trying to figure out how to say offhandedly for some time now, "by the way. Your mum called."

"Ah." I checked my phone. 8:51. I had to go.

"She said you haven't answered any of her emails."

"Been busy."

Quietly, my dad said, "I just hope it's not on my account."

He wasn't looking at me. My dad had never been good with eye contact; he fixed his gaze on the thin pond of berry syrup on his plate.

"I'm sorry," I said.

He nodded once, and that was that—the end of the conversation. I got into the car at 8:53 and drove to the pool. The whole time, I drummed my fingers on the wheel and tried not to think of my mother's emails. When they arrived, I marked them as read and archived them unopened. I was fairly sure my mum knew I did this, so she'd been making the subject lines increasingly like clickbait. *You'll never believe what I found out about your grandfather!* And: *FYI, I ran into an old friend of yours...* And: *Check this essay I wrote about you for errors?*

I parked in my usual spot at the far corner of the lot. My dad drove a 1996 Toyota Camry, gray. We called it the Ship of Theseus after the old thought experiment—if you swap every piece of a ship one by one, is it a new ship?

Getting out of the car sent another stab of pain through my left side, and with every step I took toward the pool, my faith in my ability to swim this off decreased. Usually, I said a few words to whoever was working at the front desk and to my teammates before getting in the pool. That day, I kept my head down. Scanned my pass, changed into my swimsuit, and slid into the pool silently.

Our club had four lanes. I'd been in the fourth (the fastest) since I'd been fourteen. I led the lane unless we were swimming breaststroke, at which point I would cede lead to Thomas St. Clair. The others had already started warming up, and when they saw me waiting at the bulkhead, they paused to let me go. Thomas said something to me, possibly about Midsummer. I couldn't remember if he'd been there or not. I also couldn't totally process what he was saying because the feeling of the chlorine on my shoulder blade was akin to how I imagined it would feel to be splattered with acid.

I swam one hundred meters. My tumble turn, at the halfway point, hurt so badly I did not breathe for the whole fifty meters back. Thomas poked my feet the whole time, indicating not that he wanted to go by, necessarily, but that I should probably speed up. When I got back to the bulkhead, my coach was squatting by the water bottles and staring at me.

I pushed my goggles onto my forehead and looked up at him.

His name was Dan. He'd swum for UCLA, and he'd been helping me contact US university coaches.

"What's wrong with your shoulder?" Dan said.

"Could you tell from my stroke?"

"I could tell from the obvious wound."

I put a hand to the space between the straps of my swimsuit. It felt raw there, the skin uneven. "I hit a rock."

Dan's dark eyes fixed on me. "You went cliff diving."

"I didn't."

"You know how I feel about that. The kind of risk—"

"I was pulling someone out of the water," I said. "At Midsummer."

I wasn't sure Dan believed me—his mouth was still flattened into a fine line—but he nodded anyway.

"Get out of the water," he said.

"Am I in trouble?"

"Only if you've actually hurt yourself."

I clung to the edge of the bulkhead. "I think I just need a bandage."

"Really?" he said. "Because I could also tell from your stroke." He picked up my gear bag, pull buoy, and fins and tossed them toward my backpack, which was sitting on one of the benches against the wall. When I still didn't move, he grabbed my water bottle and threw it with the rest. "Go see a doctor," he said.

We kept staring at each other.

"Don't tell me you can't get out of the pool."

"Remains to be seen," I said.

"Jesus Christ, Tess."

I felt a hot, burning shame as I ducked under the lane lines, passing through lane three, two, one, until I reached the ladder. Even that, hauling myself out on the ladder's silver arms, made my body shake. I tore off my cap and goggles. Yanked my hair out of its bun.

"A doctor soon, please," Dan called after me.

As the other swimmers came in, I could feel their eyes on me. I wouldn't look back at any of them. This wasn't serious, I told myself. It couldn't be. Because I could not go to university in Stenland and I did not have money to go elsewhere and swimming was the way I was going to get a scholarship to the US; I already had coaches emailing me. Swimming was how I got out of Stenland. I did not have a backup plan.

There was no one available to look at my shoulder for a week. I made the appointment sitting in the Ship of Theseus, watching people with flip-flops and big backpacks come and go through the pool's double doors. I briefly considered asking my dad's hot date, Anna-from-the-hospital, if she knew anything about shoulder injuries.

My dad respected my drive to leave Stenland, which meant that he also respected my swimming. He came to every meet, paid every fee, and bought every new swimsuit. It was an investment, we told ourselves—some money now, free university later. Assuming I was fast enough. Assuming coaches were interested. Assuming I didn't get injured.

I didn't want to get home so soon after I'd left, which I knew would stress him out, so I sat in the parking lot googling scapular fractures for an hour. It was neither reassuring nor helpful.

When I did get home—around the same time practice normally ended—I got a call from Linnea. As a rule, Linnea never texted and Kitty never called. Sometimes I ended up coordinating their plans to hang out when I wasn't even going to be there.

"Hey."

"Are you done with practice yet?" Linnea asked.

"No. Currently swimming. Glub, glub, glub."

"Oh," she said. "Yeah, right, of course, because how else would you pick up the phone? Anyway, I have a preposition for you."

In the background, Kitty yelled, *"Proposition."*

"No," Linnea said. "My preposition is *with*. As in, I'm going on a date, and will you please come with?"

I threw my bag onto the couch and the keys onto the counter. Linnea going on a date was not particularly unusual. She'd been going on dates for years now and had already had two serious-ish relationships, which we defined as one that lasted more than six months. She had lapped both Kitty and me; neither of us had dated anyone. In my case, it was because I didn't want to date anyone Stennish. In Kitty's case, it was because she was in love with Linnea.

"Why do you want me on your date?" I asked.

"I don't want it to be too romantic. You have to feel things out, you know? Establish a rapport. And then, if it's good, we can have a romantic date next."

"Who is 'we,' exactly?"

"Oh, Henrik! He was so sweet last night. We just sat on the beach for hours after you and Kitty left, and he made me laugh and said all sorts of kind things about how much he liked talking to me."

Kitty made a loud vomiting noise.

"Kitty is less sure of him," Linnea added.

"Will Kitty also be coming on this date that will not be too romantic?" I asked.

"Kitty will not be in attendance!" she called.

"That would be *too* unromantic," Linnea clarified. "Because he's her cousin and all."

"I'm sorry," I said. "What about Kitty's cousin?"

"Oh, that's right—Soren will be there."

I had been in the middle of inspecting the fridge for snacks, but when Linnea said that, I stopped moving and stood in the refrigerated glow. "No," I said.

"Why not?"

"You know why not."

"Yes," Linnea said, "I do hear you, but this was actually Henrik's idea, and Soren is his best friend, so if Henrik thinks it's a good idea, then who are we to disagree? So it's a double date, and we're meeting at Hedda's at six after my shift, so I'll see you there—okay, bye!"

Linnea ended the call.

I looked down at my phone.

I thought of the way my skin had felt when Soren had touched me. Yes, I had been somewhat delirious from pain, but also, even now, thinking of his fingers running over my neck and his breath against the back of my head, I could feel my pulse in my stomach. I had always imagined that boys didn't talk to each other about feelings, but now I had the idea in my head of Soren telling Henrik that he liked me and Henrik telling Linnea and the pair of them constructing this double-date scenario to contrive us together. And I liked the thought of it: Soren and Henrik driving down the road together in Soren's banged-up white truck on the way to Midsummer; Soren admitting that he hoped I would be there. But then I thought of my mother, she of the many unanswered emails. I almost texted Linnea to tell her I wasn't interested, but then I went into my bedroom and saw Soren's red sweater hanging over my footboard.

I smoothed down the wool, picturing Soren handing it to me without letting his fingers touch mine. The sweater had to get back to him somehow; maybe if tonight was awful, I could pretend that I'd just wanted to return it. That I had not been particularly interested in his presence. That it did not drive me to distraction that of all the people on this island my mother might have killed, it had been the Fells.

My dad was just about to leave for his date when I left for mine. He was sporting a pale blue button-up and a vaguely nauseated expression. When he saw me, he squinted at my outfit and said, "Where are you going?"

I looked down at myself and wished I had time to change again. I was wearing black high-waisted jeans and a gray crop top, plus a massive sherpa jacket that had belonged to my dad in high school. When Linnea had said we were meeting at Hedda's, the downtown café/diner/post office where Linnea had worked since we'd been fifteen, I hadn't been sure if she'd meant we were staying at Hedda's or just picking her up and going elsewhere. If we were eating at Hedda's, the crop top was a bit much. If we were going to a party, the sherpa jacket was a bit stained with motor oil. I could've called Linnea and asked for clarification, but that would have revealed that I cared, and I was studiously trying to convince myself I didn't.

"I have no idea," I said.

"Well," my dad said, still looking puzzled, "I'm sure you'll be fine."

I walked into town with my hands shoved into the pockets of my dad's coat. I had Soren's sweater, freshly washed, tucked under one arm. Lundwall, the capital of Stenland and the only town that occasionally tried to call itself a city, had been built on the side of a hill. All the roads sloped downward toward the harbor like the island wanted to drain us into the ocean. There was no footpath, so when I heard a car behind me, I had to step into the wet grass or onto the nearest stone fence until it passed. That time of year, everything was lush—the lawns and the roofs and those mossy stone fences—and not yet windswept to death.

Hedda's was there along the ocean, the first thing you saw climbing off the ferry. Next door, the pub's parking lot was already full of battered thirty-year-old Škodas and Vauxhalls. Just beyond, an imposing cement church glowered down at the town. It had been built over top of a five-hundred-year-old stave church by some notable brutalist in the 1960s, and it was regularly featured on worst-of architectural lists. Behind it, just within view on the black-green hillside, there was a graveyard full of statues that had not been carved or cast but born.

I opened the door to Hedda's with my boot. A bell jingled. Hedda's was a blunt and unpretentious place. The tables were sticky and squeezed close together. On the counter, there was a coffee pot, a case of grainy-looking pastries, and a sign advertising postage stamps. It smelled vaguely of fermented fish. Behind the register (*CASH ONLY I MEAN IT*) hung a painting of Madonna and child, but I also knew that out back, Hedda kept an earthen mug of sheep's bones for the wight that might or might not have lived in the alley. That was the Stennish way: Jesus inside, paganism out back.

Only two of the tables were taken. One by a group of backpackers, twentysomethings, speaking loudly in an assortment of accents. A tall boy had his passport sticking out of the water-bottle pouch on the side of his backpack, right where anyone could grab it. I felt a wave of prickly irritation.

At the other occupied table, a booth, Henrik was studying a menu like it hadn't been the same for our entire lives. When I approached, his big face broke into a smile.

"Hey," he said.

I slid into the booth across from him. Was that correct double-date etiquette? Next to your date, not across from them? Too late to move now.

There was an awkward pause. I had been in school with Henrik for as long as I could remember, but he had never been someone I talked to. Actually, I didn't talk to anyone except for Kitty, Linnea, and other swimmers. I was saved by Linnea, who was hanging her apron on a hook and hurrying toward us. She was wearing a knee-length dress, lacy, which didn't answer the question of where we were going tonight.

"Formula One," Linnea said, a little breathless as she slid into the booth beside Henrik.

"Sorry?" he said.

"That's what you two should talk about. When you're looking so terribly awkward. You both like Formula One."

Henrik shot me a nervous look, as if I might contradict this. But I nodded my agreement, and Henrik gave a big, full-body sigh of relief. "Well, you should've said so. Linnea, you and your friends are intimidating."

"I am *not* intimidating," said Linnea, who nonetheless looked delighted. "Tess is, somewhat, but she has a gentle and delicate heart."

"Do I?" I asked.

"You cried when we watched *Titanic*."

"Yes, because Kitty was making hot chocolate and spilled boiling water on my arm."

Linnea scrunched up her face. "Really?"

The bell on the door jingled, and my face swung toward it with embarrassing speed. It was just Hedda. She regarded us suspiciously. There was little color variation between her skin and brows—pale to the point of invisibility—and her hair was short and feathery. Linnea waved cheerily, and Hedda disappeared into the kitchen.

Hedda had run her café for years before she'd become mayor of Lundwall and then a minister of Stenland, and now she ran her café again. She could've been prime minister, but she said bureaucracy was tedious and she preferred yeast. The actual prime minister was a thirty-nine-year-old woman who had studied at Cambridge and now lived by the water with her fisherman husband. Every election, the whole island crammed into Hedda's and drank strong coffee and gossiped until Hedda finally taped her list of political endorsements on the pastry case, and those were the people who would win.

I felt Henrik's gaze on me, and I was agonizingly conscious of the Soren-shaped hole in the booth. I wasn't about to ask where he was, but I also wished Henrik would offer the information.

"So, Linnea," Henrik said, "you're the expert. What should I order? What should I definitely not order?"

She giggled, and I shifted uncomfortably in my seat.

"Do order: any of the breakfast food, the fish and chips, and the cider. Do not order: the soup of the day, the wine, and anything Hedda's marked as a local favorite."

"Do I want to know what's wrong with those things?" Henrik asked.

"You do not!" Linnea said brightly.

The bells on the door jingled again, and this time, I forced myself not to look up. I studied my menu even though I got the exact same thing every time I came to Hedda's and she probably wouldn't even bother asking for my order. Linnea whispered something to Henrik, and I stared at the menu with increased fervor. I didn't look up until a shadow passed over the table, and there was Soren standing above the booth.

He looked like he'd just showered. His hair was curling slightly and a few shades darker than normal. He was wearing another sweater, this one navy, and dark jeans, clean but worn.

"Soren!" Henrik said. "Sit down. I'm just learning about why the soup of the day may or may not give me food poisoning."

"It won't give you food poisoning," Linnea said. "It'll just taste like whatever people didn't order yesterday."

"Well, that does sound tempting," he said. "Did people by chance not order pizza yesterday? Because I could go for pizza soup."

"We don't serve pizza."

"Really? Maybe you should."

Soren hovered at the head of the table. He wasn't looking at me so determinedly that I didn't see how it wasn't on purpose. This embarrassed me, and my embarrassment annoyed me, so I decided to stare at him with as much concentration as he was staring at Henrik. Soren's mouth was very thin; his eyes I'd always thought of as blue, but they were actually almost gray and set under heavy brows. I thought I could make out a hint of stubble on his jaw, the color of straw, and seeing it made me think of the flash of hair across his stomach when he'd given me his sweater.

"You going to sit?" Henrik said.

"I didn't realize it wasn't just us," Soren said.

"Well, that's rude," I said. He finally glanced over at me, his eyebrows lifting.

"It was kind of rude," Henrik said apologetically.

Linnea, for her part, looked aghast. "We just thought maybe it would be fun if we did some sort of double—"

Before she could say the word *date*, Soren's head swung toward her and the expression of absolute horror on his face might've been funny if it wasn't also humiliating. Soren took a step back from the table. I hated him, truly hated him and his bad haircut and his face that looked squarish from straight on but angular from the side. I wished I was lying at home in bed in a top that wasn't cropped with an ice pack on my shoulder.

Soren seemed to regain control of his face and smoothed the horror off it. "I don't think that's a good idea." He said it like he was talking to Linnea and Henrik, but this time he kept his gaze on me.

"Yeah," I said. "Of course not." I handed him the sweater. He took it and gave Henrik one last inscrutable glance—some combination of bewilderment and annoyance.

Soren raked his free hand though his hair, making it stand up on end. He paused a minute, and I was sure he was going to say something else, but before he could, he spun, strode quickly through Hedda's, and shoved outside. Through the glass door, I could see him stop and scrape his hand through his hair again. He took two steps to the left, shook his head, and did an about-face, hurrying off in the opposite direction with his shoulders bent to the wind.

I sat stiffly on my side of the booth. How stupid I was to only realize it now: that I had hoped that if Soren did not hate me for what my mother did, then I no longer had to hate myself for it.

"Well," Henrik said finally. "That could have gone worse."

"I thought you said he wanted to go on a date with her," Linnea said.

"He does!"

"Has he actually said that to you?" she asked. "In words?"

"Words?" Henrik said. "No."

I pressed my fingers to my temples. "Linnea, please bring me the soup of the day. Extra food poisoning."

"I feel like you two are angry at me," Henrik said.

"We're not angry," Linnea said. "We're just embarrassed."

I liked that she said *we*, like our feelings were a packaged deal. We grimaced at each other over the table.

"Wait, why would you be embarrassed?" Henrik said. "Are you really? I'm sorry. I figured you knew, or at least mostly knew."

"Knew what?" I asked.

"That he likes you. Well." He rubbed the side of his face. "I say he likes you. What I mean is that he has been more or less in love with you since we were twelve."

Linnea propped her elbows on the table. "Again, has he said that in words?"

"Well, no, but that's because he's conflicted. On account of—of his parents."

"Maybe he's not interested in dating," she said. "Or girls."

"I'm pretty sure he is. I just think he's only interested in Tess."

Linnea looked pensive. "Is that the way teenage boys work? Media has told me they're not particularly specific in their interests."

Henrik's cheeks flushed. "I mean, maybe some of them, but Soren's really… He's just serious. Look, he talks about her all the time. *Tess got a better grade on her essay than me—do you think her mum helped her write it?* That sort of thing."

"My mum doesn't help me write my essays," I said.

Henrik raised his hands defensively. "Okay, well, he says other stuff too. Like, he asked me if I thought you were dating Thomas St. Clair."

"I find myself grateful we're having this conversation now and not ten minutes before he showed up," I said. "Imagine how demoralizing that would've been."

"He is in love with you," Henrik insisted. "I mean, I think he is."

"You think," Linnea said.

"There's also a chance he resents you." He sounded concerned. "Honestly, I didn't consider that."

I stood up. "And on that note, enjoy your date."

Linnea's eyes were wide with concern. "Want me to walk you home?"

I looked at her, then at Henrik, so hapless and earnest. Whenever his eyes found Linnea, he blushed like she was the most gorgeous girl in Stenland. Which, for the record, she was; but it was nice to see someone else noticing. I liked him despite myself. I liked him even though he'd architected the shortest double date of all time.

"No," I said. "I'm fine."

I was halfway out the door when Henrik called after me, "I still think he's in love with you! Ninety percent sure!" Then the door closed behind me, swallowing his voice. I dug my hands into my pockets and ducked my head to the wind, and as I walked home alone, I reminded myself that I didn't want to date a Stenn anyway, much less one who belonged on this island the way the wind belonged on this island, like neither would be alive without the other.

Meet

2013

"You have to tell her," Kitty said.

"Actually," I said, "I do not."

"You do. Reason one—friendship and trust. Reason two—I am tired. Reason three—would it be the worst thing in the world if Linnea realized that being Faerie Queen has consequences? No. Shall I go on?"

We were sitting in the metal stands overlooking the pool. The noise was cacophonous: coaches shouting and bodies splashing and younger siblings having meltdowns by the snack bar, where two mums were selling oatcakes and fudge. The pool was a hulking cement building, one fifty-metre lap pool and one irregularly shaped kiddie pool. The tiles were that yellowish-brownish color where you couldn't tell if they were supposed to look like that or if they used to be white but had gotten stained.

It was my first swim meet of my last club season—or rather, it should've been. My eventual diagnosis, once I'd made it to the hospital, was a fractured scapula. The doctor had told me I'd been very lucky not to have fractured anything else; I'd said lucky was exactly how I felt. There was nothing to give it but time. I didn't have a sling or a cast, which saved me from talking about it. It had been two months since Midsummer, and I was back in the pool, but only twice a week for easy, slow laps. So the first meet was going on without me. Dan had asked if I'd come cheer on the others. For team morale. For my part, morale was low. Dan had not provided me with any cheerleaders.

It didn't help that Lukas Fell was in the stands. Soren's younger brother. He didn't look anything like Soren, really—Lukas's hair was brown and curly, and where Soren was lanky, Lukas was solid. The only family member Lukas really looked like was his uncle—Kitty's dad. When Lukas walked into the pool complex, he looked at Kitty and then at Kitty's shirt and promptly looked away again.

The shirt in question said *Go Tess! Do swimming!* Kitty had worn it to all my swim meets since age eleven, and she kept insisting she would stop wearing it when she grew out of it, but that hadn't happened yet. I was wearing a plain black sweater because when I'd seen my reflection that morning, wearing my Stenland National Swim Club T-shirt, I'd started to cry.

Crying: that was new. I figured it had something to do with my abrupt ceasing of physical activity. Whatever endorphins I'd been relying on to regulate my mood had vacated my body and left me sleeping badly and eating at only bizarre hours. Linnea knew I wasn't swimming because I was dealing with some obscure injury, but I'd never told her exactly what it was, and I certainly hadn't told her how I'd gotten it. She had offered to come sit in the stands with me today too, but I didn't think I could bear it, and Kitty didn't think she could bear Henrik, so we'd both been relieved when they'd decided to go picnic by the gorge instead.

"You sound bitter," I said.

"I am bitter," Kitty shot back. "I am bitter like black coffee spiked with vodka. I am bitter like kale that has not been properly massaged. I am bitter like a woman scorned."

"Have you been scorned, though?"

"I feel scorned. That counts for something."

"Speaking of telling Linnea things," I said.

She gave me a murderous look. "Right. That would go well. 'Hey, Linnie, I know you're really keen on your brick of a boyfriend these days, but have you perhaps considered that I am both wittier and nicer to look at? Also, I can braid your hair that way you like, and I already know you snore. Shall we? Become wedded?'"

"I don't know," I said. "Sounds pretty good to me."

"I'm not saying any of that."

"Why not? If it's making you miserable."

"At least this misery is vaguely romantic. If I tell her and she shoots me down, then I'm just the loser who got rejected. No offense."

The first event was starting. The glare through the windows was so intense, I could hardly see the swimmers. I squinted at the pool and grunted, which was all the response Kitty's comment deserved.

A grainy voice said over the speaker system: *"Take your mark."* My heart upended in my chest in anticipation; I heard that voice in my dreams. A loud *beep.* I heard that in my dreams too. The swimmers launched off their blocks, and my head seemed to think I was swimming with them. I pressed my palms against the stands.

"Oh, forget it," Kitty said. "You're Robot Tess, beep boop. What is love? Cannot compute."

"If I were not a robot, I would find that hurtful."

Kitty threw herself back, tossing an arm dramatically across the row of seats behind her. "Why is it that Linnea's the one who can talk about feelings, but she's also the only one I can't talk to about these feelings? And you're the one who has this whole angry bisexual energy going on—don't look at me that way—except you have too much of a hard-on for swimming to even figure it out."

Kitty had told me she was fairly sure she was in love with Linnea last April. She said she wasn't yet sure if she was gay or bi or just into Linnea specifically but that she would continue to assess the situation and report back in detail. I had felt a stab of panic at the time. There'd been a part of me that had thought I was perhaps too interested in Tana Jonsson's comings and goings from swim practice, and there had also been a time where we'd been sitting next to each other on a team outing to the movie theater and I had wanted to reach over and grab her hand so badly I'd thought I might die. But when Kitty had told me she was in love with Linnea, I'd felt overcome by the fear that if I could date Kitty, I had to. And I did not want to date Kitty. The thought of dating Kitty made me feel like I was being shoved into a steamer trunk. Although she was indeed very witty and very nice to look at, she nonetheless hated sports and was basically my sister and never fucking shut up. So I'd neatly boxed any feelings I might or might not have had for Tana Jonsson, and I put them on a high shelf with a label that said *DO NOT OPEN UNTIL UNIVERSITY.*

Angry bisexual energy. I did not dignify Kitty with a response.

"Is this one of the switch-y stroke events?" Kitty asked, squinting at the swimmers. "I could've sworn they were just doing butterfly."

"They are doing butterfly."

"Are you sure? I thought butterfly was the...you know, *whoosh* underwater one."

"That's breaststroke."

"Huh. You'd think I'd know all this by now."

"You would," I said, "think that."

"You should sit on the sides and explain more often. This is way more fun than when you're in the pool. I mean, it's fun to watch you swim and stuff, assuming you win. Honestly, kind of a buzzkill when you don't. It was a big relief for all of us when you got good." Kitty yawned and stretched. "Tess. Tess." She grabbed my arm. "TessTessTess—"

"What."

Her eyes were fixed on the doors, and I thought, yes, of course, it was Soren—probably coming to glower at me. But then, Kitty didn't care when Soren walked into a room, and she had no reason to know that I did, that my heart went *TessTessTess* when he stepped through a door looking windswept and serious. I followed her gaze to the door, and even as I stared at the person standing there, it wasn't until she spoke that I processed who it was.

Kitty said, "Your mum is here."

She was wearing a long camel-colored trench coat and dark sunglasses. Her fair hair was pulled back with a claw clip. She looked, I thought, like a celebrity trying to hide her identity from the paparazzi.

I stood up without knowing I was doing it. I started clambering down the stands, but her gaze was fixed on the swimmers in the water—searching for me, probably. She didn't look at me until I was right next to her.

"Oh!" she said. "Tess. What are you doing? Why aren't you in the pool?"

I set my jaw.

"I did email you," she said, "that I was coming. I thought I'd watch your race, but you aren't..." I couldn't see her eyes behind her sunglasses. There was a part of me that still flinched when her eyes met mine, like there might still be some remnant of curse lingering there. Also because we had the same eyes. Everyone said so.

"I came all this way," she said finally.

In the background, I could hear that voice: *"Take your mark."*

I gestured to the door with my chin and brushed past her. She hesitated, then followed. Outside, the parking lot was damp. It wasn't actively raining, but the air still had the feeling of it, and the sky was full of lumbering clouds. Just beyond the lot, the tumbling grass rose into a hill, and from the top of the hill, a dark slab of stone stared down at us. It had a raven carved into one side and Norse runes along the edges. Surrounding it was a half-hearted attempt at a fence. On the whole, it felt like an apt summary of Stenland.

My mum took off her sunglasses and slid them into her handbag. When our eyes met, I flinched, and she regarded me coolly.

"Are you going to acknowledge me at all, then?" she asked.

"Why are you here?"

"I wanted to see you swim. I look at all your race results, you know. You're good."

"Well, I'm not swimming. Obviously."

"Why not?"

"Injury."

Her frown deepened. "Why didn't you say anything? Is it serious? You know the doctors here are— Well. If it's something serious—"

"I'm fine."

We watched each other. A gust of wind came tearing through, throwing water off the rooftops and splattering my cheeks. The air smelled of chlorine, and I could hear that voice again, *"Take your mark."* My mum was waiting for me to say something, but she ran out of patience before I did.

"I don't know what your dad told you to make you hate me so much—"

"Dad has never said a single bad thing about you." Heavy in the air was the implication of the reverse: that my mum had said plenty about him.

"Well, what am I supposed to think? You don't answer my emails, you don't pick up my calls… I show up here to be supportive, and you act like I'm victimizing you somehow."

I looked away from her. Fixed my gaze on the Ship of Theseus, parked in its usual corner. A puffin landed on the roof and picked at his feathers.

"Your dad mentioned you were looking at American universities," my mum said. "I think that's great. Broadening your horizons. I wish I would've done it." She waited for me to speak, then continued. "Kitty's mum told me how well you did on your SAT. That's got to really help. Show the coaches you're not just a swimmer, you know?" When I still didn't respond, she added: "I can help you write your essay, if you'd like. I've started doing some freelance work, and I've edited personal essays. I mean, I can't do much right, apparently, but at least we know I have a grasp of narrative nonfiction."

I couldn't bear the weight of her eyes on me. I just wanted her to look away, at her phone, at anything else. The puffin cocked his head at me curiously.

"You're behaving like a child," she said.

"Okay."

"I don't know what you think I did to deserve this."

"You killed someone." I finally looked at her. "You turned two people to stone, and then you made a career talking about it. And—and telling people how stupid and backward we all are, Dad and me and everyone else. And now you act like we should celebrate you for it."

"I thought you wanted to get out of Stenland."

"That doesn't mean I want you to call Dad stupid."

"I never said that," she said. "And you really think that little of me? That I set out to profit off what happened to those people?"

"The Fells."

"Yes."

"And it's not what happened to them. It's what you did to them."

"It's what this island did to them," she said. "It's what this island did to me—and to every woman who's come before us and everyone who's been turned to stone. You think I'm the only one who's forgotten to look in the mirror before walking out the door?"

I didn't answer.

"I should've been more careful," she said. "But I've already paid for it. I left so it would never happen to me again." When I still didn't say anything, she said: "I just hope, for your sake, you get out of this place while you can."

Another gust of wind whipped up the hillside, but I felt immovable, stone. I watched my mother cross to a familiar car, and I realized it was Mrs. Sjöberg's BMW. They were still friends, I supposed. The car was out of the lot with a spray of its tires. I sat on the wet curb and pressed my fingers against my eyes. A car door opened, then closed gently, and I hoped whoever it was would go into the pool without acknowledging my existence. But they didn't, so I was forced to look up, from muddy shoes to a familiar red sweater, and there was Soren.

I hadn't spoken to him since the double date that wasn't. We had most of our classes together, but between his tendencies toward not speaking and mine, we managed to avoid interaction. He had his hands shoved into his pockets, and just like the last time I'd seen him, his hair was damp and curling at the bottom.

"What could you possibly want?" I said.

"I didn't mean to overhear," he said.

"Oh, for fuck's sake."

"My window was open. I was parked right there."

And sure enough, there was his truck, just on the other side of an SUV. I pressed my palms against my cheeks and made a low, dejected sound, which made the edge of Soren's lips turn briefly upward.

"Thank you," he said. His voice was very level when he said it, and his gaze. I thought about what Henrik had said about Soren, that he was serious, but I thought maybe a better word for him was *deliberate*. You got the sense that he didn't do anything accidentally.

"I didn't know you were there," I said.

"I figured."

"Why were you there?"

His eyes moved briefly to the wet stretch of curb beside me, like he was considering sitting, then away again. "My brother wanted to watch the meet."

"Why?"

"His girlfriend is swimming."

"Oh," I said. "And you were waiting in your car?"

Soren nodded once.

"Why?"

"Because I didn't want to go in."

"Why?" I asked again.

"Because I didn't want to see you."

A beat of silence. Soren scraped a hand up through the back of his hair.

"That's...rude?"

"You said the same thing to me at Hedda's."

I pursed my lips. "Well, take the opportunity to recognize these patterns as they arise." That earned me a laugh, and I wished I didn't like the sound as much as I did. Maybe I was still high on adrenaline from the meeting with my mum, or maybe I figured Soren's rudeness gave me permission to be rude in return, but I found myself saying, "Henrik tells me you either hate me or have been in love with me since we were twelve years old."

Soren was quiet a moment. "Henrik," he said finally, "should talk less."

I raised my eyebrows at him. He raised his right back. Neither of us said anything, though it was quite possible I'd never wanted to say something more. The silence stretched for so long that it became awkward, and then it became funny—because we both had the same trick and neither of us wanted to lose.

I crossed my arms.

He tilted his head to the side.

I checked the time on my phone.

Soren sighed and looked over his shoulder.

"I'll see you around," he said finally.

"You didn't answer my question."

"It wasn't a question."

I wanted to say *Then which one is it?* but to this point, I could almost play off the conversation as a joke—just two of Henrik's friends laughing about the ridiculous things he said. If I pressed again, it would be woefully obvious that it wasn't a joke, really. I didn't think I could bear to hear Soren say *I hate you, actually*, but what would be worse was the likelier answer *I don't know where Henrik came up with that; I think you're very nice; it's just, you know, your mother killed my parents.*

"I'm going to go back inside," I said, standing up. My butt was wet from the curb. I tried to wipe it off, but felt stupid doing it. "Are you coming?" I realized after I said it that he'd already said *See you around.*

"Ah. No. I have…errands."

"I thought Lukas was inside."

"I'll pick him up later."

I waited for him to leave, but he didn't. Maybe he was waiting for me to leave too.

"I think you sat in some bird shit," he said.

I looked down at my jeans.

"Bye," Soren said quietly, "Tess."

He got back into his car and drove away. I stood in the parking lot for longer than was dignified. When I went back inside, I texted Kitty from the locker room. She arrived a minute later and said, "What happened with your mum?"

"I sat in bird shit, Kitty."

"Oh. That's…not good?"

I wanted to tell her about my conversation with Soren in unsparing detail. I wanted her to hear every syllable he'd spoken, and I wanted her to visualize every time he'd swept his hand through his hair. I wanted her to tell me it was obvious he loved me and, thus, that any feelings I might or might not have had would not wind up hurting me. In the end, I couldn't make myself say his name at all.

Better

2022

When I got back to Sjö with the birthday cake, I put the car in Park but didn't open the door. Through the dark tinted windows, I watched guests trickle in and pretended I was not waiting for anyone in particular. Had he left the bakery just behind me? Had he made a stop along the way, biding his time so we didn't run into each other again any earlier than necessary?

I heard the familiar rumble of a grumpy engine, and a Camry puffed into view. My dad was driving. For a moment, I thought he was looking at me—I lifted a hand, but it was dark and my windows were tinted. His gaze remained fixed forward, his face slack.

I climbed out of the car with the cake as he parked. It took him a minute to notice me—a raven was cawing and cawing from the nearest light post, and the fog seemed to swallow all other noise—but then finally I said, "Hi."

He turned. For a minute it seemed like he might rush at me, that we would be a happy chaos of limbs, but then he hesitated, rocking forward on his heels, rocking back again.

I smiled at him, feeling nervous and guilty and uncertain, and he smiled back—or tried to, getting there in the mouth if not in the eyes. He took the cake box and placed it gingerly on the roof of his car, then he folded me into his arms. I tried to think of what to say first—that I loved him or that I'd missed him. Each time I left Stenland, I stayed away longer, and each time I came back, I felt more like a tourist: not just on the roads or in the restaurants but within the relationships that shaped me.

"Happy birthday," he said quietly.

"It's so nice to see you."

"I recorded the Grand Prix, if you want to watch it together when we get home?"

"Sure," I said, and he kissed the top of my head.

"You've seen Linnea and Kitty?" he asked.

"We got ready together."

"That's good. That's very good."

When Soren's truck appeared, we both looked up. He parked as far from us as possible but still nodded in a cordial, forced sort of way as he passed. The wind flattened his hair, blowing it back from his face.

I thought of other times I had seen him like this, facing down the wind: his hair light with California sun, tousled in a eucalyptus breeze; his hands deep in his pockets, chin to his chest, as he made his solitary way across the croft. I wished I could tell Kitty and Linnea how I felt, but I wasn't sure how to say it in a way that wouldn't sound like I still loved him, because I didn't. It was just that so much of what I felt when I thought of Stenland was shame. I was ashamed I'd been born here and ashamed I'd left. I was ashamed of the distance between me and my dad—between me and everyone. And when

I saw Soren, who was clever and beautiful and good, who knew me as well as anyone could, who'd loved me but not forever: it was just a shame.

"Well," my dad said, lifting the cake. "Better get this inside."

Kitty texted me.

Kitty: Alert, alert, Soren has arrived. You are hot/brilliant and I love you!!!

A few seconds later, from Linnea:

Linnea: Hi love—just fyi soren is here now. I didn't want you to be surprised. Rehearsal starts soon hope all is going okay with the cake x

I felt my dad watching me. I blinked, staring straight forward.

"You have good friends," he said.

"I do."

"It'll get better."

"What?"

He nodded at the door. "Seeing him. Maybe you can, you know, be friends someday."

I pressed my fingers into my shoulder, trying to force the tension from the muscle. Sometimes I could still feel a pang when I did that, the memory of injury.

"I don't think that's— I think I would find that difficult."

My dad didn't argue. He never did. He just smoothed the hair out of my face and told me we'd better go inside.

The Croft

2013

It was entirely possible that Soren and I would have continued to only speak to each other in situations where one of us had not known the other was going to be there if our literature teacher had not decided that he was sick of everyone partnering up with their friends for group projects and that he would be pairing us off alphabetically instead. There was no one between *Eriksson* and *Fell*, which was how I ended up with plans to go to Soren's house on a Thursday evening in October. I had by then increased from two to three swim practices a week, which was progress, but not nearly enough. Thursday was one of my off days.

My dad took the opportunity to invite Anna (from the hospital) over to the house for dinner. When I passed him in the kitchen, he was making ravioli.

"It's odd to think of that boy in a classroom," my dad said.

"Soren?"

"In my head, he's twenty-seven."

Soren lived on the farthest northern tip of Stenland. Once I'd made it around the mountains, the road turned narrow and gravelly. To my right, the hills sprawled green gold and treeless. To my left, whitecaps frothed across a flinty sea. A single power line heralded the curves of the road. I saw no other cars but sheep in every form: a cluster by a stone fence, a ram on the far side of a creek, a bloodied corpse on the edge of the gravel. It took forty-five minutes to get there, and as someone who had never lived farther than a few hundred feet from wherever I wanted to go, I could not imagine driving all that distance every day.

Soren's house was bigger than mine. The ground floor was carefully laid gray rock, and the first was black wood. The turf roof had openings for skylights and chimneys. Each of the windows was fitted with a red frame, and from inside, the light glowed gingery gold. Behind the house, a craggy hillside stepped into the clouds. There were old legends that said Stenland had been formed when a giant had been turned to stone, and out here, you could see why.

I got out of my car and swung my feet onto the soggy ground. My breath turned misty in the air. The silence was so profound, I might as well have arrived in another century: no cars, no TVs, no fishing boats clanging their bells. Even the ocean was muffled by fog.

Lukas answered the door when I knocked. It was only five, but he was already wearing flannel pajama bottoms. His dark curls were sticking up at the back, like maybe he'd just been asleep.

"Oh," he said, "it's Tess Eriksson."

It was a normal Stennish introduction—the sort of thing you say to someone with whom you've never had a chat but know anyway because everyone knows everyone, because your family has hurt their family, because you are unable to feign casualness when you are already linked together with iron chains. So instead, you just acknowledge: *I know exactly who you are.* I wondered if he remembered what my mum looked like, if he was thinking how much I resembled her.

"Lukas Fell," I said.

"Come in, I guess. Soren's off… I don't know. You can sit in the kitchen and wait for him or whatever."

I followed Lukas through the house. From the outside, I'd expected something that felt old, but it was warm and neat. I knew via Kitty that Soren's grandmother—his dad's mother, from the Fell side of the family—had moved in with the boys after their parents had died. Among the boots and raincoats by the door, one set was fuchsia.

Lukas flopped across a yellow couch and pressed Play on whatever violent show he was watching. I'd arrived just in time to hear someone's head get chopped off. Over the kitchen table, there was a window with a view of the ocean, all pewter and steel under the fog. I sat down and examined the vase at the center of the table. Stenland was too far north for most trees and flowers, but the vase was filled with branches of some kind. From a willow bush, maybe. Their leaves were a pale, grayish-blue, and they were lovely in a sparse, delicate sort of way.

"He did that this morning," Lukas said.

I turned in my seat. Lukas didn't bother looking away from his show, but he nodded vaguely in my direction.

"The vase. He did it this morning."

"Oh," I said.

"I think it looks stupid," Lukas added.

"Does he…often put out vases?"

Kitty had a signature expression, a kind of disappointed scowl that made you feel like you were the stupidest person on Earth. I'd always thought it was unique to Kitty, but maybe it was inherited after all because Lukas gave me the exact same look.

A back door opened somewhere, and Soren called, "Lukas?" The stamping of wet boots. "Did Tess's car pull up? Because I just saw—" He came up short on the other side of the room. I had never seen someone so entirely covered in mud. It was across his chest, on his knees, splattered up the side of his face. He looked almost violently startled to see me, and when he did, he touched the mud on his jaw.

"I think you sat in some sheep shit," I said.

"Touché," Soren said.

Lukas snorted and turned up the volume.

"Give me a minute," Soren said. He gestured vaguely at the kitchen. "Grab whatever you want." On the way past the TV, he turned the volume down again, which made Lukas throw a sock at him.

Once Soren was gone, Lukas said, "Not whatever you want. Like, don't take anything good."

"If I get hungry, I'll be sure to eat something that looks terrible."

"Thanks."

Sitting in the Fells' kitchen, I fidgeted in my chair while I waited, mentally rehearsing what I could say, if I should say anything at all, to explain how I resented my mother, how sorry I was for what happened, how desperate I was for their forgiveness. There were no words good enough.

Soren reappeared a few minutes later in new clothes. His face looked bright pink and freshly scrubbed. He cast his gaze around the room—Lukas pointedly turned up the volume of the TV again—before saying, somewhat grudgingly, "I suppose we can work in my room."

I followed him up a set of stairs, narrow and steep. I had never been inside a boy's bedroom before, and there was something about it that felt vaguely illicit. Soren's room was at the top of the house, with a slanting ceiling and some of the skylights I'd noticed from outside. There was a small wooden desk and a small chest of drawers and a small radiator tucked beneath the window. The only things that were not small were the bookshelves. There were two of them, and the tops seemed to have been cut at custom angles to accommodate the triangular ceiling. He'd stacked the books horizontally and then begun to double-stack them in places, and now the shelves were bowing dangerously. There was another collection beginning on his side table and a few more poking out from beneath his bed.

"No wonder you get offended when I get better essay grades than you," I said.

"Not offended," he said. "Merely bemused."

"I didn't know you read so much."

"I don't. I just like the aesthetic."

I picked the nearest two books off the shelf. *Hamlet* and *The Hunger Games.* "Eclectic," I said.

"Do you read much?" He said it casually, as if the answer did not matter much, as if a person could possibly own this many books and approve of any answer besides *Yes, emphatically.*

"I feel like this is a test," I said.

"Not a test."

I held up the books. "Both of these have characters named Claudius. Do I pass?"

"It wasn't a test."

"They also both have characters named Peeta."

"There's no one named Peeta in *Hamlet.*"

"Sure. He's friends with Rosencrantz."

"Ah, yes," Soren said. "The iconic trio—Rosencrantz, Guildenstern, and Peeta."

"I love the Peeta soliloquy in Act Two."

Soren took the books out of my hands and put them back on his shelf. "Again," he said, "I wouldn't test you."

As I started pulling textbooks and notes out of my school

bag, my eyes kept flicking toward his shelves. I couldn't say what he read, other than everything. Fat fantasy epics were squished next to thin literary novels. Books had to be shipped to Stenland from the UK and were priced accordingly, so I was aware I was looking at a precious collection. I wanted to go through them, pulling out titles I'd read, but Soren had already turned to our homework, the papers for which he was spreading across the desk. He had long fingers, the nails cut short and scrubbed clean. They might have been elegant, his hands, if not for the patchwork of scars and scrapes across them. I realized I was staring, so I cleared my throat and looked at the assignment.

We'd been tasked with translating a four-hundred-year-old ballad from Stennish to English using a stapled packet of grammar and vocabulary from our teacher. According to my dad, translation didn't used to be part of the curriculum. It was a new thing the education council wanted high schoolers studying. There was just one university in Stenland, a small campus with six compact buildings, and Stennish Studies was one of their limited number of departments. I wanted to ask Soren if he ever thought about going to the university, with grades like his, or maybe to a university somewhere else, but it felt too personal.

We started translating, moving word by word and line by line. I tried to surreptitiously find an online translator on my phone and discovered only one, which appeared to have been created at the dawn of computers and never subsequently updated. If I was with Kitty, I would've made a joke about the pointlessness of studying a language the internet had not even bothered to learn.

I kept looking at the last stanza, which was one from a sailor's perspective as he left his love behind, and eventually, I said, "I don't think he's sailing off."

"No?"

"I think he's been turned to stone, and now the sea is eroding his body."

Soren frowned at our paper. "You reckon?"

"That's why he's so sad."

"I think he's just heartbroken to be leaving her," he said. "They love each other. That's the point. Love amplifies normal experiences."

I sat back in my chair. "Well, I think she killed him."

Soren looked over at me, smiling slightly, and my stomach did something complicated. We'd shifted our chairs closer together as we worked, and there was a very small corner of my knee that was brushing his thigh. Did he not move because he didn't feel it? Or because he did and wanted it there?

"You're a much better partner than Henrik," Soren said.

"Yes, well, it helps to know how to read."

The humor vanished from Soren's face. He shifted his leg away from mine abruptly and started gathering our papers.

"I'm sorry. That was mean. I don't know why I said that."

But I did know why I'd said it. I'd said it because we'd been talking about books earlier, and there was a part of me that still felt like I was taking a test. Soren had done all the cleverest bits of translation, and surely he'd noticed that he was better at it than I was, that he could untangle the words and reincarnate them into something beautiful.

Soren said nothing. He slid the papers back into the folder and closed it with an air of finality.

"I'm sorry," I said again.

"Henrik isn't stupid," Soren said.

"I know. I—wanted you to think I was smart. I didn't mean it."

He nodded, but he didn't say anything more. Linnea would've been so hurt if she'd heard me. Linnea, who'd been teased our whole lives about not gliding through school with Kitty's and my grace or luck. When Soren led the way back downstairs, silent still, I felt a dull flush of embarrassed anger.

Lukas was still watching his show on the couch. Oh, a sex scene—lovely. I was just grabbing my coat from the back of one of the kitchen chairs, where I'd left it, when the door swung open and Soren's grandmother came in, a sheepdog nipping at her heels. I recognized her vaguely from assorted school functions; she was so tall you couldn't not notice her, so tall it was difficult not to point it out. Elin, I thought. Elin Fell. Her gray hair was tied back into a ponytail, and her clothes were muddy, though not nearly as muddy as Soren's had been. I braced myself for her disapproval.

"Ah," she said, nodding at me like it was no surprise to see me in her kitchen, "Tess Eriksson." She strode over to me, the dog still trailing her, and shook my hand three times. On the third time, she said, "Your car's in a state."

I frowned.

"Go on," she said, gesturing with her head toward the door. "Have a look."

Outside, the mist had turned to rain, a drizzle spat from low-slung clouds. I flicked on the flashlight of my phone to make it across the muddy driveway. It wasn't until I reached my car that I realized Soren had followed me and the dog had followed him.

I crouched by the wheel. The tire was as flat as a tire could be, squished into the earth like it had melted. I thought I saw a gleam of something gray reflecting back the beam of my flashlight, and when I touched it, I found the flat head of a nail pressed against the rubber.

"Do you leave many nails lying around?" I asked Soren.

His hand was on the dog's head. He was watching me, but he had an absent expression on his face, like his mind had been elsewhere. He blinked and said, "Yes, on purpose. To surprise weary travelers."

"I have a spare," I said.

But I never got as far as opening my trunk because my back tire was flat too, and when I dropped into a squat next to it, I found another nail protruding from the rubber.

"Do you really?" I asked.

He frowned at me.

"Leave nails lying around," I clarified.

His face went very blank. "Is that tire also flat?"

I leaned to the side so he could see.

"I'll be right back," he said.

The dog trailed him back up the steps to his house, tail wagging. I sent my dad a picture of the tire. He immediately texted back a gif of Sam from *Holes* saying *I can fix that.* Then he quickly added the message *you can fix that! There was a series of enthusiastic emojis.

I sent him a picture of the other tire.

He sent me a frowny face.

I looked over my shoulder at the house, and through the kitchen window, I could see Lukas sprawled on the couch while Soren stood over him. Soren had the look of someone tightly controlling their anger. Lukas had the look of someone who didn't particularly care. In the kitchen, their grandmother was scrubbing potatoes and looking at the boys from under raised eyebrows.

Soren came back outside a moment later. He stopped on the bottom step and put his hands in his pockets.

"It seems," he said, "my brother put nails in your tires."

"Ah."

"I'll pay for new ones. I'm sorry. About all this."

I looked at my phone. It was eight forty-five. I could call my dad, who could probably borrow the neighbor's car, the Ship of Theseus being the only one between us. Kitty and her mum were in London for a long weekend to see a show, and Linnea didn't have her license.

"I can drive you home," Soren said.

"Are there any nails in your tires?"

"I should bloody well hope not."

But I hoped that there were. Which was stupid. I hoped it anyway.

"And after school tomorrow," he said, "we can get new tires in town and you can drive back here with me to pick up your car."

"That's a lot of driving," I said.

He raked a hand through his hair, which I was coming to realize was his habit, the thing he did when he'd already decided what he was going to say, but hadn't yet said it.

"You could just stay," he said.

"I suppose," I said, "that would be the most environmentally conscious option."

"You could take my room." Quickly, he added, "I fall asleep on the couch all the time anyway."

"Should I be concerned Lukas will spear me with nails while I sleep?"

"No. He's… I'm sorry. Maybe he thought it would be funny. I don't know what he was trying to prove."

"Trying to prove?"

"You know," he said.

Soren was looking at me. I could only see his silhouette and the faintest shine of his eyes. He tilted back on his heels, waiting for an answer.

Warmth spread from my stomach up my chest and down my legs. I wanted to call Kitty and Linnea immediately and tell them I was staying the night at a boy's house. Even Linnea hadn't done that—she and Henrik only ever had sex in his car or the beach caves. I also wanted to not tell Kitty and Linnea, perhaps ever, because there was something secret and perfect about this quiet house at the end of the world, and in front of it, Soren.

"I should tell my dad," I said.

Soren exhaled softly, then coughed once to cover it. "I'll tell Elin." He went back inside again, and I walked a loop around my car. I didn't want to call my dad; I felt like he'd be able to hear the hormones in my voice. I turned away from the house and toward the blackness of the sea and pressed his name.

"Tess?" my dad said.

I focused on the waves. "Is it okay if I stay here tonight? Because of the tires."

"I suppose so. You always make good choices. Is Elin there?"

"Yes."

"Are you dating Soren?"

"No."

"Because keep in mind that he's twenty-seven."

"He's eighteen."

"He has the air," my dad said, "of someone who is twenty-seven."

"Can I stay here or not?"

Again, my dad said, "You always make good choices," as if to reassure himself as much as me. As a parenting philosophy, I found it both endearing and sad. Endearing because he trusted me. Sad because it spoke to my dad's conviction that I was already more capable of making intelligent decisions and didn't have much need for him.

Back inside, Soren had started chopping the potatoes. Elin was inspecting something in the oven that looked like mutton, but I wasn't sure. Despite the legions of sheep across the island, it wasn't that common in the grocery store. My dad and I tended to buy frozen things imported from elsewhere, like mince pies and fish sticks.

Without preamble, Elin handed me an onion. "Knives in the block," she said. "Sorry my grandson's a clod."

"Which one?" I said.

"Ha ha," Soren said.

"Both of them."

I glanced over at Lukas to see if he cared, but he was still staring at the TV. I wanted to ask if he was always this useless, but I didn't think I'd yet established that much rapport with Elin.

By the time we sat down to eat, it was nine thirty. There were mashed potatoes with sweet sheep's butter and soft rolls and mutton with rosemary and roasted onion. Elin selected two beers from the fridge with a practiced habit, then said, "Oh, would you like one, Tess?"

My dad hardly drank, and never at dinner with me, but I said, "Sure. Thanks."

"I'd like one," Lukas said.

"Too bad."

"You've been giving Soren beer since he was fourteen."

Soren smiled pleasantly at his brother as he pried the lid off a bottle and handed it to me.

"Do you not see that?" Lukas insisted, waving at his grandmother. "The way he's smirking at me?"

"Oh, bother," Elin said. "I must've missed it." She turned to me. "Sorry we're eating so late. It gets busy out here. Chores, and that."

"What do you grow?" I asked.

"Abject misery?" Lukas suggested.

"Depends on the year," Elin said. "How good the soil looks, and whether we can hire help. The sheep are our constant."

"Do you need to hire much help?" I wasn't sure if I was being nosy; I was genuinely curious, and I'd never wanted to ask Kitty any of these questions for fear of looking too interested.

"Less so now that Soren's older. We get by, the two of us, but it'll look better once he's not in school anymore."

Soren ripped a roll in half. He didn't react to what Elin said, but he wouldn't look at me either. I had more questions—like why she said *the two of us* instead of *the three of us*, and whether Soren, who was so clearly excellent with literature, would have time for university—but I ate my potatoes instead of asking.

After we finished, Lukas wandered off without offering to help clean up. Soren scrubbed and I dried and Elin put away. When Soren handed me things, our fingers would brush, his skin hot and soapy.

"I don't need to tell you not to fall asleep in the same room tonight, do I?" Elin asked abruptly.

Heat rushed to my cheeks. "No."

"Well. I would say you should take Lukas's, since it's his fault you're stuck here, but he's probably already barricaded his door."

"I was going to take the couch," Soren said.

"I'm happy on the couch," I said.

Elin waved me away. "Let him be gallant."

Soren pulled spare sheets out of a hall closet, and Elin gave me a pair of pajamas. In the bathroom, which was painted soft red and lit dimly, she'd laid out a new toothbrush for me, still in the packaging. I brushed longer than was strictly necessary. My hair looked scraggly, and my cheeks were flushed. Elin's pajamas were a matching plaid set, bottoms and a button-up shirt. I put on the bottoms but not the shirt, instead wearing the black tank top I'd had on beneath my sweater. When I tried to walk, the excess fabric caught beneath my feet.

Soren wasn't on the couch when I went back outside. I wasn't sure where he was. Another bathroom, maybe. In the kitchen, I lingered longer than necessary, drinking a glass of water and then washing the glass. When Soren didn't reappear, I walked up the stairs to his room, but I didn't close the door behind me.

What an odd and personal thing, to be in someone else's bedroom. The bed he slept on and read on and had maybe had sex on. The window he looked out every day, the glass a perfect mirror in night. There were no actual mirrors in here, of course, because Soren did not need to wake up every day and search his reflection for the sudden appearance of a skeld's mark.

I sat lightly on the edge of the bed. It seemed impossible that I could be here, only a few feet through space from Soren, and we would just go to sleep. I looked at the open door and imagined him coming up the stairs. The house was quiet. I stood up again.

Light footsteps on the stairs. I watched the shadows shifting across the walls, waiting for them to solidify into a person.

That was probably the moment I gave up pretending I did not want Soren completely—hearing those footsteps. Because I knew that if it was Lukas coming to poke at me with nails or Elin coming to see that I'd gotten settled in all right, my heart would plummet through the floorboards and land on the couch next to Soren. I wanted him—him and his serious gray eyes and his pianist fingers and his thin, fine mouth, and when I saw it was indeed him leaning against the door frame, I couldn't remember, if I was being honest, the last time I had not wanted him.

"I forgot something," Soren said.

"Oh," I said. "What?"

"The excuse I was going to make about forgetting something."

I laughed, and the sound that came out of my mouth was unfamiliar, breathy and uncertain. Soren was wearing a gray T-shirt that fit him snugly across his shoulders.

"A book," he said. "I always read before bed."

I turned to the nearest bookshelf because my cheeks felt warm. "Reading doesn't make me tired, really."

"Me neither," he said. "But it's before bed or not at all."

Soren came up behind me, his feet quiet on the wooden floor. I didn't want to turn and look at him because then he might realize we were standing too close together and move back. I could feel him over my shoulder, gazing at the bookshelf, maybe assessing the spines where my fingers lingered.

"What do you read?" he said.

I considered saying something that I thought might impress him—tossing out the few classics I had actually read outside of school and of my own volition. I felt like he'd see through me. "Mostly fantasy. The weirder, the better."

He made a soft *hmm* noise over my shoulder.

"That surprises you?"

I was more aware of his body than I had ever been of anyone's body: the space it took and the air around it, the creak of the floorboards as he leaned his weight to one foot, the sound of him breathing quietly. My skin felt hot and flushed, and if I turned, I would be turning directly into him. If I stepped backward, my spine would meet his chest and his mouth would be at my ear.

"I figured you'd be a nonfiction person," he said.

"Why?" I asked.

"You're very practical."

"I suppose I like reading about curses," I said, "worse than ours."

Outside, I could hear rain pattering against glass. A sheep bleated. Beneath it all was the steady *inhale, exhale* of the sea, the background music to every moment I had ever lived.

"Tess," Soren whispered.

I turned.

His expression wasn't at all what I'd expected. He looked pained, almost, his jaw tight. And he was close, so close that if we inhaled at the same time, our chests would brush. Reflected light from the window cast raindrop shadows across his face, and as I watched, they slid down the length of his nose, across the planes of his cheeks, around his jaw.

"You really hate this place," he said.

I opened my mouth to say that I didn't because for a moment, I forgot that I did. I forgot that I was going to leave this island and never come back. "Don't you?"

"It's home."

"Why read if not to escape?"

"If I do it in my head," he said, "then in real life, I don't have to."

I swallowed. Tried to think of something intelligent and witty but got lost along the way. Knew I was staring at him; could not stop.

Soren took my wrist between his thumb and forefinger. I was sure he must've been able to feel my pulse; I could feel it, beating out under his touch. There was a smudge of dirt running up the inside of my arm, probably from leaning against my tire. He wiped it carefully with his thumb, bending his head so I couldn't see his eyes through the fringe of his lashes. His hair shadowed his forehead. The dirt was gone, but he didn't let go of my wrist. He laid the rest of his fingers gently across my forearm. When he took a breath, the sound scratched, hoarse, and there was nothing he could've said that would've made me want him more than that: the bare truth of how much he wanted me back.

"Soren?" I said.

He pressed me against the bookshelf and kissed me.

It took me a moment to react. When I kissed him back, he sighed against my mouth and drew his hands to either side of my head, his fingers winding up through my hair. His lips were soft and tasted like toothpaste. There was nothing but him, nothing in the world, just his chest blocking my view of the room and his head tilted down to meet mine.

He kissed the way he spoke: slowly, deliberately, with a control that did not match the tremor in his hands as they moved down my neck, my chest, as they settled around my waist and held me to him.

I kissed him back the way he kissed me, slowly at first, then harder, with a breathless sort of desperation. When I arched my hips against his, he pushed back, making his body taut against mine. It might've hurt, pressed so tightly against the bookshelf, but his hands moved, one to the small of my back, one to my head, keeping the shelves from digging into me.

Downstairs, a creak. Soren's lips left mine. He looked at me, those eyes and that flush in his cheeks—god, god—and then he was on the other side of the room, shutting the door quietly and locking it behind him.

Then he was back, gathering me into his arms and holding me to him. We were turning, and I felt myself pulling him toward the bed.

My knees met the back of his mattress and folded. The weight of him on top of me—I'd expected him to feel heavy, but he didn't. He was braced with an arm on either side of me, one knee between my legs.

When he kissed me again, there was no more rhythm, no more restraint. The sound of his breathing was ragged and came from the back of his throat. I knew the exact places where our bodies touched and all the places they didn't, but I wanted them to. My hand found his waistband. I ran my fingers along the fabric, then just beneath, along the smooth skin under the elastic waist of his boxers. He exhaled something that sounded like my name into my mouth, and I made a sound I'd never made before, something desperate and wanting.

He was taking off my tank top, and I was taking off his shirt, and it was not possible to be embarrassed with him looking at me the way he was looking at me. I touched his back carefully, and he shivered. There was just so much of it, this vast expanse of skin, all flat and graceful lines.

"Have you ever…?" he whispered.

I shook my head. "Have you?"

"No." He was lit from above, silhouetted by the overhead light, and it made him look filigreed, like a Renaissance painting. I wanted to stare at him, memorize him, touch him, have him—I wanted and I wanted and I wanted. "Should we stop?"

I had it in my head that you weren't supposed to do everything all at once—not at first, at least—and that had sounded fine to me in theory. There were steps; you took them one at a time and not out of order and not in a mad rush. But I had underestimated the power of instinct. The fact that my body would know, so clearly, what it wanted to do. This was what I wanted, all I wanted, to be closer than our bodies were, to be as close as our bodies could be.

"I don't want to stop," I said. "Unless you do."

Soren kissed me again. Our legs were wound together. His hands were touching my body so carefully, exploring, his fingers against my chest and around my waist and against the inside of my thigh.

I slid my hand along the inside of his waistband again, watching his expression. He let out a pained little sound, and my whole body went hot, shivering cold, then hot again.

"Tess," he said. "I want—"

A knock at the door.

Soren went still, propped above me. His jaw was tight as he breathed to a count of three and then, eyes still on me, said, "What."

From the other side of the door, Elin said, "I have a phone call for the very gallant young man who offered to sleep on the couch tonight."

Soren looked up slowly, staring at the headboard. I could see his heart beating at his throat, right where you'd take a pulse. He shut his eyes briefly. His voice was very flat, betraying nothing, when he said, "One second."

He climbed off me and pulled his shirt back over his head. Abruptly, I felt bare, exposed, uncertain, all the instinct that had been telling me I was doing everything the right way vanishing the moment Soren's weight had. I pulled the comforter to my chin.

When Soren opened the door, he stood between it and the frame, shielding me from Elin's view. I curled farther under the quilt.

"It's Jamieson," Elin was saying. "He says the flock is on the road. We must have a fence down."

Soren was quiet. I risked a glance at his back and saw the muscles tense beneath his shirt.

"Don't ask me to get them for you," Elin said.

"I wasn't going to."

"It's your croft, Soren."

"I'll go get them," he said.

Neither of them said anything else for a moment, and I got the sense some silent conversation was transpiring in the expressions between them. I couldn't see either of their faces, but when Soren closed the door and turned back to me, he looked, briefly, like he was a thousand years old. He leaned against the door and exhaled, and then he scrounged a half smile from somewhere.

"Don't go anywhere," he said.

"Where would I possibly go?"

He gestured vaguely at the books. At his dresser, he started pulling out clothes. His back was to me, so I let myself watch in fascination as he stripped off his pajamas, replacing them with jeans and a sweater.

"Do you need help?" I asked.

"No. I'll be right back." He made it as far as the door, ran his hand through his hair, and then looped back just long enough to kiss me again, fast and desperate. "Jesus Christ," he said, pulling away. "I fucking hate sheep."

Then he was gone.

Through his window, I saw the arcing beam of a flashlight. I heard a dog bark twice. I touched my face and my lips like they had been remade and were now unfamiliar territories for me to rediscover. Once he was gone, the enormity of my desire felt like a black hole. It should not have been possible. Someone should have warned me. I thought of Soren saying, *Love amplifies normal experiences.* I wanted him to come back and tell me he loved me cataclysmically, and I wanted him to take off all his clothes and have sex with me, and I wanted him to never see me again so that I would not have to face the truth of the matter, that you could feel so much for one person, that someone could walk into your brain and change it.

I curled on the bed and waited for him, but at some point, I must've slipped into sleep, thinking of him out there in the rain and the wind and all that billowing quiet here at the end of the world.

When I went downstairs the morning after Soren and I did not sleep together, I found Elin making coffee in the kitchen and Lukas eating his breakfast without looking at it, gaze fixed on his phone. The sheets on the couch had been neatly refolded.

Elin said good morning, and though her voice was perfectly level, I convinced myself she was either reproachful or laughing at me.

"He's taking the sheep to graze," she said.

"They can't graze here?"

"If they only grazed here, they'd run out of things to eat, wouldn't they?"

"And then they'd all be dead," Lukas said, still looking at his phone. "Which would be terrible."

To Lukas, Elin said, "Offer Tess some porridge."

"Can't Tess get her own porridge?"

"It's polite to offer."

"I can get my own porridge," I said. "Thanks."

Breakfast was quiet. I wanted something to do with my hands, but I was afraid Elin would like me less if I took out my phone, so I flipped through our translation for class. I kept glancing at Elin out of the corner of my eye, wondering what she, the mother of a son turned to stone, thought of me, the daughter of the mother who'd done it. I knew Elin had been a skeld—once, when she'd been my age, then a second time twenty or so years back. No one really talked about those uneventful skeld seasons when no one had been turned to stone. I assumed that to women like Elin, who had faced down the curse and emerged unscathed, women like my mother seemed impossibly reckless. Or impossibly stupid.

When I heard Soren at the door, I stared fixedly at the paper so no one would see me blush. I risked a glance as he was scooping himself porridge, but he was looking at Elin. Between bites, he told her something I didn't understand about a fence down at a field with a name I didn't know. Their back and forth was efficient and practiced, and it made me acutely aware of how little I knew of this world they lived in. When Soren looked at me, his eyes didn't linger. When he passed behind my chair, he didn't brush against me. It made me feel like last night existed entirely in my head, but I also knew I would be embarrassed if he said or did anything romantic in front of Elin.

It was still dark when we climbed into Soren's truck. I expected Lukas to take the passenger seat, but he clambered into the cramped back row without a word.

Soren put the truck in First. It was a manual, old as rocks, but well maintained. I liked watching people drive cars they had a relationship with; I thought it revealed something about them, about the way they took care of themselves. Soren's hand was light on the gear lever, the other hand loose around the wheel. His eyes were steady on the dirt road ahead.

Lukas stuck his head between our seats. "You should always drive to school with us," he told me. "And then I wouldn't have to listen to any agonizing audiobooks."

"Is that why you put nails in my tires?"

"I already told Soren I didn't do that," Lukas said.

Soren glanced back at his brother. "Not convincingly."

"Whatever," Lukas said. "Hey, you know Eva, right?"

"Rendall? Sure. She swims the 200 butterfly."

"She's my girlfriend. She says you're bloody quick."

I'd never learned how to accept a compliment, so I didn't. "I haven't competed in months."

"Why not?"

I shrugged uncomfortably. "Injury."

"What happened?"

"Just...overuse."

I noticed Soren frowning at me in my peripheral vision, but I kept staring at the dark road ahead.

"Oh," Lukas said. "Well, you're going to fix it, right? Because Eva said you're so fast, you're going to go swim at an American university and that they'll pay you to be there and everything. And that you and your coach have been talking to all the schools already."

The truth was that I was only very fast, not astonishingly fast. I wasn't good enough in Year Eleven to get an offer from any school that could also pay the exorbitant US tuition fees, but my times were improving enough that a few coaches told me to stay in touch. By October, I was meant to have dropped four seconds off my 400-freestyle time, but when I'd tried to swim it two weeks before, I'd gone forty-six seconds slower. The pace I'd swum in Year Seven. Part of me already knew that there was no way, at this point, I could get fast enough before the recruiting deadlines. But it had been my plan for so long that I didn't know what else I was supposed to do. I thought of my mum in the parking lot, offering to help me write an essay, and I felt a cold wash of panic.

"I think it'd be mad if you went to university in America," Lukas was saying. "Like, dorms and frats and American football and all that. Then you could get a job there and never again have to eat an animal you named."

"Cut it out," Soren said.

"Just because *you* get off on shit weather and wool sweaters..."

"I do get off on wool sweaters," Soren said. "That's why I have that sexy-wool-sweater-of-the-month calendar."

Lukas made a disgusted noise, and it was so over the top I couldn't tell if he was taking the piss. To me, he said, "You get it, right? You don't want to stay on this fucking rock your whole life?"

I was slow to answer because I didn't want to agree with him about anything, but eventually I said, "Not really, no."

"See?" he said to Soren. "You never listen to me, but maybe if she says it—"

"Lukas."

"Or I guess we can just stay here and get turned to fucking statues! That's fine too! Not like our parents would be offended by that or anything."

The truck was painfully quiet. Across the hills, faint fingers of sun began to cast the world in gold. I pressed myself farther back into my seat. Lukas muttered something unintelligible and slid on a pair of headphones. I had always thought of Soren's silences as an offensive, rather than a defensive, strategy. But in this case, it seemed more like he was protecting himself and Lukas both from an argument that wouldn't lead anywhere good.

I didn't say anything, but I reached for the gear lever and touched the back of his hand with my pinkie. It was a question, or maybe a few questions. He looked over at me, and just like that, I was all full up of want again.

He drew my hand to his side of the car, and he pressed his lips to the inside of my wrist.

We didn't speak for the rest of the drive to school. It didn't feel like we had to.

What You Will

2013

Soren and I didn't set out to be a secret. Or, at least, I didn't. It just happened that way.

I didn't tell Kitty because I didn't want her to feel like a fifth wheel; I didn't tell Linnea because sometimes Linnea made offhanded comments about the floral arrangements she'd have at her wedding to Henrik, and if she started talking about me and Soren that way, I thought I might lock myself in a cupboard until graduation.

Not long after whatever was happening between us had started, I was sitting in my history class finishing a reading, and I heard a group of boys come rumbling through the door. One of the others from the soccer team was calling his name: *Soren, oi, Soren!* He had a book held to his chest in the crook of one arm. Our eyes met as he slid into his seat on the other side of the room. Someone was still jockeying for his attention.

He only looked at me. It seemed to me like the sexiest thing in the world: that no one but us knew I had seen him naked twelve hours before.

My dad probably knew there was something going on with Soren and me, and Elin definitely did, but neither of them brought it up. The only person who confronted me was Dan, my swim coach, who intercepted me on the way to the locker room after an uninspired practice by saying, "What, have you started dating someone, or something?"

I felt exposed on the pool deck and wrapped my towel tighter around myself. "Why would you say that?"

"Because you're still only doing three practices a week. Because you didn't even mention the email from the Davis coach. Because it's like you don't care anymore."

I flinched.

The email from the Davis coach had been much like the emails from all the other coaches we'd received recently—Dear Tess, sorry to hear about your injury; unfortunately; not able to offer you a spot at this time; feel free to apply by the regular academic deadline, and we can consider you as a walk-on. The only remaining coach who had not yet sent such an email was from the University of Maine, and I was fairly sure she was just holding off because her dad was Scottish and she felt a certain North Atlantic kinship with me. Maine hadn't even been on my list, originally, because it seemed cold and north and remote and altogether too close to Stenland. More recently, it had started to feel like fate because would it be the worst thing in the world if I were only five time zones from Stenland instead of eight? Would it be the worst thing if I lived somewhere with mist and wind and frigid Atlantic waters that reminded me of Soren and of home?

I pushed past Dan without saying anything. The next day, for the first time in ten years, I skipped swim practice.

★★★

Someone at school got the bright idea that we should celebrate the end of term by breaking into Ramna Skaill. When Linnea told us we had to go, I said I would rather drink cleaning fluid.

"That may well be what's on tap," Kitty said.

"Please?" Linnea said. "I really want to go. Henrik said it'll be fun."

"Well, if Henrik said."

Linnea ignored Kitty and turned her big eyes on me. "If you're leaving me in eight months, you have to do fun things with me now. Those are the rules."

"I'm not breaking into Ramna Skaill," I said. "Doesn't that seem like tempting fate?"

"No?" she said. "I feel like I never see you anymore."

"You see me all the time."

"Actually," Kitty said, "I'm with Linnea on this."

"How surprising," I said.

"You didn't go to Hedda's with us for brunch last weekend. And you bailed on our study date on Tuesday."

"I've been busy."

Kitty gave me her most suspicious look. "Doing?"

That was how I ended up at Ramna Skaill.

Kitty and I got ready at Linnea's house. The keep was on the northeastern edge of the island, so Henrik was going to drive us. Linnea's parents thought we were spending the night at Kitty's house, and Kitty's parents thought we were spending the night at Linnea's, and my dad wasn't about to ask. We dressed in skirts that were too short for the weather and our puffiest jackets. Linnea did our hair because she was the best at hair, and Kitty did our makeup because she was the best at makeup, and I snuck into the Sundstroms' pantry to nick a bottle of gin because I was the best at keeping my face blank and unassuming when I'd been caught doing something I wasn't supposed to be doing. Every few minutes, Linnea's fifteen-year-old sister, Saffi, would invent an urgent reason to come bother us and gaze around the room with wide eyes. When she stared at us, it made me feel vaguely like a celebrity. Linnea shooed her out again every time.

When Kitty was working on Linnea's eyeliner, I sat in the corner of Linnea's nest of turquoise pillows with the gin. My phone buzzed, and I looked at it covertly.

Soren: Henrik is composing a song for Linnea

Soren: He may sing it tonight

Me: You must stop him

Me: This is your quest

Soren: May I request a different quest

Me: No

A pause.

Soren: Driving over now

Soren: Henrik wants to know who I'm texting

"What are you smiling at?" Kitty said.

I looked up. "Nothing."

"Bullshit."

"I saw a meme," I said. "I would share it with you, but I've already scrolled past. Such is the ephemeral nature of the internet."

Kitty rolled her eyes at me, a habit she never grew out of, and resumed perfecting Linnea's already perfect makeup.

★★★

When Henrik's car pulled up in Linnea's driveway, Soren climbed out of the passenger seat and into the back.

Linnea protested. "You have longer legs than me."

"All good," Soren said.

He sat in the middle of the back, between me and Kitty. With one hand, he held a beer. With the other, he ran his thumb down the hem of my skirt across the outside of my thigh. The car was too dark for anyone to see him do it. He was able to maintain a perfectly normal conversation with Kitty about our history exam, but when I tried to speak, my voice came out scratchy.

When Henrik parked in the dirt lot and we climbed out of the car, Kitty grabbed me by the arm and said, "I don't mean to alarm you, but I think Soren might be into you."

"Interesting," I said.

"I mean, he wasn't trying to sit next to *me*."

"Maybe he wanted to have a pleasant conversation with his favorite cousin."

"Right," she said. "I hope you know your face is red."

Ramna Skaill sat at the far end of a peninsula that looked, from some angles, like an island. It was connected to the mainland by just a narrow spit of land, which rose out of the ocean like a spine. Someone had already undone the padlock on the gate, and now it hung open, its rusty hinges creaking in the wind. As we walked down the path, I had to force myself not to look down. I wasn't afraid of heights, but the land gave way on either side of me in steep, tumbling cliffs. The waves crashed against the rocks, like they could erode them clean through at any second.

The keep itself was a sixteenth-century tower: four narrow stories of moss-covered stone with intricate rams and ravens carved into the bartizans. That was where the skelds stayed. Next to the tower, there was a compact cottage, where the keepers stayed. The keepers were there to keep the skelds in or to keep everyone else out, depending on the era. They were also supposed to bring the skelds food and medicine. Before phones, there'd been some elaborate system of bells they used to communicate.

Through the windows, the light glowed cider yellow. A speaker was blaring music that sounded fuzzy and pleasantly familiar, some 2000s indie-folk-pop hit I couldn't place. Thomas St. Clair and Delia Haugen were kissing in the courtyard.

Henrik leaned his shoulder into the wooden door until it opened. Inside, darkness fluttered in and out as flashlight beams swept past. Someone had lit a fire in the hearth, but it wasn't quickly heating the hollow space. Presumably, they only turned the power on during a skeld season. I'd never had reason to wonder about it before.

"Beer?" Henrik said, making finger guns at us. "Tess? Soren, almost done with that one? I'll get you all beers. Don't worry—I'm driving. Wait here."

He disappeared into the crowd, Linnea at his elbow.

"God, I hate him," Kitty said. "No one's that nice unless they're secretly a murderer."

"Except Henrik," Soren said.

"Well, then, maybe you should date him," Kitty said.

"Tempting. I'll have to pass for the time being."

"Well, then, maybe you should date Tess."

"Kitty."

Soren looked at me over Kitty's shoulder. His eyes softened. "Interesting."

"She's surprisingly strong, which could be useful should you need to move heavy furniture. Additionally, she's an excellent math tutor, and she won't make you feel stupid even when you nearly fail your calculus exam."

"You got an eighty-seven," I said.

"Really?" Soren said. "I got a ninety-three."

Kitty pointed at him. "No one asked you. Also, Tess got a ninety-eight, so piss off."

Soren tilted his beer back, watching us over the top of the bottle. There was a long silence. In my stomach, I felt an unexpected sense of weightlessness. He lowered the beer and said, "Okay."

Another pause.

"Well," Kitty said to me, "do with that what you will, I guess."

I didn't know Linnea had come back until I felt her tap my shoulder. "I need to pee," she announced. "Tess, Kitty?"

I glanced at Soren, but he was already wandering off toward a group of soccer players by the fire. Linnea led us beyond the densest part of the crowd and up a stone staircase. It was even colder there, and darker, and though we were standing by a window, the sky outside was black.

"She doesn't actually need to pee," Kitty said.

"I gathered," I said.

"What's going on with you and Soren?" Linnea said.

The temperature of her tone caught me off guard. I wrapped my arms around my torso, sticking my hands under my armpits, and shrugged.

"A nuanced explanation as always," Kitty said. "Thank you for apprising us."

"Why are you two being so..." Linnea's brows drew together. "You know. First you two get angry at Henrik and me for trying to set you up, and now you're—"

"I wasn't angry at you and Henrik," I said. "Was Soren angry?"

Kitty leaned toward me—her way of establishing sides. "I think you're overreacting."

"Overreacting!" Linnea said. "I tell both of you every time I'm interested in anyone. I ask for your advice, and I tell you how it's going, and neither of you ever tell me anything. It's like you think I'm stupid or something, or that I wouldn't be able to understand your feelings because—"

"Linnea," Kitty said, raising her hands.

"Because you two think it's pathetic to fall in love with someone Stennish when you're both going to run away and fall in love with someone so much better."

Linnea turned and disappeared back down the stairs. Kitty and I stayed there in the darkness listening to the wind howl against the edges of the tower.

"Well, fuck," Kitty said finally.

My body felt too heavy suddenly. I leaned against the wall, which was the sort of cold that felt like it was sucking the heat from your skin.

"You and Soren, though?" she asked. "Are you, like, dating?"

"I don't know."

"How can you not know?"

"We haven't talked about it."

"Wow," Kitty said, "you two, struggling with communication? Shocking. Are you having sex?"

I pressed my hands against my face.

"Oh my god!"

"Kitty…"

"This is much better gossip than when Linnea started having sex. Because, you know, that was personally devastating re: my whole being in love with her thing. But you! Tell me all about it! Wait, don't. He's my cousin. Tell me all about it for you, and we'll just pretend he's not part of the equation."

I made a pained noise into my hands.

"The humiliation will cease once you start providing details. How long has this been going on?"

"Two months?"

"Two months!"

"Are you angry?"

"As if I could get angry at anyone for not telling their friends who they're into," Kitty said. "Why didn't you tell us, though?"

"I don't know," I said. "I guess I didn't want anyone to think it meant I suddenly wanted to stay here for the rest of my life."

"If you ever start talking that way, I'll pull you onto the next ferry by the ankles."

"Please."

When we got back downstairs, I found Soren feeding more peat to the fire as a few of the other members of the soccer team talked to his back. You could tell he was listening, crouched at the hearth with his head turned slightly. I liked that I knew those things about him, the little things.

"Yeah, no," Magnus Invers was saying. "Mum was friends with her before she lost it."

"How many people was it in the end, do you reckon?"

"Eighteen, I think."

"Nineteen, definitely nineteen. My aunt was one of them. Nan makes us do a candle thing about it every Christmas."

They were talking about Matilda. The one who'd *lost it*. She always came up on nights like these: in the dark, with beer, when boys tried to frighten each other.

I touched Soren's shoulder, and his hand moved automatically on top of mine. Distantly, I was aware of the trailed-off ends of sentences from the soccer boys, but most of my brain space was occupied with the glow of the fire across his face. Soren's teeth seemed very white against the darkness, and his eyes too dark to see at all, like maybe they were just pupil.

Magnus said, "All right there, Tess?"

I turned, slow to respond. "Yeah, fine."

"How's the swimming? Heard you're going to the US for it. That's brilliant."

I laughed noncommittally. Soren straightened, and I looked back at him.

"Should we go check on Kitty?" he said.

When I nodded, he made off back in the direction of the stairs. I ran a few steps to catch him, and then I said, "You didn't actually want to check on Kitty, did you?"

"Does she need checking on?"

"No."

"I assumed your pointed look meant *Make up an excuse—let's leave.*"

"It did," I said.

Once we were up to the second floor, Soren slid his hand through mine. My eyes adjusted to the darkness and began to pick out the spots of light: the glint of mirrors, the ghostly glow of wineglasses in a cabinet. When we reached the third floor, Soren stopped and kissed me so suddenly I had to steady myself against the wall. He raked his hands through my hair and touched his teeth to my lips, and then he was taking me by the hand again and walking faster down the hall.

"In a hurry to get somewhere?" I asked.

"Yes, actually."

He almost opened a door, then pulled back when a voice drifted out. I recognized the laugh—Thomas St. Clair, I thought.

Soren took my hand and led me farther down the hall.

"How do you know your way around?" I asked.

"This may not be my first time breaking in."

"Should I be jealous?"

"It may not be Delia's first time breaking in either."

"You never told me you and Delia were a thing."

"We weren't a thing. We just kissed on the roof once."

"I was fine not knowing that," I said.

Soren stopped at another door. This one, he opened. He stepped into the blackness and turned back to look at me over his shoulder, down the length of his arm and up the length of mine. I couldn't see anything but him.

He held up his phone to illuminate the room: a mattress

stripped of bedding, a hearth with a stack of driftwood, a side table with a lamp. I went over to the lamp and flicked the switch, but it didn't turn on.

Soren knelt in front of the hearth on a sheepskin rug and began arranging the driftwood. It was set up like someone had planned this—maybe for the party or maybe because the hearths were always ready for a skeld season to begin. I rubbed my hands against my legs. I felt off-balance in here, in this place I had spent my whole life afraid of.

I listened to the scratch of a match striking, the hiss of catching newspaper.

"Henrik said you'd never liked anyone but me," I said.

"Did he?"

"After Midsummer."

Soren didn't respond. In front of him, the fire bloomed.

"Is it true?"

"I don't know," he said. "Maybe."

I joined him on the sheepskin. When he turned to look at me, his face was lit from the side in wobbly honey light. He took my hand and pulled me toward him, into his lap. I was pushing his shoulders down and lying on top of him, my knees on either side of his hips. His breathing went shallow. I could only see him in flickers of gold: the edge of his jaw, the blink of an eye. Beneath him, the sheepskin curled white and pale. I reached my hands up the inside of his sweater, spreading my fingers across his stomach and chest, and he shivered.

"Are you too cold?" I said.

"For this? No." His hands found my wrists, and then he was guiding me to pull the sweater over his head. Another flash of firelight on the plane of his chest. He took off my shirt next, running his fingers across the lace of my bra.

"Are you worried someone will catch us?" I asked.

"No."

"Because you don't think they will, or because you wouldn't care if they did?"

His hands slid down to my thighs, still on either side of his stomach, and rested there. "Is this a trick question?"

"No," I said.

"I would care because it might embarrass you," he said.

"Is it bad that we haven't told anyone about us?"

He was quiet. I couldn't tell if he was uncomfortable or just considering the question. "I didn't know you wanted to."

"I didn't."

"Didn't?" he said.

"What would I even say?" I asked. "That we're..."

"Dating?"

"Are we?"

"I make you dinner twice a week, and we're figuratively sleeping together," he said.

I ran my fingers down the lines of his stomach, trying to conjure a picture of his body in my mind. I imagined him the way he'd looked the first time I'd ever seen him like this, the night in his room with our translation homework in my backpack.

"Linnea and Henrik go on picnic dates," I said. "And then they post about them on social media."

"Do you want to go on picnic dates and post about them on social media?"

"Not really."

Soren caught my wrist as it traveled across his chest. He pressed his hand on top of mine, flattening my palm to his heart. "We're not Linnea and Henrik, Tess."

"What are we?"

"I don't know," he said. "Us."

Quietly, I asked, "Does that scare you?"

He gave one of his exhaled laughs, like he hadn't expected the question. "All the time." He ran his thumb across my hand, light circles that shouldn't have commanded the whole attention of my body but did anyway. "Do I ever scare you?"

"You don't," I said. Then: "I scare myself, though."

"What scares you?"

"How much I can want another person."

His thumb stilled on my hand. He made a soft noise, and then he was unhooking my bra, and I was unbuttoning his jeans, and he was tugging at my skirt. We were acres of bare skin, all of it touching. His fingers were on my hips, and he was guiding us together, and I was wanting and wanting and wanting. My hands pressed against his chest, and he whispered my name until it stopped being a word and became just a sound. No clothes, no lights; we could've been two people from any time, any at all, hidden away in the darkness with no sense left but the feeling of one body and another.

After we finished, there was a quiet retrieval of clothes and a gentle kiss on my temple. My stomach was still on fire. Soren had asked what I was afraid of, and the answer was this. That he could expend his desire, but for me, it only ever seemed to grow. Linnea had accused me of thinking it was pathetic to fall in love with someone Stennish, and she was right. How pathetic, to fall in love when you were too young for it to last. How pathetic to seal your fate to someone who happened to be in the right place at the right time. How pathetic to stay when you could leave.

I wanted Soren before we had sex and while we were having sex and after we were done. I wanted him when he was funny and when he was gentle and when he was kicking the mud off his boots after bringing the sheep back home. I wanted Soren in the cosmic sense that I had wanted him for many lifetimes before this one and might still for many lifetimes after.

I told Soren he didn't scare me, but that wasn't exactly true.

Soren terrified me because if he offered to ruin my life, I might say yes.

To Leave a Place

2013

I woke with a sense of complete wrongness.

My eyes opened. Thin daylight was beginning to stream through the curtains, which meant it must've been nine or ten in the morning. I saw the texture of the walls, which had been obscured in night: pale stone etched with knots, spirals, and ravens. I was lying on a sheepskin rug, cold prickling through from the floor. My face was turned toward the embers of a fire. Soren's chest was pressed to my back, his jacket bundled under our heads like a pillow. We were dressed like we'd meant to go back to the party; of course we had. We fell asleep. *We fell asleep.*

A scream.

That was what had woken me up.

Someone screamed, and I shut my eyes so hard I saw red dots.

I felt Soren shifting behind me, still asleep or just sleepy as he tried to draw me closer to his chest. I ripped myself away from him. He said my name or something like it, but I'd already started stumbling toward the door.

It happened, of course. People fell asleep together and when they woke up and looked at each other, one of them was a skeld and one of them was stone. And when it happened, I had always thought: How could anyone be so stupid? How could anyone be so careless?

I touched my face, searching for a mark. I felt nothing, but that didn't mean it wasn't there. The scream came again, and this time, I could tell where it was coming from: through the wall, one room over. I reached blindly for the doorknob. Once through, I slammed the door shut again behind me.

Just for a second, I opened my eyes. Long enough to see my bare feet on the stone floor, to see the shadows moving as a door creaked open down the hall and a figure emerged. Delia, moving toward the stairs.

I ran after her. My eyes were open, closed, open again. She must've heard my footsteps because she started to turn, and I pressed my eyes shut so hard it hurt. They were gritty with dried makeup, and I couldn't feel my hands or feet, and my mouth tasted like gin and stomach acid.

I slammed into Delia. We both went down, and I kept thinking *Eyes shut, eyes shut,* and I kept them that way even as my body crashed into the floor, even as the pain ricocheted through my shoulder and made my hands fly open. My lungs searched for air that wasn't there. The blackness was complete. Eyes shut, eyes shut.

"Thomas," Delia was saying. "Thomas, he was… He's not…"

She kept trying to writhe out of my grasp, but I kept my arms around her.

"Stop it," I said. "Delia. Delia!"

Eyes shut. Delia's hair was curled against my face. I could feel her body shudder every time she gasped for breath. Eyes shut.

"Thomas was right there. He was just…" With every word, her voice got louder, shriller.

"Stop moving!"

Delia didn't. She was starting to scratch my arms, hyperventilating now. I tried to grab at her face and felt wetness on her cheeks, tears or the sweat of panic. She kept saying Thomas's name. Could she hear me? Did she know I was there at all? I thought I heard footsteps, and I called out some warning; what I said, I didn't know.

My phone dug into my rib cage. It was in the pocket of my jacket, which had ridden up and left my stomach bare against the stone. I did the only thing I could think of; I covered Delia's eyes with my hand, and then I dared to open my own. Just long enough to take the phone from my pocket, find my mother's contact, and touch her name.

Delia tried to break away again. Before she could manage it, my mother answered.

"Hello? Tess? Is everything okay?" Her voice was staticky and distant. I shut my eyes again and shoved the phone at Delia's face.

"Tess?"

Delia was going heavy and still in my arms.

"Tess…"

Finally, Delia whispered: "Something's wrong."

I laid my head against the ground.

"Okay, honey, it's okay. Who is this? Is this Linnea?"

"It's Delia Haugen."

"Delia? This is Alice. It's Tess's mom, honey. I know you're scared right now, but you're going to be okay. Are you breathing? I want you to breathe for me."

I listened distantly as my mother asked Delia where she was, then instructed her to stand up and walk very carefully to the fourth floor of the tower; she could wait there. She told Delia to keep her head down. To keep her eyes closed if she could.

She knew the way up the stairs, didn't she? Of course she did. There's a good girl.

I wasn't sure if I was supposed to follow Delia. I didn't. Just let her leave. That was the point I realized I was crying. My face was sticky with tears and dust. Chunks of my hair clung to my temples. I managed to raise myself onto my hands and knees, and only then did I open my eyes again, not looking in front of me but at the splay of my fingers across the stone. My fingers were lavender with cold. Across my arms, blood welled in long, nail-shaped scratches.

As I crawled to the bedroom where Delia had spent the night, my stomach tensed and flexed like it wanted me to vomit. I kept hearing my mum's voice echoing in my ears, as if she'd been talking to me: *Are you breathing? I want you to breathe for me.*

It was just like the room where Soren and I had slept. A fire dying in the hearth; symbols etched on the walls. Thomas's feet were pointed toward the door, so at first all I could see were the bottoms of his shoes. Black runners, the tread caked with sand, like he'd been out on the beach before this. I kept crawling, and I saw his jeans and then his sweatshirt—oh, god, he was wearing a swim-team sweatshirt—and then his face.

One of his hands was pillowed under his ear. His wavy hair was flopping to the side of his head in this boyish sort of way. I had always loved the expression he wore when he finished a set in the pool behind me. He'd never been annoyed to be outpaced by a girl. He'd touch the wall and lift his head out of the water and laugh; his lips would curl in this playful little smile, and he'd say something like, *I don't know what I'd do if I couldn't coast along on your feet, Tess.*

That was the smile. The one frozen on his face. That playful little smile, now immortalized in smooth, gray stone.

I touched his cheekbones. I was crying now, really crying. He still looked so alive; his clothes weren't even cold yet. I realized I was lying in the divot of rug where Delia must've slept. They'd slept facing each other. They'd woken up facing each other. Thomas's eyes were sleepy and happy because it all must've happened too quickly for him to realize he was dead.

"Tess?" Soren said from the door.

I clenched my eyes shut. More tears slid down my cheeks and into the sheepskin. I could hear Soren stepping carefully toward me, but I just buried my face against Thomas, into the soft swim-team sweatshirt stretched across an unbreathing chest.

"Tess," Soren whispered, and he was right behind me now, leaning over me; I could tell from the shadows behind my eyelids.

"Go away."

He was smoothing my hair out of my face, and I tried to wrench away from him, tried to bury myself in Thomas's unmoving embrace.

"You don't have it," Soren said. "There's no mark."

I didn't believe him. How would he know? He had not spent every morning of his life staring at his own reflection, wondering at every smudge and shadow and spot. He had not been trained to examine his face for a monstrosity that felt like a promise. When wind whispered through the tower as we slept, some fickle god of the island looking for girls to ruin, it did not go looking for him.

From the time we were born, we knew the rules. Spend the night with someone if you must, but wake up alone. Always wake up alone. Look at your reflection before you let anyone else see you because if you don't, the first person to gaze into your eyes may pay a price that can't ever be repaid.

"You're not a skeld, Tess," Soren said. He was still running his hand through my hair. Touching my forehead where I was sure there were three dark lines he was too stupid to see.

I grabbed his wrist and flung it away from me. Maybe I

swore at him. My words were muddled in my own ears, like I was hearing someone else say them from a distance.

I had never been so happy to hear him leave. Footsteps growing quieter on the stone, and I started to sob. Full-body, wracking sobs, holding my face against the soft darkness of Thomas's sweatshirt. It smelled like chlorine and sex. Every few minutes, I would remember that Delia had done this and not me. I had not killed him, but I could've. I did not this time, but there would always be another skeld season.

In the space between remembering, I would feel a guilt like being buried alive. Here it was, the crescendo of panic: Why, *why*, why had I not run away from this place when I'd had the chance? If it was Delia and not me, Thomas and not Soren, it was just luck. Soren could be dead right now, and it would be my fault.

I was in my bedroom with my comforter pulled over my face when my dad brought my phone back. Delia's father had delivered it, apparently. He was going to be one of the three keepers. Of course he was. Delia, Delia's mother, Delia's grandmother: those were the three skelds this time.

I hadn't left Thomas's body until Kitty and Linnea had found me. When they'd told me I wasn't marked, I'd believed them where I hadn't believed Soren, but there'd still been a part of me that was afraid to look anyone in the eye until I'd made it home and stared at myself in my mirror. I was bruised and scratched and matted and altogether torn apart by the island in every way except for my forehead, which was bare and unmarked.

My dad sat on the end of my bed. "I don't think she'll have to do any jail time, if that makes you feel better."

I kept my comforter over my head. "Why would that make me feel better?"

"Jon, from the station, he thinks they'll rule it criminal negligence. But she's still seventeen. Community service, maybe, or a fine."

There was a hierarchy of badness when it came to skeld killings. Stories like Matilda's, about skelds who left the keep, who turned people to stone on purpose, those were the very worst, but they were rare. Second were stories like my mum's, skelds who were too careless to check themselves for a mark before wandering out in public. Then you had cases like Delia's—cases where women accidentally fell asleep with a loved one—and those usually got treated with some degree of mercy, maybe because it was so obviously accidental, so obviously horrible. And then there were keeper deaths. Keepers were more likely to die than anyone else. It just sort of happened, never on purpose, and everyone treated the keeper like a hero afterward.

"Would you look at me?" my dad said.

I yanked down the comforter. When he met my eyes, he flinched. Just for a second, but it was there.

"You called your mum," he said.

I shrugged, like I could unseat the weight on my shoulders.

"That was a good idea. It sounds like she helped Delia keep everyone safe. It sounds like you helped keep everyone safe. It could've been much worse today, for Delia and everyone in the keep."

I didn't want to be told how much worse it could've been. My hands were numb, like they were still pressing against the cold stone of Thomas's face.

"Do you hate Mum?" I asked.

"Of course not."

"No, really. Because I do sometimes."

"I don't hate your mum," he said. "I resent her for being careless, but what do I know? I've never been a woman in Stenland." A pause. "Besides. I'm the one who convinced her to stay."

"You did?"

"She wanted to move after high school. Travel, see the world. I didn't care about any of that. So maybe you should hate me sometimes too."

"Why did you want to stay, though?" I asked.

My dad set my phone on the bed. He looked tired and scruffy. There was a grease stain on his shirt. "It's not easy to leave a place."

"You could've gotten a job somewhere else. They have cars other places. More of them, actually."

"But then a job would've been all I had. No family, no friends. No coffee from Hedda's. No darts at the pub. I'm—you know I'm no good with words. Not like you. I don't know how to explain. I never wanted to leave because it never occurred to me I could. It's like asking me why I never bought a rocket ship to Mars."

"You could've left, though. Mum did eventually. There are ways."

He looked down at his lap. "You aren't like me, Tess. You think the school is paying your friend Henrik to take SAT courses?"

"Henrik's not stupid," I said quickly, and my dad shook his head.

"I didn't say he was. I just mean… We pick people, you know? The island picks people, like you and Kitty, who we just know are going to do great things. Bigger things than I was ever going to do. Your mum too, she's like that. We all get to live through her, off being a writer, doing things the rest of us don't even bother dreaming of."

My dad stood up. His eyes were still downcast. It made me feel awful, like I'd done this to him, made him feel ashamed or like he wasn't good enough. I wanted to tell him that it wasn't true at all, but I couldn't find a way to say it. I didn't know when he'd decided I was good with words. "I'm going to make soup for dinner. Let me know if you want any."

I sat there for a minute, staring at the poster on my far wall, the one Kitty had given me. *I don't have anything nice to say.* I looked at my bookshelf with its collection of fantasy books about places with curses worse than ours and my ribbons for swimming faster than everyone else. When I picked up my phone, I saw I had a missed call from Soren and another from my mum. An email too, and I wondered if my dad had seen the preview before he'd brought my phone back in here. You didn't need to open it to know what it was about. It was from the coach at the University of Maine. The preview said: *Hi, Tess. I've got some bad news…*

My phone only had three percent left. I plugged it into the charger by my bed and made the call.

After a few rings, the voice on the other end said, "Tess? Are you doing okay?"

I stared at the ribbons, and then I shut my eyes. "Can you help me?"

"What's wrong?"

"I'm not going to get a swimming scholarship, and I don't know how else I'm supposed to afford college, and I have to get off this island."

There was a pause. I heard the sound of a computer turning on. Keys tapping.

"Okay," my mum said. "Let's see what we can do."

Dear Tess

2014

Delia's first day back at school was also the day Harvard and Yale emailed me with the news *sorry, unfortunately, but thanks for applying.* I was standing with Kitty, Linnea, and Henrik on the sidelines of Soren's soccer game. My phone said it was past nine at night, but because people kept falling over and looking woefully injured, the game dragged ever onward.

Henrik kept saying, "See, this is why I prefer rugby."

Kitty kept saying, "See, this is why I prefer stabbing myself with knitting needles."

I had enough of a natural intuition for sports to know that Soren was good. Probably not the best, but a solid contender for second. He was a midfielder, which seemed to involve a lot of running back and forth very quickly. Every time he went past us, his hair all sweaty and windswept, Linnea would cheer and Kitty would hurl abuse, just to see if he'd react. He didn't. I didn't cheer because being yelled at sounded distracting and embarrassing for both of us, but I was wearing one of his jerseys, a green one with his number and the name *Fell* on the back in block letters. It was the most girlfriend-y thing I had perhaps ever done, and I had taken it off and put it back on again four times before Kitty and Linnea had dragged me to the game.

Delia stood slightly farther down the field with two of her friends. I'd seen her in school, and we'd made eye contact briefly before she'd looked away again. According to my mum, Delia had called her a few more times from Ramna Skaill. My mum hadn't told me what they'd talked about. *Just skeld things* was all she'd said.

Thomas's funeral had been on Christmas Eve. I'd sat between Soren and my dad and kept thinking I was going to cry but never did.

My phone vibrated just as Soren passed the ball to someone else on his team. I looked at it covertly and saw the emails. Kitty shot me a sharp look, and I hid my face with my hair.

She was the only one who knew which schools I'd applied to, or that I'd applied at all, now that it was obvious I wouldn't be swimming at a university level. Linnea hadn't asked. Soren studiously mentioned nothing further than one month in the future. Kitty, however, who'd gotten her acceptance to Oxford weeks ago, had berated me until I'd told her the list of universities my mum and I had put together.

It had been too late, by then, to apply to Oxford too. And since Stenland, in a fit of patriotic isolationism, had declined to join the EU, there was no great financial benefit to choosing a European university over an American one.

When I looked at my list of schools—Harvard, Yale, Stanford, etcetera—I felt like someone was going to laugh at me. I hadn't meant to apply exclusively to schools with impossible acceptance rates, nor did I think I was smart enough to do well at them. But the only American universities that offered financial aid to international students were the ones with endowments greater than the entire economy of Stenland. According to the statistics my mum had emailed me, my grades and test scores were average for accepted students. Most schools did not have any students from Stenland, which might've worked in my favor if they wanted to add another country to their tally. But mostly, I was relying on the personal essay my mum had helped me write. It was about curses and translating Stennish poetry and being hewn by a place you wanted to escape. I thought it was good. The Ivies did not. Stanford would email me the next day, but my hope for a different answer was so small I couldn't look directly at it. I buried my phone in my pocket and stared at the soccer pitch.

If I was accepted nowhere, I supposed I could go live with my mum. But she was seminomadic, bouncing from tourist visa to tourist visa, always circling Edinburgh but never putting roots down full-time. And besides, what sort of life would I have? Trailing her around the world, wondering if my dad considered it a betrayal? I thought of him telling me that the island picked people they believed could do bigger things, and I wondered if escaping counted as a bigger thing even if you weren't escaping to anything.

Soren stole the ball from someone on the other team just as they were lining up for a shot to tie the game. When the referee blew the final whistle moments later, all our classmates started cheering. Soren fought his way through hands clapping him on the shoulder, and he picked me up and kissed me in front of everyone. His lips tasted salty, like sweat. Everyone cheered even louder then, and when he started to pull away, I kissed him harder.

Kitty must've known the Stanford decision was coming the next day because she suggested the five of us hike up the highest point in Stenland to keep me from checking my phone every four seconds. She spent the whole time complaining, but her complaints were charming and specific: "There's a very sharp rock in my shoe whom I've decided to name Edgar, and though he is small, he is mighty, like the proletariat to the oligarch that is my foot."

It was called Fell Mountain; Soren claimed no relation, but there had probably, at some point, been one. The land sloped down on either side of us, scraggly hills of green and gold and red. We hiked along a ridge of crumbling rocks until we reached the summit, and from there we could see the ocean in three directions. There was a cairn at the top, taller than Kitty but not as tall as Linnea. About my height. Soren put another flat stone on the tower, and it wobbled but didn't fall. Henrik opened his backpack and started distributing oatcakes he'd bought at Hedda's, then whiskey he'd stolen from his mother.

"You can see Ramna Skaill from up here," Linnea said, pointing.

We all followed her finger. The tower looked so innocent in the soft spring light—a historical artifact from an age already gone by. The waves against the shore were bright and gentle. I could see, scattered around the perimeter of the island, some of the statues left like sentinels, a warning. But from up here, they could have been anything. Just craggy bits of stone on this craggy bit of island.

"If we ever become skelds," Linnea said, "you two would be keepers, right?"

"Of course," Henrik said, but at the same time, and more loudly, Kitty said, "Well, don't fucking jinx us."

"I was just wondering," Linnea said.

"Soren and Lukas and I talked about it ages ago," Henrik said, as casually as if he were discussing what he'd eaten for breakfast. It was the first time it had ever occurred to me that Henrik and Soren might feel the weight of the island's certainty—that Kitty, Linnea, and I would become skelds—the same way we did. "We made a pact."

"It doesn't matter," I said. "Because we're not going to become skelds."

At the edge of the ridge, the ground fell away. We were as high as the misty clouds rolling off the sea. My cheeks felt damp with fog and sweat. I yelled, and my voice ricocheted around the hills and across the waves.

Kitty made a frustrated noise and pressed a hand to her ear. "Warn a person before you do that."

Henrik scrambled to his feet to stand next to me and started shouting, "Echo! Echo! Echo!"

When I felt Soren behind me, I put my hand out automatically. The backs of our fingers touched. He didn't shout anything; he just gazed out at the rocks rolling into grass rolling into sea with this perfect, peaceful expression. He shut his eyes, just for a second, and then tilted his head to the sky. When he exhaled, I could see the mist of his breath. Then he looked at me, and the expression didn't change. Like he cared for the island the way he cared for me. Or like he cared for me the way he cared for the island.

I had gotten so good at not thinking about leaving him.

We all went back to Soren's house for dinner since he lived the closest to the trailhead.

"It is the only useful thing you live near," Kitty said in the car. "And it's not, if I'm being honest, that useful."

"Not true," Soren said. "I also live near Stenland's only puffin sanctuary."

"Well, thank god for that," Kitty said.

Elin was out of town for the weekend visiting a cousin in Tórshavn, but Lukas was there when we got back to the house, sprawled on the couch with his phone in front of his face.

A few weeks before, I'd finally decided we'd known each

other long enough that I could ask him to explain the nails in my tires. We'd been alone in the kitchen at the time. He'd been making himself pre-dinner and had his back turned when I'd asked.

"Because I wanted Soren to make a move, and he was never fucking going to, was he?"

I'd blinked. "I always assumed it was because you hated me."

"Hated you?"

"Because of my mum."

Lukas had gone quiet. Finally: "Maybe that too."

"It's okay if you did. Or do. Only fair."

I'd watched the tension in his back, the defensive curl of his shoulders. "Can you imagine what it's like? To have him as a brother? He just does everything he's supposed to and doesn't complain. He has no idea how it feels to be angry all the time." A pause. "I owe him so much." Another pause. "Sorry about the tires."

I'd reached out, taken his hand, and squeezed it. He still had not turned to face me. Then he'd squeezed my hand back and walked away, and we never talked about it again.

After the hike, when we got back to the house, Lukas said, "Oh, good. I was getting hungry."

"You could've made dinner," Kitty said.

"I don't come into your home and judge you," he said.

"You absolutely do. When I was fourteen, you said my room was too pink."

"It was very pink," I told her.

"That's unfeminist."

Kitty, Linnea, and Henrik joined Lukas on and around the couch and put on a film about superheroes that looked remarkably like the other films about superheroes. I sat on the counter, swinging my legs while Soren chopped things. Over the past few months, Elin had decided she was going to become a baker, so she'd left Soren with mounds of pizza dough.

It all struck me as very fancy and gourmet, having homemade pizza, aside from the fact that we would be topping it with sheep-milk cheese. Since beginning to date Soren, I had eaten my body weight in sheep-milk cheese.

"You have flour on your nose," I told him.

"Mmm?" he said.

I reached out a hand to brush it off. He stood between my legs and stared at me like making pizza was not currently his top priority.

"You look good cooking," I told him.

"You just think that because you hate cooking."

"Possibly," I said.

Quietly enough that no one should've been able to hear over the explosions happening in the film, he said, "You looked good with my name on your back."

A rush of heat. How scary, how stupid to joke about exchanging names, to tease that I would take his. But there it was: *Tess Fell.* I'd always liked his name. Fell, Fell, even though I'd never wanted to marry my name away. I should've made a face and told him so, but instead I squeezed my knees together lightly, pressing them on either side of his hips. "Give me more free shirts, and I'll wear your name more often."

"I didn't realize I was giving you my jersey permanently."

"You were."

His lips against my hair. "Okay."

From the couch, Kitty yelled, "Keep it in your pants, Eriksson!"

I flipped her off, and Soren kissed me and went back to cutting things.

When Soren put the pizzas in the oven, I went to the bathroom with the gentle lighting and the red walls. I was wondering who was planning on spending the night here. Usually when I slept over, Soren would retreat to the couch in the living room once we started to get sleepy. I'd brought over a compact mirror, which now lived on his bedside table, and every morning, I woke up and checked my reflection in it. If everyone stayed, I supposed Henrik and Soren could share the living room and Kitty or Linnea could take Elin's bed. Maybe that wasn't smart, though; maybe there wasn't quite enough space for everyone to wake up and find a mirror before they saw anyone. I looked at Soren's toothbrush in the cup on the sink and thought about his name on my back.

I reached for my phone to tell my dad I wouldn't be back until the next day.

The email said: Dear Tess, congratulati—

I looked at my reflection. The person looking back at me was confused.

I looked at my phone again. Opened the email.

It said: Dear Tess, congratulations! It is with great pleasure that the Admission Committee invites you to join the Stanford University class of 2018.

It went on. I didn't read it. I put my phone back in my pocket and walked out of the bathroom. Soren was leaning against the wall of the kitchen watching someone on the TV jump off a building of improbable height. He lifted an arm for me to step under without really looking at me, and I slid against his chest and stared at the TV.

Dear Tess!

"Are you cold?" he asked.

"No."

"You're shaking."

I was. *Dear Tess!!!*

"I'll get a sweater." I left again. Went back to his bedroom and sat on the floor in front of his bookshelves. This time, I scrolled through the whole email, but I still didn't read it. I took a screenshot and sent it to both of my parents—my mum, then my dad—wondering if it was perhaps a rejection that my brain was too delusional to read correctly. After I did it, I felt bad about sending it to my mum first.

Both of them called. I didn't pick up. Both of them texted.

Mum: TESS!!!!!!!!!!!!!!!

Dad: I am literally crying right now :) :) :)

I lay down on Soren's floor and pressed my hands into my eyes. There was a knock at the door, and it was Kitty and Linnea, looking concerned.

"Are you okay?" Linnea said. "You don't look quite okay."

"I knew it," Kitty said. "She's pregnant."

"That's not funny," Linnea said.

"Sure it is! I'd be an aunt. Or a…cousin-aunt? Whatever."

I held the phone out to them. Kitty took it and started swearing enthusiastically.

A minute later, probably on account of the fact that Linnea had shrieked, Henrik and Soren and even Lukas came thundering up the stairs.

"Why are you crying?" Henrik asked Linnea, and she insisted they were happy tears.

Soren looked at me with his eyebrows knitting together, and Kitty handed him the phone. I watched him read with the feeling that I was stepping out of a plane and not sure whether I was wearing a parachute. He frowned in concentration and scrolled slowly, reading all the words I had not yet been able to read. When he finally finished, he handed Kitty back the phone and sat down on the floor and wrapped his arms around me. Linnea was explaining to Henrik and Lukas; Lukas was shouting gleeful things about American football at Kitty.

Soren kissed me slowly, my shoulder and my temple, and we were rocking slightly on the floor with his arms around me and all the noise swirling above us. I told myself I didn't need him to say anything, but it wasn't true. When the oven timer rang, he helped me to my feet and kissed me again, on the mouth this time, and led me by the hand down the stairs.

But he never did. Say anything.

Spar

2014

When I invited my mum to Kitty's and my going-away party, Linnea started to cry because she thought that was just so beautiful. "Love heals everything," she said, wiping her face with the sleeves of her cardigan. Linnea had been crying with increasing frequency throughout the spring and summer. "I think it's my new birth control," she'd say, and Kitty would say, "No, it's because you're going to miss me."

We had the party at the Sjöbergs' house on account of the Sjöbergs having more money than anyone else in Stenland and a home that reflected this fact. It was designed as if on purpose to let out as much heat as possible. The ceilings were so high, the cleaner had to use a ladder to dust off the cobwebs. When Kitty's dad was home, he turned up the heaters until you had to strip down to your T-shirt. And all along the west side of the house, there were no walls, just windows, providing an obstructed view of the ocean in all her grumpy September glory.

The party didn't technically start until six, but everyone had been over at the Sjöbergs' getting ready for hours. Linnea and Kitty were blowing up balloons in the living room. Their mothers had run to the shops to buy drinks. Outside, all the men were doing whatever it was men deemed acceptable to help prepare for a party, which seemed to mostly include grilling things and making a fire in the fire pit. When I looked out the window, Soren was the one making the fire; Henrik and my dad were grilling; Mr. Sjöberg seemed to be "supervising," by which I mean drinking a beer and talking loudly.

Ostensibly, I was helping my mother cook. Really, I just leaned against the refrigerator and occasionally found ingredients for her. It had been Soren's suggestion to invite her, though she hadn't believed this when I'd told her. The question of how much Soren resented her remained unresolved; I knew I should have asked, but the longer I waited, the harder it became. Sometimes I felt as if I knew Soren completely, but other times I wondered if I only knew him well in comparison to everyone else. He never told me how he felt about my mum or how he felt that I was her daughter.

My mum, for her part, brimmed with frantic energy. She had decided the party would be a disaster if it didn't have pastelillos de guayaba, which were some sort of fried guava pastry she'd eaten on a recent trip to Puerto Rico. Her hair had come out of its bun and was starting to look disheveled. Every few minutes, she muttered a curse at her pastry dough.

"You know," I said, "you could serve us white bread and tell us it was a recipe from New Zealand."

"What's your point?" she said.

"That this is less about the pastries and more about proving you've been outside the country."

She glared at her bowl. "You'll understand soon enough."

Soren came into the kitchen to get a lighter for the fire pit at one point, and my mum, in a voice far too loud for normal conversation, said, "Oh! Soren! Hello!"

As far as I knew, it was the first time they had spoken since Soren's parents had died.

He touched the small of my back like a question, and I wrapped an arm around his waist, trying to silently communicate my support.

"Hi, Ms. Eriksson."

"Alice! Please."

Soren nodded once. His face was formal and blank, the way he looked when we ran into Father Andersson, of whom we were all terrified. I wondered what my mum saw when she looked at him and if she saw the same person I did—his handsomeness, his adultness, how whole he was despite everything that had happened.

"Tess mentioned you read that book I sent?"

That book—which I never bothered opening but which Soren found on my bedside table—had some tragic title like *In the Wake of Their Passing.* It was about this man and this woman who married a pair of fraternal twins only to realize they loved each other more than the people they'd married. They almost ran away together, but instead they decided to stay in their mediocre marriages and raise their children and continue with their careers. And then, in the epilogue, their respective spouses had conveniently died and their children were all grown-up, so they ran away and fucked on a train.

"I liked it very much," Soren said.

"No, he didn't," I said. "He called it saccharine."

Soren looked pained.

My mum laughed. "Should've known better than to give a boy a love story. I'll find something with more trench warfare next time."

He shot me a pleading look.

"He doesn't sit around reading war books either, Mum," I said, feeling defensive.

She raised a spoon in my direction. "That book was excellent. It was long-listed for the National Book Award."

"The prose was great," Soren said.

"Saccharine," my mother said, shaking her head.

He shifted his weight. This was the usual moment at which he'd leave a conversation, considering himself no longer an integral part, but talking about books seemed to make his feet heavier, to make him that little bit more reluctant to walk away. "Not saccharine," he said. "I just didn't like that we were supposed to think it was a happy ending, them being together, when they'd forced themselves to be apart for thirty years."

"But they ended up together."

"I'd rather have the middle than the ending," Soren said.

My mother looked up at him—really looked at him, squinting slightly, and he held her gaze, hands in his pockets, rocking back on his heels.

"Huh," she said.

Henrik called Soren's name from outside, and he pressed a quick kiss against my temple before retreating again. I wondered if my mum was also listening to his footsteps, waiting.

"You want to say something about him," I told her.

"I'm thinking," she said.

"About?"

"He's not who I would've expected you to date in high school."

"Why not?" I asked.

She gestured at the air. "He's so...solemn. That's not the right word. He's just intense. You two are intense. It all strikes me as a bit serious for a high school relationship. What are you going to do when you leave?"

"We haven't talked about it."

My mum turned and stared at me. She set down her spoon for full effect. "You fly tomorrow."

I crossed my arms. Behind me, the refrigerator hummed loudly.

"Are you breaking up? Doing long distance?"

I shrugged.

"Don't you *care*?" she asked.

Did I care. I was pleased she'd asked, pleased I had successfully convinced her I was the kind of chill and laissez-faire type of girlfriend who might not.

Since my acceptance to Stanford, I'd begun to imagine the holes in my conversations with Soren as a kind of currency. Every time I repressed the urge to ask him if we had a future, I felt like I'd won something. Each day closer we crept to my departure, I waited for him to ask me to stay, and he didn't. I waited for him to say he'd call me every night, and he didn't. I waited for him to buy a plane ticket to visit me over Christmas, and he didn't. It was an arms race of weaponized silence, neither of us willing to admit we had more to lose even as we hurtled toward our mutually assured destruction.

Did I care.

Somewhere upward of a hundred people came to the party, including my dad's somewhat-serious girlfriend, Anna (from the hospital). I never saw her and my mum standing in the same room, which was probably strategic on one or both of their parts.

Hedda gave me a leather passport case. The Sjöbergs had gotten me a Longchamp duffel bag that probably did not pair with the flannel shirt I had on over my dress. From Linnea, I got a massive collage of photos of the three of us from infancy to present. Perhaps my most surprising gift was from Lukas, who handed me a newspaper-wrapped book of sudokus. Inside the cover, he'd written *To keep you busy on the plane ride. I hope I can come visit you in California.* When he gave it to me, he blushed to the tips of his ears.

After we ate, there were toasts, and my dad raised his beer to my future mechanical engineering degree and a lifetime designing cars he hoped to someday fix. Soren sat with his arm over my shoulder, and I pressed my face into his chest so no one saw me cry.

Once almost everyone had gone, Soren took my hand and tilted his head questioningly toward the door. My mum was staying with the Sjöbergs, and my dad had rather conspicuously announced he was going to Anna's house and would I be okay alone? When I said goodbye and thank-you to everyone who was left, Linnea started crying again, even though she was going to the airport with Kitty and me in the morning.

Soren and I stepped into the misty night and the dribbles of conversation were swallowed up behind us. I leaned against his shoulder as we walked. With the hand that wasn't holding mine, he reached across his chest to stroke the ends of my hair.

When we got back to my empty house, I flipped on the kitchen light. Soren held me from behind, arms wrapped around me, chin against my shoulder.

"I got you something," he said.

"Something good?"

He reached into his pocket—I felt him doing it—and pulled out a small black box. When he held it in front of me, I felt like the floor was dropping out, like I'd stumbled out of the set for my own film and into an entirely different one.

"Open it," he said.

"No."

He laughed into my hair. "What do you mean, no?"

"That's a ring box."

"It's just a box."

"Why are you giving me a ring?"

"Christ, Tess." He flicked it open, and inside I saw that it was not in fact a ring but a necklace with a fine silver chain. The pendant at the end was an intricate knot with a crystal in the middle, mostly clear with veins like frost around the edges. It wasn't a large necklace, but it wasn't delicate either, and I liked it the second I saw it. "Can I put it on you?"

I nodded. He brushed my hair out of the way and fastened it behind my neck. The pendant hung at my breastbone.

"It's spar," he said. "The stone. There's a theory that sailors used to use it to find the sun when it was cloudy. They called it sunstone." He paused. "I had a romantic speech planned here, but you can figure out the tortured metaphor for yourself."

I turned to look at him, touching the pendant with one hand. "Thank you."

"Do you like it?"

"A lot."

"It was my mum's."

A flutter of panic. "You can't give me your mum's necklace."

"Why not?"

"It's too important."

He pressed his lips together. "Calm down. It's not like I gave you an engagement ring."

"You gave me an engagement-ring box."

"I didn't think about it, okay? It was just the box the necklace was sitting in. I'm sorry you thought I was *proposing*."

"We're nineteen," I said.

He lifted his chin, staring at the ceiling in this *god give me strength* sort of way, and it struck me as the most patronizing thing anyone had ever done. "Thank you. I had forgotten."

I took off the necklace and held it out for him to take.

His hands stayed at his sides. "What are you doing?" he said tiredly.

"Take it. I don't want it."

"You said you liked it."

"That was before I knew it was your mum's."

He just shook his head at me, at the necklace, at the whole thing.

I set it on the kitchen counter and crossed my arms. "I don't even know what this is supposed to be," I said. "Is it supposed to remind me of you? Am I supposed to wear it to scare off other men? Or is this, like, some sort of goodbye, thanks-for-the-sex-while-it-lasted gift—"

His expression slid from horror to betrayal to anger in the span of a breath. I watched it like I was watching myself knock a glass of the edge of a table. He picked up the necklace and shoved it into his pocket.

"Why did you even date me if you thought that's who I was?" he said.

"Did?" I asked.

Time slowed down. He hunched his shoulders. A pressure was building behind my eyes, and I told myself that if I started to cry I would never forgive myself. We had never said it, that we were in love, except when we teased each other about being in love since age twelve, and that never quite felt like it counted.

"I kept waiting for you to say something," Soren told me.

"You could've said something."

"You're the one who's leaving," he said.

My back straightened of its own accord. "You're not allowed to be angry at me for leaving. For wanting...more than this."

"Who said I was angry at you?"

"You just want me to stay here and marry you and have kids and—and never see what the rest of the world is like or see what I could be or..." I was beginning to shake, my hands clenching into fists and my nails digging into my palms. "You think I should, what, turn down Stanford? Stay here and do Stennish studies?"

"Don't say it like that. I'm doing Stennish studies."

That made me pause. "You never said you were taking university classes."

I wasn't sure he'd ever looked at me as unkindly as he looked at me then.

"Maybe you should've asked," he said.

I wrapped my arms around myself. He kept standing there like he was waiting for something, but we'd reached a dead end in the maze and I didn't see where else we could go.

"Were you always planning on breaking up with me tonight?" I said.

I wanted him to say *We're not breaking up, Tess.*

"No," he said.

"But," I said.

"Do you ever see yourself coming back here?" he said. "If we kept dating and you graduated and it was four years from now. Do you think—" His voice cracked, and for a second, just a second, I thought there was another turn in the maze after all, another path, another road to take that was not this. "Do you think there's even a chance you would consider living here again?"

I thought of Delia screaming.

I thought of the smell of Thomas's sweatshirt.

I thought of the uncountable number of times I had been told that there was no escaping it, not for the three of us, not for Linnea and Kitty and me, not if we stayed on this island.

"No," I said.

Soren exhaled. Nodded once. He turned and made it all the way to the door, and as he went, I felt like there was a rubber band stretching between my heart and his, just waiting to snap. At the door, he paused. Ran his hand through his hair.

He looked back at me over his shoulder and said, “I don’t understand how you could’ve loved me when it seems like I’m everything you hate.”

I couldn’t look at him. “I never said I loved you.”

“No,” he said. “I guess you never did.”

The Rehearsal

2022

While most of the room drank, the wedding party practiced walking up and down an imaginary aisle. I was paired with Magnus Invers, who was, apparently, Henrik's cousin; I'd forgotten that. Because we were at the back, Magnus and I were in charge of sweeping heather brooms down the aisle, which was tradition but made me feel like an old witch. Kitty was paired with Henrik's older brother, who kept having to dash off to help his wife with their kids, a one-year-old son and a three-year-old daughter who were experiencing simultaneous meltdowns. I did not understand why so many people had to be here if they weren't even part of the rehearsal. I did not understand why they looked so amused, watching us as they drank their wine. Soren and Saffi practiced standing right behind Linnea and Henrik, and if you held up your bouquet to blot out the center two figures, it looked like they were the ones getting married.

Once we were done learning how to walk and stand, the seven of us—the wedding party, sans Henrik's brother, who was still trying to sort out his toddler—were seated at a table at the head of the room, over by the big windows. There were handwritten cards with our names on them. I was placed between Kitty and Magnus. Soren was seated directly opposite me, almost as if whoever had created the seating arrangement had wanted to put as much distance between the two of us as possible. Consequently, he was constantly in my line of sight.

Around the same time the soup arrived, Henrik's father came over from the parents' table to say hello. He spouted a series of logistical details that entered my left ear and puddled out my right. Then he clapped a hand on Soren's shoulder and said, "See if Father Andersson's schedule is free for the best man and the maid of honor after, eh?"

"Dad," Henrik said, and I took a lingering sip of wine.

Saffi laughed. Soren did not.

When Henrik's dad left, Magnus asked me if it was true I was building cars now.

"Not whole cars," I said. "Just one sensor, actually."

"I feel like I'm back at the nerd table in high school," Magnus said, leaning over the table to bump Henrik's shoulder. "Kitty, Tess, Fell—gang's all here."

Linnea pursed her lips at her plate. I groped for something to say that wouldn't draw even more attention to the line Magnus cut between us. Before I could find anything, Saffi said, "Soren got an offer to do a PhD at Oxford."

"You did?" I said.

I didn't mean to say it. The whole table shifted in discomfort.

"He's not going to go, though," Saffi added.

I waited for Soren to confirm this. He just shrugged. I couldn't read his mind anymore.

"You still swimming?" Magnus asked me.

I opened my mouth, but Kitty said, "With staggering speed and delphine grace."

"And, um," Magnus said, "liking Frisco?"

"Frisco!" Kitty said, swatting my arm with the back of her hand. "You're right—that is worse than San Fran."

Everyone else looked at her blankly, except for Soren, who said, "Don't be shitty."

The silence was dense and claustrophobic. Magnus, who still looked unsure how, exactly, he'd been made fun of, said, "Oh, right, Fell, I forgot that you lived—"

Then he thought better of it and shut his mouth.

Another silence.

"This soup is incredible," Henrik said to Linnea. "Isn't it incredible?"

"Mmm," she said. Her face was turned toward the table, but I could see pink splotches on her cheeks.

Kitty poked at a white lump in her bowl. "What do you think this is?"

"Potato," I said.

"How sure are you?"

"Pretty sure."

"Because remember that time in Paris when you ordered soup and it had sheep testicles in it?"

I choked on my spoon.

"Right?" Kitty said. "*La vie est trop courte* to eat testicle soup, etcetera, etcetera."

Linnea stood up, her chair squeaking. She hurried in the direction of the bathroom.

Henrik threw his napkin onto the table. "You're better than that."

"What?" Kitty said. "If she doesn't want us having a pleasant soup conversation, then she shouldn't have served soup."

A vein in Henrik's neck twitched. He stood up and went after Linnea.

"Do you think it's the word *testicle*?" Kitty whispered to me. "Because I know—gross, but we may have to give her a talk before this wedding goes through."

I snorted, not quietly enough, which made Saffi get up and follow the others.

"And then there were four," Kitty said.

Soren leaned back in his chair, his arms crossed.

"So..." Magnus said. "What did that soup taste like?"

"Don't encourage them," Soren said.

"Encourage what?" I asked.

He gave me a look that said *You know exactly what.*

"If Linnea has a problem," Kitty said, "maybe she should tell us instead of running away like a disconsolate Victorian orphan who's just been denied another bowl of porridge."

"I don't think Victorian orphans did a lot of running," I said. "On account of the malnutrition."

"Point, Tess!"

Soren made a disgusted noise.

"Problem?" Kitty asked.

He stood up. It seemed like he was answering Kitty, but he was looking at me. "We already know you think you're better than us." He followed the others and left behind a carcinogenic silence. Even the tables around us caught it.

"I wasn't thinking about it that way," I said.

"Of course you were," Kitty said. "I want more wine."

"No," I said. "We should go apologize."

"For what? Living our lives? Having been to Paris? Are we expected to sit around listening to them talk about the fucking weather all day? Breaking news—it rained."

I started to stand, but Kitty grabbed my wrist and yanked me back down.

"Oh, don't do that, don't join the exodus. If Linnea has a problem, she should say something."

"It's her wedding," I said.

She sighed. "Fine. It's not you she's angry with anyway. I'll go make nice with the parents, and everyone will come back. Parents love me." She pushed herself to her feet and away from the table, and then it was just Magnus and me.

"Shit," he said finally. "I'm not drunk enough for this."

Kitty was right, though; once she left, the others came out of whatever bathroom they'd been in and sat back down at the table. Linnea's eyes were puffy, but her makeup was still perfect. Probably Saffi had fixed it. I was angry it hadn't been me. I didn't want to embarrass Linnea, so I texted her under the table.

Me: I'm sorry, Lin

Me: I wasn't thinking

Me: I love you

Linnea: It's okay

Linnea: It's not you

I wished it was, though, because if it was me, I could fix it. I wanted to grab hold of Kitty with one hand and Linnea with the other and force them to stare at each other until this was better. The thought of Linnea and Kitty not liking each other, truly not liking each other, made me feel like my childhood had been a lie.

When Noah and I had moved in together, he'd had a giant cardboard box labeled *SENTIMENTAL SHIT.* A Chicago Cubs flag, a photo from his sister's bat mitzvah, a highly impractical bong. When he looked at my boxes, full of disassembled IKEA furniture and textbooks, he told me, *Sometimes it seems like you sprang to life fully formed at age nineteen.*

I wondered if he knew I thought about that every day.

Kitty never came back to the table. I watched her in my peripheral vision as she artfully ducked from one table to another, chattering and laughing and looking for all the world like she was having a grand time. My table mostly ignored me. At one point, Soren said something too quiet for me to hear, meant for Saffi alone, and she laughed and laughed. She seemed to laugh so easily, Saffi. I'd always liked her. I still did. Really. She kissed him, right in the hollow below his cheekbone. It was a normal amount of jealousy. The same amount I would feel if Saffi kissed Noah in front of me. Maybe a little more, but only because you never forget the first person you fell in love with. Soren looked up at me through his eyelashes, and I turned away, my cheeks hot from having been caught.

Someone dimmed the lights, and a procession of waiters brought out a cake with twenty-six candles. When my mother had been twenty-six, she'd had a seven-year-old daughter.

It was too rich to eat but very pretty: velvet layers of fudge on chocolate cake with a sticky caramel drizzle. I was wondering if there was some sort of geometric proof for how you could rearrange cake to get the maximum ratio of *looking eaten* to *actually eaten* when Lukas dropped heavily into Kitty's empty seat.

"Tess fucking Eriksson!" he said. "I'm offended I wasn't the first person you came to see."

Lukas sent me emails still. Long diary entries about the island (too cold) and the croft (so dull) and whatever girl he was seeing (always, by his telling, more interested in him than he was in return). I responded infrequently, afraid to reveal my own interest in the world I'd left behind. The stiffness of my replies didn't deter him. I imagined, to him, pressing Send on those emails was the emotional equivalent of launching garbage into space; I was too far away for it to matter.

"How's the job?" he asked.

"Oh, fine," I said. He waited expectantly. "How are you?"

"Oh, you know. Same as usual."

I did know, and it was the same as usual. He gave me all the details anyway, talking until everyone else at our table had stood up to clean or mingle or put their toddlers down for the night. While Lukas was regaling me with a story about the sheepdogs, Soren helped Saffi to her feet, his hand brushing her waist. Lukas must've seen me watching, because he said, "But you don't give a shit about that, do you? Tell me about you. How's the boyfriend? Can I see a picture?"

I scrolled for a while before I found one I liked. Noah was more handsome in person than he was in photos. I settled on one from after his company's holiday party—lying on a couch, dressed in a suit, thumb to his lips. Byronic and idle.

Lukas said, "I reckon he looks like me."

I looked again at the photo. At Lukas. "Sure," I said. Noah texted me again then, like he could sense he was being talked about.

Noah: Found a spider but trapped it in a cup and brought it outside instead of killing it

Noah: Made me think of you

I stared at this message and tried to remember if I was someone who trapped spiders in cups or squished them. I couldn't remember. Could not. A buzzing filled my ears; it wasn't a natural buzz, not like bees, so I'd started to think of it like static, like I was a character in a little box, but the TV was losing reception. *Bzzz.* I didn't know why the spider, or the trapping, made Noah think of me. I thought I would sound inane if I asked.

"Are you okay?" Lukas asked.

"I should go home." It was impossible to know at what volume I said this.

I found my dad standing with Linnea's and Kitty's mums, his hands in his pockets and his shoulders near his ears. We nodded in mutual agreement at the door. On the way out, we passed a hallway from which I could hear Saffi's clear, easy laugh.

In the car, I rolled the windows down even though it was too cold.

"Do I set bugs free or kill them?" I asked my dad.

"I suppose I've seen you do both," he said. "Why?"

The static was getting louder again. "I can't remember."

Back at home, in my childhood bedroom turned guest room, I stripped off my dress and curled under the quilts in just my underwear. I was both sweating and shivering.

I looked at last-minute flights on my phone; there was nothing until the next afternoon. Curses always find you when you're sleeping, so I decided not to sleep. Not until it was time for me to leave. I would sway deliriously through the ceremony, and I would not laugh at any of Kitty's inside jokes, and I would clap when Saffi caught the bouquet. Outside, the wind smashed against the sides of the house. The ceiling distended. My skin felt too thick and too heavy, probably just dry from the travel, but I would've sworn it was spreading, the dryness, calcifying. Thirty-six hours. I would leave in thirty-six hours.

I really didn't mean to fall asleep.

The dream always looked like this:

I went into the kitchen wearing faded jeans and a blue cardigan, no shoes. It was morning, cool and bright. Our daughter was eating carrot sticks.

"Carrots for breakfast?" I asked.

"If I eat a lot of them," she said, "I'll be able to see through walls."

She was seven. We had argued about whether she would end up liking words or numbers better, but as it turned out, she liked bugs. Bugs! Whose daughter liked bugs? Ours did.

Soren handed me a cup of coffee. "How fast can you drink that?"

"Are we running late?"

"Depends how fast you can drink that."

I drank it in one go and handed him the cup. He still had coffee grounds on his fingers. He was wearing that red sweater he'd given me after I'd pulled Linnea out of the ocean; it was pristine.

"No longer running late," he said.

I was on car-seat duty. Our daughter hated the car seat—it was always an ordeal—but I bribed her by telling her the plane would probably have a bug film on the in-flight entertainment. We had so much luggage—we always did—in our boring little suitcases with the yellow ribbons on the handles so we could find them at the carousel more easily. Our daughter had a backpack shaped like a ladybug. It had room for exactly two outfits, so of course it was instead jammed with embroidery thread so she could braid friendship bracelets to add to the fourteen thousand already on her wrists.

We sat at the gate underneath a big sign that said our destination on it. Soren bought muffins and more coffees from the café by our gate.

"You have a problem," I said.

He passed me one of the coffee cups. "Fortunately, so do you."

I put my head on his shoulder, and we watched our daughter braid her long, neon threads. It was so boring. We were so boring. Some people spent their whole lives without ever getting to taste such warm and magnificent boredom.

We got on the plane and found a bug film. An hour in, Soren gestured for me to take off my headphones. He set a hand on our daughter's head—she always sat between us—and said, "This is just *King Lear* with butterflies."

"Daddy." She tugged at his sweater. "You're not paying attention."

"I already know how it ends. Because it's *King Lear*."

"With butterflies," I said.

That was when the plane started to shake. Everything went weightless. I heard this buzzing, and at first I thought it was bees, and then I thought it was static, and then I realized it was the sound of a plane ripping apart bolt by bolt. She was screaming. Then—impact.

Everything was black, and then everything was blue and cold. I kicked my way to the surface. Plane bits were scattered around me, bobbing on the sea, but no one else was there. Just empty seats, dangling seat belts, tray tables, and dinners still wrapped in plastic.

I screamed Soren's name over and over again, but where was everyone else? Why wasn't anyone else swimming? When the safety crew arrived to rescue us, they were sailing a yacht called *Serena*. I was on the deck with no recollection of how I got there. A man in an orange vest was putting a crinkly reflective blanket over my shoulders. I kept screaming Soren's name.

"You're the only one we've found so far," the man said, and then I remembered that it was Noah. I grabbed him by the vest.

"You have to get them back," I said.

"They'll come if they hear you calling," Noah said. "But you don't even remember your daughter's name, do you?"

That was always when I woke up.

There were some details that were always the same. Soren's sweater. The way the little girl braided those bracelets, her hands tiny and nimble. Other details never stuck no matter how hard I tried to remember. Like where the house was, Palo Alto or Stenland or suburban nowhere. Whether we were leaving home or coming back. It never occurred to my dream self to wonder. I hated her, dream Tess, like I had never hated anyone. I hated that I didn't know if she had a career. I hated that she was soft and maternal and unbothered, right up until the crash. The crash was punishment for daring to feel so mundanely complete.

I cried with my blankets pulled over my face so my dad wouldn't hear. How were you supposed to grieve something that wasn't real? I'd asked Noah once if he ever had dreams about his exes. He'd said yeah, but it was no big deal, just the way memory went sometimes.

I hauled myself out of bed and pressed the heels of my hands into my eyes. They were going to be red. My eyes always stayed red and puffy for hours after I cried. Maybe Kitty could fix me with enough makeup. I dropped my hands and looked at my reflection in the mirror, and I watched my mouth form the soundless word—oh.

I called Kitty first, not quite knowing why her and not Linnea. She picked up on the second ring.

"My alarm wasn't set for another seven minutes," she said. "I begrudge you those seven minutes."

"Look in the mirror," I said.

A pause. The rustling of blankets.

"Kitty?"

"We should call Linnea," she said.

I could not stop staring at myself. At the black lines seared across my skin. I touched them, expecting them to smudge. They didn't, of course. It was as dark as a fresh tattoo, except the skin wasn't raised. Just above my brows, in line with the bridge of my nose, were the three jagged lines, just the size of a raven's talon.

I added Linnea to the call. It rang and rang. I called her again. This time, she answered groggily.

"Tess?" she said. "Is everything okay?"

"Tell me you're not with Henrik," I said.

"It's bad luck to see the bride on the day of the wedding. Oh my god. I'm getting married today."

"Or not," Kitty said.

"Look in the mirror, Linnea," I said.

A pause.

"Oh" was all she said.

And then we all went silent, all three of us. I wondered how many times we had cumulatively been told this was our destiny. I wondered how everyone had known, like they had seen this story before, like they already knew the ending—the way I had always known, on some level, that I would end up accidentally killing Soren.

When my reflection stared back at me, it didn't feel so much like my face had been altered as I slept, but rather like a lie had been scrubbed away to reveal the truth of what had lain underneath.

This was how the story always went.

Stanford

2014

When I showed up for International Student Orientation, I was given a key to a room with two small mattresses wrapped in blue nylon. To orient us, they told us important cultural things, like that Americans took lines very seriously, and if you cut them at the waffle station, they would hunt you down and murder your family. There was only one other international student on my hall, and for the first few days, we were the only ones there. His name was Samir. We met in the hallway on the way to the bathrooms, both of us holding toothbrushes.

He said hi. I said hi.

"Are you enjoying learning how to stand in line?" he asked.

"I'm more intrigued by the waffle station, to be honest."

He told me his name, and I told him mine, and then he asked where I was from, which seemed like more of a formality than an actual question because it said where I was from on the piece of paper the RAs had taped to my door.

"Stenland," I said. "You?"

"My mum's Jordanian," he said. "My dad's Brazilian. I grew up in Quebec. Complicated, but whose life isn't?"

"My mum's Stennish. My dad's Stennish. I grew up in Stenland."

"I suppose that's not very complicated," he conceded. "Which one's Stenland again?"

"East of the Faroe Islands, north of Shetland."

"Near Norway?"

"West of that."

"So…middle of nowhere?"

I nodded.

"Is it the one with the whale hunts or the one with the stone disease?" Samir asked.

"The latter."

He whistled. It was a nice sound. He was a nice-looking person, all thick hair and dimples when he smiled. His build was like Henrik's, that of someone who lifted up a lot of heavy things and set them down again. He wasn't Soren; I reminded myself this was a good thing and not a bad one.

We made plans to get dinner together that night; I put my number in his phone, and he texted me right away with a smiley face. When I saw the shape of his name on my screen, I thought, for a second, it was *Soren*. For the rest of the time I would know Samir, every time he texted me, I would look at my screen out of the corner of my eye and think it said *Soren*.

The American students poured in a few days later. Flustered parents wore red hoodies. RAs offered to help unpack IKEA lamps with fanatical intensity. I met my roommate, Bianca. She was from DC, and everything she owned was yellow.

We were all so squished together that I fell into step with the rest of my dorm without really thinking about it. Samir and I went swimming at the pool. Bianca helped me choose classes. In the early mornings, when it was afternoon for Kitty and Linnea, I'd call them and show them around campus with my phone camera. On account of her hatred of calls, Kitty only sometimes picked up, but when she did, I felt the knot in my chest loosen like a hand unclenching.

"And this is another palm tree," I'd say, panning my camera. "And this is a fountain, but there's no water in it because we're in a drought."

"It feels like you're a million miles away," Linnea said.

"And a million miles closer to the sun," Kitty said. "Your video gives me a headache."

The campus left me with the sensation that I'd accidentally stumbled out of one genre and into another. I wasn't used to the color palette, all red roofs and dusty earth and azure sky. I wasn't used to the smell of eucalyptus trees and freshly mown grass. Even the speed of the world seemed to shift, though I couldn't tell if it was going faster or slower. Maybe the world was going faster, but I was moving through it more slowly. I got it in my head that I would feel normal again as soon as it rained, but it never did. It was never even cloudy. If you had a sunstone here, you'd never need to use it.

I declared a mechanical engineering major in my second month. My academic advisor told me it was quite early, and wouldn't I rather explore my options? I said no thanks.

For Christmas, my dad tried to convince me to come home, but now that I was gone, I was positive, absolutely certain that I would become a skeld the moment I went back. I told him the plane ticket was too expensive.

One of the local students from my hall, a guy named Damian, told me I could crash in his guest house while the dorms were closed, no sweat. It was roughly the size of Kitty's home.

I wondered if there was any way to sufficiently thank his parents for having me and concluded there was not. To be unobtrusive, I spent the break doing math problems from the next quarter's textbooks. When that started to make my head hurt, I read winding fantasy sagas and watched nature documentaries on the guest house TV. Sometimes I'd go for walks in a December air so warm I didn't need a jacket and listen to podcasts about global affairs, reminding myself that the world was wider than Stenland.

On Christmas, when my phone lit up with a new text, my heart exploded into a thousand tiny pieces. It was Samir asking if Damian's house was as posh as rumors would lead him to believe. I put my phone in a drawer and didn't let myself look at it for the rest of the day.

As the end of the academic year crept closer, my dad started asking me to come home again. I frantically applied for jobs until I had one, as a lifeguard and swim instructor at a summer camp at Lake Tahoe. My dad congratulated me and said, "This Christmas, though?"

I was beginning to wonder if I could go my entire life without going back.

By May, Damian had decided my dating life was getting tragic and that he would set me up with someone as a present. I was at dinner with him and Bianca at the time.

"I don't think I want to be set up with someone," I said.

"Sure you do!" Damian said. "It'll be fun."

We were eating burrito bowls that had one uniform flavor despite containing seventeen ingredients. Our table was a sticky diner-style booth. Every few minutes, a group of people we knew would pass, some dressed for studying, some dressed for going out. We were dressed for going out already; I'd been informed we would be going to the Row and attending a frat party at one of the houses some of our dormmates had joined.

I had also been informed that staying in my room doing math was not an option.

"Mmm," I said.

"Come on. How long has it been since you got laid?"

Bianca swatted Damian on the chest. "Don't be reductive."

He frowned like he was thinking. "Is it reductive, really, or just indelicate?"

"Soren was eons ago," Bianca said. "It doesn't seem like the worst thing to get back out there."

Hearing her say his name made me feel ill. I pushed away my burrito bowl.

Something I'd learned quickly upon my arrival was that one's sexual history was a seemingly inexhaustible mine of gossip and conversational value. Everyone had dug through everyone's social media, and I had been informed that Soren was "actually pretty hot, especially if he got a better haircut." Even though none of these people had ever met him, it elevated my standing among them that he had deemed me worthy. Everyone constantly tried to outdo everyone else's exploits while pretending they weren't actually that titillated by the competition.

In my first week, in a game of Never Have I Ever, the first thing out of Damian's mouth had been, *Never have I ever been caught fucking in my car in a parking lot by a mall cop.*

Half the people I'd been sitting with had clapped their hands and put a finger down, and I must've looked confused because someone had turned to me and very sympathetically said, *Have you never had sex?*

I'd said, *I've never been to a mall.*

There was a strange tension to the whole thing because everyone spoke rather exhaustingly about how having a lot of sex or a bit of sex or no sex at all were equally great choices. Spunky RAs threw condoms at us but also reminded us that abstinence was neat too, if that was what we were into. For all their insistence that none of it mattered, everyone seemed to care a lot.

And I didn't hate being asked about it. Because it gave me an excuse to talk about Soren. To show off a picture so I could be told he was actually pretty hot. If I was feeling boring and tame for spending so much time doing homework, I could casually mention that we'd once had sex in a sixteenth-century tower. If I was feeling bitter, I could rehash the story of our breakup in exacting detail. At the end, someone would say, *He just expected you to throw your whole life away to stay there? What a dick.*

Even when I said terrible things about Soren, I always liked saying them. Because it was the only thing I still had of him, and it was the only thing I still had of the version of me I was with him.

"He hasn't texted you, has he?" Damian asked. "Classic ex thing to do. Text you right when you're getting over them."

"No," I said. "He hasn't texted me."

"And thank god for that," Bianca said. "I still can't believe that bastard wanted you to just stay there for him."

"Thanks, Bianca."

"You're welcome. Let's get drunk."

The floor of the frat was so sticky it felt like my shoes were suction-cupped to the tile. Over the speakers, the bass thumped loudly enough that you couldn't hear other parts of the song. I thought of how excited Lukas had been about the prospect of American frat parties. If I saw him again, I would explain the rules to rage cage.

I was wearing a thin black dress and white tennis shoes that probably wouldn't be white much longer. Outside, it was too cold, but as soon as I stepped inside, it was too hot. Bianca handed me a beer of unknown origin, and Damian made a beeline for our most attractive RA, who would be allowed to date members of our dorm at year's end.

A hand reached through the crowd and grabbed me. I startled, but then relaxed again when I found myself chest to chest with Samir.

"That's a great dress!" he shouted into my ear.

I nodded my thanks.

"How's the night going?"

I gave him a thumbs-up.

"You really don't say that much, do you?"

I laughed and yelled, "It's just loud," and he said something to that, but I couldn't make out what and didn't ask him to repeat himself.

People kept jostling me from behind, and every time Samir and I got pressed closer, we didn't move apart again. He was sweaty and I was sweaty and the music was too loud to think over. I felt, in my stomach, some of that old want that had felt so big I thought it would consume me. When I kissed him, he kissed me back.

At some point he started shouting about whether or not I wanted to go back to the dorm, and I shouted that I did. The walk back wasn't as cold as the walk out had been. We got to our hall, and he asked if I wanted to go to his room. I said yes again. On his bed, we started kissing, and he asked if I wanted to have sex, so I said yes a third time and he went to lock the door and text his roommate to go get some mozzarella sticks at Late Night for a while.

I lay back on his pillows, and he climbed on top of me, his dark hair a wave off his forehead.

"These are nice pillowcases," I said.

"I think they're bamboo."

"Ah. Sustainable."

"You know what they say. Nothing sexier than sustainable home goods."

He took off his own shirt. This might not have been weird in the abstract, but I'd always taken off Soren's clothing and he'd always taken off mine, so it struck me as transactional and presumptive to remove your own. Just to be fair, I took off my dress.

Objectively, Samir was probably better at sex than Soren. He did things that felt good, and he kept asking what I liked. I kept saying, "That's great." It seemed to last a long time, which literature had taught me to believe meant it was good, but mostly I felt tired. When it was done, I didn't feel an insatiable pit of want, but I wasn't sure I felt satisfied either. He didn't kiss my temple.

"That was fun," he said.

"Yeah," I said. "Same."

"See you in line for waffles tomorrow?"

"I'll try not to cut."

I gathered up my dress and shoes and went to take a shower. I had a feeling the two of us wouldn't do that again, Samir and me. In the hot water, I stared at the tile and let my arms hang by my sides.

I didn't know why I would feel like I belonged to Soren less after sleeping with someone else, since I'd never felt like having sex made me his. But I felt further from him now, more my own person, less his girlfriend, less someone who was hoping he would change his mind. *I have now had sex with two people.* I wondered, in this place where that seemed to be such a valuable currency, if this in turn made me a more interesting person.

The hot water never ran out. It just went and went and went. I felt so much better. I felt so much worse.

August

2016

I met August at the start of my third year; at the time, I was swimming at the outdoor pool. There was still something novel about that, a pool with no roof, and even though I didn't swim particularly fast anymore, I did swim most mornings. I cut through the water, bright ultramarine in the shattering sunlight, swimming backstroke until I saw the red-and-white flags bobbing overhead. On one side of the pool, there was a gym with windows behind which students played basketball and ellipticaled. On the other side of the pool, a grassy hill rose toward the street. People on towels, at least one of whom appeared to be reading a Java textbook, lay on the grass in swimsuits.

Bianca thought swimming was just protracted drowning, but she came to the pool with me a few times a month anyway. When I reached the end of my set and looked for her, I saw her sitting in the grass, shading her face with a paperback as she spoke to a guy in pastel shorts.

I pulled off my cap and goggles and wrapped my towel around myself before going to join them.

Bianca looked up at the guy. “Have you two met?”

He was considering me intently. His eyelashes were dark and his eyes jarringly blue. A square jaw tapered to a square chin. On the curve of symmetricalness, he was beyond attractive and into the uncanny valley. There was something immediately intimidating about him, but I wasn’t sure if it was his build—tall and muscular—or his clothes—sharp and fitted in a way that made his parents’ socioeconomic status abundantly clear.

“I don’t think we have,” he said.

I offered the hand that wasn’t holding my cap and goggles. “Tess.”

He shook. “August.”

“Tess is my roommate,” Bianca said. “August is poli-sci with me.”

“I was just on my way to brunch,” he said. “You two want to join?”

Over pancakes (me) and omelets (August and Bianca), I learned that August was from Connecticut and had two older brothers. I asked if their names were June and July. He said, “Connor and Thomas, actually,” and without meaning to or stopping to consider, I found myself saying, “I had a friend named Thomas who got turned to stone.”

“What the fuck, Tess!” Bianca said. “You never thought to mention that?”

I shrugged and ate my pancake and wished I hadn’t spoken.

“But, like, are you okay?” Bianca pressed.

“I left, didn’t I?” I said, which I thought was a fair answer but didn’t seem to make her happy.

“My uncle actually died that way,” August said, so casually it took me a prolonged moment to process what he'd said. When I did, I frowned at him, a bit of pancake halfway to my mouth.

"What?"

"My uncle," August repeated. "He went to Stenland on a trip just before I was born and got turned to stone. That's where you're from, right? Stenland?"

I nodded.

"Sounds like a crazy place," August said, then went back to eating his omelet.

To Bianca, I said, "Did you know about this?"

She just shrugged and shot me a knowing look, though what she knew was unclear. It seemed impossible that someone else whose life had been touched by a skeld could cross my path accidentally. Surely Bianca must've set up this meeting for us, or maybe August knew who I was all along and sought me out. When it seemed like neither of those things were the case, I told myself that it was fate.

"Damian's been saying for years that he should do a documentary on Stenland," Bianca said.

"Really?" August asked.

"No," I said.

"That's what she always says."

Flatly, I told Bianca I would rather die. If August found this abrupt and off-putting, he got over it quickly. He asked me if I wanted to go on a date while we were bussing our plates. I hadn't gone on any dates at school, though over the course of my sophomore year and the first month of junior year, I'd slept with two other men, which had been fine, and one woman, which had been both more and less terrifying than the men. Less because she'd been funny and relaxed. More because I'd had no idea what I was doing. Though I'd considered asking all three of these people if they wanted to go on dates, I had a fear that I would no longer find them attractive the moment I was committed to them.

I told August I'd think about it.

Linnea video called me a few hours later. I was alone in my room working on a problem set. Through my window, I could see people playing beer pong on a lawn. I answered the call, and Linnea's face filled my screen.

"Tess!"

"Linnie."

"What are you doing? Are you doing maths again? Is that all you ever do?"

"Yes," I said. "Where are you?" It was loud behind her, and her cheeks were flushed.

"Huh? Oh, my house. It's Saffi's birthday." She panned the camera around, but I caught only flashes—bodies without faces, voices without names. "She's eighteen. Isn't that weird? It makes me feel decrepit."

I set down my pencil and tucked my feet up on my chair, wrapping an arm around my knees. "How are you?"

"I am medium. Kitty hasn't been answering my calls."

"Has Kitty ever answered calls?"

"She hasn't been answering my texts either. I think—oh my god. Someone is eating my rosemary plant. I'll be right back. Henrik, take Tess."

I had the sense of being jostled as the party flashed around me again. My room felt very quiet, very warm and still in comparison.

Henrik stared down at me from an unflattering below-the-chin angle. "Oh, hi Tess!"

He'd started growing a beard, I noticed. It was reddish, which surprised me because his hair was dark blond.

"How are the cars?" I asked.

"They're good. Your dad is good. I replaced a transmission today. You'll be going to watch the Grand Prix in person next week?"

"It's in Texas," I said. "Too far away. I'll stream it, though."

"Go Lewis," Henrik said.

"Go Lewis," I agreed.

"Hey, sorry, I gotta pee. Here—I'll be right back."

The party swirled around me again. A familiar voice said, "Hey, don't—"

And then I was looking at Soren.

Two years and one month.

"Hi, Tess," he said softly.

His eyes really were such a pale blue they looked gray; whose eyes were gray? I'd forgotten they actually looked like that, that it wasn't just something I'd invented in retrospect.

"You cut your hair," I said. It wasn't lumpy anymore. Shorter on the sides now, which made it a shade darker. He looked older; I supposed that he was.

"So did you," he said.

I touched the ends of my hair. It went to my collarbones now, but the last time he'd seen me, it had been down to my ribs. Kitty and I had gotten the same haircut on the same day, via FaceTime, and now Linnea was the only one left with long hair.

"It's really nice," Soren said.

We stared at each other for longer than two friends would stare at each other, longer even than two people who were dating would have any cause to stare at each other. My stomach was weightless inside me like I'd just stepped off the edge of something high. I told myself it was nostalgia, that a pixelated version of him in a screen could make me feel more want and hurt and love and loneliness than anyone who had touched me in the past two years and one month.

"How are things?" I asked.

He nodded, which I took to mean *Good.* "Lukas misses you."

"I heard he didn't get into any American universities."

"I know you read his essays," Soren said. "Thanks for that, by the way. It meant a lot to him."

"Sorry I couldn't do more."

He shrugged. "Linnea said you're studying cars?"

I smiled faintly at that. "Mechanical engineering."

Usually, when I talked to someone on a video call, I could see their eyes on the corner of their screen, watching themselves the whole time. I didn't mind because I did it too. But with Soren, it felt like he was looking right at me.

"That makes me happy," he said.

"Are you still doing Stennish studies?" I asked.

"Slowly but surely. I—really love it."

Want and hurt and love and loneliness. "That's great," I said quietly.

Someone jostled him out of frame, and he turned a smile on whoever it was. They were saying his name, tugging at his arm, and he was still smiling as he gently detached himself. The camera tilted, and I felt a jolt on seeing a pale face and long hair that I thought, at first, belonged to Linnea. But no—it was her sister, Saffi, so much more adult and so much more beautiful than the last time I'd seen her. It wasn't fair to be jealous.

When Soren looked back at me again, I heard myself saying, "So, are you seeing anyone these days?"

His smile faltered. "Ah," he said. "Yeah. She's— You don't know her. She's Canadian. She was just backpacking through for a week but really liked it here, so she applied for Stennish studies." When I didn't say anything, he added, "Her name's Abigail."

It didn't surprise me that Soren would fall in love with someone who would fight to live in Stenland instead of to escape it. I was sure it was a good match. Better than the two of us anyway.

"She sounds great," I said, but I didn't sound like I meant it.

"What about you?" he asked.

I rubbed the corner of my desk. There was an ink mark there from where I'd chewed the top off a pen last week. "Actually," I said, "I have a date tonight."

The phone got passed back to Henrik, and then it got passed back to Linnea, and I chatted with them for as long as I could bear, which was only about ten minutes. When I was done, I found August on Facebook and sent him a message.

Me: I'm done thinking about it. Dinner tonight?

He responded right away.

August: Tonight? Mmm

August: Let me check my calendar

August: Okay. For you, I'm free

Me: Off campus somewhere?

August: I'll make a reservation. 7?

Me: Where?

August: It's a surprise

Me: No, tell me

Me: So I know how to dress and whether my bank account will start crying

August: Nah my treat

August: It's a surprise :)

August: I'm sure you'll look beautiful

Me: Seriously, where are we going?

August: :)

I ran my hands through my hair. It was still sticky with chlorine. I'd meant to shower after swimming, but I hadn't had time before we'd gone to brunch.

A surprise restaurant. I didn't like surprises. I also didn't know if I liked being treated to dinner, but I told myself that if he wasn't going to let me have a say in where we were going to eat, it was his fault if he ended up paying a very large bill.

Before I could think better of it, I typed Soren's name into my phone. The last time he had texted me was the day of my going away party. He was asking if he should bring my mum a book to make her like him. It made my heart feel numb to look at it, so I tried not to.

Me: For what it's worth

Me: I really am happy you love Stennish studies

Unlike August, Soren didn't respond right away. He had on read receipts, probably because read receipts were the final word in letting someone know your lack of a response was the response. He read the message. Did not write back. I set my phone face down and tried not to look at it again. About an hour before my date, as I was trying to put on eyeliner and wishing Kitty were there, it buzzed. I told myself it was August, but when I flipped it over, I saw Soren's name, and for the first time in a long time, it actually was Soren's name.

Soren: For what it's worth

Soren: It was really nice talking to you

It was two in the morning in Stenland. I wondered if he was back home now or with our friends still or at Abigail's house. I wondered if he was imagining me getting ready for my date and hating that it was not with him.

I almost responded, but I left him on read instead.

Nostos

2017

"I just think," August was saying, "that there's not much point in studying abroad when your whole college experience is already abroad."

"I've been promising Kitty I'd do a quarter in Oxford since freshman year."

"Yeah, well, if Kitty was really your friend, she'd understand."

"I've already bought my plane ticket."

He made a dismissive sound that implied *Yes, and I could buy you a different one.*

When August had invited me to spend spring break with his family on a boat in the Caribbean, I'd told him thanks, but I'd probably just head to England early. The next day, he'd slipped a plane ticket to Martinique under my door. I'd found it when I'd been going to brush my teeth. Damian had said, "Damn, he spoils you."

The Van Andel family boat was not actually a boat. It was a yacht, or perhaps a compact hotel, and it was called *Serena.* There were enough bedrooms for Mr. and Mrs. Van Andel, who did not invite me to call them by their first names, and for all three Van Andel brothers and their girlfriends. Connor, the oldest brother, was dating a woman named Samantha. Connor was stocky and did coke in the bathroom and worked on Wall Street. Samantha had wrists so slender that the hair ties she kept there slid around freely. August's middle brother, Thomas, had declined to come because he was in a feud with his father over his decision to pursue a career in DJing.

At present, Connor and Samantha were lying on deck chairs on the other side of the boat while also answering work emails for their respective and vague business jobs. Mr. and Mrs. Van Andel had retreated to argue, which they only did in private. That left August and me standing by the railing as the sun began to drown in a bath of crimson light. I was wearing sandals that didn't quite fit and a white dress that twisted around my calves in the warm breeze.

"But spring quarter's the best time to be on campus," August said. "You'll miss everything."

"I promised Kitty."

He leaned against the railing. "Well, then, maybe I should come to Oxford with you."

"The deadline already passed."

"No need to sound panicked. I was just suggesting things." August kissed me once on the corner of my lips to let me know he wasn't actually angry—he never was—before going to talk to Connor and Samantha. I waited for him to turn the corner.

Then I took a picture of the ocean and sent it to Soren.

Even though it was late in Stenland, my phone buzzed within a few seconds.

Soren: How's yachting?

Me: Like a cross between Moby Dick and Gatsby

Soren: In that Mum Van Andel has a peg leg and Dad Van Andel is making gin in the bathtub?

Me: In that it's a waste of resources

Soren: Hey

Soren: I like Moby Dick

Me: No one likes Moby Dick

Soren: I do

Soren: It has a lot of dick jokes

Soren: I like being reminded that people in the 1800s were just like us

Me: Did they also lie about which books they liked?

For the past six months, Soren and I had texted each other almost every day. It was a combative conversational style; sometimes I lay in bed playing through fictional conversations in which I was so exceptionally clever he conceded defeat. If he'd ever done that in real life, I would've been disappointed.

I told myself it wasn't flirting because we never mentioned anything like feelings for each other, and also because we would quite possibly never see each other again. But I also knew it was not the way I texted Kitty and Linnea. I imagined it was not the way Soren texted anyone else either because there wasn't enough time in the day.

Me: How's Abigail?

This earned me a pause. Sometimes I wondered if we inflicted punishments on each other for asking questions we didn't want to answer. The long gap between replies. The stiff response when you'd been searching for banter. We both did it, and it had begun to feel like its own sort of grammar. When he employed a tactic that made me feel particularly outplayed, I would file it away for my own future use.

Soren: She says hi

Like that.

Me: Ask her if she thinks you actually like Moby Dick

Another pause.

Soren: How's August?

I put my phone away so he had to use his imagination.

We ate dinner on the upper deck of the boat that was too big to be a boat. Dinner with the Van Andel parents should've been difficult because I had approximately zero things in common with them, but it was actually tremendously easy so long as I didn't try to be myself. I imagined I was playing a character in a period-piece drama and behaved accordingly. Mr. and Mrs. Van Andel rarely spoke to Samantha or me, so we just took dainty bites of our food and sat with good posture.

I was debating slipping off to the bathroom to see if I had another text from Soren even though he was almost surely asleep already when Mr. Van Andel asked August if he'd heard back from their "mutual friend" about the DNC internship yet.

"Not yet," August said. "Any day now, I'm sure."

Mr. Van Andel said, "Sure, sure—just let me know if you need me to send an email."

August looked faintly embarrassed by that, so he said, "Tess, have you heard back from anywhere yet?"

I had applied to twenty-four internships. Anything that had anything to do with cars. "Not yet."

"I'm sure you will," Mr. Van Andel said. "Companies are starving for female engineers."

"And Tess is a great candidate," August said. Under the table, he squeezed my knee.

"Did you apply for anything back in Scotland?" Connor asked.

"Stenland, actually," I said.

"Yeah, but isn't Stenland part of Scotland?"

"That's Shetland."

"Stenland's part of Shetland?"

I smiled as serenely as possible. "Shetland is part of Scotland. Stenland is independent as of 1921."

"Ah," Connor said. "What do you speak?"

Samantha gave Connor a look that said *Please stop*, but he didn't seem to notice.

"English," I said.

"Like, what did you grow up speaking?"

"Yeah," I said, "English."

August interjected smoothly: "I've been saying for years that we should do a documentary on Stenland. You know my friend Damian? He's studying film? We think it'd be amazing.

Everything about skelds, the isolation of the island, the declining opportunities in rural communities..."

My throat felt tight. The only reason I didn't tell August that his idea made me feel voyeured was because of his uncle, the one who died by a skeld.

With a note of finality, Connor said, "Well, I'd love to go someday."

There was a brief pause; a scraping of a fork against a plate that made Mrs. Van Andel wince. It seemed like I needed to apologize for my country somehow.

"I was sorry to hear about your uncle's time in Stenland," I said to Connor.

He pursed his lips at August. I assumed the look was meant to chastise August for revealing family secrets. I looked at my lap and went back to not speaking.

The bedroom August and I were sharing had a nautical theme, should you forget you were on a boat. The ceiling was about three-quarters the height of a normal ceiling, so you couldn't raise your hands over your head when you got changed. It made me feel like I was in a very expensive coffin.

I was lying in bed with a book when August looked over at me.

"What are you reading?"

I showed him the cover.

"In the Wake of Their Passing," he said. "That sounds uplifting."

"My mum really liked it. I've been meaning to read it for ages."

"What's it about?"

"Sad people," I said.

"Do you want to have sex?"

I closed the book and set it on the bedside table. "How thin are the walls?"

"Not very."

I considered him. His rectangular face and his Ken-doll smooth skin. He was wearing a silky pajama shirt, which I thought was the least arousing article of clothing any man had ever donned. I didn't tell him this because he already thought I made fun of him for being wealthy.

"Do you think your parents like me?" I asked.

"Of course. They love you."

"What would they love about me?" I said.

"You're beautiful and brilliant and charming."

"Name a single beautiful or brilliant or charming thing I have done since getting on this boat."

August shook his head. "Why are you being so hard on yourself?"

This was the moment I realized I did not find myself beautiful or brilliant or charming, though perhaps I had at some point in the past. My period-piece character was a docile automaton shell whose skin I inhabited. The most interesting thing about me with the Van Andels was that I was playing a game of not being myself, and they didn't even know I was doing it.

August propped himself up on an elbow. "I think they're just protective of me. Because, you know, Val."

"Your high school girlfriend?"

"Yeah," he said. "Since she cheated on me."

"You never said she cheated on you." My tone should've been sympathetic and comforting. Instead, it came out accusatory. August was always saying things like that, saying things that should've been important, but that he mentioned breezily. *My mom actually had breast cancer when I was a kid. I got kidnapped on vacation in Italy when I was ten. I was going to go to a ski academy for high school, but I shattered my knee in eighth grade.* There were times when I found myself thinking that August was the most boring person I'd ever met because as far as I could tell, he didn't read, didn't do a sport, and didn't work all that hard.

And then he would say something like that, and I would realize I only saw fragments of his giant life. I convinced myself it was my fault. That I wasn't very good at asking questions. That I didn't make him feel safe. Besides, it wasn't as if I told him everything about my life either.

"Yeah, well," August said. "I caught her with my best friend. Wouldn't recommend the experience, if you're considering it."

"I'm sorry. That's awful."

"If only there was a way to help me forget about my deep emotional wounds."

"How thin are the walls again?"

"They're actually concrete. Really thick concrete."

August had very nice abs. He took off his shirt, and I admired them. When we had sex, I felt myself stepping inside a different character, this one not my period-piece lady, but my action-film femme fatale. She flipped her hair a lot. Despite being very tough and competent, she gasped dramatically like this whole sex thing was rather startling to her. Right before August came, he told me he loved me. The femme fatale said it back.

As soon as he was done, I went to the bathroom and peed.

"Is it nice to be in a place where you can actually go to sleep next to someone?" he asked when I got back. He really was handsome; there was no taking that away. I wondered what he'd look like when he was fifty. I wondered what I'd look like. I wondered if we'd have three sons who also went to Stanford and wore pastel shorts.

"It's great," I said.

Every night on the boat, I woke up at three in the morning and couldn't fall back asleep. I went outside in my pajamas and stared at the black ocean. You could jump over the railing and just start swimming. How far to Stenland? How many thousands of miles?

In honor of being on a boat, Samantha had been reading a retelling of *The Odyssey*. She'd mentioned to me, while we'd passed each other in the kitchen, that she had always thought *nostalgia* meant fond memory, but actually, in the Greek sense, it meant suffering because you so badly wanted to return home. I'd asked her, defensively, why she was telling me. She'd said, *Okay, fine, never mind.*

Static started to fill my ears. I sat down on the deck and pressed my face against the white painted bars of the railing.

What kind of person would miss a place like that.

Oxford

2017

When Kitty met me at the airport, she screamed.

I had planned something dignified and cute. Perhaps she had too. Instead, she screamed and I started crying and dropped my suitcases and we flung our arms around each other.

"You're here!" she said. "You're here, you're here, and we're going to do whatever it is people want to do when they visit England, like eat fish and chips or see those men with the stupid tall hats because you're here and I love you and you're never allowed to leave me again."

Kitty gave me an abridged and entirely inaccurate tour of London as we swept through the city. "Piccadilly Circus really *is* a circus, you know, but only on leap years when there's a full moon out. And you'll want to see Paddington Station, obviously, since it's named after the UK's first ursine prime minister."

When we got to Oxford, she started reeling off a list of

restaurants at which we could eat, and I told her it had to be a pub.

"A pub!" she said. "A pub!"

"Palo Alto doesn't do pubs," I said.

"Perhaps Palo Alto is onto something."

"I just want to order a pie and be brought something with meat instead of apples."

"A pub. You are very lucky I love you."

"I know."

For the past few months, Kitty had been dating a fellow economics student named Georgia. I'd met her on FaceTime before, but dinner at the pub was the first I'd seen her in person. She was about a thousand feet tall, with olive-toned skin and curly hair and all black clothes. She surprised me as a match for Kitty, not because they didn't suit each other but because she was so not like Linnea. At dinner, Georgia leaned back in her chair with her arms crossed and looked endlessly amused by Kitty. Every time she spoke, I marveled at her accent, which was the poshest I'd ever heard. I asked how they'd met, and Georgia told me she'd struck up a conversation in class with Kitty about cycling, to which Kitty had replied that she was an avid cyclist. Georgia had invited her to cycle to Aston, a couple hours away, and Kitty had showed up on a cruiser bike with no gears.

"I cycled quite convincingly," Kitty told me.

"She didn't," Georgia said. "We made it to the edge of town, and I asked if she wanted a coffee instead."

"And conveniently enough, I did want a coffee."

Georgia sipped her beer, looking pleased, then said, "Kitty tells me you're dating an absolute dick."

"Georgia!" Kitty said. "We were supposed to ease into that. Over many weeks and with soothing tea."

I waited for myself to feel offended on August's behalf. It didn't happen. It felt like I was hearing about someone else's boyfriend—maybe the boyfriend of that action-film femme fatale.

"It's not that I think he's a dick," Kitty said. "Here, eat more of my chips. It's just—you never seem particularly excited about him when we talk, and he seems kind of manipulative when—"

"He's not manipulative," I said, surprised. It was hard for me to imagine August manipulating me into doing anything; it was hard for me to imagine him even having an opinion. "I actually think he adores me, for whatever reason."

"Because you're adorable," Kitty said.

My phone buzzed, and I glanced down at it under the table. I smiled before I could stop myself.

"See," Kitty said to Georgia. "He can't be terrible if he makes her happy. What did he say?"

I cleared my throat. "'How's Kitty doing?'"

"Oh, he remembers me. That's sweet."

"'Tell her,'" I read, "'she still has my copy of *Beowulf*.'"

"No!" Kitty said.

"You lent August a copy of *Beowulf*?" Georgia asked. "I can't say I see the point in owning one, except to tell people you do. He really does seem like a dick."

"She's not texting August," Kitty said, giving me an evil look. "She's texting Soren."

Georgia looked mildly intrigued. "Soren your cousin?"

"Soren her ex."

"Small towns seem amusing," Georgia said.

"Since when do you text Soren, Tess? Care to share with the class?"

"Anyone want another beer?" I asked.

As I left, Kitty called after me, "We're not done talking about this! And get me a cider!"

At the bar, I ordered three more drinks. While I waited for them, I took my phone out of my pocket again.

Me: Kitty's girlfriend thinks you're smug for reading Beowulf

Soren: "We are the companions of Hygelac; Smug is my name"

Me: Why would you assume I would understand that reference

Me: If you have passages of Beowulf memorized, I don't want to talk to you anymore

Soren: I may have done a quick google

Me: This disappoints me somehow

Soren: It's weird that we're in the same time zone

Me: Yeah

Me: Not far at all

When he didn't respond to that, I pictured him looking at airfare prices, then told myself to stop. As penance, I texted August.

Me: Meeting Kitty's girlfriend!

August: Aw

August: I am sure she will love my sweet girl <3

I put my phone away again, feeling off-kilter in a way I hadn't since my plane had touched down.

Academically, my quarter at Oxford was harder than anything I'd yet done at Stanford. I made the mistake of sharing this with Kitty, who proceeded to bring it up to everyone we met for the rest of the term.

My scholastic performance was not helped by the fact that I became suddenly and inexplicably extroverted in the third week of my stay. It was like a switch flipped on a circuit board. Georgia invited me to a house-warming party a few of her school friends were having; I surprised myself by saying yes. I surprised myself further by going out the four subsequent nights as well.

It rained all the time. My mum showed up unannounced on three occasions. Stenland was just one plane ride away. It was, in short, everything I had wanted to avoid when I'd gone off to college.

August was supposed to visit me halfway through the quarter and then again when classes ended. He had to cancel the first visit because he was supposed to go meet someone important about his upcoming internship with the DNC. When he told me he wouldn't be coming, he had a bouquet of two dozen red roses delivered. There was some sort of mix-up, so they ended up going to the guy across the hall from me instead, another Stanford student studying abroad. Noah. When he knocked on my door with headphones around his neck and the massive bouquet in his hands, I said, "I didn't know you felt this way."

Noah handed me the bouquet. "Devastated to realize these weren't for me."

The note that came with them said *We'll be together before you know it. Romantic weekend in Paris? Love with all my heart, A.*

"You can keep them, if you want," I said.

He looked uncertain. "That seems weird."

"Yeah," I said. "I guess."

I probably didn't put them in enough water because they started to rot right away. The petals fell and got trapped behind my desk and made my room smell like musty potpourri.

August was going to show up on my last day and whisk me

around Europe for the week before his internship started. It was unclear what I was going to do after that. Of the internships I'd applied for, only one had bothered to interview me before saying they'd chosen another candidate. A few had sent form rejections. What I really wanted was a place at a Formula One team, but none of them responded to me. When I told August about this over FaceTime, he said, "Oh, I think one of Connor's friends ended up at one of those teams. Someone from his frat, maybe? I'll make a call."

The thought of August getting me a job was the most horrifying suggestion I could imagine, though I couldn't have said why. "Please don't."

"This is how people get internships. I forget you don't know how all this works."

"Seriously," I said. "Don't."

"It's one call. It's really no sweat."

"I will break up with you," I said, and I found that I meant it.

A pause. "Jesus. Sorry for trying to help."

The end of the term came barreling toward us, and I still had no internship. I had drunk my weight in lager; I had learned how to ride a bike with clip-in pedals, courtesy of Georgia; I had spent nearly every night eating chips and doing readings with Kitty, whose friendship, it turned out, was not something I had ever come close to replicating in college. And yet.

Outside, the spring weather was tantalizing and the lawns were that deep shade of green California could never imitate. We were at a table in the library, Kitty and me, ostensibly working on our final projects, though Kitty seemed to be spending most of her time online shopping for the trip to Greece she had planned with Georgia. I'd assumed she was still looking at sundresses when she said, "Didn't you say August's uncle was killed by a skeld just before he was born?"

"Yes?"

She turned her laptop toward me. There was an Excel spreadsheet on it with dates and numbers, none of which meant anything to me. I shook my head blankly.

"My project," she said. "I'm looking at the economic impact of skeld seasons. Like, does being in the news drive tourism up or scare people away."

"And?"

She pointed at the 1996 column. "No one got killed by a skeld in ninety-six."

"Well, maybe it happened earlier than that. He didn't say exactly when."

"I don't think any tourists got killed by skelds in the nineties. A few locals. Some keepers, two husbands. I mean, I can pull up the names, but..."

I stared at the screen with a rising sense of déjà vu, as if I was being told something someone had already told me. When I texted August asking if he could remind me what had happened to his uncle, he didn't respond for two hours. When he finally did respond, Kitty and I were leaving the library.

August: Wow

August: I know you didn't mean it that way, but that's a kind of crass way to ask about a family tragedy

Once, when I'd been ten or so, my dad had taken me camping. We'd bought a brand-new tent. It had been packed into this tiny little bag, and when we'd tried to put it away again, we couldn't do it. It was like the fabric had expanded overnight, all the poles growing longer and more unwieldy.

As I picked through memories of conversations with August, that was what it felt like. Like once I'd taken them out and examined them, I could no longer stuff them back where they'd been hidden.

I found myself googling his name with every variety of

story tacked onto it. August van Andel ski results. August van Andel kidnapping. Van Andel skeld. I found nothing and nothing and nothing, and I kept scrolling.

Me: Did your uncle actually get killed by a skeld?

August: Tess

August: Come on

August: What are you even accusing me of?

Me: Did your uncle actually get killed by a skeld?

August: Okay, I think you need some time to calm down

August: I'll see you in a few days

August: I still love you, you know that

"Dump him," Georgia said.

"What if he's telling the truth?"

We were in the same pub Kitty had taken me on my first day in Oxford. The waitstaff knew us now; they brought me my beer without asking my order.

"Oh my god," Kitty said. "He's not telling the truth. You know in your gut that he is a slimy little weasel liar, and you've known it all along. Dump. Him."

"I don't want him to be lying," I said.

"Why not?" Kitty demanded.

I leaned against the window. It was cool against my forehead. "Because then I'm an idiot."

When my phone buzzed, I was certain it would be August, and I was certain he would say something apologetic and believable and confusing. When I saw it was Soren, I felt like I had just been pushed out of the path of a train and wrapped in something warm. It didn't even matter what the message said; I couldn't remember what we'd been talking about. Nothing important. What was important was that I had tried to convince myself I could be with a man who made me feel like I was, at all times, about to get hit by a train.

"I should dump him," I said.

"Oh, thank god. Call him. Call him right now."

"What if he says he wants to come here in person?" I asked. "What if he talks me out of it?"

"Text him, then," Kitty said. "Refuse to talk to him."

"Is that fair?"

"I don't care! Want me to text him for you? Here, give me your phone. I'll eviscerate him within an inch of his smarmy little life."

Georgia looked at her admiringly. "Remind me never to break up with you."

"I shall," Kitty said. "Regularly. Give me your phone."

"No," I said, "I can do it."

"Are you sure? I've always wanted to write a break-up message. Something eloquent but scathing. Something with just enough inside jokes that it really cuts to the bone, you know, but also doesn't imply you'll miss them too much? I've actually been brainstorming this for a while. It's a little long, but hear me out."

"Sent," I said.

Kitty blinked. "Sent?"

Me: We're done.

"Efficient," Georgia said. "I like it."

August did not.

This Place

2017

Once I'd turned in my final assignment of the term and started packing my suitcases, I was left with the same uprooted sensation that had marked the beginning of my time at Stanford. Everyone else was going off to work or travel, and I didn't know what I was meant to do. Kitty and Georgia had invited me to Greece with them, but the trip was supposed to be romantic and perfect. I said thanks but no. The obvious solution was for me to go to Stenland, where at least I could work for my dad for the summer. It was a job involving cars, after all, which was more than I'd been able to get on my own. The prospect of seeing people was also tempting—Linnea, Henrik. Soren. I even wanted to see Delia, who Kitty told me had had the tremendously bad luck of becoming a skeld a second time last year. No one had died this time.

On the other hand, I had the feeling that I had insulted the island by leaving and if I went back, it would punish me by turning me immediately into a skeld. Also, if I was being honest, I desperately did not want to meet Abigail.

I decided to stop packing and FaceTime Bianca, thinking absently that maybe she wanted to offer me a place on her floor for the summer. When she picked up, she was sitting with her feet in a fountain. Damian was next to her. They were both wearing sunglasses and looking celebratory.

We exchanged the usual pleasantries. It had been weeks since I'd spoken to either of them—a long time for my supposed closest college friends—but we all bobbed through the conversation like nothing was wrong. When I told them August and I had broken up, they looked relieved.

"Oh," Damian said. "Good. I mean, you two never made that much sense anyway."

"What he means," Bianca said, "is that we hope you're doing okay."

"You didn't think we made sense?" I asked.

I was sitting on top of my suitcase with my back against the bed frame. The wood was digging into my spine, but I didn't move.

"August is just quirky," Bianca said. "You knew that."

Did I?

"Right," I said, "well, I think he lied to me about things." I hurried to add, "Nothing that important," but I wasn't sure why I was defending him.

Damian and Bianca nodded. "Yeah, classic August," Damian said.

Classic August—of course, classic August. The static was coming back, the ringing in my ears that was becoming an increasingly regular companion. I was glad I was already sitting down. As if through water, I heard myself say, "Did he lie to you about something?"

"Oh, god," Bianca said to Damian. "Remember the kidnapping story?"

Damian laughed. He responded, but I didn't hear what he said.

I wanted to say *Is that really the same thing as being quirky?* I wanted to say *Jesus fucking Christ, why didn't you tell me?*

They assumed I knew. Who would be so stupid not to? Who could possibly be so naive? What a sad, small world I came from.

I ended the call with an abrupt goodbye. In the hallway, there were two male voices, and though neither of them sounded quite like August, I was suddenly and utterly convinced he would be knocking on my door within the hour. It was the day he'd originally intended to fly in; who was to say he hadn't just gotten on the plane anyway?

In response to my text, August had said he was sorry things had been so distant over the past few months. He'd said he hoped I was doing well.

He had not said he was not flying out to see me.

I called Kitty and asked if she and Georgia could drive me to the airport. I put her on speaker and started looking at tickets.

"Wait, right now?" Kitty said. "Where are you going?"

"Home," I said.

Part of me thought I'd see Stenland through the fog as my plane came in to land and feel—love, I supposed. But as the hills resolved themselves and the little toy buildings sharpened into focus, I felt the first swells of panic. When I'd flown into London, seeing all that rained-on green and old stone, it had felt like coming home. But as the plane jostled its way toward the runway, I was so aware of the lack of city beyond the airport. When I stepped outside with my bags, the air was quiet of all human noise. Just ravens and that fog.

I checked my phone and had no messages from August,

which made me feel like maybe I'd invented this fantasy in my head, the fact that he was coming to find me. It made me feel both relieved and guilty. I called my dad, realizing that I probably should've called him sooner to let him know I was coming, but it went to voicemail. Linnea still didn't have her license. I briefly considered calling Soren but remembered Abigail.

How did tourists get to their Lundwall hotels from the airport? I'd never needed to consider it before. We certainly didn't have an underground; I didn't even think we had a bus. Maybe you were required by law to rent a car. Or there was a single driver who ferried everyone back and forth very slowly.

In the end, I called Kitty's mum.

She answered on the second ring, sounding breathless. Upbeat, folksy music twanged in the background.

"Tess," she said. "Is Kitty okay?"

I stared at the small parking lot in front of the airport and kicked a bit of gravel with my toe. Beyond the flatness of the lot rose a golden green hill flecked with blooming crowberry bushes. We were too boxed in by fog to see the ocean, but I could sense it, maybe in the saltiness hanging in the air. "Kitty's great, Mrs. Sjöberg."

"You're twenty-one, honey. I think you can call me Michelle."

Over the music in the background, I thought I could hear someone calling out instructions.

"Are you at a dance class?"

"At the community center. Are *you* okay?"

"Never mind," I said. "Sorry to interrupt."

"Tess Eriksson, you are near enough my own daughter to know you cannot possibly get away with this *sorry to interrupt* act. Tell me why you called and tell me what I can do."

"I might be at the airport," I said.

She paused. "I'll be there in fifteen minutes."

Twelve minutes later, I was climbing into the passenger

seat of Michelle's car. It was a new one, still a BMW but now small and sporty instead of giant and meant for lugging around three girls.

"Is this an M3?" I said.

"As always, your father's daughter."

Growing up, I'd always thought the Sjöbergs were the richest people in the world. It had been hard to imagine what you'd do with more money than they had. It was still hard for me to imagine, actually. Like Kitty, Mr. Sjöberg had gone off to study something business related at Oxford. He'd spent the next decade working in London and Paris and Hong Kong. He'd met Kitty's mum, started investing in businesses and properties back in Stenland, and moved home just before Kitty was born.

"Do you like living here?" I asked.

She glanced over at me as she threaded the car through a roundabout. "So we're not going to talk about why you hopped on a plane without telling anyone you were coming? Okay, that's fine. Yes, I do like living here. I love my friends and I love my husband and I love my life. I hate the weather, and I could die happy if I never again ate herring. But do I like Stenland? I do."

"Did you always?"

"Of course not. I'd never been anywhere with people who were so polite yet so cold. And I knew we were having a girl, which was horrifying once I realized skelds were real. I'd always thought they were folklore—like elves or something. Mind you, I also thought narwhals were folklore. Bit of a shock all around. But when I found out—I've never shouted so much in my whole life. My voice was gone the next day. I was so angry Kitty's father would bring her to a place she might end up cursed. It never even occurred to me that *I* might. Hasn't happened, but—if there were a way to bear the curse for someone else, I'd do it. I can't say I wasn't relieved when you and Kitty left. I was always sure the three of you…"

I tucked my feet up on the seat. "Why stay?"

She made a soft thinking noise, an *mmm*, and we both gazed out the windshield as Lundwall winked into view. Red buildings; turf roofs. Stone fences essing like snakes through the grass. At the center of town, right in front of the parliament house that I'd come to realize was the size of a normal city hall, there was a bronze sculpture. She was maybe twice life-size, her hair flowing out behind her and her arms raised like she was summoning something. Her skin was gleaming from the wetness in the air. A simple dress from an indiscernible era fluttered around her legs. In one hand, she held a length of fabric that had, perhaps, been tied recently around her eyes. Her lids were closed, but you got the sense she could open them whenever she wanted to.

"This place gets in your veins," Michelle said finally. "You know?"

"I know," I said.

Michelle dropped me at my dad's house. She asked if I needed her to hang around in case I couldn't find him, but he hadn't locked his front door in years, so I said I'd be fine. From his workshop, I could see the flicker of lights. It was only seven at night, and the sky wasn't even pink yet, so I figured he was probably bent over the guts of a car fiddling with something. My palms were sweaty. I readjusted my grip on my bags and walked toward the garage door. It was rolled open. From inside, I heard a trickle of voices and the occasional clank of metal.

"—the red house," a man's voice was saying.

"But it's so close to the cemetery," a woman said, and my heart swooped in my chest.

"That's probably why the price is so low!" the man said cheerfully.

I stepped through the garage door.

Henrik was leaning against a car with the hood propped, a

wrench in one hand. His beard had grown thicker and his face had rounded out, but he had the same pink cheeks, the same bright blue eyes as always.

Linnea sat on a tall worktable, her legs swinging. She was wearing a lavender dress and a cardigan. Her hair was in loose waves down her back like she'd just taken it out of a braid. No one had ever in history looked more like a goddess of springtime.

She saw me before Henrik did.

His gaze was still fixed on her when he said, "We can afford it if we let my parents chip in. And we'll pay them back, obviously. Promise me you'll think about it."

Linnea's lips parted.

"Hi," I said.

She toppled forward off the worktable and flung herself at me. I'd forgotten how tall she was, and when we crashed together, I had to catch myself on the car Henrik was working on to keep us both from hitting the concrete. A rain of kisses descended on my head.

"Henrik!" Linnea said. "Henrik, I found Tess!"

I laughed and tried to wriggle out of her grasp without success.

"I can see that," Henrik said. He set down the wrench and approached more cautiously. "I'm covered in grease. Can I hug you anyway?"

I nodded, and Henrik wrapped his arms around both of us, pinning us together in a knot. When we finally disentangled, Linnea's cheeks were bright. She looked like she might cry; if she did, I would too.

"Are you here for the weekend?" Linnea asked.

I felt that I needed to ask their permission. "The summer, I think."

She shrieked, then pressed her fingertips to her lips.

"Is my dad here?" I asked.

"He's at dinner," Henrik said. "With Anna. They should be back any minute, though."

On cue, I heard the hiss of tires against wet stone. Three years. I hadn't seen my dad in person in almost three years because he never left Stenland and I never came back, and FaceTime was fine, but it wasn't the same as seeing him make toast while singing off-key to Adele. I turned and took a step out of the garage—god, I was definitely going to cry—but then out of the driver's seat of a muddy white truck swung Soren.

His feet hit the ground.

A precarious hope hovered between my throat and my heart. We stared at each other, maybe both in shock, though it was probably fairer for him to be shocked as he wasn't the one who was supposed to be a thousand miles away. He looked taller than the last time I'd seen him. Or older, maybe, with his hair shorter and his shoulders broader and his face narrower. The eyes, though, same as always, under those heavy brows, behind those long lashes.

Linnea pushed between my shoulder blades. I took a stumbling step, and that seemed to jar Soren too because the next minute, his arms were wrapped around me and my nose was in his collarbone.

Soap and sea and earth and toothpaste. You never forget what a person smells like once you've been in love with them.

We stayed like that until I started wondering how long you were allowed to hug your ex without it being weird. He was the one who let go, which felt the same way it felt when he texted me something too clever to counter.

"I don't..." he said. "What?"

"She's here for the summer," Henrik said.

I watched Soren's face for clues about how this news was received. He still looked vaguely dazed.

"Okay," he said.

"What are you doing here?" I asked.

"What am *I* doing here?"

"We were going to get dinner," Henrik supplied.

I wondered if dinner plans included Abigail, but was afraid of how it would sound if I asked. Before I could think of a way to say it without reminding everyone of just how long I had hugged Soren, another car pulled into park in front of the house, and when I turned, there was my dad.

No dazed hesitation this time. I ran straight to him and he was saying my name like a question and then I hugged him for the first time in three years. He was already crying.

"Can I stay with you for the summer?" I said. "I probably should've asked sooner."

He said yes, then, oh my gosh, then, of course, absolutely, all summer?

"If that's okay."

"Oh my gosh," he said again. "Of course. Absolutely. I thought you'd be working again."

"I didn't get any internship offers," I said.

They all frowned sympathetically like they were wondering if this condition was terminal. It had felt that way when I'd been talking to my classmates, but I supposed none of the people currently assembled had ever done an internship because, if we were being honest, it was a bit of a stupid premise anyway.

Once my dad had his bearings, he remembered to step out of the way so I could say hello to Anna (whom I should probably have long since stopped calling "Anna from the hospital"). She wore practical shoes and had her gray-brown hair in a ponytail and her round face free of makeup. When she hugged me, it felt soft and sincere.

My dad showed me to my room while Anna chatted in the driveway with the others. It was funny, my dad leading me through the house, like I might've forgotten the way. When he opened my door, he said apologetically, "Sorry I didn't keep it like it was. I figured you wouldn't have wanted me to, since I knew you didn't want to—well."

It was a clean and bright guest room. My swim ribbons had been packed away, as had my child-sized bed. Everything was blue and white now, and the curtains were open to let in the evening sun. I had a feeling Anna had contributed to the redecorating effort because it was hard to imagine my dad selecting throw pillows.

I was glad he'd changed it, and I told him so. I didn't want a dusty shrine.

The six of us crammed together in the kitchen, and I was regaled with town gossip. Lukas had started dating someone named Johanna; a politician had been fined for bicycling drunk. Soren didn't say much, but he never stood more than an arm's length from me. Once, I glanced up and found him leaning against the fridge, his hands in his pockets, his eyes soft on mine. I looked away again quickly. No one offered any gossip about the current whereabouts of Abigail; I was still too embarrassed to ask.

Once we'd been huddled in the kitchen for nearly two hours, my dad said, "Oh, you were all meant to go get dinner, weren't you?"

"I didn't want to complain," Henrik said, "but I may faint."

My dad shooed us out the door, and Anna waved. We left the cars behind and walked to Hedda's. The mist had mostly blown off, so I could see all the way to the ocean. It was past nine, but coming up on the longest day of the year, the sky was still a pale and powdery blue.

When we pushed open the door to Hedda's, her voice rang out from the kitchen in warning that they were closed.

"It's me!" Linnea called back.

We sat in the booth where we always used to sit, in the places we used to claim: me next to Soren and Linnea next to Henrik. We would drag a chair to the end of the table for Kitty, and I wished we needed to now.

Hedda swept past us with a rag over her shoulder, muttering about how we'd better just want the usual. Then she stopped. Turned back toward us.

I waved.

"What year is this?" she said. "Should I expect Kitty to come blowing through my door next?"

"I can lock up." Linnea blinked her big eyes up at Hedda. "If the kitchen's still open..."

"I was just about to turn the griddle off," Hedda said.

"Please? It wouldn't be right for Tess to eat someone else's cooking on her first day back."

Hedda gave Linnea a mutinous look. "Fine."

"I'd love some pancakes," I said helpfully.

"I know what your order is," she snapped, and she stalked away before anyone else could try to tell her what they wanted.

"I missed her," I said.

"You know," Linnea said, "you can tell she missed you too."

It was painful, how normal it was. How normal it used to be. Hedda brought two coffees (me, Soren) and two hot chocolates with whipped cream (Linnea, Henrik). A few minutes later, she brought pancakes (me) and fish and chips (Soren) and a burger (Henrik) and two eggs and a slice of cake (Linnea). Linnea told us she'd been thinking about quitting, actually; Anna had convinced her to enroll in the nursing course at the university the prior autumn, but she hadn't yet committed to a second year.

"I just don't want to leave Hedda's," Linnea said. "Also, what if I have a terrible bedside manner?"

"You wouldn't," Henrik said. To me, as an aside, he added: "She'd be so bloody good at it."

"Henrik thinks I'd be good at everything."

"Well," he said, "you are."

Conversation veered, as I knew it would, toward Kitty's absence. Linnea told me that aside from a happy birthday message, Kitty hadn't texted her all spring, much less called. I tried to keep my expression neutral, but I made a mental note to berate Kitty; she'd promised me she was keeping in touch and that Linnea was just being dramatic.

"She'll come around," I told Linnea. "You know how wrapped up people get in new relationships."

Linnea's fork clattered against her plate. "Kitty's in a relationship?"

I blinked a few times. "You knew this. Georgia's been in the room while I've FaceTimed you."

"Kitty's dating *Georgia*?"

"You knew this!" I said.

"I thought they were just really good friends!"

"Well—" I started to say something like *they haven't been together that long*, but that wasn't actually true. "They're also good friends?"

"Kitty's *gay*?" Linnea said.

We all stared at her.

She whipped an accusatory look at Henrik and Soren. "Did you two know?"

In what was perhaps not his most tactful moment, Soren said, "How did you not?"

I kicked him under the table.

"I didn't know," Henrik said. "For whatever that's worth. I definitely did not know."

Linnea was gripping her fork so tightly I could see the white ridges of her knuckles. Had I not told her on purpose? Had Kitty not told her on purpose? I hoped I hadn't just spoiled a secret, something Kitty was safeguarding, but it had been so long since she'd cared for Linnea in that way that it hadn't even occurred to me that Linnea might still not know.

I cleared my throat uncomfortably. "So," I said. "Where's Abigail?"

If I had hoped to find a less awkward conversational topic, I had, apparently, failed because Henrik and Linnea both went very still on their side of the table.

"Ah," Soren said.

A long pause.

"Toronto," he said, "one assumes."

I felt lightheaded. "One assumes?"

"We broke up," Soren said.

"Ah."

"About a month ago."

"Mmm."

Another silence. Linnea broke it with, "Well, at least I am not the only one who doesn't get told anything."

I was suddenly uniquely conscious of Soren's leg beneath the table. His knee was an inch from mine. When he shifted his weight, the bench shifted under us.

"What happened?" I asked. "You don't have to say."

He made an uncomfortable noise. Linnea and Henrik pretended to be very interested in their hot chocolates.

"She…ah. Told me she loved me. In March." Soren ran his hand through the back of his hair. "And I said I couldn't say it back yet. She said, you know, no worries. But she said it again in April." He winced. "And then when she said it in May, and I still didn't say it back, she asked if I thought I'd ever be able to. I said I didn't know. So she left."

"Oh." My voice sounded high and strained. "Well. It can be hard to know. If you love someone."

He finally looked over at me. Then he let out this helpless laugh, which made me laugh back, which made Henrik and Linnea laugh, and it was good that they did because I'd forgotten they were sitting there.

"How's August?" Soren asked.

"What?"

"Van Andel," he clarified.

I tried to keep my voice level. "We broke up. Actually."

Soren's face remained fastidiously devoid of emotion. "You did," he said. "Ah."

"You didn't," Linnea said.

I frowned at her. "Last week."

Her voice pitching higher, she said, *"Why doesn't anyone tell me things?"*

Soren and I looked at each other. Henrik put a concerned arm over Linnea's shoulder.

"I'm sorry?" I said.

She was going alarmingly pale. "You really should've said."

"I should've. We can get breakfast together tomorrow. We'll catch up on everything."

"No," Linnea insisted. "You really should have said."

I opened my mouth. Then: "Oh."

"Oh, what?" Henrik asked.

"He's coming here, isn't he?"

"He messaged me on Facebook right after you got here," Linnea said. "He just said he wanted to surprise you, that I shouldn't say anything. Tess, I'm so sorry. I didn't know—"

I couldn't string the words together. A part of me wanted to ask that they hide me somewhere, but most of me thought that sounded melodramatic. Because what had August done wrong, really? He was no physical danger to me. Maybe this was my own fault, for being too much of a coward to break up with him in person or at least over the phone.

"Tess hates surprises," Soren said. It wasn't accusatory, exactly—but it wasn't not that either.

"I'm sorry," Linnea said again.

That was when the bell on the door jingled.

There is a very specific, incongruous sound when a man in expensive shoes walks across a floor that needs mopping.

There's that faint heel-tap and the shifting of leather, and then, beneath it, the staticky noise of a sole clinging to sticky tile. A shadow crossed in front of the table, and I looked up, and there was August.

He was wearing pale yellow shorts and a Patagonia vest, and he had a North Face duffel bag slung over one shoulder that made him look more outdoorsy than he was. His sunglasses were propped, pushing his hair off his forehead. Behind him, through the windows, the sky was awash with pink midnight light.

"Surprise," he said. He said it pleasantly. He said everything pleasantly. August Van Andel was not a scary person; it was not fair that I felt scared.

"Oh," I said.

He smiled at Linnea. "Hi, Linnea. Great to meet you in person." His eyes drifted over Henrik, whose arm was still around Linnea's shoulders, and then found their way to Soren. When they did, his smile thinned.

Soren extended a hand without standing up. It forced August to hunch if he wanted to shake, which of course he did, because August was nothing if not polite.

"Soren," Soren said.

"August."

I wondered if August knew. I'd never spoken Soren's name aloud in front of him—very carefully, actually, like I'd been conserving a precious resource—and had only ever referred to him on the odd time he'd come up as *my high school boyfriend.* But there were artifacts. Old Facebook posts we'd both been tagged in. I could picture this one particular photo Kitty had taken after one of Soren's soccer games, me in his jersey, him standing behind me with his arms draped over my shoulders. I wondered if August had seen it. I wondered if he was picturing the same photo.

"What are you doing here?" I asked.

"Surprising you," he said. "I thought, hey, what's the point of money if you're not going to use it to book a last-minute flight from London to Copenhagen to Stenland to visit your girlfriend?"

Soren had been rolling a balled-up straw wrapper back and forth across the table, and at the word *girlfriend*, his finger stilled, just for a second. "I'm sure you could find a rainforest foundation that would take your money instead," he said.

Linnea laughed like she wanted to melt into the floor.

"So," August said, "it's probably been a while since you all saw Tess, huh? I don't mean to steal her away. I'm sure she's been catching you up on everything she's done since leaving, right? Stanford, America—she must be a celebrity around here."

"Yeah," Henrik said uncomfortably. "She was just telling us."

August turned his smile, still pleasant, on him. "Sorry—what was your name?"

"Henrik."

"Ah," August said. "Linnea's boyfriend?"

Henrik looked surprised he would know this. I wasn't. August had a good memory. He was always saying so. Reminding people he did. Suggesting, pleasantly, that perhaps your memory was not quite as good as his.

To Soren, August said, "And you're…?"

Soren looked at him for a long time. August shifted his weight. Readjusted his bag.

"Kitty's cousin," Soren said.

"Funny," August said. "I haven't heard anything about you."

"Interesting."

"I actually don't find it all that interesting that I wouldn't have heard about you."

"No," Soren said. "I think it's interesting that you'd rather be the one she talks about than the one she talks to."

"Excuse me?" August said.

Soren turned his head away from August so his temple pressed against the back of the booth and his eyes fixed on mine.

"August," I said, "I think we should talk outside."

"Yeah," he said. "Great."

Soren had to stand to let me out of the booth, and when he did, August's eyes swept across him. I felt a pang of secondhand embarrassment as his eyes lingered on Soren's muddy shoes, on the hole in that sweater that he had long-since worn to death. Soren slipped his hands into his pockets and leaned against the edge of the table. When August looked down at him, it was like he was pleased to find he was taller.

"Do you want me to come with you?" Linnea said nervously.

"It's fine, Lin." I kept my eyes on August. "We're good."

I followed August out the door. The bells jingled again. August started walking down the street, not even looking back at me, and though there was a part of me that wanted to stay where my friends could see us, I was too embarrassed to let them. I followed him until we'd passed the last of Hedda's windows, and then I grabbed his arm.

"What are you doing here?" I said.

He turned.

The path ran along the harbor; all to my right, the ocean lapped against hulls and docks and cement posts. When the wind skated in, it ruffled August's hair, and he frowned like the gust was a personal inconvenience.

"Were you trying to embarrass me?" he asked. I was surprised by his voice—how tight it was, how quiet.

"Why are you here?" I said again.

"Do you know how shitty that felt? To fly all the way to fucking London just for the guy across the hall to tell me, 'Oh, sorry, Tess left an hour ago'?"

I lifted my chin and stared at the waves.

"Fine," he said. "I can talk. I knew you were mad at me

about something. I figured it was just the distance, or maybe you were pissed I didn't come visit you. But it was just a fight, okay? We had a fight, but I figured we'd still go on our trip. I mean, fuck, I was going to ask if you wanted to live with me over the summer, since you clearly don't have anywhere else to go." When he said this, he gestured at the harbor. At the fishing boats with their fishing-boat smells and their incriminating bloodstains.

"Are you really from Connecticut?" I asked.

He looked blankly back at me. "What kind of question is that? Where else would I be from?"

"Did you get kidnapped in Italy when you were ten? Did you almost go to a ski academy until you broke your leg? Did your high school girlfriend cheat on you?"

August's lips parted.

"Did your uncle get turned to stone by a skeld?"

"Look. Maybe I… Maybe I exaggerate sometimes, okay? For the sake of a good story. Maybe it speaks to some youngest-child thing or some repressed insecurity, but…" He shook his head. "You think I lied to you? Tess, come on. I know you. I know how much this matters to you."

I had always been afraid of being trapped, but I had pictured being trapped in a place: a small island, a small home, a small life. What I realized, standing there with August, was that there were more ways of being trapped. By someone else's power, money, family. Inside someone else's version of reality, as a supporting character in the story they wanted to tell. I tried to walk away, but he took my arm.

"Please just look at me," he said. And I did. His frighteningly blue eyes and his kohl-black eyelashes. The polished, even teeth. "It's about that guy, then?"

"No."

"Because you know what happened with Val," he said, "and I've got to say, this is starting to feel really fucking familiar.

Girlfriend promises she loves you, you start to trust her, goes and hooks up with her ex—"

"Your best friend," I said.

"What?"

"You told me Val cheated on you with your best friend. Not her ex."

His eyes narrowed slightly. "I guess you must've misheard me, then. Because I don't know why I would've said that."

"We're done, August. Go home."

He let out a sharp, unbelieving laugh. "Right," he said. "Okay. Have a good time with your fucking farmer. I'm sure the ME degree will serve you really well here."

"Don't be a dick."

"I'm not a dick," he said. "You're just mad because you know it's true."

"What's true?"

He gestured at the empty boats, the exhausted cars parked along the street, the railing gone rusty from sea spray. There was a garbage can coated in bird shit and a dog barking where it was tied outside the pub and up the hillside, just visible, all the stone statues in the church graveyard. I imagined how he saw it: not as a home but as a subject for examination from a safe remove. The lucky recipient of his pitying interest.

"This *place*," he said.

Before he walked away, I said, "I don't know what you mean."

But we both knew I did.

Ramna Skaill

2022

My dad drove me to Ramna Skaill on what should have been Linnea and Henrik's wedding day. I lay flat in the back seat of the car because I didn't want anyone to see me. I had a beanie pulled down over my eyes, but I kept them shut anyway. My dad wasn't singing along to his music, but I asked him to. Just to make sure he was still alive.

He stopped the car. Opened the door. A burst of wind came rushing off the water, so loud my dad had to yell to be heard.

"Need a hand?"

I took it. He led me down the stairs. I remembered walking this path the night of that party in Year 12; I remembered how narrow it was, penned in by an angry ocean. I had the uneasy sensation of being walked down an aisle: veiled, blinded, and given away.

"We're in front of the door," my dad said. "Do you want me to wait with you?"

"No. Please." Linnea and Kitty would be there soon. We'd made a schedule.

My dad paused. I could picture him with that look on his face—the nervous one, when he was afraid he'd say the wrong thing.

"Do you want me to stay out here?" he asked finally. "In the cottage?"

"You have to run the shop."

"I could work during the day and come back at night. In case you need anything."

"Don't. We'll be fine, Dad. I promise."

He pulled me in for a tight hug. Once he was gone, I shut the door and took off the beanie. Puffs of wool clung to my eyelashes. I could still hear the wind outside: howling, gathering its breath, howling again. It was dark in the keep, the curtains drawn, the power off. This was the room where everyone had danced at that party. Now the stone was swept clean. A rug the color of wine stretched across the floor, and a hearth sat empty behind it. Above the mantle, where you'd expect to find a painting, there was instead a carving done straight into the wall. Interlocking knots formed a ring around three ravens. Where the stone had been chipped away, it was lined with red ink.

Each floor was narrow, with just a few rooms. The kitchen and bathrooms had modern appliances; I'd half expected chamber pots.

There were three bedrooms upstairs. It seemed obvious I should take the one at the end of the third floor, seeing as I'd had sex in it, but once I stepped inside, I felt ill. I considered moving my duffel bag to one of the others, but I could hear voices downstairs—Kitty arriving—so I just shut myself inside until I was sure her mother had left.

The heat turned on around the same time Linnea showed up. There were promises of bedding and shampoo and homemade casseroles, which would have to be scheduled and delivered with painstaking care. For the first time, the three of us uncovered our eyes together in the hearth room.

Skelds can't turn each other to stone. That's the only consolation, really: company.

Linnea's hair was tangled messily across her forehead, almost obscuring the three black lines. Kitty had her hair pulled back into a bun, putting the mark on defiant display. I looked at them, and the skeld's mark, with the unmoored sensation that I'd seen them like this before and would see them like this again.

"I'm supposed to be getting married right now," Linnea said.

"We know that," Kitty told her.

"Well, I wanted to remind everyone anyway."

I got the fire going, and then we sat in front of it in a circle with our knees touching. Where my body didn't face the flames, my skin tingled. I'd expected the cold, but I hadn't realized it would be like this: a sapping, like the stone of the keep was bleeding heat out of me.

"We need to pick keepers," Linnea said.

"We don't," I said. "We absolutely do not."

"It's a good idea to have someone nearby in case something goes wrong."

"That's why they invented the cell phone."

"Come on, Tess," Kitty said. "We all know it's as much about the island's safety as it is ours. They'll want people to keep an eye on us in case we go mad and decide to go turn everyone to stone for fun."

"That's horrible," Linnea said. "Don't even joke about that."

"I think I'd look good as a madwoman," Kitty said.

"Shut up."

We both looked at Linnea. She had never told us—perhaps anyone—to shut up.

"You're not funny," Linnea said, then looked away.

Kitty cleared her throat. "Right."

I gazed into the fire. They were both right: we were in danger; we were dangerous. But keepers were more likely than anyone else to die during a skeld season. It was just the terrible sort of thing we expected to happen at Ramna Skaill. I watched a twig smolder to charcoal at its axis and finally snap, falling into the embers. Outside, a gust of wind spat rain across the mottled windows. If you listened closely, you could hear bells clanging from somewhere—probably a fishing boat just offshore.

"We could ask Hedda," Linnea said.

"Hedda is somewhat busy running the entire island," Kitty said.

"But she'd make us food."

"And the rest of the island would starve."

"What about our mums?" Linnea asked.

"I am not asking my mum to spend three months living in an ancient cottage with a fucking blindfold on. She has better things to do. I don't see why we're even debating this. We already know who it's going to be."

I pulled myself away from the fire and looked at Kitty. "What's that mean?"

"They made a pact. Like, eight years ago."

"No," I said.

"Henrik, Soren, and Lukas?" Linnea asked.

"That was—" They both turned to me. "Different."

Linnea hugged her knees into her chest. "Henrik has already left me about four voicemails about it."

"And Soren and Lukas are my cousins," Kitty said. "And they already promised. Remember?"

There was a long silence. I looked down at my hands, the purpling of my fingernails in the cold. Finally, quietly: "Don't make me say it."

"Say what?" Kitty asked, even though she knew exactly what.

"Not Soren," I said.

"He's my cousin."

"It's not right." I looked at Linnea. "He's— I wouldn't want Saffi to think—"

"Saffi knows you're still friends," Linnea said.

"We aren't friends. We're uncomfortable acquaintances. And you can't hold him to a promise he made when we were eighteen and dating."

"I don't understand why you have so little faith in Soren's ability to make his own decisions," Linnea said.

I blinked.

"Ooh," Kitty said. "Harsh."

"I'm sorry, but he can keep himself safe. You don't need to spend your whole life trying to protect him."

"Yeah," Kitty said. "Think of all the free time you'll have once you quash that hobby."

I stood. "I need air."

"You can't go outside."

"Then just—please, just give me a minute."

I could feel their eyes on my back as I went up the stairs. In my room, I wiped my palms on my thighs and paced the stone floor, trying to steady my breathing. A raven shrieked outside, and I startled so hard I slammed into the bed frame.

I pulled my phone from my pocket and found his name. When he answered, there was a lag before he spoke, and in that pause, I could hear his surroundings: the wind; the sea.

"No," I said.

"No?"

"I don't want you here."

"It's important to Linnea and Kitty."

"Well, it's important to me that you're far away, okay?"

"Tess," Soren said softly. "It's fine. I'm not afraid of you."

"Don't flatter yourself. Maybe I just don't want you around."

"I know it's a risk. You think I'd let Henrik and Lukas take it without me? And besides, Kitty's my cousin, and Linnea's one of my best friends. I trust all of you. This is something I want to do."

I kicked the door hard, and the hinges clanged. My eyes were burning from the pressure of not crying. "You're not listening to me."

"And you're not listening to me."

"I didn't throw my home away just so you could fucking die! Is that what you want me to say? You want me to admit that I don't want you dead?"

"Is that how you feel about Stenland?" he said. "Like you had to throw it away?"

I focused on swallowing the knot in my throat instead of trying to answer.

"Tess."

"I don't want you," I said.

"I'm sure your boyfriend will be relieved to hear that."

Heat spread up my throat. "As a keeper," I said. "Dick."

"In case you're forgetting," Soren said, "one of us has seen a lot more skeld seasons than the other. And I've been able to take care of myself so far."

"I don't want you to do this," I said.

"Well fucking aware."

"But you're going to be a keeper anyway."

"Yeah, actually, I am."

"Because you think Stenland needs protection from me."

"Because you fucking matter to me!" he said.

I stopped pacing. Listened to the rattle of his breath. Behind him, the wind howled.

I pressed my forehead against the stone wall and let my eyes fall shut. "It would be better if I didn't."

He said, "Obviously, Tess."

Bruise

2017

The morning after August left Stenland, I woke at noon to see that he had posted a photo on Instagram of his complimentary champagne in the airport lounge at Charles de Gaulle. I gave him a like. Just to be nice.

In the afternoon, I went for a hike with Linnea, just the two of us. When we reached the top of Fell Mountain, we sat down next to the cairn and looked out at the island. It was in perfect form. The sky was a chipper blue, innocently pretending it looked like that all the time. Sheep dotted the hillsides like kids' drawings of clouds, lumpy and white.

Linnea pulled a flask out of her backpack and offered it to me.

"Oh," I said after I sipped. "That's much better than whiskey."

"I know, right? Elderflower liqueur. Girls-only hiking trips!

Hang on—I have chocolate too." She rummaged around in her bag. "Oh, that's where my birth control went."

I choked on my drink, and Linnea waved a hand.

"Don't worry," she said. "I just missed, like, a day or two."

"You're giving me secondhand panic."

"Hasn't caught up with me so far," she said, finally extricating a chocolate bar from the depths of her backpack. She broke off a square and passed it to me.

We ate our chocolate in companionable silence for a few moments, just watching the wind bob through the grass, before Linnea asked, "Does Kitty hate me?"

"Never," I said.

"I wish she did. That would be better than feeling like she's outgrown me."

I looked over at her. Her cheeks were pink from the walking and the sun. She had her elbows wrapped around her knees, one long blond braid nearly touching the grass on either side of her.

"Do I make you feel that way?"

"No," Linnea said quickly. When I gave her a look, she smiled grudgingly. "A little. Maybe. It's hard—being left behind."

"The world's still out there waiting for you," I said.

"Do you think less of me for not caring that much?"

"No. No, of course not."

"Henrik and I are thinking of buying a house."

I raised my eyebrows.

"I know," she said. "It's serious. It's like, how much do you love your partner? Are you willing to bet all your money on it? But I think I am. Besides, money is mostly imaginary anyway."

"Sure," I said, skating past this point for the time being. "Do you think you'll get married?"

"Oh, someday. Not yet. I'd rather just live together." She handed me another piece of chocolate. "Henrik said that Soren said you were having dinner at the croft tonight?"

"Mmm."

"And?" Linnea said.

"Apparently Lukas and Elin want to see me."

She gave a delighted laugh. "Yes. Elin Fell wants to see you. That's why you're going. No other reason."

"I don't know, Lin..."

"Do you think I don't know that you've been texting him for months now? I've never seen someone go from totally indifferent to their phone to completely addicted in less time. He's still in love with you."

"He can't still be what he never was."

"I might not be as smart as you or Kitty." When I started to protest, Linnea held up a hand. "No, look, I was never good with school the way you two were. But I know people. I know what it looks like when someone's in love."

I almost told her that she clearly didn't, given the whole Kitty situation, but I thought better of it. Instead, I said, "Even if we did...care about each other, I'm only here for the summer."

"So you're here for the summer. You don't know where you'll be in five years." I opened my mouth to insist that I did, I always had, and the answer was *not Stenland*, but Linnea barged onward. "And he doesn't know where he'll be in five years."

My throat felt tight. "You just want someone to go on double dates with."

"No," she said. "I just want my best friend to be happy." She paused. "And also I wouldn't mind the double dates." She stood and brushed the dirt off her leggings, then offered me a hand. I took it, and she pulled me to my feet. "Now let's go so you have time to shower before your date with Elin."

On the drive to the Fells', I played a news podcast at full volume from the speaker of my phone so that I couldn't think too hard. As I parked the car, a *New York Times* columnist shouted in the cup holder about gerrymandering.

A dog started barking when I opened my door. The driveway had been lined with gravel since I'd last been there, but other than that, it was the same as always. The windswept grass; the moss-furred stone; a blue-gray ocean beneath a blue-gray sky, both of them stretching so far in every direction you'd swear you could see the earth curving.

I thought I was more nervous to see Elin than Soren since I'd already seen Soren and the thought of parental disapproval made me anxious. But when I knocked on the front door and Elin opened it, I felt a rush of relief. So maybe I was more nervous about Soren after all.

Since I'd last seen her, Elin's hair had grown wispier; it was now less the color of steel and more the color of ash. She'd never been someone who wasted smiles, and I didn't get one, but I did get a hard, appraising look, like she cared enough to make sure I hadn't grievously injured myself since leaving.

"One of the neighbor's horses started foaling," she said by way of greeting. "He'll be back when he's back."

I got the sense Elin was daring me to voice annoyance at this turn of events. Like she thought I might insist we call Soren away from his equine midwifery. I just nodded.

The kitchen smelled like lamb and rosemary. Elin gestured vaguely toward the fridge in what I thought was a *get yourself a beer* signal, so I did. She was already drinking one. I glanced around for Lukas, but he wasn't in his usual place on the couch. Answering my unspoken question, Elin said, "Lukas is out with the chickens. Don't look so surprised. He does help sometimes, you know."

As I chopped potatoes and onions for Elin, I kept glancing through the window, waiting for Soren's silhouette to appear in the hazy light of the drive. When I finally heard the door open, my knife skittered off a potato, and Elin snorted. It was Lukas.

His face cracked open in a smile, and he strode across the kitchen to hug me. His body was bigger and broader than I'd remembered, oddly mannish, and the hug went on just long enough that I started to feel uncomfortable. Then he stepped back and grinned down at me. He'd let his hair grow long; it was pulled into a bun at the back of his head. I'd never thought he looked much like photos of Soren's mum, but he did now. Something in the nose, maybe.

"Jesus fucking Christ," he said. "Never thought you'd be stupid enough to come back here."

Elin clicked her tongue, but Lukas looked undeterred.

"How's California? Do you have pictures?"

"I didn't think anyone ever wanted to see someone else's travel pictures," I said.

"I expect an exhausting recap."

"Exhaustive," Elin said.

Lukas just shrugged, still looking pleased. "How late are you staying? Is this, like, a slumber party sort of scenario, or—"

"Lukas," Elin said, "take a shower. You smell like manure."

He made a face, but ducked out of the kitchen anyway. When it was just Elin and me again, the silence felt thicker than it had before. I kept waiting for her to say something about Soren: *Don't hurt him* or *Stay away from him* or *He hasn't been the same without you.* She didn't say any of these things, which made me feel oddly disappointed, like perhaps Elin didn't think anything that might or might not happen between Soren and me was of particular import.

When the clock on the oven read 10:00 and Soren still wasn't back, I went to the bathroom and splashed water on my face. Maybe it was because I'd never seen a horse give birth, but I felt nervously fascinated by the thought of Soren helping with it. I liked that while my classmates and I were learning niche and computer-based skills so we could work for start-ups, Soren could tumble any number of generations back through time and still be useful and steady and competent. Like if I were giving birth and the power went out and the roads were flooded, Soren would know what to do.

I went back into the kitchen and hovered awkwardly in front of the fridge. Dinner was long since done; Elin was just keeping it warm. She'd turned her attention to a jigsaw puzzle set up on a card table in the living room. Lukas was eating a bowl of cereal for pre-dinner.

When Soren finally appeared, his cheeks were pink and his eyes were bright. He must have cleaned up at the neighbor's house before coming back because as far as I could tell, he wasn't covered in any horsey birth bits.

"Sorry," he said to the room, sounding breathless. "She was upside down. Beautiful, though. She looks just like her mother."

I hadn't even noticed Elin look up, but she must've because she said, "You get kicked in the arm?"

Soren was peeling off his sweater. He wore a gray T-shirt underneath, and right at the edge of the sleeve, on his upper arm, a reddish-purple bruise was spreading. "Grazed."

"Do I need to tell you to put ice on that?" Elin asked, fitting another piece into her puzzle.

Soren was smiling at me; he still looked twitchy and pleased from the evening's work, bruise aside. I smiled back hesitantly. Once the moment had gone on a little too long, Soren lifted me by the waist and moved me a foot to the left. He opened the freezer door and grabbed an icepack. I went to find the salt shaker so he wouldn't see me blush.

Lukas drove the conversation while we ate, asking if I surfed (no) and if I'd been to American football games (yes, but I didn't really get it) and if the food was brilliant (I grudgingly admitted acai bowls were fairly brilliant). Soren and I sat next to each other, and at one point, when he reached for the water jug, his knee touched mine. It stayed touching mine, and I felt like every cell in my body had gone to sleep except for the ones in that knee. It seemed impossible that it was an accident, but then again, my foot was actually edged up against Lukas's, and I hadn't noticed that at all. I pressed my knee a little harder against Soren's, and he held up the water jug in question. I nodded, and he poured. He didn't move his leg away.

No one has ever washed dishes more slowly than Soren and I washed those dinner dishes. I kept waiting for Lukas and Elin to leave so that I didn't need to be conspicuous about wanting to be alone with Soren. But Lukas turned on the TV; Elin puttered at her puzzle.

I picked up the glasses one by one. I handed them back to Soren and said I could still see soap in them even though I couldn't. He washed them again. The countertops weren't dirty, but I wiped them down anyway.

After a half hour of this, Elin said, "For god's sake, just make up an excuse about showing her a book or something."

Soren turned the water off. His ears were pink, and he looked down at his hands, flicking water in the sink. Then he met my gaze and tilted his head toward the stairs with a question in his eyes.

I nodded back.

While we were on the stairs, I heard Elin tell Lukas, "Mimes would do better."

Soren went into the room first, so I was the one left on the threshold wondering whether to close the door. He met my gaze as I was hesitating, and his lips twitched toward a smile.

I kept my hand wrapped indecisively around the side of the door. Soren leaned against one of his bookshelves and crossed his arms.

"You got another shelf," I said.

"I got a lot more books. For school."

"I hope you're still the smartest person in class."

"*Smartest* is a stretch."

"If it makes you feel better, I am easily the most confused person in any class I take."

He laughed under his breath and shook his head, which I appreciated even though it was completely true.

I ran my fingers down the painted wood of the door. It creaked under my weight.

"What are we doing?" I asked.

His lips inched up at one corner again. "Rationalizing."

"What are you rationalizing?"

"You know."

"Breaking up with you was shit," I said. "I don't want to do it again."

"Then let's not."

"Start anything?"

"End anything."

I opened my mouth but couldn't think of how you were meant to respond to something like that. He rested his elbows on the shelf behind him. It stretched the gray T-shirt across his chest. Through the window: a summer dim sun and fog against the glass.

"I have to leave at the end of the summer," I finally said. "And I still don't want to live in Stenland after."

"Okay," he said.

"But you do."

"Do I?"

"You just came back from a horse birth looking like you won an award. This place is—who you are."

He shrugged.

"So what are you suggesting, then?" I asked. "If we—if it was like the summer before I left, and it was time for me to leave again, would you..."

"I don't know," he said.

I swallowed. My throat felt raw, like it was lined in sandpaper. I closed the door slowly, watching him. It clicked shut.

The bedroom wasn't big, but it felt that way, him on one side, me on the other.

He moved toward me. Not all the way; just to the bed. He sat on the edge of it and looked up at me.

I took a step closer, then another. Our socked toes touched.

"Do you really think you're everything I hate?" I asked. When he shook his head, confused, I said, "The day we broke up. You said you didn't see how I could've loved you because you represent everything I hate."

"And you said you didn't love me."

"That's not exactly what I said."

He swallowed. I watched his throat bob, like he was working to keep his face from showing too much. He touched my waist with bird-light hands, so careful, as if I might skitter away. When I didn't, his fingers became solid against me, his thumbs just beneath the hem of my shirt, the faintest press of bare skin.

I climbed onto his lap, resting a knee on either side of his legs. His hands never left my waist; he pulled me closer to him so our hips were fitted together, and our chests. He tilted his chin up to look at me, and it wasn't until I watched my fingers touch the sides of his face that I realized they were trembling.

We leaned together. Our noses brushed, and our lips, not quite, as if there was a decision to be made, as if we were coming back from this. I could feel his pulse in his throat and his chest. His hands moved up my waist, around my chest, through my hair. He was so close I couldn't see him anymore; it was just his lips so near to mine I could feel the heat of them.

"Do you want this?" he whispered.

Like I had not wanted anything since I was nineteen.

I kissed him, and whatever force had kept him so carefully controlled before was gone. He stood, lifting me, kissing me as I clung to him. I was landing back against his pillows, and he was leaning over me, his lips on my neck, my breastbone, the line of my bra. I fumbled with his belt as he pulled my sweater over my head. My jeans against his boxers; my bare stomach against his shirt. Too many clothes, still too many, but his fingers were at the button at my waist, and my hands were reaching up his chest. Just underwear, then not even that, and he let out a sound like pain.

His eyes were intent on mine as he slid his hand up my thigh, then slid it higher. I made a noise without meaning to, and his lips went up at one corner. I told him he looked pleased with himself. He told me he rather was, thanks.

When I rolled on top of him, I held his wrists against the pillows. He rocked his hips slowly against mine, and even when he shut his eyes and lifted his chin, he reached to push my hair behind my ears and cradle my face in his hands. He whispered my name, and I thought, *You must know how much I'm in love with you.*

In the stillness after, he set a ten-minute timer on his phone so we wouldn't fall asleep. He lay on his back with one hand under his head and the other tracing idle circles across my arm. His eyes were closed. I lay on my side and watched him. The bruise from where he'd gotten kicked by the horse was turning a vivid shade of purple.

It was both terrifying and relieving to find I could still want someone as much as I wanted him. For most of my relationship with August, I'd felt ambivalent about sex, like maybe we'd both have been better off if we'd just handled our own urges when they'd struck. But there had been a certain power in that. August had wanted me more than I'd wanted him. With Soren—this was the same fear I'd felt when I'd been nineteen, staring into that chasm of longing and thinking I was hopeless up against a force as big as all that.

When Soren's phone timer rang, he made a sleepy noise and dragged himself unwillingly around the room to collect his clothes. He tilted my chin upward and kissed me once, all sweetness and no passion.

"Sleep well," he said.

I curled my knees to my chest. "Good night."

His footsteps were soft on the stairs. From below, I heard murmured voices; maybe Lukas was still watching TV.

I lay back down and touched the empty pillow on the other side of the bed. The faintest static buzzed in my ears. It was that trapped feeling, that claustrophobic feeling coming back. I'd tried to convince myself it was August-specific, but here it was again.

The pillowcase was cold beneath my fingers. I traced the outline of a shadow running down its middle. The static was getting worse, louder, and I thought about calling Soren. I thought about telling him everything and resting my head against his chest and letting myself cry.

When I tried to think of what Soren had said or done that had made me feel this way, I couldn't find anything. So maybe it wasn't him. Maybe it was me. Maybe this was a thing I did and would always do to myself: invent cages that shrank whenever I breathed in.

Maybe loving someone always meant trapping yourself.

Ten Thousand Years

2017

It was both humbling and embarrassing to realize how bad I was at fixing cars. Despite a childhood in the vicinity of cars and three-quarters of a mechanical engineering degree, I had little in the way of practical knowledge. On one of my first days in the shop, someone brought in a car that needed a new transmission. Henrik said, "Longitudinal powertrain, I hope?" My dad said, "Nah, it's a transverse." They sighed and laughed and made reference to how they'd need more coffee. I said, "Well, if you need anyone to use Bernoulli's principle for something, just let me know." As it turned out, they did not. I got us all coffees.

Damian and I only talked once, and when I explained to him what I was doing, he asked a string of curious and polite questions about my dad and Henrik that implied they were a peculiar species of animal he'd happened across at the zoo.

He said they must've been very grateful for my help; I assured him they really weren't.

Whenever I wasn't working, I was with Soren. Sometimes also Linnea or Lukas or even Delia, but mostly Soren. He was busier than I was, so we spent most of our time at his house. We'd wander the hills together, dogs galloping through the grass ahead, relocating the sheep or searching for a broken pipe. Sometimes, out there in the mist, when it felt like we were the first two people on earth, we would lie in the tall grass and the world would shrink to the size of Soren above me. The first time we went out there, he called me *kere*, which he pronounced as *care*; I asked him later about it, and he said, in Stennish, it meant "that which is precious to me." That was when Soren seemed most Soren: in the hills, undone, speaking Stennish.

It felt needy to ask for more of his time than I already had, so I didn't, even though I felt restless every night we didn't see each other. Every time we saw each other, we exchanged books—I would give him something sexy and adventurous, and he would give me something dense and thoughtful. I read these books with the sense of peering into his brain and beginning to resolve the pieces of him that remained enigmatic to me. There was no limit to how much of him I wanted to have. I didn't realize just how much time he was already carving for me until a man in tweed dropped off a decrepit car and greeted my dad familiarly. He was Anna's brother, my dad explained, and he was a professor of Stennish studies at the university.

We shook hands and he introduced himself as Kirk Sandison. I recognized him by face, though we'd never been introduced. When I told him my name, his eyebrows pinched together.

"Ah," he said, "yes, Tess. Of course. I'd forgotten. You're Soren Fell's..."

I must've looked confused—if not affronted—that Soren's professors knew I was his *dot-dot-dot* because Kirk hurried to add, "I'm his advisor. He was meant to come with me to Edinburgh this summer. Now I see why he didn't."

"Oh."

"Never mind that," Kirk said. I was busily deciding I liked him less than Anna. "He's a bright young man. He'll land on his feet."

It had never once occurred to me that I might've been the one standing in the way of Soren's education rather than the other way around. The embarrassment, though, came with a pulse of hope because if Soren was becoming the type of person who might go abroad for academic conferences, maybe he was also becoming a person who did not need to stay in Stenland forever.

"Do you think he'll be an academic, then?" I asked.

Kirk considered me. "He's special enough that there are opportunities out there, if he wishes to seize them. But he's not so special that the opportunities will seize him. Now, Erik—about these squeaky brakes."

All summer, the weather was tauntingly nice, like the island had conspired to make me forget its true nature. I kept catching myself glancing at little houses with For Sale signs, then abruptly feeling like someone had dumped ice water over my head.

The first—and only—hot day of summer arrived in late July. My dad had gone to spend the night at Anna's, which left Soren and me alone in the house playing at real adults. Well—I felt like I was playing. Soren carried himself with the same intent seriousness as he always did: cooking the chicken, wiping down the counter with a tea towel.

In my bedroom, Soren opened the windows, letting in a breeze that tasted like salt. It was light out, and it would be for hours, but not in the oppressively bright way of a California afternoon. Here, the sky was the golden gray of falling dust.

I lay back on my bed as he looked out the window. "I met Kirk Sandison," I said.

"Oh?"

"He said you worked together."

"That might be a stretch."

"What are you working on? You never talk about it."

He turned toward me. Where his hair didn't lie flat, the light turned the strands white. "I didn't think you'd want to hear." I must've looked hurt; he added: "Because it's Stennish. I know it's not—the same for you. As it is for me."

"I want to hear," I said. "Really."

He crossed the room, the curtains twirling behind him. When he lay beside me on the bed, the mattress caved slightly, tilting me toward him. Outside, seabirds called to each other: long, searching cries.

"You know there's not much left of the Stennish language?" he said. "The carvings in the cairns. A prayer and a poem here and there."

I nodded.

"It's just translation work. Seeing how much of a dictionary we can build. If we can find more fragments. That sort of thing."

"Why?" I said. "I don't mean it in a bad way."

He laced his hands behind his head and looked at my ceiling. "There's this word in Russian—*razbliuto*—that means something like 'the feeling you have toward someone you've fallen out of love with.' And in Old English, *sorhlufu*, which meant 'sorrow-love.' Feeling love and fear at the same time, or loving someone even when it's painful." When he blinked, slow flutters of his long, pale lashes, spidery shadows moved across his cheeks. He tilted his head to me. "I guess I'm looking for words like that."

"In Stennish?"

"Sometimes I think..." He took a breath. "I'd only be able to say the thing I really mean if I could say it in Stennish."

"What's the thing you really mean?"

Soren took my hand. His skin was cool against the summer air. When he pressed his lips to my fingers, he looked at me over the ridges of my knuckles. He kissed the inside of my wrist, my elbow, the hollow where my neck met my collarbone. His hands breathed down the sides of my body, coming to rest where the top of my jeans met the bottom of my shirt. Then they were off and his were pushed haplessly to the floor, my quilt kicked to meet them.

I held his jaw in my palm. Ran my thumb across the plane of his cheekbone.

"You know how I feel," I told him.

"Do I?"

"You always know."

I touched his chest, the width of it, and his waist, the narrowness.

"Tell me anyway," he said.

The fine golden hairs at his stomach; the cord of muscle along his thigh.

"Maybe if I knew Stennish," I said.

He shut his eyes and tilted up his chin. His voice was so thin I had to ask him to say it again. It was my name: once, softly, like that was all there was.

After, when I thought he'd started dozing off, he said: "Sometimes I think I'm only me when I'm with you."

Linnea and Henrik had decided to put a down payment on the little house by the cemetery, so she asked me to come with her for a final inspection. The estate agent stood by the door texting while Linnea showed me around the house. Ostensibly, she wanted my opinion because I was practical and not prone to daydreaming about DIY renovation. But she was distant in a way I couldn't quite place. At one point, she rested her elbows on the kitchen counter and gazed out the back window, where there was a view of a miniature yard and an empty plot of soil. I had to say her name three times before she heard me.

"It's cute," I said.

"Do you think it's too small?"

"No smaller than my house."

"It's three bedrooms," Linnea said.

"Okay, great. One for you, one for Henrik, and one for yoga. Or painting. Or a dog."

She chewed on her lip. "It's really more of a closet."

"So use it as a closet. Besides, we grew up in closet-sized bedrooms and turned out fine."

"I just don't want to outgrow this place, you know? I want to put art on the walls and plant things in the backyard, and I want to feel permanent. Does that make sense?"

No, actually—the idea of anchoring myself in one place sounded terrifying—but I took her point. I reminded myself that I wasn't the one who was making these permanent decisions and tried to look at the house objectively.

It *was* small. Three bedrooms, yes, but none bigger than the beds that would snug inside them. The kitchen had lots of light, and the fixtures looked like they were from this century. My least favorite thing about the house was its proximity to the church and the cemetery; from the front steps, you could see long rows of headstones and tombs and, towering above them like guardian angels, the stone statues of those who hadn't had flesh left to bury. To preserve their modesty, the statues were draped in traditional Stennish clothes—red woolen skirts and bodices laced with silvery chains, tunics with fine buttons and delicate embroidery. There was a group, mostly older women, who made and repaired the clothes. You couldn't go as far as the grocery store without seeing ten flyers inviting you to come join them. *Preserve local tradition; honor our families. Sewing circles every Wednesday and Saturday at the cultural center.* They were beautiful, the clothes, but they also made the statues look eerie, like they'd only been turned to stone a moment ago, like maybe you'd just done it.

"I'm just worried, I guess—" Linnea started, but before I could find out what she was worried about, my phone vibrated in my pocket. I gestured that I wouldn't pick it up, and she gestured that I should.

"Hello?"

"Hey," Soren said. His voice sounded echoey and grainy, like he was driving through a tunnel. "I did something stupid."

"Who is it?" Linnea asked.

"Soren. He did something stupid." Into the phone, I asked, "How stupid?"

"Six out of ten," he said. "I twisted my ankle, and now I can't drive home because I can't use the clutch. Can you pick me up?"

"I'm just at the new house with Linnea—"

She made a shooing motion, mouthing, *Go, go.* I nodded my thanks.

"Are you at a soccer game?" I asked.

"Fairhowe," he said.

"The cairn?" I asked. "Or the ice cream place in the visitors' center?"

"The cairn."

"Disappointing."

"Please?" he said. "The tourists are starting to stare at me."

I apologized again to Linnea; whatever she'd been thinking about telling me seemed to have slipped back out of reach. I promised myself I wouldn't forget about it and got in my car.

At Fairhowe, I parked by a discarded waffle cone and sent a collection of curious puffins scattering. Soren's truck was in the corner of the lot, but he wasn't in it. When I tried to text him, the message wouldn't go through.

From here, the cairn just looked like a mound in the earth, grass patchy and golden in places. Between us stood two fences, four informational plaques, and a bored-looking woman with a name tag whom I recognized as Eva Rendall from swim team.

I squeezed past a family of Italian tourists—who didn't look particularly pleased with me—and tapped Eva's shoulder.

"If your ticket—oh. Hi, Tess. You must be here for Soren."

"Is he inside?"

"Looking very sorry for himself."

I ducked under her arm—earning me another annoyed look from the line of tourists—and approached the cairn. It was smaller than I'd remembered. I had to duck to get through the entrance. There was the *drip drip drip* of water against stone, the echo of my shaky breathing.

I emerged into the main chamber, the one with the stone man and woman on opposite walls, staring at each other for eternity. When I stepped into the line of sight of the male statue, I was, for a moment, convinced I knew this man: the long lines of his lean body and the precise shape of his fine lips. What he looked like—what I had not realized as a child because Soren had still been a child then too—was that the statue looked like him, like Soren, like the contents of my heart turned to stone and perfectly preserved. And in the right light, if you didn't look too hard, you could almost convince yourself the woman looked like me.

I dragged my eyes away from the statues and scanned around for Soren. He was tucked behind an upright slab of stone, seated on the damp floor and facing the wall.

"Do you often hang out in tombs when I'm not around?" I said.

Soren looked up at me through his eyelashes. The greenish light made hollows of his cheeks. "I twisted my ankle."

"So you said. On what?"

"Outside. Before I came in. Eva told me that if I was going to look pitiful, I may as well look pitiful while I stare at my wall."

"This is your wall?"

"Hardly," Soren said, so bitterly I laughed.

I squatted next to him and looked at the stone slab. There were carvings in it, some more elegant than others. *M + F*, *Genesis 3:7*, something that looked angular and runic. It felt like I was being offered a rare and breakable glimpse inside of his head, or his heart.

Carefully, I said, "Why are you looking at this wall?"

He seemed to consider the question for longer than it needed considering. Finally he said, "I'm meant to be editing this paper."

"But you're on break."

"Not a school paper. Academic."

"You wrote a paper?"

"Just helped, really."

"And it's getting published somewhere?"

Soren shrugged. "Don't know. Sandison thinks I should have it so I can apply to master's programs."

I was simultaneously excited by the thought that Soren might leave Stenland after all and annoyed he'd never brought it up with me. Keeping my voice neutral, I said, "So what's this wall?"

He pointed to, but didn't quite touch, a line of text carved at ankle height. The markings were thin and precise, but it was dark enough that I couldn't read what they said.

"What language is that?"

"English," Soren said. "'Let me not dwell in this bare island by your spell.' It's Shakespeare. *The Tempest*."

"Who put it there?"

"Unclear. Sandison thinks it's from the 1870s."

"What does it mean?"

"It's from the end of the play," he said. "*The Tempest* takes place in this island full of magic, and in the epilogue, Prospero—he's a sorcerer who's been trapped there—asks the audience to free him by applauding."

I was distracted by a sharp burst of laughter. The Italian family, who'd come in behind me, was taking pictures of the male statue. I couldn't tell what they were saying, but I felt almost violently protective. I forced myself to swallow and look away. Soren was leaning toward the lines, his teeth pressing into his lip.

"So you wrote a paper on why someone would carve that here?" I asked.

"Not that line, specifically. It's—it's the fact that Prospero says *in*. He doesn't say '*on* this bare island.' He says '*in* this bare island.'"

"Oh. Like how Stenns say we live *in* Stenland, but tourists say they're staying *on* Stenland."

He nodded. "That's what the paper is about. We looked at all these old texts to see when someone used *in* and when someone used *on*. Because when you say you're *on* an island, it's like saying you're above it. But if you're *in* it, if you're part of it, it's—" He stopped abruptly. "I just think it's an odd line to choose. You have all of Shakespeare sitting in front of you, and you choose that."

"A line about being trapped," I said.

"A line about being part of a place," he said.

I heard footsteps—the family leaving. For a moment, we were alone, just me and Soren and the statues and the graffiti. Our breathing echoed. It felt momentarily like we were inside the body of a giant, listening to the pump of his heart and the rasp of his lungs.

"A master's program?" I asked.

"I don't know." He touched the stone with the tip of his index finger, exquisitely careful. "Sometimes I think none of this matters at all. Sometimes I think it's the only thing that does."

I set a hand on his cheek and tilted his face to mine. He kissed me, slowly, gently, comfortably, like we'd done it a thousand times and would do it a thousand more.

"I can't believe you twisted your ankle," I said.

"I was looking at my phone. Henrik has started sending me dog memes that were probably not funny when they were first created circa 2009."

"That really doesn't make it better."

"No," Soren agreed. "Help me up?"

I stood up, dusted off my hands, then offered them to him. "My damsel in distress."

"My knight in shining armor," he said.

"Ice cream?"

He put his arm around my shoulder. Now that I saw it, his ankle really did look terrible—swollen and discolored in the dim light. He leaned his weight against me, and when he looked at me, I could see the glow of the bulbs reflected in his eyes, the darkness filling the hollows of his face.

While I waited for ice cream, Soren safely seated on the hood of my car, I googled *Fairhowe cairn runes*. I opened the Wikipedia page. Under the "Graffiti" section, there was no mention of *The Tempest*. It did, however, explain the largest inscription running across the length of one wall, carved circa 1500 in Stennish, and when I read the translation, I felt as though I was happening upon a bit of information I'd known my whole life. When I returned to the car with our ice creams, I asked Soren if he was familiar with that inscription.

He said, "Everyone's familiar with that inscription. Oh, strawberry—I love you."

"Sorry?"

He looked slowly up at me. "Ah," he said. "Fuck."

I laughed because I didn't know what else to do. After a minute, he did too, setting his cup of ice cream on the car so he could take my hand. I let him.

"Just imagine if I'd brought you chocolate," I said.

"You don't have to say it," he told me.

"Soren."

"Tess."

"Did you actually mean that, or is it just because I bought you an ice cream?"

"That's not a real question," he said.

"Of course it's a real question. You've never said it before."

"That's not fair. Henrik told you years ago."

I was about to say, *That doesn't count because you had just walked out of our first would-be double date*, but before I could, I spotted Eva hurrying through the parking lot toward us. Her eyes looked red, and her cheeks.

As she went by, I reached out to brush her arm.

"Mia," she said.

I shook my head uncomprehendingly.

She didn't say anything else. She just got into her car, slammed the door, and screeched out of the parking lot. Soren was watching the place where her car had been, grimacing against the sun.

"Mia?" I asked.

"Her little sister," Soren said.

We wouldn't know the full story until that night, when gossip reached us via Saffi, who was friends with Eva. It went like this: three girls had a sleepover. They stayed up too late and drank liters of chocolate milk. When they woke up, they found black talon marks had appeared on each other's foreheads. Afraid they would get in trouble, they hid in the cellar of one of the girl's houses until their parents banged down the door to get them out. The girls were smart enough to close their eyes. They probably shouldn't have been sleeping in the same room at all, really, in case the curse had caught just one of them rather than all three. But no one really policed that rule until girls became young women, which these girls were not. It had been a long time since anyone had heard of such a thing: three skelds, just eight years old.

Soren and I didn't say anything else about love on the drive home. It was by silent agreement that he crawled into my bed that night; I would not wake up a skeld in the morning—because another skeld season had already begun.

As I brushed my teeth, I scrolled through my phone looking for more news about the girls. A text from Linnea: Coffee tomorrow morning? It's urgent... I remembered that I'd meant to figure out what was wrong. I told her I could meet at seven, before work, and she said that was fine.

I wondered if she, like me, felt her edges fraying. Three little girls, eight years old. Why not the three of us? Why them? I didn't know the girls, but I felt a cavernous maternal instinct thinking of them: I would take every skeld season if it meant those girls never had to. They would spend three months cooking and cleaning for themselves, pretending to be adults, and when their time was up, that was how they'd be treated. Like women. Like goddesses. Like witches. If one of them killed someone, she would never forgive herself, and I would never forgive Stenland.

I spat out my toothpaste and closed the newspaper's website. The tab behind it was still open, the one on the Fairhowe Cairn. It had a photo of the scratchy engraved letters and, below it, a caption that said:

Do you feel like the two of us
have been falling in love for ten thousand years?

The next morning, over coffee, Linnea told me she was pregnant.

White and Pink

2017

"I mean," Linnea said, "fairly sure."

"You've taken a test?"

"No, I decided to rely on reading tea leaves. Yes, of course I've taken a test."

"You sounded like Kitty just then," I said.

"And you sounded like my mum."

We were in our usual booth at Hedda's. Linnea was wearing her apron and name tag, and an American-looking man in a Yankees hat kept glancing over at us like he couldn't understand why she wouldn't pop up and take his order. From the back, I could hear the usual clanging and cursing that meant Hedda was making bread.

Our drinks—my coffee, Linnea's hot chocolate—sat untouched in the middle of the table. Linnea's fingers were knotted together.

"You've told your mum, then?" I asked.

"No. I just mean you sounded like she would. I haven't told anyone."

"Henrik?"

"I don't know how to break the news it's not his," she said.

"What?"

"You're really not in the mood for sarcasm today, are you?"

"I didn't know you had a sarcasm setting," I said.

"Maybe it's a sign that the baby will be sarcastic."

I gripped my coffee cup so tightly my knuckles turned white. "What do you want to do?"

Linnea looked down at her hands on the table. Her hair fell forward into her face. It looked tangled, like maybe she hadn't brushed it, but instead of making her look messy, it just made her look wild, like someone you'd happen upon running barefoot through a brook. Faerie Queen, like Kitty said. I wondered how old the man in the Yankees hat thought she was; you'd look at her one moment and she was thirty, then you'd catch a glimpse of her in a different light and, flash, she was fifteen.

"If it were you, you'd get rid of it," Linnea said.

I tried to keep my face neutral. "Yes. But you're you."

"And you wouldn't judge me if I wanted to have the baby?"

"I would just worry it would keep you from doing everything you wanted to do with life. But I wouldn't judge you."

"But what if *this*—" Linnea gestured around the café "—is what I want to do with life? Live here. Be with Henrik. Have kids and take them hiking and teach them to dance. Would that be so bad?"

"Whatever you decide," I finally said, "I'm here."

She exhaled and leaned back against the booth. It was such a complete expression of relief that I wondered if I should be offended; she'd been certain, it seemed, I would say something awful.

"I have a doctor's appointment later today," she said. "I'll tell Henrik once I'm sure. But the test really did look positive."

"It *looked* positive?"

"I mean," Linnea said, "the second line was kind of faint. But it wasn't not there, you know? Also, I didn't get my period this month."

"That's not necessarily proof," I said. "I miss my period, like, every other month."

"Really? Why didn't I know this?"

"Why would I tell you that?"

"You know," she said, "I really thought you were going to make fun of me for missing my pills."

"It concerns me how mean you think I am."

She snorted and lifted her hot chocolate, which I took to indicate she was feeling slightly more like herself again. "When was the last time you missed a birth control pill?"

"Never."

"Never? Like, not ever?"

"That is what never means."

"Right. I briefly forgot that I was talking to Robot Tess."

"Hey," I said. "You're going to hurt my feeling."

As we sat there, the Yankees man growing increasingly impatient, I rolled the thought of Linnea as a mum around in my head. In some ways, she'd always been the most maternal of the three of us—the most likely to coo at small children and the quickest to offer a compassionate word and a shoulder to cry on. On the other hand, she'd also always been the one who'd most wanted to be parented; Kitty and I had been in a hurry to be treated like adults, easily embarrassed by affection.

I hoped Henrik would say all the right things. I wasn't sure what those things were, but I hoped Henrik knew instinctively. *Be kind to her,* I thought. *Just, please, be kind to her.*

On the walk back home, my feet led me into the grocery store of their own accord. I was only half paying attention. I had my phone open, the newspaper's website again, and was reading about the three little girls. Apparently, one of the windows at Ramna Skaill had shattered in the night. Constables were unsure whether it was a malicious act by someone from town, a panicked gesture from one of the girls, or a freak weather incident. I considered each of the options in turn, swirling downward through them and hating each one more the longer it festered in my brain. My hatred for the girls' parents came on so vividly that for a moment, I couldn't see anything. Why hadn't their parents moved? Why hadn't their parents taken them away from this place? The shelves refigured in front of me, and I found myself staring at a row of white-and-pink boxes.

I swept one into my basket and proceeded to cover it up with other things I did not need, as if that would prevent the cashier from noticing it. Chocolate milk? Sure. Shampoo? Fine, let's get some. I stared at my phone as my items were scanned—*beep*, *beep*, pause, *beep*—and kept refreshing the newspaper's comment section.

Back at home, I shouted to my dad in the garage that I'd be there in a minute. I brought my bags into the bathroom with me without unloading the groceries. I opened the white-and-pink box and read the instructions twice. As I'd told Linnea, I missed my period every other month. Sometimes two months in a row. As someone prone to panic, I'd long since schooled myself into not panicking about this. Like Linnea had said, I was Robot Tess; I took my birth control every day. I took it perfectly.

I sat on the toilet seat and waited.

That evening, Soren came over to make dinner with me because my dad was at Anna's house again. I talked for a while, and he slowly set down the knife he was using to cut potatoes, and because he wasn't saying anything, when Linnea called me, I accepted it.

"Not pregnant!" she shouted. "Oh my god. So the doctor thinks I read my test wrong or didn't wait long enough or something? I don't know. I'm embarrassed. But actually, I had no idea how relieved I was going to feel getting the news. Thank you for being there for me this morning."

"No problem," I said, still watching Soren. "I'm so happy you're happy."

"Literally so happy! Can we do drinks? Want to hang out?"

"Actually, can I call you back later?"

"Oh," she said. "Yeah, sure, of course. I love you, in case you forgot. Not pregnant!"

I set my phone face down on the kitchen counter.

"Are you sure?" Soren finally asked.

"I mean," I said, "fairly sure."

Mifepristone

2017

Soren drove me to the doctor that weekend. I told him I could drive myself; it wasn't like I was dying.

He said, "I am so utterly useless in this entire situation. Please just let me drive you."

If I didn't know what I'd wanted Henrik to say to Linnea, I certainly didn't know what I wanted Soren to say to me. I would've been angry if he'd tried to make a decision for me, but I also found I was angry at his complete unwillingness to reveal any opinion on the matter.

He parked the car, but neither of us got out. I realized belatedly that his ankle must've started feeling better.

I'd already been here once. On Wednesday. I'd taken a test and scheduled a follow-up. The nurse had very kindly explained everything that would happen: I would take a dose of mifepristone at the hospital and then a dose of misoprostol at home two days later. Some women experienced cramping, but the nurse had assured me it wasn't always bad. She'd said I should find something good on Netflix and make myself brownies. I'd said I would.

"Tess."

I wasn't sure how long I'd been sitting in the car; it felt like it might've been a while.

Soren took my hand lightly in his, like he thought I might pull away. I didn't. I studied the length of his fingers, the veins in the back of his hand, the white-gold hair on his forearms. I tried to look at his face, the sharp jaw and the narrow lips and the thin nose, like we were strangers and I was seeing him for the first time, but I couldn't do it. I couldn't imagine not knowing him. For just a moment, I was savagely proud that my child was half his. Then the moment was gone and the guilt crashed in, and I felt once more like I was being punished for my bottomless well of want.

"You wish I was keeping it," I told Soren.

"Excuse me?"

"You wish I wanted to keep the baby and that we'd stay here and get married and be like our parents."

He let go of my hand. I could still smell his toothpaste.

"You're not going to say anything," I said. "Right."

"I'm trying to figure out how to respond. I think that's the worst thing you've ever said to me."

"Well, it's true, isn't it?"

"Of course it's not true," he said.

"So you want me to go in there?"

He looked like he wasn't sure whether to be angry or confused, which made two of us. "Yes!"

"Well, you never said so. You never even asked what I was going to do."

"Christ, Tess, you know this isn't my first time meeting you?

Of course you don't want to have a child. Why do you think *I* would want that?"

"Because—you're you."

"What," he said, "someone who seems like they'd really love to spend more time changing diapers?"

"Someone who stays here," I said.

"Sometimes you sound just like a tourist."

I winced. He looked away.

"The choice between being an engineer and having a kid isn't actually binary," he said. "Some people do both. Some people—and this may shock you—do neither."

"I didn't say I never wanted kids."

"Of course you never want kids."

"Okay," I said. "Since you know me so well."

I got out and slammed the door before he could respond, or not. I went into the hospital alone. After my first appointment, I'd expected the same nurse, so I was surprised when this time Anna came into the room with a pill in a wax paper cup. She was in bright yellow scrubs. Her expression was pleasant and practical and completely without pity, which made me feel better.

"Please don't tell my dad," I said.

"That would be illegal," Anna said. "And also against my conscience. But he wouldn't be upset with you, if that's what you're worried about."

"I don't like the thought of him knowing I've had sex."

"Ah," Anna said. "I'm sorry, sweetheart, but I think he's figured it out by now."

I took the pill. I'd been worried I would feel an immediate wave of wrongness, but instead I felt rightness: like my body was being returned to its correct shape. Anna patted my shoulder comfortingly. I said I was sorry and that I wasn't sure why I was crying.

"Maybe because it's frightening to stand at a crossroads, no matter how sure you are which path is yours?" She gave me the second pill and my instructions to take it in two days' time. "Is anyone here with you?"

"Soren's in the car," I said. And then, because I was still angry at him, I added, "Unless he's decided to drive off."

"Now you're just fishing."

"Fishing for what?"

"For me to tell you that if you think that boy would drive off, you have never paid attention to the way he looks at you."

It was the word *boy* that did it. Made me start crying again. With relief, mostly. Because if I hadn't taken that pill, she probably would've called him a man.

When I got back to the parking lot, Soren had not, in fact, decided to drive off. His head was bent against the steering wheel, but he looked up when I opened the door.

"Are you okay?" he asked.

I nodded and slid into the passenger seat. Shut the door again, cocooning us in silence.

"I just keeping thinking of the girls," I said. My voice came out hoarse.

"The skelds?"

"I just keep thinking someone should've protected them."

"There's nothing anyone could've done," he said.

"Except leave."

Neither of us spoke for a minute. He ran his hands up and down the steering wheel. Outside, a man in a wheelchair was pushing himself toward the automatic doors.

"For the record," Soren said, "even if I did want a kid right now, I never would've wanted you to have one. I love you a lot more than I could love the idea of a child."

"You said you love me."

"I know. On purpose and everything."

I rested my temple against the headrest, looking at him. I

reached out to push his hair off his forehead, and he took my hand and pressed his lips against my palm.

"You know I love you too, right?" I said.

He moved his thumb where his lips had been, running slow circles around the center of my hand. I wondered if he could tell I'd been crying.

"The last time we saw each other before you moved..." he started.

"I loved you then too."

"Huh."

"You haven't really been in love with me since we were twelve," I said.

"Oh, at least. That's why I started reading so much. My mum said you were the smartest kid in our class and I had to read a lot if I wanted to impress you."

"That's not true."

He shrugged like it didn't much matter to him whether I believed his story or not. I didn't, but then again, when I thought back, I couldn't quite remember if I had always been infinitely aware of Soren or if it was just in retrospect that he occupied so much of my memory. I couldn't remember exactly when I'd fallen in love with him any more than I could remember exactly when we'd met; it was more like it had been true from the start.

Casually, I said, "What if you came to California with me?"

He put the car in Reverse. Stretched one arm behind the back of my seat and looked over his shoulder, steering with just his palm flat against the wheel. As we turned left away from the hospital, I began to wonder if I had only imagined speaking.

"Yeah," Soren said then. "Okay."

Freestyle

2022

I stayed in my room while Henrik moved his things into the keepers' cottage. Linnea and Kitty went down to chat with the men—to thank them, I supposed.

Kitty texted me to say it was time for dinner and that Lukas had made something of unsubstantiated gustatory delight. I considered staying in my room but decided that would be too childish, so I texted back saying I was coming to substantiate presently.

We ate in the hearth room on the first floor, where someone had dragged a table and six chairs in front of the fire. The men had sleep masks over their eyes. It used to be that the skelds had worn the blindfolds, even in the keep, but in the past decade, most people had decided it wasn't fair to make us helpless in the one place we were meant to feel safe. While I was glad not to be blindfolded, I was nonetheless so embarrassed for the keepers that my skin hurt.

"Tess is here," Linnea announced.

"I'm starving," Lukas said. "Someone put food on my plate and hand me a fork."

I asked warily if we were going to do this every night, and Linnea said, "Oh, no, of course not—just to sort out some details real quick."

I took the seat between Linnea and Kitty on one side of the table, opposite Lukas, who was feeling around impatiently for his cutlery. Henrik was indiscreetly nudging Linnea's leg under the table, smiling pleasantly to himself like this was a fine way to spend his would-be wedding day. For his part, Soren sat utterly still, jaw clenched, head tilted to the side, like he was trying to hear better to make up for not seeing.

"Okay!" Linnea said. "So, just to catch everyone up—Henrik is going to live in the cottage, but Soren and Lukas will come by every day to keep him company and make sure everything is going all right."

"Because they're lazy?" Kitty asked.

Linnea folded her hands primly on the table. I got the sense that she felt she was the leader of our skeld season, that it was her fault for bringing us back, so she would make sure nothing went wrong. "Because they have important farm things to do."

"She means making sure the sheep fuck each other properly," Lukas said.

"They know what she means," Soren said.

Linnea continued: they would cover their eyes if they were in the keep, and we would cover our eyes if we left, though we were only supposed to go outside if there was some sort of emergency. If we were dying for fresh air, the windows on the fourth floor opened, but we should cover our eyes anyway because we might glimpse someone walking around down below. When closed, the windows were too mottled to see through clearly; no one had ever been turned to stone through them. The rest of the island had, of course, been made aware of the situation, and no one but Henrik, Lukas, and Soren would be allowed down the road to Ramna Skaill. Linnea had a printout of phone numbers we could call in case of assorted emergencies: fire, nervous breakdown, accidental poisoning.

"What about intentional poisoning?" Kitty asked.

"I'm not sure that's actually helpful at this juncture," Linnea said. "Thanks, though."

Once Linnea was finished, Lukas declared he would keel over dead if he was not given something to eat, so Linnea slopped big spoonfuls of gustatory delight onto every plate.

"It's shepherd's pie," Lukas explained.

Kitty poked it experimentally with her fork. "Is it?"

"I was telling Soren and Henrik. *You* can see."

"That is one opinion," she said.

"Okay, so Kitty will be cooking for herself this skeld season."

"God, I didn't even think of that. Have they invented delivery here yet?"

"Yes," I said, "but it's just one sheep with a scooter."

"So that's where she went," Soren said.

I laughed, but no one else did. Everyone else just looked uncomfortable. I clattered my fork against my plate and wished the ceiling would cave in.

Soren and Lukas got up to leave soon after. Henrik lingered at the table with Linnea, whispering something into her ear, which left me wondering if I was allowed to ask if they were planning to embrace abstinence this skeld season.

Kitty took Soren by the arm and led him to the door, which left me with Lukas. He allowed himself to be guided, but he was so much larger than me that I felt off balance.

"How's Noah taking it?" Lukas asked.

"Noah."

"What did he say when you told him about skeld season?"

Kitty and Soren had stopped at the threshold, and they were quiet like they were listening.

"He said, 'Wow, you were right all along.'"

"Has to be weird. You're not going to see him for three months."

"Right," I said.

I dropped his arm and stepped back inside, by Kitty.

"Do you two want anything tomorrow?" Lukas asked. "Board games. Knitting needles. Whatever it is Kitty does for fun when she's not making spreadsheets."

"Bring me books," Kitty said, "so I may emerge from this hellhole morally and intellectually superior."

To Soren, Lukas said, "That's on you, Captain Superior."

Soren shrugged and said he'd take a look.

We left Linnea and Henrik to engage in whatever ill-advised activity they were determined to engage in and went upstairs. Kitty declared she was going to take a three-month bath. I went to my room and lay back on my bed, wondering if this was the bed my mum had slept on after she'd killed Mattias and Sara Fell. I also wondered if anyone had noticed, when Lukas had asked me about Noah, that it was the first time I'd realized I had not yet told him.

So I called him. When he picked up, he asked me how the wedding was.

"Change of plans," I said.

"They didn't call it off, did they?"

"Temporarily."

There were loud voices in the background and what sounded like an acoustic guitar. In all the time we had dated, I had never once heard Noah turn down an invitation. Sometimes he went to two dinners in the same night. He usually didn't make a show about it when I didn't want to go—which was always—but I felt guilty anyway. My first thought when I heard that discordant acoustic guitar was *Thank god I don't have to go to a house party for three months.*

"Why?"

"Skeld season."

He repeated it back to me, louder and pitching high at the end. I heard the music falter and wished he'd take this call somewhere else. I could've asked him to step outside, but I was hoping he'd think to do it for himself.

"So," I said, "I guess I'll see you in three months."

"Wait, shit, really? What does this mean for your job?"

"I have to send some emails. Hopefully I can work remotely."

"What if you leave?" he asked. "Get on a boat to Iceland or something?"

"I'll still be cursed for three months. I'll just be cursed in Iceland."

"Can you do video calls? Does the curse work that way?"

"I don't know. I don't think anyone's ever tested it."

"Why not? Should we?"

"You're going to risk being turned into stone so you can have a video call?"

"Oh," he said. "Fair point."

He wasn't stepping outside. The music had stopped altogether, but I could hear voices murmuring in the background. I caught *On Shetland* and then *No, it's Stenland* and then *Why did I think she was Danish?*

"Anyway," I said. "Just wanted to let you know."

"I'm so sorry, Tess. Shit luck. Let me know if you need anything."

What I needed was for him to step outside. I needed for him to understand that my mum had killed two people and that their stone bodies were currently standing in a cemetery of other stone bodies, some a thousand years old. I needed for him to get it because I could not bear to explain.

But he would never be able to understand how Stenland had

shaped me because I had not given him the opportunity—with him, I had done my best job yet of becoming un-Stennish. His sound briefly cut out, and I felt a pressure in my throat at the distance, the absence of him, the fear that I had not let him see the truth of who I was.

"I love you," I said.

"I love you too. This'll be over before you know it."

I ended the call and hoped he was right.

That night, I woke up just past one because I'd been dreaming about Soren. Not the one with the plane and the dead daughter. In this dream, we were having sex under a Christmas tree while snow fell tastefully from the ceiling. During, I thought: *I forgot that this is what he looks like up close.* When I woke up, I realized I obviously hadn't forgotten. Good try, though.

I punched my pillow into a more reasonable shape and fell asleep again after some hours.

This time, I had the dream about the plane and the dead daughter.

When I considered the fact that I was still attracted to Soren, it made me feel sinful and grotesque, like an evil stepmother from a fairy tale. To combat this, I mentally appended everything he said with the phrase *because I am so in love with Saffi.* I chose this phrase for two reasons. The first was that it made me deeply uncomfortable, which I felt I deserved. The second was because my subconscious could clearly use the fucking reminder.

While we were eating breakfast on the third day of our captivity, he called—Kitty, not me—and got put on speakerphone.

"I'm going to the store," he said, "*because I am so in love with Saffi.* Do you need anything?"

"Wine," Kitty said.

"And?"

"Just wine for me, thanks."

"Linnea," he said, "can I get you anything? *Because I am so in love with Saffi?*"

"I wouldn't mind ingredients to make some sort of kringle. So, you know. Kringle things."

"Text me." There was a pause. "Tess?"

"Coffee. Please. The beans in the blue bag."

"I know which bag," he said, *"because I am so in love with Saffi."*

I told myself it was normal to still be attracted to other people outside your relationship as long as you didn't do anything about it, which I never would. I also told myself that this was clearly a sign I needed to keep busy, so I threw myself violently into work. My supervisor, Carla, was fine with me working remotely for three months, but she asked if I wouldn't rather just take some sick leave or something. I said, *No, thanks, please don't make me.*

When Soren deposited the groceries on our front step, he also left behind a cardboard box of books. Kitty spread them across the table and said, "It's like he's trying to prove a point."

"What point?" Linnea asked.

"That he's the cleverest boy in all the land."

There were thirty books, give or take, in a variety of genres. I recognized some of them from his shelves and bedside tables over the years: the one on Neolithic structures he'd taken camping in California, and *The Tempest*, and *Independent People*. There was *Downwelling*, the only Stennish novel to win the Booker Prize. There were mysteries and a box-set fantasy series Soren had read all of, thousands of pages of sexy elves and dragons, just because I'd loved it.

Kitty picked up *Beowulf* and said, "Ah, fuck, I probably have to read this now that he's gone and made a point about it." She opened to the first page, frowned, and said, "Then again, maybe I won't and say I did."

Linnea picked up something with a blue cover. "I can't help but notice there are no shirtless men on any of these."

"Yes, perhaps Soren is withholding his supply of erotica."

Linnea sniffed. "I want sex and a happily-ever-after. He'll have to make a trip to the library. Here, Tess, this one's for you."

She tried to pass me the book with the blue cover, but I flinched. "What do you mean, for me?"

"Go on," Linnea said. "It's obviously for you."

When I still didn't take it, she set it on the table by my laptop. *Freestyle*, the cover said, *A Memoir by Elsa Bergquist*. Elsa Bergquist was Stenland's only Olympic medalist; she'd swum the 800 free in the eighties. She hadn't lived in Stenland for years, but she still occasionally made the news for attempting frigid and shark-filled channel crossings. Her book had been published two years prior. I had been given it as a gift three times and never read past the first page.

I finally opened it that night. Unlike my three gifted copies, stiff and sterile, this one had all the ease of a pre-read book. The pages didn't lie flat. There was a tear in the inside cover flap.

Eventually, past midnight, I got to the end. Soren had drawn a box around the last page, underlining sentences he liked. There were other underlines throughout the book, but this page had the most of them.

Distance swimmers know that you can't think about anything in the water for more than seven minutes. That's the cutoff. Once you're swimming for longer than seven minutes continuously, you stop noticing your body is a body at all. You're just a pillow of saltwater in a bath of saltwater, dreaming your way through the waves.

I swam this morning, and while I was out, I saw the biggest shark fin, as tall as my forearm. All around me, the clouds were heavy and the waves were thrashing. It's not that I wasn't afraid; it's that I was busier being awestruck.

That's the thing we're all after, I think: awe. We should all endeavor to be awed at least once a day. Awe makes your body transparent and lets everything flow in and out again. How you manufacture awe, I'm not sure. Perhaps there's no way. Perhaps that's the whole point.

In the meantime, I will keep swimming.

I texted Noah as soon as I finished to tell him he had to read it, the way I used to text Soren about everything I read, and Noah wrote back to say, Looks good, I'll check it out! I did not actually think he would ever check it out.

Noah and I loved each other, but were not obsessed with each other. He had never felt the need to crawl inside my brain and make sense of what he found. It was healthier this way, I thought—just to be comfortable.

I thought about texting Soren too, to tell him thank you. I wrote the text. Deleted it. Wondered if there was any way to speak to him that would not feel morally suspect. Maybe there were some people who couldn't just exist in the periphery of your life; maybe Soren was my all or nothing. Because I would tell him I loved the book, and then he would ask for a recommendation from me, and back and forth we'd go, just like when I'd dated August. I couldn't do it to Noah, to Saffi, to Soren, to myself. *We should all endeavor to be awed once a day*, Elsa Bergquist had said, and what awed me then was this: that even if Soren and I never spoke again, there was no excising him from me because we had already done too much to each other when we were too young to know any better.

Palo Alto

2017

The woman at the gate called us Mr. Fell and Ms. Eriksson. Soren said he felt unduly fancy. I told him it was the flannel that tipped him over the edge.

It was an eleven-and-a-half-hour flight from Frankfurt to SFO. I told Soren he should take the window since he'd never flown farther than Tórshavn before. He told me I should take the window because the eleven and a half hours would be plenty exciting from the middle seat.

When the plane took off, Soren suggested we watch a documentary on Le Mans. I suggested we watch one about British people digging through mud for shards of pottery. The man sitting in the aisle seat said we sounded just like him and his wife, except that his wife would probably want to watch one of her rom-coms. Soren and I smiled indulgently at each other and decided not to tell the man that we were nothing like him and his wife, actually, because we were better at being in love than anyone who'd ever tried it before.

We watched both. When it came time to go to sleep, Soren rested his head on my lap and I ran my fingers through his hair, staring out the window at a black expanse of sky and an ocean just as dark.

Soren had a visitor visa. It lasted six months, and he couldn't work on it. He'd also applied for an agriculture visa, but those could take months to process. When we told Elin about our plan, he'd been quick to mention the agriculture visa—that he'd be working, making money, learning about other farms in other places. But when it was just the two of us, I'd gotten the impression he wasn't eager for that visa to get approved; it would mean working with animals that weren't his on land he didn't know, trapped under a hot, inland sun with little pay, probably at least a two-hour drive away from me.

So he was going to live in my room. The Bay Area was too expensive for him to get his own apartment. My senior-year housing was a pseudo-apartment on campus; I'd have a kitchen and a bedroom and a living space I shared with a woman I didn't know, but who I hoped would keep to herself enough that she wouldn't notice or care that she had two roommates instead of one. It was against Stanford's policies, technically, and as plans went, it wasn't particularly well thought out. But it was the first illegal thing either of us had done, and we were rather in love with ourselves over it, doing something daring in the name of romance.

Elin had said, "Jesus, Mary, Joseph, you'll be bored out of your mind."

"I won't," Soren had said stubbornly. "I'll be applying to master's programs. And reading."

She'd grunted. It was the closest thing we got to her approval.

When I'd told my dad Soren was coming to California with me, he'd been making pancakes. He'd stared at the griddle for a while, then said, "For how long?"

"I don't know," I'd said. "Indefinitely?"

"You two are moving back here when you graduate?"

"No. Why would you think that?"

"I just figured," my dad had said. "He goes where you want to be for a while, then you go where he wants to be."

"Maybe he doesn't want to be in Stenland anymore," I'd said.

"Right. Of course. Don't mind me, Tessie—I'm sure you've thought about all this more than me."

My mum had been the bluntest. I'd told her on the phone, and she'd said, "You cannot be serious. He's going to live in your tiny bedroom? In a country he's never been to? With no friends, no family, and no work to keep him occupied?"

"He'll be applying to master's programs."

"You're putting him in a position where he's going to be incredibly needy. You'll end up killing him. Or breaking his heart."

"Oh, because you're such an expert on relationships?" I'd said.

She'd hung up on me, which had been immature, but also a relief. I hadn't wanted to hear what else she'd had to say.

Linnea had thought it was a great idea. So had Kitty. In Linnea's case, she'd thought it meant both Soren and I would end up coming back to Stenland at some point. In Kitty's case, she'd thought it meant neither of us would. I'd begun to see it as a kind of Rorschach test for whether someone was a stayer or a leaver, which of the two they thought Soren and I would end up doing. I knew beyond doubt that we weren't going back, but I also knew it made me sound cold and uncompromising to say so, so I didn't. Soren knew, though. He'd known when he'd agreed to be with me again. That was the deal. I was almost entirely sure of it.

★★★

Probably because of what my mum had said, I was afraid I would begin to resent the space Soren took. I kept waiting, as we picked up my key and made our way to my apartment. I waited as he unpacked his books on my shelf and his clothes into the wardrobe. I waited as he hung up the painting Kitty had given me half a lifetime ago.

"It's a very small bed they've provided," Soren said.

"Almost as if they don't want two people sleeping in it."

"You can just sleep on top of me. I'll lie very still."

"Hot," I said.

The first night back, we went off campus for dinner. Over pizza—"What kind of pizza costs twenty-eight dollars?" Soren asked—I introduced him to Damian and Bianca and a handful of our other mutual friends. No one mentioned August.

In the bathroom, while we were washing our hands, Bianca said, "Fucking hell, Tess, is everyone on Stenland that hot?"

"No," I said smugly, "just him."

When we got back to the table, Damian was asking Soren what he thought about a hard-hitting documentary about the skelds, and Soren was staring blankly at him like he was wondering if he'd misheard.

"Tess says you're really into Stennish history," Damian was saying. "I figured you'd be great for something like that."

"People have done documentaries before," Soren said.

"But all of them are shitty. No one ever gets the local perspective."

"Can't imagine why," Soren said.

When Damian saw me, his smile faltered. "Just think about it, yeah? You deserve to tell the story your way for once."

Once the conversation had moved on, Soren glanced at me, but he was too polite to make his feelings any more obvious.

Even when we were alone again, he never said he didn't like my friends, but I knew he didn't. I thought it probably had to do with the way they acted like I was engaging in some sort of exciting anthropological study by dating someone who had not even once interned at Goldman Sachs.

We didn't spend much time with them after that—my friends. I told myself it was a small sacrifice to make to get to spend more time with Soren, who, after all, had no one but me. It didn't occur to me until later that having no friends but me was worse than having friends about whom he was only lukewarm.

The calendar said it was autumn, but the air still tasted like summer. I woke up looking at Soren every morning. He sent me on long voyages to the library to collect textbooks and novels and bound theses that almost certainly no one had read in years. My head filled with new equations and programming languages, and my arms ached from sanding bits of metal clean for class projects. And Soren was always there.

For the first time in my life, I felt like an adult: we bought vacuum-sealed packages of gnocchi from Trader Joe's and bottles of red wine, and we walked hand-in-hand with our reusable grocery bags back home through the eucalyptus trees. When a warm breeze came through, the pale green leaves spun on their axes. Soren had never been so tan. I could just make out the shape of his eyes through his sunglasses as he gazed at the bright sky, the fluttering leaves, the squirrels racing up rainbow-barked trunks. At the apartment, he cooked with a tea towel over one shoulder. I ostensibly did a problem set at the table, but mostly I watched his back—the way his shoulders moved beneath his T-shirt, the way he poured two glasses of wine and wiped a stray drop clean with his thumb.

We had so much sex.

Most of the campus emptied out for Thanksgiving. Soren and I had no reason to celebrate American Thanksgiving, so we drove to Santa Cruz and walked through the surf.

"I have something for you," he said. He pulled a cardboard box from the inner pocket of his jacket and handed it to me.

"Oh," I said, "Toaster Strudel. You shouldn't have."

"Open it."

I did, and inside sat his mother's necklace—the silver chain and the pendant with its ice-white crystal. I handed him the empty box and fastened the necklace around my throat.

"I didn't want you to think it was a ring," he said.

"It's just a shame there weren't also Toaster Strudels in there."

"I'll buy you more."

We stood in the ocean until my feet began to ache with cold. I tried to pull him out, but for the longest time, he wouldn't budge. He just kept staring at the ocean, looking at the waves like he was searching for something he couldn't find. Eventually, I took off my shirt and threw it at the back of his head. He caught it, realized what it was, and looked back over his shoulder at me.

"Interesting tactic," he said.

"I'm very cold."

"Whose fault is that?"

"Can we get burritos?" I asked.

"Can I keep your shirt?"

"Only if you buy the burritos."

Finally, he stepped out of the ocean after me. Neither of us said *I love you.* It seemed too obvious to bother.

When I got out of the shower back at home, I wrapped a towel around myself that was probably too small to try to wrap around myself. I noticed myself doing things like that often: pretending I didn't notice how low my shirt had slipped down my chest or how high my skirt had ridden up my hips. Maybe it should've felt like an act, the way it had with August. Maybe it did feel like an act. I kept doing it anyway. I felt at my most powerful when Soren wanted me and my least powerful when he didn't.

So when I found Soren sitting on the side of the bed, hunched over, phone pressed to his ear, the annoyance came half a second before the concern. When I heard the voice thinly through the other end—Lukas, sounding panicked—I sat next to Soren and put a hand on his knee. He set his hand on top of mine absently.

"Okay," Soren said. "Love you too."

When he put down the phone, I expected him to tell me what the call was about. He didn't; he just held my hand where it was and looked down at our tangled fingers.

"Lukas?" I asked.

He nodded.

"What's wrong?"

"The girls," Soren said. "The skelds."

I was ashamed how little I'd thought of them since getting back to California; as if they no longer represented me, or my theoretical daughter, now that I wasn't in Stenland. I nodded, and slowly, haltingly, Soren told me the story.

It was the last week of their time as skelds. Wasn't it always? The worst always seemed to happen right at the very end. Right when you started to think you'd escaped.

They'd been making dinner. Heating up a casserole that one of the keepers had left at the door. One of the girls was taking the dish out of the oven, but it was heavier and hotter than she'd expected, hot even through the potholders, so she'd dropped it and the glass and molten food landed on one of the other girl's feet. Mia. Eva's little sister. Mia wasn't wearing any shoes, not even socks, and her feet were burned and bones were broken. She passed out from the pain, but the other little girls had been good, so good, calling their keepers and dutifully wrapping blinds around their eyes and around Mia's.

They hadn't wanted to take her out of Ramna Skaill, but

there were so many tiny bone fragments that she needed surgery. So one of the keepers, an aunt, found an old pair of ski goggles and covered the lenses in fabric and secured it so it would definitely not come off. When Mia woke up—I kept imagining it, the darkness, the sterile lemon smell, the *beep beep beep* of machinery—she didn't remember what she was. She'd torn the goggles off her face before anyone had realized she was awake.

There were three people in the room at the time. One was Mia's father, who had gone to sleep with a blindfold around his eyes as a precaution. While he'd slept, it had slid up his forehead, exposing his eyes. Of course they'd opened when his daughter screamed. And now he was dead.

The other two people, a senior nurse and a new student, had come to change the bandages on Mia's feet. They'd been keeping their eyes carefully averted from the girl, just to be safe, but when a child shrieks, you look. You just look. It's so hard not to.

The student managed to shut her eyes again just in time. Mia had looked at the senior nurse first.

Soren said, "Tess, I'm really sorry."

He told me that Linnea had survived, and Anna had not.

The funerals would be in three days' time.

Soren and I spent the night curled around each other in our too-small bed with my phone, set to Speaker, sitting on the mattress. It was hours to dawn in Stenland, but everyone was awake. We talked to my dad, to Linnea and Henrik, to Kitty, to Elin. Everyone was crying. Someone would say, *That poor little girl.* Then someone would say, *But if she'd just kept on the mask…*

My spine pressed against the curve of Soren's chest and stomach. He ran his hands through my hair until it was smooth and fine. None of us talked all that much, not on either end of the phone. We just sat together in our bubble of mourning, Soren and me and our family on the other side of the world. You could escape Stenland, but you couldn't escape being Stennish.

Between calls, he got up to get me a glass of water. When he settled himself around me again, he called me *kere* in his softest voice.

"Please don't," I said.

"Don't what?"

"Bring it here."

"Stennish?" he asked.

"Why can't you just hate it already?"

I felt his forehead press against the back of my neck. His muffled answer: "I don't know."

"But your parents…"

"I don't know, okay?"

It wasn't. "You should hate the island and the curse and my mum and me. You just should."

But then Kitty's mum called, checking in, so he never ended up responding. Finally, when my phone was dead and it was just the two of us again, I told Soren that I would never let my daughter set foot in Stenland.

"Yeah," he said. It was only when I heard his voice that I realized he was crying. "Yeah, I know."

Everything Else in the World

2018

We didn't go back for the funerals. I asked my dad if he wanted me to come home for Christmas, but he surprised me by saying he was going to stay with my mum in Edinburgh. I didn't think there was anything romantic about it. But I was relieved to hear it anyway—that I didn't have to go back to that place. That island.

And life kept going.

In January, Lukas flew out from Stenland, and Kitty and Georgia from England. I was almost certain Kitty's parents had paid for Lukas's ticket. Linnea and Henrik had wanted to come, but flights were too expensive.

Georgia had insisted we find some tall Californian trees and sleep under them. We spent the first few hours shuffling uncomfortably through grief and awkwardness, through Soren trying to talk about home and Lukas changing the conversation to anything else. But there was solace among the leviathan trees. You got the sense that your problems were small and your life was short, so why not just breathe? We all began to unfurl, then to curl back into each other, rediscovering our old rhythms.

On the first evening of our camping trip, we got back from a hike to discover a black bear pawing through the wreckage of our campsite. It looked up at us, startled, and Kitty said, "Maybe he's looking for marmalade."

Lukas said, "If that's the last thing I hear before I die, I'll be gutted."

"Perhaps literally," Kitty said.

There had been a sign near the entrance to the campsite warning about bears and how you shouldn't leave food or deodorant or feminine hygiene products where a bear could reach them, including your tent or your car because apparently bears could smell through steel. I hadn't paid much attention to these warnings because being afraid of bears felt fanciful, like being afraid of quicksand or dragons.

We backed away slowly from the bear, who was making a low, rumbling growl. I unlocked the rental car.

That night, we'd meant to make burrito bowls and s'mores over a campfire. Instead, I drove us to the nearest service station, where we bought seven sleeves of Oreos. When we got back to the campsite, the bear was gone. We set the tents back up as well as we could, which mostly involved throwing things away.

"We go back to civilization now, right?" Lukas asked.

"Nah," Georgia said. "What are the odds it comes back?"

"Medium?" he said.

We started feeling queasy after about five Oreos, but Lukas made us eat all of them so the bear wouldn't have anything left to smell.

"Besides us," Kitty pointed out.

Lukas decided to sleep in the car. Kitty and Georgia took the tent the bear had ignored, which left Soren and me in a tent with two broken poles and a hole in the side that we fastened shut with a hair tie. We curled in our sleeping bags facing each other. Soren was illuminated by the angled beam of a flashlight. He was wearing a gray beanie pulled over the tips of his ears.

"Remember when we got attacked by a predatory mammal in Stenland?" Soren said.

"There are no predatory mammals in Stenland," I said.

"Exactly."

His visitor visa lasted two more months. He'd applied for master's programs across the US and the UK; I'd applied for jobs everywhere that might even theoretically hire me. It had occurred to me that the visa process might be simpler if we were married, but that seemed like a stupid thing to bring up, so I didn't.

"Are you tired?" I asked.

"I just saw a bear, then ate fourteen Oreos. Not really."

"If only there was some way to amuse ourselves for a while."

"Good point." He turned away from me for a moment, rummaging around in his bag. He retrieved a book, which he proceeded to open and start reading under the glow of the flashlight.

"That's not what I had in mind," I said.

"Surely I don't know what you're talking about." He flipped a page.

"I can tell you're not actually reading."

He flipped another page. "I am reading. About construction techniques in Neolithic Orkney."

"Is that a euphemism for porn?"

"No. Sorry."

As it turned out, the tents were not as soundproof as previously assumed; from a few feet away, Kitty yelled: "Soren brought porn on a camping trip?"

"I didn't know they made analogue porn anymore," Georgia said.

Soren lowered his book. "I bet John Aubrey didn't have to live like this."

The next morning, we packed up the scraps of our dew-soaked tent. The air was so thick with fog, you couldn't see where the trees ended. Milky beams of light slotted through the branches as the sun began to break. Soren wrapped his arms around me from behind as I was stuffing the tent into the back of the car. "Coffee?" he said into my shoulder.

"Probably not until we find that service station again," I said.

"No, I made coffee. With the gas kettle thing."

I turned in his arms to face him. "You brought instant coffee?"

"I brought a pour-over and some filters."

"Have I ever told you that you are a very handsome man whose propensity for reading about Neolithic construction techniques is actually quite admirable?"

He sniffed. The tip of his nose was pink from cold. "It doesn't hurt to hear it again."

I had the thought, loud enough to be jarring: *this is the happiest I have ever been.* And then, just as abruptly, the natural follow-up: *this is the happiest I will ever be.*

When we got back to campus, I bought Lukas a twenty-dollar acai bowl. He said he never wanted to leave. I think it was supposed to come out like a joke, but his voice cracked on the word *leave.* When we dropped Lukas at the airport, Soren spent the whole time quizzing him about how things were going on the croft. The men they'd hired to help in Soren's absence? The sheep? Elin? Lukas kept changing the subject.

The last thing he said to me before he left, he said in a whisper while he hugged me, a little too long and a little too tight. "It's better going back knowing you're here, you know?" He didn't say it loud enough for Soren to hear. Like the two of us were in a little club—those who didn't love Stenland.

Kitty and Georgia flew back to London the next day. I reminded Kitty to text Linnea once in a while; she promised she would.

Once it was just Soren and me again, he seemed more subdued. We fell back into our normal routine: I did problem sets, applied for jobs, swam. He read, applied to universities, went on trail runs that lasted hours. Every night, we went to sleep in the same bed, and every morning, we woke up facing each other.

A month before Soren's visa was due to expire, he booked a flight home. He booked it for just two days before the expiration date, which I took as a good sign. When I asked if he'd be coming back as soon as possible, he said, "I mean, I guess, why not?"

Three days before Soren's flight to Stenland, one of my professors asked me to stay after class. Everyone called him Tim, though as far as I could tell that was neither his first nor his last name. Before starting Tim's class, I'd been warned that he only paid attention to how well you did on the first project and gave you the same grade on everything thereafter, so I made sure I did well on the first project. I was pretty sure he liked me despite the fact that I was a decidedly middling student in most regards.

"Did you ever meet Carla Tapia?" Tim asked without preamble.

I shook my head.

"Really? She graduated last year. Also ME. She's working at a self-driving car start-up now."

"The name sounds familiar," I said, even though it didn't.

"She was one of my advisees," he said. "She was tearing her hair out this time last year trying to figure out if she could get a job that would sponsor her—she's from Chile—and I know you're from Scotland, so I figured maybe you were doing the same."

I decided now was not the time to inform him about the Stennish Treaty of Secession. "I am," I said. "No one's getting back to me."

"Email Carla," Tim said. "Tell her I told you to. I know her company's hiring—we had coffee last week."

I told him I would and stumbled through my thank-yous. On the way back to my dorm, I felt like I was being propelled upward—like when you're swimming right on someone's toes and their wake slips under your stomach, buoying you to the surface. I had never been so glad Soren lived in my room. I had never wanted to tell anyone something so badly.

When I got back, the room was empty. His running shoes were gone. I sat at my laptop and searched around for a Carla Tapia in the alumni directory. I drafted a friendly email, removed two of four exclamation marks, and pressed Send. Still no Soren. I fidgeted over my problem set. Ate dinner and set aside a plate for Soren. Carla wrote back—oh, god—and she wanted to get coffee! Coffee like an interview? I said yes, sure, absolutely, and I left in all my exclamation marks. Soren still had not returned.

I ended up drifting off around midnight, still fully dressed. When I heard the door open, I watched Soren through my eyelashes. His shirt and shorts were soaked through with sweat, and his hair was plastered against his head. I didn't say anything because I felt like I was punishing him, not sharing my good news because he'd taken so long to return and hadn't intuited that I'd wanted to tell him something. I pretended I was asleep.

Soren walked very quietly to the desk chair and sat down in it. I watched him unlace his shoes. But once they were unlaced, he just stayed like that, eyes trained on the floor, head in his hands. He was breathing so hard—from the run, I thought—

that the silhouette of his body shook even though he never made a sound.

I should've stopped pretending to be asleep, and I should've asked him if he was okay. Instead, I imagined laying a circle of flat stones around myself like the ones in Fairhowe Cairn. A perfect, even ring turning into a perfect, even wall.

That was when I knew he was not coming back.

Like being in the middle of a car crash, time slowed down in the two days before Soren's flight to give me full opportunity to realize how obvious it had been all along.

When I woke up the next morning after an uneven sleep, Soren was already gone. He'd texted me: Going to Philz. Want coffee? The message was already an hour old. I was angry that he used a period instead of a comma in his text even though the period was more correct. He had told me once he could not abide a comma splice. At the time, I'd thought it was funny.

I opened the top drawer of the desk. Soren's drawer. I never went through it, not even when I'd glimpsed an envelope in there with his name written in a curling, feminine hand. The envelope was still there. I pulled the card out of it, feeling mean and destructive. It was a birthday card from Linnea's little sister, Saffi. She'd said she hoped Soren got to eat lots of strawberry ice cream (*your favorite!*) and signed it *xxxxxx*. The card was only five sentences long. There were two comma splices.

Also in the drawer, Soren had a neat bundle of traveling paperwork—a printed ticket, a Stennish travel declaration, all things that existed happily on his phone but that he'd chosen to print anyway, as if he was terrified of being turned away at the airport, as if that would be the worst thing.

I found a notebook—one of mine, the paper gridded instead of lined. I wanted to find diary entries and love poetry. Instead, I found notes, all written in a self-consciously tidy hand, as if he imagined someone riffling through these papers for evidence of his brilliance.

Grimm's law

Posited by Jacob Grimm (of Brothers fame)

Linguistic theory that certain letters/sounds shift to other specific letters/sounds in Germanic languages

P becomes f and t becomes th, for example, so Latin pater *becomes English* father

Languages layering on top of each other... Like archaeology—buildings on top of buildings, stories on top of stories...

Palimpsests all the way down

Below that, he'd started doodling: little sketches of stones slotted on top of stones, a cairn covered in dirt. I didn't know the word *palimpsest*, which annoyed me, so I looked it up on my phone. *Parchment whose text has been erased (through scraping or washing) either fully or partially so the page can be used again.*

The desk drawer rattled when I shut it. I started angrily taking off my pajamas and angrily putting on my jeans. When it came time for me to leave for class, he still had not returned. I left the sunstone necklace on the desk, as if I'd forgotten to put it on.

I couldn't concentrate during Tim's lecture. I kept thinking about that word, *palimpsest*, and about the amorphous anger I felt building toward Soren. Anger was a palimpsest—a feeling on top of a feeling on top of a feeling. It didn't matter why you'd been angry last time, if it was for the same reason or a new one. It just mattered that the anger was there: layer upon layer, building over time.

I was angry that he hadn't told me what the word *palimpsest* meant. I was angry that he didn't think I would be clever enough to get it or that he didn't think it wouldn't have meant something to me the way it meant something to him.

He was gone again when I got back home. So were his running shoes. When we'd first moved in, I'd been grateful to learn that my roommate had mostly planned to live with her boyfriend on the other side of campus, but now I longed for her company—for anyone's company other than my own. I banged around the kitchen loudly making dinner, even though the only person I was annoying was myself. Around the time the pasta was done cooking, I'd worn myself out and begun to feel childish. I poured two glasses of wine and sat at the table to wait.

It was because of what my mum had said—that Soren would suffocate me. All this time, I'd been on high alert for signs of my own discomfort. Selfishly, it hadn't occurred to me that Soren might be the one to leave me. I still thought of myself as the leaver.

By the time he got home, the pasta was cold. He was soaked in sweat again, a dark line down the middle of his chest, cleaving his heart in two. I didn't understand how he hadn't hurt himself yet, hadn't run his feet clean off. Sometimes it seemed like he was trying to. He examined the pasta on the stove.

"Just leave it." I was so tired. "It won't be any good anymore."

He scooped himself a bowl anyway and came to join me at the table. He lifted the mostly empty bottle of wine. "Jesus," he said.

"You could've texted me."

"You knew I was out for a run," he said. "It's not like I have anywhere else to go."

I didn't have anything to say to that. I drank the rest of my wine even though it was starting to taste sour and my head was already throbbing. He ate silently and methodically and did not complain that the pasta and the sauce had congealed in the pot.

"I got in," he said abruptly.

"To a master's program?"

He nodded.

"Which one?"

"All of them," he said.

Which meant Edinburgh, Oxford, Trinity, Berkeley, UW, Stenland. He'd applied to slightly different programs at each of them—*None more likely than the others to make me any money*, he'd joked—depending on what they offered.

"Oh," I said, feeling lightheaded. I wondered how long he'd known, but I was afraid to ask. Afraid to sound shrill. "Congratulations. That's great."

His fork shrieked against the plate, and he winced. "Thanks."

"And you're leaning toward…?" I said.

"I might defer a year," he said. "Just to make sure the croft's okay."

The words hit me with a sharp sting of betrayal. He wouldn't look at me, like he knew what expression I'd be wearing and didn't want to bother seeing it.

"I got a job interview," I said; even I thought my voice sounded too combative. "At a self-driving car company."

"That's great, Tess."

Never before had two people sounded less happy for each other.

"It's based in SF," I said. "So, if you went to Berkeley…"

He kept his gaze fixed on his plate.

I leaned back in my chair and crossed my arms.

He got up, did the dishes, and got into the shower. We didn't even say good-night to each other.

As I lay in bed, trying to find a centimeter of space on the tiny bed where I would not touch Soren, I wondered if people were doomed to always act the age they'd been when their relationship had started. If we stagnated in love but grew with heartbreak. Here we were, Soren and I, and we had not changed at all.

The day of the flight, I borrowed Damian's brand-new Tesla to drive Soren to the airport. We made it halfway there before I couldn't take it anymore. Soren won. Fine.

"Were you ever going to tell me?" I said.

"Tell you what?"

"You're not coming back."

A pause. "I was still making up my mind."

"You could've told me that there was something to make your mind up about."

He leaned his head against the window. Finally, quietly, he said: "I'm so tired."

"Maybe that's because you go on four-hour runs to avoid being in the same room as me."

"I hate it here, Tess. Is that what you want me to say? I hate the way people look at me, like I don't belong, and the way they talk to me, like I'm an idiot. I hate that it's so bright and dusty all the time. I hate that this car costs more than I'll ever have in my bank account, and I hate that all anyone here talks about is how hard they're working all the goddamn time. I hate that this is not Stenland. I hate that I am not in Stenland. And I hate you a little bit for making me choose."

I kept my eyes fixed forward on the road. My hands tightened around the wheel. "And I hate you a little bit," I said, "for loving an island that turned those girls into monsters."

"No one but you would call them monsters," he said.

"I'm sure they call themselves that."

"Don't lecture me about the curse. Not me. Of all people."

"You're right," I said. "You should be mad. You should hate me more than a little bit."

"Please stop."

"I'd rather you just say it for once. That my mum killed your parents. You never talk about it, but it's always just sitting there."

"That was never your fault. And even if I thought it was, once, I forgave you years ago. You're the one still holding on to that."

"I don't think that's the truth," I said.

"Sometimes," he said, "I wonder if you only want to be with me because you want absolution."

I turned to look at him. His head was still pressed against the glass. I said: "Sometimes I wonder if you only want to be with me because forgiving me means you've forgiven Stenland."

We made it all the way to the airport before either of us spoke again. I gestured to the directional signs—drop-off or parking?—and Soren said tiredly, "Just drop me off."

I pulled the car up to the curb. Soren unbuckled his seat belt.

"So you're not going to go to Berkeley," I said.

"Can we figure this out later?"

"It sounds like you've already figured it out on your own."

We looked at each other. I knew his face better than I knew my own. Every angle and plane and hollow of it. I felt possessive, jealous, livid, lonely, humiliated. I felt tired.

"I guess I have," he said.

"Is this an ultimatum?" I asked. "I move back to Stenland, or we're over?"

"It's not an ultimatum. I already know what you'd say."

"Oh."

We were done, then. I had known it was coming; I hadn't really *known*, though.

"So," I said, "you don't love me anymore."

"Don't. You know that's not it." He shut his eyes. Exhaled unsteadily. "I'll always love you, Tess. I just thought I could love you more than everything else in the world put together. And I can't."

He climbed out of the car. Collected his suitcases. Went through the double doors and didn't look back.

I realized, once he was gone, that my hand was on my throat. I was touching his mother's sunstone necklace. For a moment, I considered calling him so I could give it back, so I could tell him not to go.

Instead, I drove away.

I would not see him again for four years.

Maps

2018

After Soren left, I went home and sat on my bed that still smelled like him. I waited to cry but didn't. Eventually, I called Bianca and asked if she wanted to go to a party. She said sure.

The party was loud, dark, and sticky. In the comparative peace of the row house's kitchen, I told Bianca that Soren and I were done.

"Thank god, honestly," she said. "I didn't want to say anything, but he was so controlling. We never saw you anymore."

I didn't think this was fair, but I didn't feel like being fair to Soren, so I said, "Yeah, true."

"It's a good thing," she said. "Why is it only women who are expected to sacrifice their careers? Like, hello, go back to 1930."

"We should dance," I said. We went back to the loud and dark and sticky part of the house and danced. I hadn't been to a frat party since the winter of my junior year; I'd asked Soren if he'd wanted to go to one, just to see what it was like, and he'd laughed at me, not meanly, but like he'd thought it was a joke. I'd felt embarrassed at the time because I liked dissolving in the loud/dark/sticky of parties.

Someone slid behind me and put their hands on my waist. I could feel their breath in my ear. For a moment, I had the thought that it was Soren—that he'd come back from the airport to tell me he couldn't live without me. Because I was imagining Soren, I didn't turn around. I wanted to show Soren that I was disinterested in his return; I was not grieving. But then the voice in my ear said, "Hey, Tess," and it was not Soren's Stennish accent or his particular way of saying my name; it was a smooth Connecticut accent, and it belonged to August.

I spun, and there he was. In my ear, holding me close still, he said, "I heard you broke up with your farmer."

It seemed impossible that he could have heard this so quickly, but then again, Bianca had never stopped being friends with him.

Maybe it was the lights, which were strobing, but for a minute I thought August's face was melting. He looked like a photo with the sharpness turned all the way up: I could see his pores, gaping black holes in sweat-shimmering skin. Had his eyes always been so close together? Had his teeth always been so small, like Tic Tacs?

He pressed his body against mine. I was too surprised to move away. In my ear, he was saying, "I really missed you, you know that?"

It struck me as remarkable that he thought I would be pleased at his attention. For a moment, I wondered: *Am I supposed to be pleased?* But his face, it was melting, and he would not stop pressing his hips against me like he was eager to prove just how much he really missed me.

A hand closed around my elbow.

"Oh my god," a woman's voice—not Bianca's—said. "I've been looking for you everywhere!"

Then I was being tugged away from August and out of the crowd. It felt like being pulled out of a riptide.

She was tiny, and she stood like a ballerina, her toes out to the sides. Even her hair was pulled into a bun that looked like something a dancer would wear. Her skin was light brown in the strobing light, and she didn't seem to have any pores at all.

"You looked like you needed help," she shouted into my ear.

"Thank you," I said.

"That guy's a fucking creep. He's in one of my classes this quarter. I'm AJ."

"Tess."

Someone screamed her name as they ricocheted down the stairs past us, and I got the sense that I knew of AJ. There was this term people used, the "Stanford 500," for the five hundred people who knew everyone and who everyone knew. I was whatever the opposite of that was. But AJ was Stanford 500, or maybe Stanford 50. I'd seen her tagged in Facebook things and on posters around campus, for plays or student government or a cappella shows.

"I'm actually about to go to another party," AJ said. "Want to come?"

"I should find my friend," I said. But then I remembered that Bianca had told August about Soren. And I said, "Actually, never mind. Sure. Let's go."

That was how I started dating AJ Maines.

Delayed grieving: like packing your brain in bubble wrap. For three months, I thought it meant I must've never loved Soren after all.

I expected Kitty to be ecstatic over AJ; she wasn't.

"Though I am vindicated that you are embracing the angry bisexual I have always known you to be," she said over the phone, "I was pretty excited about this whole 'you legally become my cousin' thing."

"Take it up with Soren," I said.

"I have."

"What did he say?"

"Oh, no. I'm not being your go-between. You two want to talk, call each other."

We didn't.

Right before AJ and I slept together for the first time, I started to panic. She had never slept with a man, and I had slept with almost exclusively men, and though she didn't try to make me feel bad about this, she and her friends all laughed about it in this, *Oh, aren't you in for a treat* way. It wasn't a treat, really. It was mostly similar to the first time having sex with anyone, which was to say, not as comfortable or good as with someone you knew well, but kind of exciting anyway. I wondered if there was something wrong with me for not enjoying it more.

AJ had a giant map above her bed. It was the kind where you could scratch off countries you'd visited. I felt like I'd see the little, unscratched shape of Stenland and start counting the finger-lengths between there and here. I never looked. I never, ever looked. Until I did.

AJ was in the communal bathroom down the hall. I was lying on her bed scrolling through the Instagram feed of the self-driving car start-up where I would be working, courtesy of Carla Tapia. The map was watching me. I could feel it. It throbbed like a beating heart in my peripheral vision.

I opened my own Instagram profile to distract myself and looked at all the little squares of my face. At formal! At Bay to Breakers! Since starting to date AJ, I had restyled myself. I wore makeup. I lost weight. I thought about how I didn't look as pretty as she did in photos we took together. In those photos, she was dressed more femininely, in skirts and sundresses, and I wore flannels and black jeans. I'd always worn flannels and black jeans, but now I wore them almost exclusively, like a statement. AJ said it was my aesthetic. It was closer to my aesthetic than whatever aesthetic I'd had with August, when I'd been playing my Regency-era character, but I was still conscious of the clothes as part of an act. Maybe dating was just trying on different characters until you found one you could pretend to be for the rest of your life.

I looked up at the map.

I couldn't help it.

Stenland wasn't there.

The bed creaked when I stood on the mattress. My eyes were level with the North Atlantic. North of mainland Scotland, I found Orkney, and north of Orkney, I found Shetland, and north of Shetland there was nothing, just ocean all the way to the Arctic. I pressed my finger to the place where Stenland was not.

That was how AJ found me.

"What are you doing?" she asked.

"Where's Stenland?" I said.

"Oh, is it not on the map? Huh. I guess they left it off."

"Where's Stenland?" I said again.

I think she answered; my ears were full of static.

There was a chance I had lost my mind completely. Maybe I'd made it all up; there was no Stenland, no skeld curse, no Soren or Kitty or Linnea. I was from somewhere else, Cheshire or Kansas, and there was another family, another life waiting for me there. So much static, and black pixels growing cancerously across my vision.

If Soren was not a real person, I did not want to be alive.

That was the thought that emerged fully formed in my head. I heard it like someone else was speaking it to me, word for word. If Soren was not a real person, then I had never really felt the things humans were meant to feel—love and sorrow and anguish and peace.

This would mark the end of my relationship with AJ, though I didn't know it yet. She was kind about it in the ensuing days, but I nonetheless stopped behaving like the person she'd thought she knew, the person I had so studiously become.

I went back to my room and found the sunstone necklace in the otherwise empty top drawer of my desk. I read the Wikipedia page on Stenland all the way through, just to make sure. I looked at Google Maps and found Stenland where it was supposed to be, the last thing in the North Atlantic until you reached the Arctic.

Stenland was real, which meant Soren was real, which meant I was too. I had loved him and he had loved me and we hadn't loved each other enough. I had been pregnant with his child. That had happened. His child, his genes, his eyes, his smile—all inside me, like we might've been something permanent. Our daughter would never live in Stenland. I would not let her. She would end up killing her father. I would end up killing her father. We would be monsters. And he would be dead.

I cried in the frantic way children cry. The way that feels like you might die. That was the way I cried for Soren. But worse were the slow, heaving, nauseous gasps that came after. That was the way I cried for the person I was with him, who, in retrospect, had not been a character at all.

Gallant

2019

Elin Fell died around the same time Noah asked me if I wanted to date, like, officially. I felt anxious because I hadn't dated anyone since AJ and was afraid it would end the same way. I didn't know about Elin at the time.

It was a few days before Christmas, and we were eating takeout Thai food in my kitchen. My apartment—where I had lived for a year and a half since graduating—was the second floor of a Victorian town house in the Mission. I shared it with three other Stanford grads, but all of them were consultants, usually traveling, so it felt mostly mine. There was one big window at the edge of the kitchen and on the sill, a row of miniature succulents and potted herbs. I sat on the counter next to my tidy little chrome espresso machine and ate pad see ew directly from the container.

Noah got a second beer from the fridge, and while his back

was turned, he asked the question casually, like he wasn't particularly fussed whether I said yes or no.

"Officially," I repeated.

"Yeah. You could meet my parents. I could list you as my emergency contact. You know—officially."

"Oh," I said.

Noah sipped his beer and shrugged with one shoulder.

We'd been together-ish, unofficially, for six months. Like me, he lived in a rental house with former Stanford classmates whom he only saw once every two weeks. We'd known each other from Oxford, so he'd started coming over for dinner whenever either of us had been bored or lonely. The third time it had happened, when we'd been watching a shitty horror film on my couch, he'd said, "Would it ruin things if we slept together?"

"You're kind of my only friend on this continent right now."

"Really? We don't have to."

"No," I said, "sure."

So for six months, things had proceeded the same way: Noah came over for dinner, or I went to his place; we slept together; he was still kind of my only friend on that continent.

He took another long sip of his beer, looking at me over the top of the amber bottle.

"You want me to meet your parents?" I asked.

"Sure. Come with me for New Year's."

"To Chicago?"

"Yeah. It'll be fucking freezing. My mom will ask you invasive questions about our sex life. We'll laugh about it later."

With his free hand, Noah tossed the bottle cap up into the air, watched it spin, and caught it again. It made a metallic *ting* every time it launched off his thumb. He had approximately zero body fat, so when he tilted his chin up, I could see all the bones in his jaw. His eyes were fixed on the bottle cap. By this point, I knew him well enough to see he was nervous and pretending not to be.

"Why?" I asked.

"Why will my mom ask you about our sex life? I really wish I could tell you."

"No, why do you want to date?"

He set the cap on the counter. "We're basically dating already. I have a toothbrush here. Linnea loves me."

"Linnea loves everyone," I said.

"Kitty tolerates me."

"That is rarer."

Noah had met both of them on FaceTime, and Kitty in person when she'd visited in October. Linnea had said it was wonderful, so wonderful that I had someone in my life, and Noah was actually so cute, wasn't he? Kitty had said he was fine, if I really wanted to date a tech bro. Kitty and her parents were in New Zealand for Christmas. Linnea was in Stenland. A few hours prior, she'd sent me a photo of her and Henrik at their house—the black windows, the tree glittering with white lights and red ornaments. They were drinking mugs of mulled wine, and Linnea was smiling at the camera, but Henrik was smiling at Linnea. I looked out my own window and saw the dusty gray sky of the city. No snow, no frost, no wind; just the lights of cars looking for parking.

"It's not that I don't want to," I said. "I just don't want us to do this because it's the path of least resistance."

"It's definitely not," Noah said. "You're very resistant. Like when I try to make you coffee and you pour it down the drain when you think I'm not looking."

"Look, you're very cute, but you make a shit coffee."

He gave me this smile, the uneven Noah smile I had grown, without realizing, to love. "I guess I was also thinking that it'd suck if you had to be alone for Christmas."

"You don't even celebrate Christmas."

"Yeah, but you do."

Being asked to be someone's girlfriend, officially, made me think of Soren. I had not spoken to him in almost two years, but his ghost often appeared when I was with Noah: when we were watching a film where the main characters confessed their love, or when Noah asked where the dishwasher tablets were in his own home. When Noah did that, I thought of Soren, who did not need to be told how long to microwave his leftovers or not to pour the detergent directly onto the clothes or where to find the dishwasher tablets when they were, obviously, under the sink. But if Noah was less mature than Soren, he was also quicker to laugh, more easygoing than AJ, kinder than August.

I said yeah, okay, could I think about it? Noah said no stress.

I woke up before him the next morning and checked my phone while I was making coffee. That was when I saw the text from Kitty, sent at three in the morning, telling me that Soren's grandmother had just died. I didn't stop to consider before I dialed.

The espresso machine hissed. I leaned my forehead against the cabinet in the cloud of coffee-scented steam. In my head, Elin was saying: *I have a phone call for the very gallant young man who offered to sleep on the couch tonight.*

The ringing stopped; someone picked up.

"Soren?" I said. "I'm so—"

"Tess, it's me, Henrik."

"Where's Soren? What happened?"

Henrik paused. "It was cancer. It'd been—it's been coming for a while."

"Oh."

There was someone in the background—a man's voice, faint, but I couldn't tell who it was for sure.

"Listen," Henrik said quietly. "I know you just want to help, but I think it's probably better if you just...let him be."

"Right." My throat felt dry and scraped. "Of course."

"I should— I have to go. Talk soon."

The call ended. I stared into the steam, blinking and blinking and blinking. Then I called Kitty, who didn't pick up, and Linnea, who didn't pick up, and I would've called Henrik next if he hadn't just told me to go away. The first hazy beams of morning light were streaking through the windows, yellower and brighter than a December had any right to be. Outside, a car drove past playing loud Christmas music. A plane roared overhead. When I looked at the white knuckles clenched around my phone, I was sure they didn't belong to me.

I typed: flights Stenland

I got to the part where I was supposed to enter my credit card information when Linnea called me back.

"You heard?" she asked by way of greeting.

"I'm coming home."

"What? Tess—"

"I'm booking a flight."

"I love you, Tessie," she said. "But you can't do this to him."

"Do what?"

"It's— I thought you two were done hurting each other."

I blinked again, more slowly this time, and wiped my eyes too hard with the heel of my hand. I told her right, of course, sorry, and she promised she'd call back soon. It wasn't until after the call had ended that I thought to ask if she'd known Elin had been ill all along and if she'd chosen not to tell me because she'd been afraid of what I would do. Come back, hurt Soren, leave again—was that all I ever did? It was the first time I realized that I had succeeded: Stenland was no longer my home. It no longer mattered that I had loved Elin too. I had ceded my rights—that was what Linnea thought—when I'd chosen to leave Stenland behind. I closed the tab on my phone with the flights, and then I went to the bathroom and stood in the shower until my skin was bright pink. I remade the coffees, two this time, and I brought one to Noah in bed.

"I was planning to sleep for three to six more hours," he said.

There had been a part of me, I realized, that still believed life might pull me back to Stenland, and now finally that part had been broken. No one was trying to drag me back anymore; I had won, for whatever winning was worth.

I sat on the edge of the bed and smoothed Noah's hair from his forehead, cataloguing his face for what felt like the first time: his sleepy eyes, the elegant angles of his cheekbones, the smooth tan glow of his skin. Lovely and funny and calm and easy—I could fall in love with Noah, if only I let myself.

"I got some bad news from home this morning," I said.

He propped himself up on one elbow. "Are you okay? Do you want to talk about it?"

"Not right now," I said.

"I'm here if you change your mind."

And he was there. Had been there for a long time now, and I had not been seeing him. I set my finger under his chin and tilted his mouth to meet mine, and he kissed me back slowly and sweetly, like honey.

"I think we should date," I said. "Officially."

"Whoa, whoa," he said. "Let's not be hasty with labels."

"I always underestimate how annoying you can be."

"Annoying, or charming and funny? You know what, who cares. For you, I'll be all three."

He wrapped his arms around me and pulled me into the soft burrow of the comforter, my back curled against his chest. "This makes me happy," he said quietly, and he lightly kissed my shoulder, right where the fractured bone had stitched itself together again.

Patterns of Light

2022

On Halloween in Ramna Skaill, I found Kitty in the kitchen stirring a pot of something that smelled like spices and alcohol.

"What," I said, "the fuck."

"I'm being festive."

"What are you wearing?"

She plucked her beaded dress. "I'm Zelda Fitzgerald."

"Because…?"

"It's Halloween. Here, try this." She pushed a mug into my hands. It smelled even more like alcohol in close quarters. "I also sent for turnips because I thought we could carve lanterns."

She went back to stirring. I sniffed the cup, but didn't drink.

"To my original question," I said.

"'What the fuck,'" she said, "yes. Let's all make fun of Kitty for embracing the holiday spirit."

I kept staring at her. She hummed something off-key. A

minute later, Linnea ran through the kitchen, her bare feet slapping against the stone floor. She hugged Kitty from behind. "You dressed up!" she said. "Oh my god! That's so earnest and dorky."

"See?" Kitty told me. "That was the proper response. Take notes for future reference."

Linnea asked me what I was dressed as, and if it was Grumpy Woman in Pajamas. Kitty suggested I could be Scrooge in some sort of modern, feminist Halloween interpretation of *A Christmas Carol.* I sipped Kitty's drink and told her it tasted like cinnamon rubbing alcohol. She curtsied.

I thought it was funny that they thought I was grumpy. I was afraid to admit I was the opposite.

Noah was going to a Halloween party with some of his friends. They'd all dressed up as characters from a TV show I hadn't seen. It was still lunchtime there, but they'd started drinking already. I knew because he'd sent me a series of photos of red cups and people I only sort of recognized.

"Am I old and boring if I think this looks horrible?" I asked, showing the others my phone.

Kitty said yes. Linnea said no.

"How is Noah, by the way?" Kitty asked.

"Noah is fine," I said. "He is always fine."

Sometimes Henrik ate dinner with us, and sometimes Lukas. Soren made himself known only by way of silent deliveries: groceries, books, prepared food of considerably less questionable origins than Lukas's. I talked to my dad most afternoons, if only for a few minutes, even if we didn't have anything to say.

On Halloween, I called my mum: unprompted, with no agenda, just to hear her. I'd been thinking of another Halloween, back before Soren's parents had died. I must've been seven or eight, and I'd wanted to go to the costume party Kitty had been throwing, but my mum had dragged me to the cultural center to watch the harvest ceremony. I remember standing with her, impatient, in the swiftly falling darkness. The cultural center was turf-roofed and surrounded by concentric, low stone walls. A bonfire had snapped and hissed. The man from the cultural center had told us a story I'd heard before but hadn't cared about—something about trolls and keeping the sheep safe over winter—that had already sounded young and childish to my ears. I'd told my mum I wanted to go to Kitty's, and she'd hushed me.

Then the monsters had arrived. I think they'd just been high school kids, but I hadn't known that. They'd been covered in long black tendrils of seaweed. Driftwood masks had hidden their faces. They'd leaped and laughed in the flickering bonfire light, and I'd felt something move in my chest, a feeling between pride and fear that I would come to think of as distinctly Stennish. When it had been over, my mum had driven me to Kitty's and asked if I'd had fun at the ceremony, and I'd said no because *fun* wasn't the word for it.

When she picked up the phone, she said, "Is everything okay?"

"Yeah. Just doing laundry."

"Oh. Well. How's the keep? Do you want to rip out all your fingernails yet?"

"It's okay," I said, tucking my phone between my shoulder and my ear. "I like spending so much time with Kitty and Linnea."

"You did get lucky in that respect. Imagine if you were stuck with a clompy walker. Or someone who uses the toilet with the door open."

I set down my laundry and leaned against the wall. It was stone and windowless. The fancy new washing machine seemed anachronistic against the big slabs of stone. It didn't make sense to me that a little dungeon of a room should smell like Morning Lavender.

"Have you ever considered moving back?" I asked.

"Why?" Immediate suspicion. "Is Kitty thinking about it?"

"No."

"Well, *you're* not. Are you?"

"No," I said, "obviously."

"Of course I've considered moving back," she said. "It was home for the first thirty years of my life. I miss my friends and Hedda's coffee. And I missed seeing you grow up."

"So why didn't you?"

"Because you didn't want me to."

I made a disapproving noise.

"You didn't," she said. "No one was ever going to let me forget what I did, least of all you. Or least of all me, really. So I went somewhere I could start over. Sometimes I think it was selfish, giving myself the chance to do that. Other times I think the homesickness helps pay for the crime."

"But you like traveling, don't you? And cities?"

"I love them," she said. "Most of the time, I prefer them. But they are not Stenland. Are you going to tell me the real reason you're asking?"

"No," I said.

She said okay and changed the subject.

Six weeks into skeld season, we'd carved out our routines. Kitty and I could work remotely, so we spent our days sprawled across the couches in the hearth room on our laptops. Linnea, I worried about. At first, Kitty and I had joked that Linnea had gotten a vacation, but as the weeks passed, we watched her get increasingly restless. She attacked the replanning of the wedding like it was her career, calling florists and watching long YouTube videos on DIY centerpieces. "Wedding 2.0 is going to be way better than the original," she told us while eviscerating a length of fabric she planned to turn into some sort of garland. "It's actually a silver lining, to get a do-over."

"Right," Kitty said. "Um, maybe be careful with the crafting scissors?"

When we weren't working, Linnea tried to teach us to bake and Kitty tried to teach us to knit and I tried to teach them how to do a push-up. Results were mixed. Most nights, after dinner, we read by the fire, though because Kitty kept getting distracted by her phone, she was still ostensibly on *Beowulf* by the time I'd circled back to read *Freestyle* again. We were heaped together on the same couch, with Linnea on her stomach in front of the fire reading a rom-com.

"It can't be that good," Kitty said, lifting *Beowulf.* "Look, why has Soren gone and scribbled all over it?"

I swatted her with *Freestyle.* "He just underlined things."

"He's so annoying. If I have to read one more annotation about Grendel's mother, I'll hurl myself from the roof."

"You could read something else, you know," Linnea said. "Soren hasn't annotated this one."

"Do we think Soren's read that one?" Kitty asked.

Linnea held up the cover, which said: *Once Upon a Christmas Tree Farm.* "I do hope so."

Kitty made a face and reached for my book. "Gimme. I want that one."

"Hey," I said, curling my arms protectively around it.

"You've already read it."

"If I can't swim, I'm going to read about people who can."

"You're being selfish," she said. "Don't you want me to finally learn the difference between butterfly and breaststroke?"

"No," I said. "You're beyond help. Go back to reading about Grendel's mother."

"How much do you swim these days?" Linnea asked. "When you're not in a tower, that is."

"Not that much," I said. "Three times a week, maybe."

"I never understood why you stopped."

"Because she wrecked her shoulder getting you out of the ocean," Kitty said.

There was a tense, taut silence.

Linnea's eyes were wide as she awaited confirmation.

It wasn't a secret I'd meant to keep forever. It had just—stopped being relevant. Swimming had been my way to get out of Stenland. I'd gotten out anyway.

"I hardly remember anymore," I said.

"Oh," Linnea said, standing. She blinked quickly. "Sorry, I— Bathroom."

I spent the whole rest of the evening thinking I'd upset her. But when I put my mug in the kitchen sink before bed, I found her drizzling icing on a plated pastry. She pushed it toward me and said it was a Sorry for Ruining Everything kringle. I told her it tasted so good, I'd try to fracture my scapula more often.

We ate it together on the floor of her room, just the two of us.

"I'm sorry I didn't tell you," I said.

"How can I be mad? You were just trying to protect me. I'm the one who always ruins everything." She scraped the side of her fork across the plate miserably.

"Lin."

"I made you and Kitty come back."

"Bad luck, that's all."

"We spent so much money on the wedding," she said, "and now we have to plan a new one. And you know what? I've never left Stenland."

"I don't follow," I said.

"Sometimes I just think I'm so stupid," she said.

"Linnea."

"It's nothing—I'm just—just sit there a minute." Abandoning her fork, she shifted to sit behind me. She ran her fingers through my hair, separating it into three strands. "Your hair was always the best to braid because the chlorine makes it gritty.

I think we should braid your hair for the wedding. You'll look so pretty. It'll be perfect, and then you can leave, and I'll never ask you to come back again."

I looked out her window and tried to locate the place where sky turned to ocean. It was too dark, or the window was too warped.

I wanted to tell her the truth: that I felt almost terrifyingly like myself here, as if I had been slipped back into the correct skin after a long absence. There was a fundamental rightness in the patterns of light, in the background noise of wind and tide. My body wanted to be in Stenland in some sort of basal, primordial way even when my mind didn't. I thought about swimming again in the steamy, concrete pool of my childhood and could smell the chlorine so precisely it made my chest ache. This was what I wanted to tell Linnea, but I didn't say any of it because I didn't want her to tell me what she'd said three years prior: that I could not keep hurting him. *Him* was Soren, but also my dad and Lukas and Henrik and Linnea and Hedda and everyone. I would not last here. I never did. The feeling would pass. It always had, hadn't it? It would be ridiculous to imagine such a thing—that I had been in love with Soren more or less without pause for the entirety of my adult life.

In the end, I just thanked Linnea for braiding my hair and went to bed.

Easy

2022

Weekends in the keep felt mostly the same as our weekdays, except that I spent marginally less time working. On a Saturday, I was coming back upstairs after a needlessly long lunch when I heard music from Kitty's room. Something orchestral and grim, like it was meant for a funeral. I pushed open the door and found her lying on her bed with a journal open. The pages were blank.

"What are you doing?" I asked.

"Writing," she said. "Ostensibly."

"Why?"

"Posterity's sake. I thought I should record what it's like to be here just in case I ever get tempted to come back."

I sat on the bed beside her and looked at the empty page.

"I forgot I hated writing," she said. "Especially when I know I'm my only audience."

"And the music?"

"Sad Classical for Posh Crying," she said. "I put a lot of work into this playlist. Thank you for noticing."

"But you aren't crying."

"I keep getting distracted."

"You know," I said, "I don't think I've ever seen you cry."

"Of course not. I only cry in the bath when I'm home alone and no one will bother me."

"How is it we've been friends our whole lives and I've never seen you cry?"

"Because I would simply never allow it."

I studied her. I knew, of course, how much she'd withheld from Linnea over the years. I wasn't sure why it had never occurred to me that she might hide things from me too.

"I didn't realize you ever got tempted to come back," I said.

"Not really. Maybe just around Christmas."

"Do you think you'd ever do it?"

She gave me a calculating look. "What are you planning, Eriksson?"

"Nothing."

"Nothing, except that now that you're here you're remembering how much you love the shit weather and the state-run healthcare and the proximity to your friends."

I grimaced at her.

"Come live in London with me," she said.

"I can't just move to London. I have a job. I have a boyfriend."

"He's not your boyfriend," Kitty said. "He's your roommate. Don't you get tired of pretending you're in love with him?"

I stared at her.

"Don't tell me it's not true," she said.

"It's not. That's a horrible thing to say."

She made an impatient sound. "Imagine Noah and Saffi

are dead and a meteor is hurtling toward Earth. You have ten minutes. Who are you going to see?"

"That's awful."

"Who are you going to see?"

"You and Linnea. And my dad."

"And Soren."

I stood up. My throat felt too tight to speak, too tight to breathe. "I don't know what you're trying to do."

"Just admit you still love him."

"I don't. We were so young. I'm not still—" She was giving me that look, and I couldn't bear it so I turned away. "And even if I was, what's the point?"

"I'm just trying to get you to be honest."

"So you can feel smart? So you can feel good about yourself?"

She didn't say anything to that. I went down the hall to my room, thinking she would call after me, but she didn't. On my bed, I lay back with my knees over the edge and stared at the ceiling. I pressed my hands to my face and looked through the gaps between my fingers.

If Noah and Saffi were dead and there was a meteor hurtling toward Earth.

Only then.

I rolled onto my stomach and tried to breathe through the thickness of the quilt but couldn't. It should not have persisted—not this long. It was just an emotion that should have died off but became chronic instead.

When I thought of Noah, I thought of lazy mornings, his rumpled hair when he pushed himself up in bed and blearily opened his phone. I thought of going back to campus with him for Homecoming and posing for pictures in matching red shirts and how I did not have to introduce him to anyone because he already knew everyone. I thought of comfort and ease and pleasant pastel sameness.

When I thought of Soren, I thought of the first time we'd had sex the summer I'd come back to Stenland: my face cradled in his hands, his body against mine, my name on his lips. Agony, euphoria. Misery, rapture.

I did—wish for the meteor.

I called Noah, not because I wanted to, but because it was too horrible to put it off, once I'd realized. He answered on the third ring, and when he said hello, my heart gave a dull thump: I would not hear him say hello again. This would be the last time.

"Are you there?" he asked.

No. This was a bad idea. I didn't have to break up with my boyfriend of three years just because, what, I was attracted to someone else? That was normal. Everyone felt like that sometimes.

"Tess?"

"I'm here." I sat up in my bed. Wrapped an arm around my knees. "What are you doing right now? Can you just...describe it to me?"

"Okay. I'm at my desk. I'm supposed to be debugging something, but I'm actually just responding to messages. I'm drinking some green tea I found at the back of the cupboard, but I'm pretty sure it's expired. Can green tea do that?"

I had to do it. I knew—of course I knew. My *roommate,* that was what Kitty had called him. I did love him though, didn't I?

"I don't know," I said.

"Where are you?"

"In my room."

"Is it cold?"

"Yeah."

A long pause.

"I got your email," I said. "About your work holiday party."

"Do you think you'll be back in time?"

"If I leave the day the season ends."

"You probably won't want to hang around there, though, will you?"

"Yeah, no," I said. "Of course not."

We went quiet again.

"Did you see Rob and Annie got engaged?" he asked.

"Which Rob and Annie?"

"They were in my freshman dorm. They started dating week two or something."

"Oh," I said. "Wow."

I stared at the stack of books on my bedside table. Took a breath; let it out again. It wasn't about Soren, really, because I already knew there was no future for us, and I wouldn't do that to him or Saffi. But it also was, sort of, because if I had never loved Soren, I might not have ever wondered if love could be more than this.

"Do you love me?" I asked.

"What? Of course."

"No, I mean it. Do you really?"

More slowly, he said, "Yes. I mean—yeah, I guess."

"You guess?"

"It's a weird question. You caught me off guard."

"I'm not angry with you for answering it that way," I said. "I just—don't you think it shouldn't be a guess?"

I heard him shift in his chair. "I don't know. Do you love me?"

"I don't know."

It was so quiet on the other end I thought maybe the call had dropped. Finally, he said, "Well, fuck, Tess, what are we supposed to do?"

"Maybe we can fix it."

"You just told me you didn't love me," he said.

"I said I didn't know."

"That's basically the same thing."

"You said you guessed."

"Because I wasn't expecting an interrogation," he said. "Do you even want to fix it?"

"Of course I want to fix it," I said. "We live together."

"That's not a reason."

I hugged my knees tighter to my chest. "Do you? Want to fix it?"

"Well, now I'm not so sure," he said.

"Maybe we should talk later."

"I don't know that we need to, actually."

"Oh," I said. "Okay. Just like that?"

He didn't say anything for a minute. Then: "You know, I was talking to my sister about how easy our relationship was. And she said, 'There's good easy, and then there's easy like you don't care what happens to it.'"

"I don't not care."

"Yeah," he said. "But it's still not enough, is it?"

I didn't say anything to that.

"Sometimes I feel like I never knew you at all," Noah said.

A cold ache spread through my chest, starting behind my ribs and spiderwebbing outward. Quietly, I said, "Don't be cruel."

"I'm not trying to be," he said. "It's just true."

When we ended the call, I turned off my phone and put it under the bed, like it was the source of the ache.

I promised myself I wouldn't tell anyone about Noah because I didn't want them to ask what I knew they would ask—if I had done it because I still loved Soren. I didn't want Saffi to worry, or Linnea. Most of all, I didn't want Soren to feel the need to tell me that he had stopped loving me a long time ago.

A week passed, and I waited for the pain of the breakup to hit me. I wondered if it would be delayed, like with Soren. I wondered if it would not come at all, like with August. If Kitty and Linnea thought I was acting differently, they didn't say.

I flicked through my email with the sense that these messages belonged to someone else and I was invading her privacy. A meeting had been rescheduled; a test engineer had a question about a malfunction. Most of my life since graduation had been about work, but now I couldn't bring myself to care. It felt suddenly shallow. I had not improved as a person; I just had more money.

The sensation burrowed deep under my skin. When I had dreaded staying in Stenland, I had dreaded not just the curse but the threat of stagnation: being trapped in a sameness, caught in deep ruts I never saw until I was too far gone to climb out again. I'd been so determined to avoid stagnation in Stenland that maybe I'd tossed myself headlong into it elsewhere.

I was so distracted by this uneasiness that I almost skimmed right past the email that did not belong. I blinked, sure I had misread. Opened it.

It was stilted and unfamiliar, like a letter to an estranged family member. I saw, in every sentence, a vision of his fingers on the keyboard, carefully deleting anything that sounded too conciliatory, anything that let on to the fact he knew exactly how this message would be received.

I read it a second time, then I went to find Kitty and Linnea.

Kitty read it first.

"He's not serious," she said. "He's serious?"

Linnea read it second.

"Oh," she said. "Oh, that's not good."

"You think?" Kitty said.

The email went like this:

Dear Tess,

I hope you are well. I am writing to you in regards to our prior discussion about a documentary on Stenland and the skelds. I have been informed that you are currently involved in a skeld season. I am sure you want the opportunity to tell your side of the story. Please let me know when you are available for an interview. We will be in town beginning on November 15.

Additionally, I would appreciate the best email addresses to contact Kitty Sjöberg and Linnea Sundstrom.

Finally, I hope you can advise on safety precautions. Despite thorough research, I have not been able to determine whether very dark sunglasses are sufficient protection against a skeld. I would also like to know whether there is any danger when looking at a skeld via a video camera. As you can imagine, safety is our highest priority.

I look forward to hearing from you.

Regards,

August van Andel

Wool

2022

I texted Noah to see if he knew anything about this. He responded, validatingly:

Noah: What? That's crazy. What a dickwad.

I also texted Bianca, with whom I had not spoken in over a year.

Bianca: Sorry, not really in touch with August these days. Hope you're well!

When I texted Damian, he did not text back but almost immediately called, as if he had been waiting for this very missive to arrive.

"Hey!" he said. "So glad you reached out about the project."

I had not spoken to Damian, like Bianca, in sixteen months.

"The project," I said.

"You know August and I have been talking about doing a documentary on Stenland since college. We actually had some rough stuff in the works, and then when we heard you were a skeld—"

"From whom?"

"What? Oh, Annie. She was at some party with Noah where everyone was talking about it? Anyway, when we heard you were a skeld, we figured this was the perfect opportunity. To tell the story from your perspective, you know?"

I was in the hearth room, pacing in front of the fire. Henrik had just come through the front door, adjusting the mask over his eyes. Linnea shut the door behind him and peered curiously at me. I turned toward the fire and pressed my phone harder against my ear.

"You can't come here," I said.

"What?" His voice was hesitant, like a child who broke something. "What do you mean?"

"It's too dangerous. The reason August can't figure out if it's safe to use dark sunglasses or cameras is because nobody knows, okay? You think this thing is—romantic, or something, but it's not. It's horrible. It kills people."

"Obviously I know that. August's uncle died that way."

"That's a lie."

A pause.

"Well," Damian said, "all the more reason not to worry. We'll be careful, Tess. You don't need to freak out on our behalf."

"I don't care about your behalf. I care that if you show up here and one of us sees you, it's going to feel like our fault."

"Frankly, I don't know how I can help with that."

"Don't come."

He let out a breath that seemed to indicate he was humoring

me with the end of his patience. "Flights are booked. Equipment is rented. We're going to tell the story of the curse, Tess—this opportunity matters. The story matters."

I stared into the white core of the fire waiting for the right words to come to me, as if there were right words, as if I could string them together like the steps of a proof. "I don't care whether the story matters. It's not worth the risk."

Damian didn't respond.

"Please. Find somewhere else to make your film."

"I'm really sorry you feel that way, Tess," Damian said. "Let me know if you change your mind."

The call ended. Linnea, who'd been standing near enough to hear his voice, said, "So, he's not coming, right?"

"No," I said. "He is."

"It sounded like he was apologizing."

"But that's not what he meant."

The three black slashes across Linnea's forehead looked especially stark against her pale skin. "They won't be allowed near Ramna Skaill, same as everyone else."

"August grew up in a house with two tennis courts. He has never once thought he's the same as everyone else."

Henrik leaned against the wall and ruffled his hair above the mask. "You know, he's the only person I've ever met who I really wanted to punch."

"Don't be macho," Linnea said. "Though, same."

"It'll be fine, Tess," Henrik said. "We'll tell Hedda. I called Lukas and Soren as soon as Linnea told me about the email, and—"

A banging at the door. It was shoved open, and in came Soren, his hair sticking up in the back where the fabric of his mask had wedged it. He was wearing muddy boots and a raincoat over his sweater. "Why are some people such utter fucking cocks?"

Lukas, closing the door behind him, said, "Rowdy Soren has joined the chat."

"Who's here?" Soren demanded.

"Everyone but Kitty," Linnea said, just as Kitty appeared on the stairs. "Oh, no—she's here now."

Henrik said, "I was just telling them we should call Hedda—"

"I already did." Soren started pacing. "On the drive over. She said she's going to tell the constable to put someone else on the road out here, just in case. And Lukas and I will stay in the cottage until they go."

"Will we?" Lukas said. "Sorry, but don't you think you might be overreacting?"

"No," Soren said. "You don't know August. He's the worst person I have ever met."

"Sure," Lukas said, "that seems objective. Look, I'm sorry this is happening, and yes, it's inconvenient, but they'll make their stupid little film and then they'll go home. They probably won't ever get anywhere near Ramna Skaill, and even if they do, it's not like they'll come inside. And if the worst happens—"

"Don't even go there."

"If the worst happens," he went on, "no one would blame you. Any of you."

I pressed my hands against my face. "It's my fault. I can't believe they're coming here."

"I can't believe you dated him," Kitty said.

"I know. I have the worst taste. Just...abominable."

"Yeah," Soren said, "no, that's fine."

Linnea grabbed my hand, prying it away from my face. She looked intently at me. "Nothing is going to go wrong," she said. "Nothing. I won't let it."

"I don't think—"

"No," Linnea said. "I brought August here last time. I brought you and Kitty back this time. I'm going to be the one who makes sure we're okay." She was squeezing my hand so hard my fingers were starting to tingle.

"It's not like they have a death wish," Lukas said. "Why do you think they're going to be so stupid?"

"Not stupid," I said. "Just not Stennish."

We only had a few weeks left of our skeld season when they arrived. I knew they'd made it because Hedda called me while I was pulling something burned out of the oven, apparently left there by Linnea some hours ago. Black, acrid smoke came belching out of oven as I answered the call.

"Tess," Hedda said. "Your friends just blew through. They told me we'd misspelled *cappuccino* on our menu and they didn't leave a tip."

"They're not my friends. You did misspell *cappuccino.* And I have never once left you a tip."

"They asked if I knew you. I misspelled it on purpose, to ferret out the assholes. And while you are not required to tip, they most certainly should have."

I grabbed a rag off the counter and started flapping it through the air, trying to dissipate the smoke. It just seemed to create more of it.

"What did you tell them?"

"That they should stay very far from Ramna Skaill unless they want to end up the next mannequins for the Historical Society's sewing circle."

"Did they listen?"

"Of course they didn't. The short one was carrying a video camera. The plastic-looking one was making phone calls. Why you have spent your life trying to be friends with those people instead of Kitty and Linnea will baffle me to my grave."

"I'm not friends with them."

"And yet you always seem to choose them."

I lowered the dishrag and tried to blink the smoke out of

my eyes. I turned away from the oven. Took a slow, shallow breath. After a minute, I said, "Hedda?"

"I know what you're going to ask. Just ask it."

What I wanted to ask was if she knew why her daughter had fled the keep. Why she'd turned nineteen people to stone. Why, for all my life, everyone had been telling the story of Matilda, the skeld who'd gone mad.

"What happened to your daughter?"

"What happened was that her father got turned to stone when she was twelve years old. Does that sound familiar? I put all my energy into Stenland, into making it a place I was still happy to call home. I didn't see her. How unhappy she was. How angry. And when the time came and she was locked in the— I don't know why she walked out that day. Maybe she hated me. Maybe she hated everyone. Maybe she was just scared."

"Hedda," I said.

"I don't need your pity, Eriksson."

"How could you stay here, after all that?"

"How could I leave?" she said. "Get your friends out of Stenland."

I thanked her for the warning, and she hung up on me because a customer came in. I rubbed the smoke out of my eyes with the back of my wrist and went back to savagely waving my rag. We weren't supposed to open the windows on the second floor in case one of the keepers happened to be walking to the cottage outside, but I thought I might asphyxiate if I didn't clear the smoke, so I went to the nearest window and tried to push it. It didn't budge. I couldn't tell if it wasn't meant to open or if it had just gone sticky with age. I blinked again, trying to clear the smoke from my eyes, and that was when I saw something small and red moving down the hillside.

The glass was fat and uneven, twisting things upside down and refracting light into rainbows across the room. The landscape was hazy and ill defined, but I could make out enough that I knew there was something moving quickly through the nearest croft.

I watched it come closer with cold dread in the bottom of my stomach. It was too small to be a car. An ATV, then, rumbling over the grass and bypassing the road entirely.

It stopped moving about a hundred feet before the narrow spit that led to the keep. The windows were not clear enough—that was what I had always been told—but still, I felt dread sink through me. They were not moving. Because they were filming something? Or because I had turned them to stone? For a moment, they were Schrödinger's documentarians, both alive and dead, and then, very slowly, the ATV reversed, and they drove away.

I exhaled. My breath fogged the glass.

That night, Henrik suggested everyone have dinner together in the keep, and this time, I didn't argue.

I didn't see the ATV at all over the course of the next week—a police car sat, unmoving, on the road to the keep, just in case—but I heard tell of spottings. Kitty's mum ran into Damian and August at the grocery store. They showed up at my dad's garage while he was working. I kept almost calling August, but I did not want him to have a recording of my voice for his film. I imagined the cold open. A shot of the keep hemmed by ominous clouds. Over the top, my voice, shrill: *Leave my fucking island before someone gets hurt.* I would not give him the satisfaction.

Henrik, Lukas, and Soren took to having dinner with us every night. I didn't ask what Saffi thought of this, but I felt bad about it anyway.

When we had only a week left of skeld season and no one had yet died, I started to believe we might actually escape the curse. Everyone had always said Linnea, Kitty, and I would become skelds; no one had ever said we would kill someone. I was getting ahead of myself, but I couldn't help it. I even caught myself humming while I washed the dinner dishes—a pop hit my dad liked while I scraped away singed layers of potato from a casserole dish. I could hear Kitty and Linnea fighting for control of the speakers; Linnea won out and the music went folksy. I shook the water from my hands and shut my eyes. It was a Stennish band, one I'd loved in high school but stopped listening to when no one in California had ever heard of them. I had anticipated, of course, all the ways coming home would be hard, but I forgot to account for all the ways it would be easy: the voices like mine and the music I'd always known; the inside jokes, the familiar stories. In San Francisco, I was forever moving at the not-quite-right speed. It was easy to start believing that people did not find me clever or interesting. But with these people, in this place, I slipped back into a self that fit naturally, some past Tess who did not need to work to make people listen, laugh, understand.

When I joined the others in the hearth room, I saw they'd shoved the table to the wall to clear space on the floor. I sat next to the hearth, which was sort of near Soren, but not exactly next to him, and I kept adjusting the fire even though it was burning perfectly well. Linnea was guiding Henrik through a complicated dance she insisted we'd all learned in primary school, but that no one else recalled. They were going to do this dance at Wedding 2.0.

"No, left," she said.

"This is left," Henrik told her.

"My left."

"I went to your left."

"Maybe you're just not a very good dancer."

"I am blindfolded," Henrik said.

"Or just a talentless hack," Lukas said. "Linnea, where are you? I'll dance with you." He stuck out his arms expectantly, and he just looked so, so stupid that I laughed, which prompted Kitty to tell him I was mocking him.

"Can't anyone take this seriously?" Linnea said. "It's for the wedding."

"What if we just eloped?" Henrik said.

"That's not funny."

"Come get married in London," Kitty said. "No curses in London."

"We are going to have a wedding, and it's going to be lovely, and the island won't do anything to ruin it because I have only ever been kind to Stenland, unlike the two of you."

There was a quiet beat where everyone tried to decide how much Linnea meant it—how much she believed that Kitty and I really had offended the island by leaving.

"Where's Tess?" Lukas said loudly. "I want to dance with Tess."

I told him Tess was a conscientious objector, but this unfortunately allowed him to locate me by the sound of my voice. He pulled me up off the floor and spun me a few times across the room, and when he finally let me go back to the fire, he said he had an announcement to make.

"Are you becoming a professional folk dancer?" Henrik asked.

"If you say yes," Kitty said, "you don't need to get me a Christmas present this year."

"I got a job. In France. I'm going to nanny some rich people's kids for three months. I start right after New Year's."

Everyone clapped. Kitty said, *"Toutes nos félicitations!"*

"Yeah, well," Lukas said. "I just thought it could be fun for a while. See the world a bit."

I looked over at Soren, who had clapped along but whose mouth was unreadable.

Lukas excused himself a few minutes later because his mask was starting to itch, and Kitty left when he did, citing her need of a bath. Henrik and Linnea stayed a few more minutes, talking in clipped tones about their wedding, which I increasingly understood as Linnea's way of reclaiming control over the curse's chaos—a perfect wedding was what the island owed her. If anyone had asked me which one of us would handle being a skeld best, I would've said Linnea. What I failed to account for was that neither Kitty nor I had ever expected the island's kindness. Eventually, Linnea and Henrik stole away to Linnea's room to engage in something almost certainly not advised in the skeld/keeper handbook, which left just two of us.

It was the first time Soren and I had been alone together since the night of the rehearsal dinner, when we'd waited for the baker to return with my cake. I wasn't sure he knew I was there, and I rubbed my palms on my jeans, wondering if I could sneak away silently before I said something awful, like, *Sometimes I wish we were about to be hit by a meteor.*

"I think he'll be good at it," Soren said.

I curled my knees to my chest and leaned closer to the fire. "What?"

"Lukas. Nannying. He's good with kids."

"Did you know?"

"He told me when he first applied."

"You two seem..." I paused. "Good."

Quietly, Soren said, "Yeah. I think we are."

The fire popped; a twig sizzled and snapped.

"I'm sorry about Elin," I said. "I miss her."

Soren rubbed his neck. The mask shifted slightly, and I flinched, but it stayed firmly fixed across his eyes. He didn't even seem to notice. "She really liked you. I know it was hard to tell sometimes."

That ache in my chest. It whittled into the bones and spread like a fracture. "I always worried she was angry with me for taking you away from home."

He let out a breath through his nose. "You never took me anywhere I didn't want to go."

I was glad he couldn't see me; my eyes were starting to water from sitting so near the fire. "Thanks for the books, by the way. I don't know if I ever said that."

"Did you like Elsa Bergquist's memoir? 'We should all endeavor to be awed at least once a day.' I think about that a lot."

"Yeah," I said. "I actually really liked it." A pause. "And are you?"

"Am I what?"

"Awed at least once a day?"

"I think so," he said.

"By?"

He was sitting with his elbows on his knees, and he was drumming his fingers slowly across his opposite forearm. "I don't know."

"No, tell me."

"Just—everything, I guess." He paused, like he was embarrassed. "The wind and the sea and the clouds and the stones."

"That doesn't count. You see those every day."

"They awe me every day."

The fracture feeling spread farther through my ribs. "Okay, Board of Stennish Propaganda," I said, though my voice sounded strained.

Another pause, then hesitantly, he said, "I was reading about riddles from the Exeter Book yesterday."

"I appreciate that you think I know what that is."

"It's a collection of Anglo-Saxon poetry. Tenth century. In it, there's this riddle that goes something like: My parents abandoned me, but a nice woman took me in like I was her own child. Eventually, once I was big and strong, I killed her other children. What am I?"

"A right dick."

He snorted. "A cuckoo."

"I don't get it."

"That's what cuckoos do. They lay their eggs in other birds' nests and take off. When I read that, my first thought was, How long did that English monk have to sit around watching cuckoos before he figured that out? But then I realized—no, not just some monk. Someone else was expected to guess the answer to the riddle. This was just something everybody knew or observed or..." He trailed off. "I guess, realizing people from a thousand years ago were paying so much attention to the world. That's what awed me yesterday."

His voice went from reverent to sheepish the longer he spoke. I felt a fierce sense of protectiveness that wasn't mine to feel.

"I had a poetry professor who reminded me of you," I said.

"Esoteric and taxing?"

"He talked like you. He made me care about poetry. And I really do not care about poetry."

"Your point?"

"Why aren't you doing a PhD?"

He turned his face to the fire. He was quiet for so long I thought maybe I had only asked the question in my head. Outside, the night air scuttled across the walls of the keep. Finally, he said, "The wind and the sea and the clouds and the stones."

The feeling in my ribs was in all my bones now: skull and arms and hips and feet. It was like homesickness, but I did not know what I was homesick for. For the wind and the sea and the clouds and the stones, maybe; for the fact that I had never once let myself love them.

"I should go to bed," I said.

"I should go back to the croft."

"Do you need a hand to the door?"

"I'm fine."

I watched him stand, and I watched him drag his fingertips along the wall as he found his way through the hearth room.

"Soren?" I said.

"Tess?"

I swallowed. "I'm sorry about your parents. I know we never really talked about it, but I'm so, so sorry."

"It's not your fault," he said. And then: "It's never been your fault."

"I didn't love you because I wanted absolution," I said.

"You loved me because you had sympathy."

"That makes it sound like I pitied you."

"Does it? I had sympathy too."

At the door, he paused like he was going to say something else, but in the end, he just let himself out and closed the door silently in his wake. I turned the word over in my head, *sympathy*, and eventually looked it up on my phone, searching for an answer to the pressure against my ribs. The dictionary said: *Sorrow for the misfortune of another.* It also said: *Shared feeling.*

The next day, Soren didn't come to dinner. I didn't see him at all. But he left another box of books on our doorstep. *Hamlet*, *The Exeter Book Riddles*, and then, slimmer than the others, a bound copy of his master's thesis. I texted him a photo of it.

Me: We don't talk enough about this pretentious streak of yours

Soren: You don't have to read it

Me: As if I would miss the chance to find a typo in your work

Soren: I hope you know that if you find a typo, I will die

Me: I love a challenge

The title was "'For Ten Thousand Years': Echoes and Allusions in Stennish Literature." I flipped through it and stopped at a photograph of Fairhowe Cairn and the Stennish inscription inside and the translation, *Do you feel like the two of us /*

have been falling in love for ten thousand years? The point of the thesis was that people in the past weren't so different from us. They were awed by history as we are awed by history. They were inspired, and they in turn became inspiration. Reading, I felt a pressure on my breastbone like a physical thing, pushing out from inside my chest and making it hard to breathe. He traced one text to another so gracefully, arguing that this poem inspired that graffiti inspired that tombstone across centuries. He wrote like he couldn't bear it not to be true.

I did not find any typos.

With three days left of skeld season, I saw them again.

I was on the stairs at the time. At first, I just glimpsed movement; and then, when I turned, I saw them. Three figures set between the keep and the sea. Through the mottled glass, I couldn't make out their faces. They were an impressionist painting: the gestural strokes of a man with a camera, a man in an expensive jacket, and a man in just a sweater and muddy jeans. Beside them was an ATV, and I could hear the low rumble of the motor.

For a moment, I didn't react because even bigger than my fury that they were standing there was my fear that they would look at me. Once I acknowledged this fear, I hated them for giving it to me.

I slammed my fist against the window. The men lurched, glanced at the keep, then quickly away again. The glass was too distorted, I figured, for the curse to do any harm, but I was afraid to look in the direction of their faces anyway. They clambered into the ATV and started to drive. Two of them, that is. The man in the sweater, a red sweater, and the muddy jeans, he stayed where his feet were planted. I waited for him to turn as August and Damian disappeared through the grass. I waited for him to turn. I waited.

My hand fell from the glass.

The wind tugged at his sweater.

I waited.

Down the stairs. I didn't remember deciding to run, but I was running. I didn't remember deciding to throw open the door, but it was open, and I was falling through it. Across the grass in bare feet. Gasping for oxygen in the too-thin air. Frost burned my skin. And still, he did not move.

He was facing away from me. Where his hair should've been blond, it was dull gray, every strand etched like it was carved by the loving hand of a master sculptor. It was pushed to the side messily, like he had just run his hand through it.

I said Soren's name. The wind ripped my voice back out to sea. I said it again, and then I stopped in front of him and stared at his face.

It took me a moment to realize. I knew so much of this face: the angle of the nose and the shape of the lips and the crease just between the brows. But it wasn't Soren. It was his father: Mattias Fell, turned to stone by my mother when he'd been hardly older than Soren was now. He was missing two of his fingers; they'd been chipped off. I touched the wool of the sweater, which was already gathering snowflakes, and I looked up at his face, seeing but not understanding.

I heard Linnea call my name. She came running through the door, and I knew what she must've seen, what she thought this was, but I couldn't find the words to explain it. Even when she saw Mattias's face, she was still calling him Soren. They looked so alike she couldn't tell. I was distantly aware of the sensation of prophecy averted. It felt like maybe I was living in two realities at the same time: one where Soren was dead, and another where he wasn't. Both seemed true, like one story was superimposed over the other—a palimpsest.

"It's not Soren," I said numbly.

"What? What do you mean?"

"It's his dad."

"How did… I don't understand."

"August," I said, because that was the only way to make sense of it. "They must've wanted a statue in front of the keep. For filming."

Linnea shrieked. I had never heard a sound like that, from her or anyone—the wild rage of it. For the first time, I noticed the way her lashes were dark with tears, and noticing made me aware for the first time of my own face, sticky and salty and cold. Every breath I took was too shallow. I felt like someone had broken all my ribs.

Linnea ran. She tore along the path where tires had flattened the grass, the soles of her bare feet flashing through the mud. I called her name, but she didn't stop.

I ran after her.

Off the isthmus and up the crest of a hill. For the first time in days, the police car had gone. Where, why? I could see the ATV in the distance—just dipping out of sight into another croft—and there was no way to catch them, but Linnea did not care. She screamed after them that she would kill them, just wait, she would follow them to the end of the island and she would kill them, and I believed her.

I only caught her because she slid on a patch of ice going down the hill. She fell, and I fell with her, and when she tried to get up, I wrapped my arms around her and held her to the ground.

"Let me go," she said.

"No."

"They—they *defiled* him. They made you think—"

"Linnea, no."

"I'll kill them," she said, but now she was crying, pressing her face against my shoulder. "What's the point of being a skeld when we can't even protect ourselves?"

"We need to go back to the keep."

"Because we could hurt someone out here, right?" She was

crying harder now. "Aren't you tired of being afraid of yourself?"

"Lin."

"I was going to protect you this time."

I swept her hair out of her collar, where it had gotten caught on a button. She accepted my hand when I offered it, and when I pulled her to her feet, she shut her eyes and tilted her head to the sky.

"I'm just so tired," she said quietly.

"I know."

We walked with our eyes on our feet. Mine were red with cold; Linnea's were ghostly purple. I thought about calling Soren to tell him about his dad or calling Henrik to tell him where we were, but I didn't have my phone. I'd run out of the keep without it.

I was so consumed with the act of not looking up that I almost did not notice. Linnea didn't. She stepped through the door of the keep with a shiver and a shaky breath. But I saw movement in my peripheral vision: Kitty's movement and her voice under her breath. I turned to see her facing the statue of Mattias, but—no, Mattias was on the other side of Ramna Skaill.

Kitty looked over at me. "Linnea screamed," she said.

I took a step forward.

"We must've both heard her," Kitty said. "I wasn't thinking. I just—I heard her out here."

Another step.

"Tess," Kitty whispered. "I didn't—"

I stopped at her side.

Looked up at Henrik.

From behind us, Linnea said, "Tess, where did you...?" Then, seeing: "Henrik?"

Keep

2022

The three of us stood on the cliffs with our shoulders touching—Linnea, then Kitty, then me.

Linnea said: "I don't understand."

Kitty said: "Fucking hell."

I didn't say anything.

I stepped forward, toward the edge of the cliffs. Faint footprints tracked a path through the frost.

Linnea made a choking sound behind me.

Where the earth gave way, right near the edge, there he stood: tall, windswept, wearing a sweater with a fraying sleeve. When the breeze blew off the ocean, the sweater flattened against his chest. Already, a layer of snow had fallen across the top of his head, the width of his shoulders, the tip of his nose. His mouth was open, like he was about to say something; he never would.

I took another step, my hand outstretched. I touched his cheekbone, and a part of me still expected it to be soft, warm, alive, but all my fingers found was stone.

The wind rushed around us, cold enough to burn.

My hand dropped from his still, stone face. When I turned, Linnea was on her knees.

"I just don't understand," she said again, her voice muffled through her hands. And then she raised her head, slowly, to look at me. She said, somewhere between question and accusation: "Tess?"

I held her gaze. Swallowed.

Then she turned, slowly, and her eyes met Kitty's. She whispered, "Kitty?"

I never should've come back.

"Linnea," Kitty said. "I didn't mean to."

"But it was you. Wasn't it?"

Kitty was shaking her head even as she said yes. Yes, it was, and she hadn't meant to, but it had just happened. Linnea had screamed, so they'd both come running. They'd both thought—

Well. It didn't matter now.

"You never liked him," Linnea whispered.

Kitty took a breath, sharp and horrible, like she'd been stabbed. "Linnea—"

Linnea climbed to her feet. She was covered in mud; her dress had a tear at the knee. She looked—oh, god, so young, with her eyes bright red and her hair wild and thistled. I tried to grab her hand, but she shook me away.

Kitty tried to say something, maybe Linnea's name again, but Linnea was already throwing open the door and disappearing into Ramna Skaill. I was distantly aware of the sound of sirens. The looming threat of more people. Somewhere, Soren.

"We have to go inside," I told Kitty.

She wasn't moving.

"Kitty. Please."

She wouldn't get arrested. It was August's fault, not Kitty's. Kitty had just been trying to protect us, to protect Linnea. For a moment, I wondered if that was what Kitty was thinking about as the sirens wailed ever closer. But when I looked at her, she was reaching a hand to Henrik. She looked so small in comparison. Her fingers touched his wide, outstretched palm.

"Kitty," I said again, quieter this time.

I didn't realize she was crying until I heard her say his name. Just once. In a whisper, as a question. Like she thought he still might respond.

The wind came whistling off the water. Kitty turned and ran, back into the keep. My legs were too heavy to move. I could not stop seeing, on the backs of my eyelids, the way Linnea had looked at Kitty: like she wished we had never been friends at all.

A voice behind me said, "Tess?"

I shut my eyes.

"It's me," Soren said. "Why are you—"

I heard, in his breath, the moment he realized. It was the longest silence I had ever endured. I kept my eyes pressed shut as tears squeezed between my lids, as Soren came closer. He didn't say anything, but he sounded like he was breathing through broken glass.

If I could've taken Henrik's place, I would've done it. I wouldn't have cared. I wouldn't have even paused. I would have been dead if it meant Henrik was not, and I wished, completely, that I was.

"We should go inside," Soren said finally, his voice hoarse and thin. "The police are— Lukas called them. About August. We didn't realize..."

"You should keep your eyes closed," I said. "I don't know where Linnea and Kitty are."

"They're closed," Soren said.

I felt his hand on my elbow. Instinctively, I started to lean into him, his warmth and his familiar smell, but I pulled away again before my body could fit against his. So we just stayed like that, barely touching—just his fingers against the crook of my elbow—as we made our way blindly back to the keep.

Through the door, I opened my eyes. Found a mask and set it in his hands. He put it on. Pressed his hands to his face.

"Tess," he said again, no more noise than a breath. "How did you— How did it happen?"

That was the first time I realized that he thought it was me.

"August wanted to get film of someone in stone by the keep," I said. "They must've gone to the cemetery. He— It was your dad. Soren, I'm sorry."

Soren lips parted slightly. He swayed slightly, as if in an invisible wind. "My dad?"

"At the back of the keep," I said. "I was in my room and I—thought it was you. I thought you were dead."

"So you ran outside."

"Yes."

"And then you—saw Henrik?"

I didn't say anything to that. It could've been me or Linnea as easily as it had been Kitty. Like it could've been Soren or Lukas as easily as it had been Henrik.

"They moved my dad?" Soren said.

"I'm sorry. It's my fault they're here. It's my fault any of this happened. I never should've—"

Soren's arms moved around me. It was not like the way we would've hugged when we'd been something more than this; we were too still, too afraid of each other. But it was desperate and necessary. His breathing was unsteady in my ear. I pressed my face against his chest and shut my eyes. We held each other like that until the sirens were right outside and someone was knocking at the door.

"I'll talk to them," he said. "Go find Kitty and Linnea."

"Soren—"

Soren what?

Soren, I wish I were dead instead of him.

Soren, I told you something like this was going to happen, and you never listened to me.

Soren, sometimes I still wonder if we're in love with each other, but maybe now we can finally stop wondering because there is no love worth this.

Eventually, the documentary would come out, released independently because they could not find anyone to back them. It was riddled, commenters said, with obvious inaccuracies. They had only managed to interview a handful of locals. One user asked if she was the only one who thought the Stenns were fucking with these shitheads. Her comment had more likes than the film.

I never saw either August or Damian again. I thought about it, sometimes. I wondered if I met them on the street, years later, if I would just keep walking or if I would stop and ask if it was worth it.

Upstairs, I knocked on Linnea's door. When she didn't answer, I pushed it open anyway. She was lying on her back on the bed with her thin fingers pressing into her eyes.

"Can I come in?"

She didn't say anything to that, which I took as a yes. I lowered myself onto the bed next to her and held a pillow against my stomach. She was crying: completely without noise even as her body shook like so many unfastened pieces rattling apart.

I touched her hair. Ran my fingers through it. Outside: the sirens shutting off, voices—Soren's. The light bruised and vanished out the window, and still Linnea and I sat. I picked the thistles and grass from her sleeves and set them in an empty mug on her bedside table. I pretended it was an important task because I didn't want to let myself think. It didn't seem fair to Linnea to cry, so I tried to watch my fingers and suppress the thick pressure in the back of my skull.

She didn't speak until after midnight.

"Please say something." Her voice was sandpapery.

"I'm so sorry."

"Something else."

"It was my fault."

"It wasn't," Linnea said. "If you—"

A knock at the door. After a pause, it creaked open. Kitty stood at the threshold with her phone in one hand, pressed against her leg.

"I just got off the phone with Soren," she said. "They've revoked all the visas of anyone involved with the film. The police don't want to charge us with anything because we were just acting in self-defence. And they know they shouldn't have left us—they got another call, probably a fake report, about shots fired near here. That's why the patrol car was gone." A long pause. "Tess, why did you tell Soren it was you?"

"I didn't."

"But you didn't tell him it was me," Kitty said.

"You only went outside because we were already there. I left the keep first."

"But it was my fault," Kitty said. "I was the one who looked at Henrik. I told Soren so. It was…" She moved her gaze to the ceiling, blinking rapidly. "Thank you, Tess. But it's never going to stop being me who looked at him last."

"Stop it!" Linnea said. I flinched, but she grabbed my wrist and squeezed it. Kitty set a hand against the door frame, like she wasn't sure if she was supposed to go. "Tess, you only went outside because you thought one of us had just killed Soren. And Kitty, you only went outside because I screamed. I'm the one who went running away from the keep, and I'm the one who Henrik thought he needed to come help, and—and it's his fault too, isn't it, because he could've been more careful, right? And maybe it's also Soren's fault, while we're at it, because if he was a better keeper, he wouldn't have left Henrik here to handle everything on his own? And Lukas? Do we want to blame Lukas, too?"

Kitty and I didn't say anything. Linnea's face was wet and shiny.

"I don't need you to fight about whose fault it was," she said.

"What do you need?" I asked.

A long pause.

"Just talk to me," Linnea said. "Please."

Kitty sat hesitantly on the edge of the bed. I listened: to the wind rattling the windows and the pop of the fire in the hearth and their breathing, Linnea's and Kitty's, in this room we had always been doomed to enter.

"You know I have thirty-seven photos of us in my flat?" Kitty said. "I counted the day before my flight here. I was trying to convince myself it was a good idea to come. There's this one from when we were, like, six. We're making something—I think it's shortbread—and it looks like it's in Linnea's kitchen, but I don't remember it at all. But in this photo, Tess is weighing ingredients on a scale, just completely focused, and Linnea has drawn little faces in this huge pile of sugar we spilled, and I'm standing on a chair with the cookbook looking so fucking annoyed." Kitty took a breath. "I guess I'm just saying that even if we never spoke to each other again, I'd still only be me because of the two of you."

When Kitty stopped talking, Linnea looked at me, like it was my turn, and I didn't know what I was going to say until I opened my mouth. When I did, I told them then about the map on AJ's wall. The one that didn't have Stenland. I told them about knowing to my bones that my life was worth fuck all if not for this place. If not for Soren and Henrik and Linnea and Kitty.

"I'm sorry I didn't stay away," I told them. "But I'm also sorry I didn't come back sooner."

Linnea let out a horrible, juddering breath. "I lied to you."

I shook my head, not understanding.

"When Elin died. I told you—I told you not to come back. That it would just hurt him."

I touched her shoulder. "That wasn't a lie, Lin. You were right."

"No, it was. Because right after the funeral, he got a flight to California. To—see you. And Henrik..." She paused, swallowed. "Henrik and I convinced him to cancel it. Because we knew how Saffi felt about him. And I was afraid if you were together, you'd both leave forever or you'd keep hurting each other, and I told myself it was the best for both of you, but really, I think I was just angry. Because you left. Because you gave up on me."

I blinked quickly, trying to clear my eyes as they began to burn. "I would never give up on you."

"But you did," Linnea said.

But I did.

"I'm sorry," I whispered. "I'm so sorry."

She shook her head frantically. "No. No, no. I should've come to see you. Both of you. I just thought if I did, it would be like when Lukas went, and he came back thinking everything here was—pathetic, or something. I just didn't want to realize my life was pathetic."

"If anyone ever makes you feel pathetic," Kitty said, "I'll rip their fucking throat out."

"I do want to go, though," Linnea said. "Visit you both."

We were all quiet for a moment, then Linnea took a sharp breath. "I'm sorry I made you both come back," she said, and then she was crying again.

I waited until Linnea and Kitty were asleep, sometime just after seven, when the sun was still hours off rising. Not long until the shortest day of the year, then Christmas, then another January to start over again.

I went to the hearth room and made a fire, slowly and deliberately, concentrating on every bit of kindling. When I opened my laptop, there was a moment before the screen lit up where I saw my reflection in the blackness: puffy, pale, hollow. I watched my fingers as I typed. The glow of the screen hurt too much. In the end, I only proofread it once, quickly, before I pressed Send.

It was a polite letter thanking Carla and the company for giving me a job three and a half years before. I said I was grateful; I meant it. I also said that due to unforeseen circumstances, I would be resigning so that I could spend more time with my family.

The Delta

2022

When I woke up two days later, I looked in the mirror and found nothing on my forehead. No mark. Like it had never existed at all.

We emerged from Ramna Skaill when the sky was still black. It reminded me of early-morning swim practices as a kid, when I'd waited just inside the doors to the pool for my dad's car to cut a warm glow through the darkness.

He parked in the dirt lot and stepped out. I shouldered my duffel bag and glanced up at him, nervous at first. He smiled cautiously back at me. My bag slid to the ground and I hugged him, and when he hugged me back, I could smell coffee and motor oil on his shirt.

In the car, I told him about the plane tickets to London and how I was maybe thinking of trying to get a job there. I told him about Noah and ending things and how my mum had offered to go move my stuff out of the apartment in case I couldn't bear to. I didn't tell him about Henrik because he already knew.

When we got back to the house, I found a mug just waiting to be filled and pancake batter at the ready beside the stove. My dad shyly handed me the mug, and I started crying before I could help it.

"I'm sorry about Anna," I said.

He put his arms around me and pulled me into his chest. I stood with the mug curled in my hands and my shoulders at my ears. "How is that your fault?" he asked.

"I'm sorry it happened. I'm sorry I wasn't with you."

"Oh, Tessie," he said. "I'm so sorry I made you grow up here."

It wasn't the reason I was crying, but I didn't know how to describe what was.

At the funeral, I ended up sitting with Linnea on one side and Soren on the other. The pews were hard and unforgiving. It was snowing outside, so someone had turned the radiators so high I felt sweat beading down the back of my neck. Soren sat very still, and when my thigh accidentally touched his, he let it stay there for one, two, three seconds before shifting away, just long enough that he could pretend he wasn't flinching at my touch. He had a book in his lap, cover-side down, and his hands rested protectively across it.

Father Andersson stood behind the pulpit and told us about hope and courage and everlasting love. My mouth tasted metallic, like I had a cut in my throat and kept swallowing the blood. In the back of the church, a child started to cry; I thought it was Henrik's nephew.

Henrik's parents both spoke. His father looked exactly like him, just bigger. When he said that Henrik was the kindest boy anyone had ever met, he said it angrily, like he was waiting for someone to contradict him. Henrik's mother swayed, tipsy, as she tried to recount some story about a tenth birthday, when Henrik and Soren had accidentally broken a window in this very church with a soccer ball, but she never got to the end of the story. Henrik's father had to go back up there to help her down. Beside me, Soren let out a tiny, strangled breath. That was the first noise I heard him make all day.

When it was Linnea's turn, she stood and closed her hands into fists, like she was going into battle. She hadn't owned any black, not a single item, so we'd had to go out to buy a dress. It was lacy and fluttery and long-sleeved. When I'd tried to pay for it, the woman at the counter wouldn't let me.

"Everyone always tells you not to fall in love when you're too young," Linnea said. Her voice echoed into the rafters. Henrik's nephew had been taken outside, but I could still hear his cries through the door. "And if you do, not to take it too seriously because it probably won't last. But I'm going to love Henrik for the rest of my life."

Soren took a breath through his nose. I tried to swallow and couldn't. In my peripheral vision, I could see his profile: jaw, mouth, eyelashes.

"I read a lot of romance books in the keep," Linnea said. "Most of them have this part at the end, an epilogue, so you can see they're still happy and in love ten years in the future." She inhaled. "But I don't think people have to be together forever for their love to mean something."

I had to stare with all my focus at Linnea's hands, wrapped around the pulpit, to keep from turning my head. My eyes were burning, but I just kept facing forward, blinking and blinking.

At the end, Linnea said that Henrik's best friend was going to read something from *Downwelling.* Soren got up, and Linnea hugged him and whispered something in his ear before she sat. He was lit around the edges, tinged gold from all the candles. It was the same suit he'd worn to the rehearsal dinner. When he swallowed, I could see the movement of his throat.

He gave no introduction. Just opened the book and read: "'The sorrow and the joy his brother had brought him seemed then of equal value. If he had not felt such pain, he would not have felt so human. There, among the young willows drooped with mourning, he felt a clarity he had never known. The stuff of life is what other people make us feel.'"

For the first time since we'd entered the church, Soren looked at me, and once he did, he didn't look anywhere else. I had a sense of falling from a catastrophic height. I was sure then that everyone in every pew knew the truth: that I loved him, would always love him, would never let him love me back for fear of what I might do to him.

"'He had always imagined,'" Soren said, eyes still on mine, "'that the difference between two people was a chasm to be crossed. Now he realized it was not a chasm but a precious entity unto itself. There is no endeavor more human than the tender examination of the delta between two souls. There is no endeavor more human than sympathy.'"

He sat back down. Father Andersson finished the service. When it was over, Linnea stood stiffly at the front of the room. Saffi wound an arm around her waist, holding and propping her both. Saffi and I nodded at each other, trying to smile for the sake of showing we didn't dislike each other but not quite getting there on account of the shittiness of the day.

"I hope you like London," Saffi told Linnea. "I hope you let yourself have fun."

Linnea said of course, a little quietly, her gaze and head elsewhere. My dad came over to hug me sideways and tell me we should think about getting to the airport soon. We'd booked our flights for the evening of the funeral, thinking that it would be good to have something to do, but now it felt like a mistake. It felt cruel to leave so soon.

Soren took a step toward us, and Saffi set her hand gently on his elbow. I told Linnea I needed some water, and would she be okay for a minute? She nodded. Soren's gaze moved to meet mine, and I pushed through the door into the hall.

In one of the bathroom stalls, Kitty was sobbing. I knew it was her because I recognized her shoes. She didn't open the door, so I crawled under it and found her sitting on the lid with her elbows on her knees.

"Don't tell Linnea" was the first thing she said.

I put a hand on her back.

"I don't want her to think I'm trying to make it about me," Kitty said.

"She wouldn't think that." I handed her clumps of balled-up toilet paper until she was done crying.

"I need five more minutes," she said. "Can I just— Sorry."

I kissed the top of her head and stepped back into the hallway alone.

"Tess?" a voice said behind me.

I turned. Lukas. I wiped my eyes, but he just gave me this smile like—no, why bother—and I let my hands drop.

"Can I give you a hug?" he asked.

I nodded, and he wrapped his arms around me. I pressed my face into his lapel, and I tried not to make any noise, but my breath came out slow and shuddering.

"Hey, hey," Lukas said, smoothing my hair. "You're okay. You're okay."

"Sorry," I whispered.

He was so much taller than me. Since when? I wanted to go back: to the Fells' kitchen, to Lukas lying on the couch and Soren at the stove and Kitty perched on the edge of the table, to Henrik and Linnea all tangled together. I wouldn't even need to be there. I just wanted to go back long enough to see them. Look through the window. Prove it was real.

"You're going to miss your flight," Lukas said.

"Yeah."

"I was thinking of visiting," he said. "If you ever need a friend in California."

I supposed, this close to the flight, it didn't matter anymore if I told him, so I said: "I might not be there. I thought I could stay with Kitty and Linnea for a while."

"In London?" Lukas asked. "What about Noah?"

I leaned my forehead against his shoulder and didn't say anything. When he spoke, I could feel the words echo in his chest. "He's not— He understands what happened here, right? I haven't heard you say anything about him in..." A pause. "Did he break up with you? Did you break up with him? Does Soren know?"

"You can't tell him."

"Why not?"

"Not until I leave."

"Tess—"

"I didn't want him to worry that I broke up with Noah because I thought he and I would..."

"End up together?" Lukas said. "Everyone has always thought that. I have always thought that. I thought I was in love with you for about six months, and even then, I still thought that."

"You thought you were in love with me?"

"Forever ago."

"You never told me."

"Of course I never told you," Lukas said. "You should've said something when you broke up with Noah."

"I didn't want to make Saffi uncomfortable."

"Not sure it would've made much of a difference," Lukas said. "They ended things the first day of skeld season, as soon as Linnea moved the wedding."

"They didn't," I said.

"Yes, they did."

"I just saw them together."

"Doing what? Talking?"

"They didn't," I said again.

"Tess."

Lukas watched me. I opened my mouth—no sound came out—then swallowed.

"You have to tell him," he said. "God, before you leave, you have to tell him."

"I can't."

"Why? Give me one good reason."

I gestured helplessly at the stone walls of the church. At the windows and the snow. At the sea and the wind and at Stenland.

"We've tried, Lukas. So many times. I don't— I can't do it to him again."

"Then just stay! Tess, I know being in Stenland can feel like being trapped at the end of the world. Jesus Christ, I get it. But it's not all that. Would it really be the worst thing? To stay?"

Jesus Christ, he got it, Tess, obviously. I knew this from his emails, which I always read, perhaps multiple times, when I had a nightmare or over coffee before Noah was awake. I read about the bloody sheep getting stuck in the mud; the cruise ships lumbering into the harbor and belching daft passengers across Lundwall; losing at darts in the pub; Soren's birthday; a hike to the bottom of the gorge with a whiskey toast to keep warm; the New Year's soccer match, played on the snow in the middle of the road because no one was driving; the smell of a peat fire. I tripped on a Pictish stone and landed in a bog; Linnea told the worst joke; I saw your dad buying coffee; Soren is currently feeding a lamb milk from a bottle in front of the fire because it's too small and it won't survive otherwise; you wouldn't believe how cold it is; you wouldn't believe how windy it is; you must feel so lucky to be somewhere else.

I pressed my eyes shut. "What if he ends up like Henrik?"

Quietly, Lukas said: "Oh, Tess."

"Neither of us even wanted the other to know we were single. He and I both know we can't try this again if we're just going to…"

"Hurt each other? Because, no offense, but you two are pretty good at that even when you're on opposite sides of the world."

I looked down at my feet, pressing my chin to my chest. "I know."

"That's not what I meant. I meant—why did you end things with Noah? Don't tell me it wasn't for Soren. I won't believe you."

"It wasn't for him," I said. "It was because I can't keep dating people I just end up comparing to him. I know we're not going to be together. But I can't just pretend I don't want to feel like that with—someone."

Lukas studied me. Finally, he just nodded and wiped my cheekbone with the side of his thumb.

"Let's meet in London, then? And you can visit me in France?"

I nodded.

"I'll email you," he promised.

"Okay."

Through the frosted window, the snow was starting to flurry. Already the sun had slipped toward the horizon, edging the island into indigo night. The waves were as big as they ever were, crashing again and again against the snow-patterned shore. I had to get to the airport. I really did want to leave—of course I wanted to leave. Because: this place, this place, *this place*—

A door creaked, and over Lukas's shoulder, I saw Soren step into the hall. His tie was undone and loose around his neck. He pressed his lips together at the sight of us, not a smile, but sort of like he was trying.

"Hey," Lukas said.

Soren nodded and leaned his head against the wall.

I stepped away from Lukas. His hands dropped to his sides.

"I should go," I said.

I had to turn sideways to get past Soren, and the goodbye stuck in my throat because it seemed too small for something so large. When I looked over my shoulder, I saw Lukas speaking urgently and Soren opening his mouth, watching me go, maybe also knowing that goodbye was too small but everything else was agony even if it was true.

I thought of Soren lying in my bed years ago, telling me he could not find the words to describe the thing he felt, but that he kept searching for them in Stennish. Maybe that was what I was missing. I could not explain the duration of my love or the depths of my fear; maybe the words only existed in a language we had lost.

In the end, how else would the two of us have left it, really? Saying: nothing. Meaning: everything.

Fairhowe

2022

Kitty bought us coffees while we were waiting for our plane. The café was a new addition to the airport, and they only served one size. When Kitty asked for oat milk, the teenage boy behind the counter gave her a suspicious look.

We sat facing the window. Outside, the world was night black even though it was only four. In California, it never got this dark. Not even at midnight. Not even in winter. The lights from the tarmac and the taxiing plane were trapped under fog that hung low like a dome overhead. Around us, the other travelers spoke in low voices, like someone nearby might be trying to sleep. Most of them were tourists, but I recognized some. Our Year Three teacher looked like he was going to come over, maybe to offer condolences, but Kitty gave him such a withering look that he changed course and bought a medium-sized coffee instead.

Linnea tucked her feet beneath her and leaned against my shoulder. "Tell me again what we'll do in London."

"Kitty gives a very good tour," I said. "She'll tell you about how Paddington Bear became prime minister."

She shut her eyes. "Keep talking. Please."

"I'm going to take you to a musical," Kitty said. "There will be big dance numbers and voluminous costumes. And then we're going to the British Museum to see how many loud comments we can make about returning artifacts before we get kicked out. Followed by a night dancing at a club in a converted button factory where all the drinks glow in the dark. Oh, Lin."

The last part was because Linnea had started crying. No sound; just tears. I ran my hands through her hair, and she turned her face to my collarbone.

The plane was the kind you had to board from a little staircase that folded out in front of the wing. We stood in the cold and wet and waited our turn. Inside, it was too hot. The lights in the cabin glowed impossibly brightly. Already, I could not see the airport, either because of the angle or the fog. It felt like we were the only people in the world.

It was not the type of plane from my dream. There were no screens above the tray tables, and the seats were in twos, not threes. Linnea and Kitty took two together, and I was alone on the other side of the aisle. There must've been something in my expression, though, because as soon as we took off, Linnea unbuckled and moved to the seat next to me.

"Tess?"

I had been looking at my phone, which I had not yet turned to Airplane Mode. As the plane shook, I kept thinking it was an incoming message. There was nothing, of course; I didn't want there to be anything. What would it say? It was better that there wasn't.

"Tess," Linnea said again. "Are you okay?"

Don't go.

That's what it would say. If I got a message.

It was better that there was no message.

"I'm okay," I said.

"Are you actually okay, or do you just think I'm less okay and you don't want to worry me?"

I gave her an almost smile, and she gave me one back.

"Did you know all along?" she asked.

"Know what?"

"About Soren and Saffi. Saffi just told me. After the funeral. It wasn't— I wasn't trying to keep it from you."

"Don't worry about it," I said. "It's not important. In the scheme of things."

"I was just thinking, if not for Noah—"

"We broke up," I said. Linnea gave me this look and opened her mouth, but I said: "In the grand scheme of things. It really doesn't matter anymore."

By *it*, I meant: the message I did not get.

Linnea rested her head on my shoulder. "Okay," she said. "If that's how you feel."

When I looked out the window, I tried to make out the shape of the island: the lights of Lundwall and the narrow black roads snaking across the coastline and the little house at the northern tip of everything. There was too much fog.

Kitty lived alone in a one-bedroom flat. I called it an apartment, and she said, in a French accent, "You stupid American."

"How much money do you make, exactly?" Linnea asked when Kitty unlocked the door.

"Honestly?" she said. "A lot."

Linnea and I set our bags by the foot of Kitty's bed, which was unnecessarily large and covered in several dozen throw pillows. Her bathroom counter was so inundated with makeup and skincare products that I knocked a bottle of perfume to the ground while I was trying to wash my hands.

"Sorry," I said.

"Don't apologize to me," she said. "Apologize to the people standing next to us on the Tube as they slowly asphyxiate on vanilla."

Linnea went to take a nap, and Kitty and I sat at her tiny kitchen table in front of cups of tea we hadn't touched.

"You don't have to try so hard to seem like you're okay," I said.

"If I stop trying so hard," she said, "I'll remember what happened."

"You know Linnea doesn't blame you."

"She does. A little. It would be weird if she didn't."

I lifted a shoulder.

More quietly, Kitty said: "I hope she likes it here."

"So much that she stays and we never have to go back?"

Kitty gave me a funny look, like she misheard me, then she shook her head and drank her tea.

We did the things Kitty said we'd do. Kitty went back to work, and Linnea and I wandered through the parks and along the Thames. We spent too long on the Tube, just rumbling through the darkness with no destination in mind. Sometimes we'd talk and laugh and get off at a station, any station, and wander until we found a bakery. Other times we'd just ride to the end of the line because we didn't have anything to say.

I scrolled through job postings on my laptop. London, New York, Melbourne. Once, Linnea came up behind me so quietly I didn't hear her, and she said, "Does that say Lundwall?"

I closed the tab. "I was just curious."

"You'd think about going back?"

"No." I felt like a traitor. "Of course not."

Two weeks in London felt longer—a whole universe inside Kitty's flat. I had counted all thirty-seven photos of the three of us. We had our places and our routines. Kitty and Linnea slept far apart on the enormous bed, and I slept on an inflatable mattress on the floor because Linnea tossed and turned so much I couldn't sleep near her. Not that I slept much anyway. Mostly, I stared at the ceiling and waited for night to be over. Once, just as I was drifting off, my phone lit up. I grabbed it, frantic, but it was just an email inviting me to Get Christmas Discounts Now.

Kitty was the one who found the article, but Linnea was the one who showed me. We were in Kitty's kitchen, and Linnea was sitting cross-legged on a wooden chair with her phone on the table beside her porridge. She was drizzling honey into the porridge, but she was looking at her phone and didn't seem to notice the rate at which her bowl was becoming more honey than oat.

"Lin?"

"Have you seen?"

I took the honey bottle. "Seen what?"

"Kitty showed me this morning, but she had to leave. For her *coffee date.* She made me promise I'd show you."

I held out my hand, and she passed me the phone. When I scrolled back to the top, I saw a familiar masthead. The *Stennish Independent*, and a picture of Fairhowe Cairn—the inside, not the outside, and the thin, scratchy writing of an inscription in the stone. The heading said: *X-ray fluorescence imaging reveals 500-year-old inscription in Neolithic monument.*

"Have you finished reading?" Linnea asked.

"Give me a second."

"How about now?"

"Linnea."

"Okay, sorry, sorry."

The new inscription had been found on the wall opposite the most famous of the Fairhowe inscriptions; they were dated to the same decade, which made noted Stennish scholar Kirk Sandison believe they'd been carved at the same time. According to Sandison, this inscription had gone unnoticed until now because it was carved over the top of a pre-existing scrawl of Norse runes, which in turn had been carved over Pictish lines. The five-hundred-year-old inscription was in Stennish, and it would provide a consuming translation project for years to come. In the interim, as a first attempt to satiate curious minds, Sandison and a small group of research assistants had translated the text as: *Pity on me should I wait ten thousand more.*

"Now?" Linnea asked.

I passed her the phone.

"Tess," she said.

"I can't," I whispered.

"You can."

"I can't go back. Not for... I can't make my life smaller for a man."

"Who said loving someone makes your life smaller?"

"My mum."

"You're not your mum," Linnea said. "You're an engineer and a swimmer and my best friend, and you don't stop being those things just because you're in California or Britain or Stenland. And a small place doesn't mean a small life."

I was blinking now, quickly, and I wished Linnea would look away, but she didn't. Outside, a car horn blared and a bare branch rapped against the window.

"You don't hate Stenland," she said. "You've never hated Stenland."

"Of course I have. Do."

"You fucking don't!" Linnea said, loudly enough that I leaned away. She looked like she couldn't decide whether to laugh or throw her porridge at me. "You love the fucking snow, and you love that fucking pool, and you love all those winding fucking roads through the hills between the sheep, and Hedda's stupid fucking coffee, and Soren fucking Fell."

"I don't."

"Yes, you do."

I looked at my hands. My shoulders curled up to my ears. When I tried to swallow, it got caught in my throat. Linnea just waited, waited for me to say something, and when I finally did, my voice was almost too quiet to hear.

"What if I kill him?" I said.

"What if you don't?"

A long pause.

"Just tell me," Linnea said. "If you could know for sure that you wouldn't hurt him, what would you do?"

"But I can't know for sure."

"Please look at me."

When I did, she took my hands in both of hers. She had honey on her thumb, and I tried to wipe it away for her, but she just shook her head and held my fingers more tightly.

"I would never take away having loved Henrik. Even if I knew how it ended. And I—I guess I can't say if Henrik would've risked it, but I—"

"We both know he would've."

Linnea hesitated, then said: "If you were eighty, and you'd spent your whole life not letting yourself love him, and he was eighty, and he'd never been turned to stone—how much would you regret it?"

I blinked again, but it didn't help this time. "You already know. Why are you asking?"

"Pity on you," Linnea said, "should you wait ten thousand more."

I started to stand, then sat again. "That place takes so much from us."

She nudged the phone with her pinkie, showing me the picture of the cairn, meaning: *Sometimes it gives us things too.*

★★★

I called Kitty in the car. When she picked up, she said, "You know I don't do phone calls."

"I know."

"And I'm in the middle of a date."

"I know."

"It's going really well, in case you were wondering. She's sitting across from me now, giving me an annoyed look for answering my phone."

In the background, a voice said: "I'm not annoyed."

"She's not annoyed," Kitty clarified. "Because I've spent the entirety of the morning providing her with backstory. And I'm actually quite eager to get back to this date, so please do ask whatever question you called me to ask."

"You think I should go? After everything?"

Kitty paused. "After everything," she said, "I do."

"But you hate the island."

"I don't *hate* the island. I hate the lack of modern art museums and underground speakeasies where the bartenders wear flapper dresses. I hate that there are no direct flights to Rome. But I don't *hate* Stenland. And, more importantly, neither do you."

"That's what Linnea said."

Kitty made an impatient sound. "Well, if I can't convince you, and Linnea can't convince you—"

"I'm in a car now," I said.

"Going?"

"Heathrow."

"Really? Shit. Really? So why did you call me?"

"Just—" I said. "Thanks."

"I'm going to hang up now," she said. "This could've been a text."

The plane cut through the fog, and I saw the tallest ridges stretching skyward like the shoulder blades of a giant. Where the snow was patchy, the earth was indigo, same as the sea.

Around the tarmac, golden lights glittered. I pressed my temple against the window, but I couldn't see Lundwall.

My heart was sitting somewhere near the base of my throat, and when the plane thumped and skittered along the runway, I felt it jump higher. Everyone was getting off the plane too slowly, clogging up the aisle and bumping around to put on their puffy jackets. When I climbed down the stairs to the tarmac, the wind came straight at me: glacially cold and too thin to breathe.

We waited, all of us, for the men in hi-vis to toss our suitcases onto a cart. I buried my hands in my pockets and stomped my feet. The ground was black, shiny, wet where they'd melted off the snow. The highly visible men called to each other, laughing. One was wearing a Santa hat. Why did I bring a bag? I didn't need a bag. I could leave without it, really, and I almost did, but then they were wheeling the cart toward us and there was an elbows-out dash for the luggage: boxes of Christmas presents and overstuffed backpacking backpacks and there, my suitcase, which I grabbed by the handle and yanked free.

In the airport, the doors were strung with pale green willow boughs and bells. Even inside, my breath came out in fog. On the far wall, probably put up by the tourism board, there was a picture of Fairhowe Cairn—five-thousand-year-old rocks dusted with freshly fallen snow. I looked at it instead of at the short line of travelers getting ready to leave on the plane that just brought me in.

I wasn't a leaver, if only for the next hour; if only until he told me to be one. So I looked at the photo of Fairhowe, and I didn't look at them, the leavers, and I probably never would have if he had not stepped out of line with a boarding pass in one hand and a book in the other and called my name.

★★★★★

Acknowledgments

Thank you to my agent, Andrea Somberg, who believed in this book from the start, and to Philippa Sitters, who brought us to the UK. I am so grateful to the incredible teams at MIRA and Hodderscape for their enthusiasm and wisdom. Thank you to my generous and thoughtful editors, Meredith Clark and Molly Powell.

Thank you to my family for entertaining my silly dreams. I love you all a lot.

Thank you to my friends in Australia and the US. Thank you to Kirsten for talking with me about swim team things and to Chantal for being my Melbourne person. Thank you to Rachel, Olivia, and Greg for reading and helping me fix things. And thank you to Ari, who always knows.

Thank you for reading.